THE BAD BOY'S GIRL

BLAIR HOLDEN

THE BAD BOY'S GIRL

Published by Blair Holden

Dedication

For my mom, I never would have had the courage to write without
you.
And for my Wattpad family, thank you for always loving this
world and these characters.

INTRODUCTION

Mom and Dad are at it again and I can hear their shouts through our thin, almost paper-like walls. They are still under the impression that if they shout downstairs, I won't be able to hear them. Yet sadly for them, and for me, I can hear each and every word crystal clear.

But that's what they do. They fight up to the point where they want to tear each other's hair out and then go to their room. Lately, however, my dad has taken to sleeping in the guest bedroom, which he sneaks out of every morning before I go to school.

He thinks I don't know, but I do.

I'm aware that things are bad between my parents but they'll never leave each other. They're stubborn like that. I get that from them, the stubbornness, but I really do hope I'm never put in a situation like theirs. Though I don't have to worry about finding someone I love and then ending up hating them, because the guy I love will never love me. He's too busy being in love with Nikki the Ho. Oh wait, let me rewind and tell you exactly why Nikki's a ho.

Nicole Andrea Bishop, also known as the reason behind every bad thing in my life, is my ex-best friend and vice-captain of the varsity dance team. I've known her since kindergarten when everything was rainbows and butterflies, and sharing a cup of Jell-O meant that we were BFFs.

Truly, that's what Nikki and I were for about ten years. Then high school happened and turned her into the spawn of Satan.

Gone was the girl with missing front teeth who used to braid my hair because I was physically incapable of doing so. Gone was the girl with severe acne who stayed up all night with me, helping me prepare for the nightmare that was my French final in junior high. Gone was the girl who'd become a sister to me, who had dinner with my family every Saturday night before we started our weekly *Gilmore Girls* marathon.

By the time freshman year ended, she had been possessed by the spirit of Regina George and I was that pesky fly that kept hovering near her. I fought to keep our friendship alive, I truly did, but there was only so much my pride could suffer.

This is the part where I tell you that I used to be fat. Oh, and when I say fat, I don't mean the kind of fat where you could wear skinny jeans and crop tops yet still find it in yourself to criticize those few extra pounds.

I weighed a whopping two hundred and thirty pounds. I was that girl who wore sweatpants and XXL hoodies with my Converse all day, every day, and didn't think twice about it. But before you begin to pity me, let me assure you that I was never conscious about my weight. In fact, I was pretty okay with it. I didn't diet, nor did I exercise (much to my mother's chagrin), and I didn't sacrifice small animals so that the gods would miraculously make me shed all the extra weight. I ate what I wanted, I stayed inside watching *Gossip Girl* on my laptop, and in school I was ignored, never bullied, but ignored.

Then Nicole joined the dance team and suddenly everyone hated me. I can still hear them, you know, the catcalls and hushed, well, not completely hushed, whispers as Nicole and I would pass the other students.

"What's Nicole Andrea Bishop doing with a girl like her?"

"How is Fatty Tessie blackmailing Nicole into being her friend?"

"Why doesn't Nicole just get rid of the extra weight?" Yeah, that one was hilarious.

Suffice it to say Nicole realized that I was damaging her reputation. So after months of avoiding my calls and not "having time" to hang out with me, she made it clear that I was now a bother to her and that we couldn't be friends anymore.

I swallowed my pride and agreed. Just like that, ten years of friendship went down the drain, all because my best friend was too big of a coward to stand up to the people who questioned our friendship. Now, if she'd stayed a coward, I would've been okay with it, but she decided that one humungous character flaw wasn't enough. Oh no, apparently the prerequisite for popularity is becoming some sort of twisted villain you find in the classic western movies. Which Nicole did.

While I returned for sophomore year eighty pounds lighter, she returned with a boyfriend. Not just any boyfriend at that. Nicole returned as the girlfriend of the boy I'd been crushing on since I was eight.

Jason "Jay" Stone was the first boy who ever got me flowers. Well, if you consider a single, roughly plucked dandelion a flower. He did this when we were in the third grade and I came to school wearing my favorite bow. He told me I looked pretty and that was it—I was in love. As time went on we became good friends. Well, he was a good friend to me. I simply became tongue-tied in his presence. He was your typical All-American Boy with his blond hair, blue eyes, and enviable baseball skills.

However, as I added pounds to my body, I became shy about my association with him. I was overweight and carried prepubescent awkwardness. I told myself that I wasn't the kind of girl who deserved to spend time with Jay Stone, and I distanced myself from him.

Nicole knew full well how I felt about him. She even encouraged me to ask him out because she claimed he had a crush on me despite my weight problems. Let's just say I was very, very opposed to the idea. However, during the summer before my sophomore year, I realized that maybe I'd finally stumbled upon a breakthrough. As I slaved over the treadmill and consumed my body weight in water, I felt that maybe this would be *the* year. The year when I'd finally have a shot, that I could finally be someone who could possibly flirt with Jay Stone.

I was in for a rude awakening.

The first time I saw Jay after that summer was in the school hallway just before the bell for first period rang. I had worn my best pair of skinny jeans, which coincidentally made my butt look good, a fitted top showing just a hint of cleavage, and some pretty badass biker boots. I'd painstakingly styled my blond hair into beachy waves with my makeup expertly applied. However, my eye makeup ran down my face not five minutes later when I saw him.

He had his tongue down my best friend's—excuse me, my ex-best friend's—throat. If I'd eaten anything at all, the contents of my stomach would surely have made their way back up. I remember clearly feeling a viselike grip around my heart, like someone was squeezing it tightly, cracking it up into minuscule pieces. Tears stung my eyes and my throat closed up. It was the worst I'd ever felt.

I had lost Jay Stone, the love of my life, to my ex-best friend, and boy, did she rub it in my face. It was like losing all that weight made no difference to them. I was destined to remain Fatty Tessie, friendless and invisible to the only guy I'd ever wanted.

***

Fast forward two years and here I am, a senior going into my second week of high school. Not quite shockingly, a senior sitting at home on a Saturday night and stalking the love of her life on Facebook. Yes, I've grown into referring to myself in third person because that's what mind-numbing boredom does to you.

I'm scrolling down his profile, which seems to be filled with photos from his girlfriend in different stages of a selfie. Sickening, that's what this level of self-obsession is.

His display picture is one of the two of them on the beach. He's lifted her up around the waist and is kissing the side of her head as she grins that evil, Grim Reaper grin at the camera.

I try blocking out the various pictures of Nicole as I veer deeper into Jay's profile. He's perfect, utterly beautiful with his messy golden hair and ocean blue eyes. His smile kills me, those dimples in his cheeks, the freckles on his nose, those sharp cheekbones . . .

How lovesick do I sound? But he won't even look at me because he's too busy swapping spit with freaking Nicole Andrea Bishop. They're the perfect couple. The kind that's most likely to be voted Prom King and Queen. The kind who would eventually get married one day because it seems like the only logical conclusion. Perfection ends up with perfection, even if said perfection has a rotten, rotten core. Why can't he see how evil his girlfriend is? How could he be blind to all her faults?

Oh wait, I remember. The fangs only come out when I'm around, and around him she's as harmless as a Chihuahua. To give him credit, Jay always goes out of his way to say hello to me, and whenever we have class he offers to carry my books. Obviously I never let him because Nicole's always just a few feet away with fire coming out of her nostrils.

I refresh his profile a couple of times because I'm feeling particularly sadistic. But my fingers freeze midway when I see a post. Not just any post, it's The Post. The one that makes me want to shriek and throw the laptop fifty feet away. The death decree staring me right in the face says:

"I'm coming home, brother. Better throw me a killer party, Jay Jay."

Curious to know who on earth could make me cower in fear, tremble in my proverbial boots, and wish that we still lived in the day and age of moats?

Well, the name that's glaring at me viciously from the screen is Cole, Cole Stone, and it's a name right up there with Nicole Andrea Bishop. The universe tends to work in mysterious ways, right? Well, at times I feel like with me the universe works with a slightly sickening sense of humor. What else would explain why the two people who have wreaked so much havoc in my life have rhyming names?

But I digress; my problem isn't rhyming names, it's the fact that Cole is . . . wait, Cole's coming back? Oh crudsticks.

Cole, for those unaware of why my skin crawls at the sound of his very name, is Jay's stepbrother and the one person apart from Nicole who seems to have made a hobby of making me miserable. He bullied me relentlessly all through elementary school and junior high. However, before

v

we started high school, he being the delinquent that he is, inevitably ended up where all the miscreants do. Military school has kept him away from me for three years now.

And now he's coming back.

Cole Stone, the reason why the nurses in the emergency room and I are on a first-name basis, is coming back to town. Oh my God, now there's going to be two of them! Cole and Nicole will combine their evil satanic powers to make my life a living, breathing slasher flick.

I gulp and shut my laptop down, tossing it aside like it's possessed.

Score one for the universe's sickening sense of humor, and none for the blonde who always ends up dead in the bathtub.

CHAPTER ONE
He's Bush and I'm Like His Mini Afghanistan

Monday morning when my dad drops me off at school, I stealthily pull on the hood of my jacket. It is a remnant of Fatty Tessie days and hence is so baggy that it almost swallows me. The mission is to be as invisible to the human eye as possible, and what better way to do that than wear something that "the new me" wouldn't be caught dead wearing? A potato sack would be more flattering.

My father eyes me curiously as I tiptoe toward the building. I can always explain it to him later that I'm trying to save my life. When he finally drives away I rush, still on my tiptoes, imitating a bad spy thriller, and merge into the crowd of ALHS—so far, so good.

The plan is to quickly grab my books from my locker, which might be the only way someone might identify me today. The strategy also involves sitting way at the back, about as noticeable as a flea on Yorkshire terrier. It's funny how easy it is to channel James Bond when you're in mortal danger.

Now, you might say that I'm overreacting and that I don't even know if Cole's going to be in school today. But the thing is, I've known that boy long enough to be aware of his twisted schemes. He will attack when I lower my defenses and that, my friends, will not be happening.

"Tessa."

My cover's been blown! I squeeze my eyes shut and start walking toward homeroom, which happens to be in the direction opposite of whomever it is that's ruining my carefully constructed plan.

"Tessa, wait!"

I keep walking, glancing to the sides, hoping that Cole won't jump out of some random corner with a paint gun in his hand. That devious baboon . . . he's got minions now, does he?

You can tell paranoia does not suit me well.

1

I try to hurry as much as I can but I'm not fast enough. A hand clasps down on my shoulder and I open my mouth to scream but then my eye falls on the bracelet on the wrist of the person holding on to me and I sigh in relief. That charm bracelet with the 'I Heart Nerds' charm is familiar, and the owner happens to be my best friend. I know for certain that she doesn't mean me physical harm, well, at least not intentionally.

"Why," she pauses to take a deep breath, "are you . . ." deep breath again, "running so fast?" She's panting like she's just run a marathon instead of chasing me down a school corridor, but in her defense, she's a bigger nerd than I am and exercise is a foreign concept for her.

"Let's get to class and I'll explain," I say, grabbing her arm and pulling her along before she attracts too much attention.

"Ooohh, I smell gossip." She rubs her hands together manically and her green eyes shimmer in delight.

Meet Megan Sharp, one of my best friends post-Nicole. We bonded over our mutual hatred of chemistry and late hours at the library. She's an honors student destined for her dream school, Princeton. In her spare time she loves nothing more than knowing everything about everyone, even though that knowledge might not be credible. Megan is stunning, with her deep red hair and flawless complexion. She looks like a porcelain doll, and I envy her ability to be petite and delicate while I am anything but.

We enter the classroom and as usual Miss Sanchez is fast asleep in her chair while paper planes are whizzing by her head. The two of us spot our other best friend, Beth, sitting by the window, scribbling furiously over her notebook, and we head over to her direction.

"Hey, Beth!" I wince at the shrill tone of Megan's voice, but you cannot tone this girl down. Her morning greeting is a way of life.

Beth doesn't look up and I realize that she's in that zone. Her "I'm writing a song; come near me and I'll kill you" zone, so I pry Megan away from her and we both silently take our seats.

Beth Romano is my other best friend post-Nicole. She transferred to our school during sophomore year so she hasn't witnessed Fatty Tessie, but what she has witnessed is Nicole's torment. She doesn't do well with bullies, and that's an understatement. If I had a penny for each time I've had to stop her from punching Nicole in the face, I'd be able to skip town and move to Timbuktu. She's got that rocker chick look nailed with her distressed jeans and band T-shirts, along with her trademark leather jacket. The ebony black hair and her piercing blue eyes only cement her intensity.

To others she might come across as a little scary, but she's one hell of a friend.

"So will you tell me why you were running away from me like

you've just killed someone and why you're dressed like . . . that?" She turns her nose up at my appearance and I try not to be offended. I dressed like this for the better part of my life and nobody ever had a problem with it then.

"You don't know?"

Apparently this is the worst thing to say to someone who feeds off gossip.

A crazed look comes over her face as her eyes become frantic. "What? What don't I know?"

"Cole Stone's coming back." I gulp and there's a telling pause. The pause that echoes what I already know. The shock that comes across Megan's face lasts for only ten seconds as pity replaces it. She places her hand over mine and solemnly says, "I'm sorry."

***

"I don't get what the big deal is. Why is this Cole person so scary?" Beth asks as she takes a bite of her cheeseburger. Her face scrunches up in disgust as she spits it all out. Two years in this place and she's not realized how bad the food is. We're sitting hidden, in the farthest corner of the cafeteria that I could find and, surprisingly, I've made it to lunch alive.

Megan cuts me off before I even open my mouth. "Cole is Tessa's stalker," she says with ease.

Beth's eyes bulge before I correct Megan. "He's not my stalker. He's just someone specifically designed to torture me," I say in an eerily calm manner.

"It can't be that bad." Beth shrugs and digs around her bag until she pulls out a half-eaten pack of chips that's been folded over repeatedly.

"Yes, it can't be bad because you know what's bad? Bad is when you run out of chocolate and Ryan Gosling during the week, Beth. Cole and his reign of terror deserve a far better title."

Once again Megan has taken to speaking for me. Hello—it's my bully we're discussing here.

"Is he hot?" Beth asks, smirking, and it takes a second for the question to register. I wait a few seconds to answer as I pull the proverbial knife from my back. Why does it matter if he's hot? Hot monsters are still monsters.

"Honey, that boy puts Michelangelo's David to shame!" Megan sighs dreamily.

I hit her arm and she pouts. "It's true, though, that guy is hot."

If only she were wrong.

***

Last period arrives without me running into either of the twin horrors, Nicole or Cole. But that's largely because Nicole's been stuck in dance practice all day. The last class is unfortunately PE and while I'm now much more comfortable with my body, the Fatty Tessie inside me still struggles to put on gym shorts while parading in front of judgmental teenage boys.

But I still have to because PE is a mandatory torture right up there with mystery meat Monday. The bell for last period allows me to put my guard down. It's safe to suppose that Cole isn't in school today and since I haven't seen Nicole, I realize that it's been a pretty good day. Too soon, these words just came out too soon. I mentally curse myself and bite my tongue when I hear her.

"Hey, Fatty." Gritting my teeth, I morph my face into a neutral expression. Turning on my heels in the locker room, I come face-to-face with the she-devil herself.

"Nicole," I say, acknowledging her presence.

She stands there in her purple-and-yellow dance outfit, which basically consists of skimpy skirt and an even skimpier cropped top. Her dark hair is pulled into a high ponytail and allows her features to stand out. Her skin is unblemished as always and the perfect caramel color. Her outfit accentuates the hazel in her eyes and her full lips are smeared with neutral gloss. My ex-best friend is a stunner and she knows it. Her Latin heritage makes her stick out amid the pale-skinned, fair-haired majority.

How she manages to look so good despite spending the day in a sweaty gym baffles me.

"I see you still aren't doing the hip reduction exercises I told you about."

Right. Mock me and my supposed huge butt.

"They don't seem to have worked on you so I decided it would be a waste of my time." The word *vomit* happens occasionally around her. I know better than to retaliate, but this day has taken its toll on me. I'm exhausted and honest-to-God sick of being afraid.

She sneers and closes the distance between us until a few inches of space separate us. She obviously means to intimidate me and it has surely worked.

"What did you say?"

"Uh-uh nothing—I said nothing," I stutter, the bravado fast disappearing.

"That's what I thought. Now move out of my way before I crush you like the roadkill you are." She growls and literally shoves me out of her way.

4

After she leaves I find myself standing in the same spot for about ten minutes, struggling to stop myself from hyperventilating. I am not good with confrontations, and God knows what propelled me to talk back to Queen Bitch. I do some of the breathing exercises I've seen on TV, which prove to be pretty pointless. Still in shock mode, I walk to my locker, which is where I stash my gym bag and phone. I've taken to changing the combination every few months after a prank by Nicole and her cronies.

It's more mortifying to walk around the school naked in real life than in any nightmare you'll ever have.

After securing my belongings, I make my way back to the gym, only to be interrupted for the third time that day. This time, however, my heart reacts in the totally opposite way to how it had reacted to seeing Nicole.

My heart flutters, it flutters!

"There you are, Tessa. I've been looking for you all day." Jason Stone comes into my line of sight, and I lean back against my locker to stop myself from fainting at the sight of his smile. He looks like a blond Adonis in his gym clothes. His strong, toned runner's legs and bulging biceps make my eyes glaze over.

"You have?" I sigh dreamily as he nears me, then mentally slap myself for sounding so silly. "You have?" I repeat with a deeper voice, yet I manage to sound like my dad when he choked on a bone last week.

"Yeah, I have. I've been meaning to talk to you since yesterday, actually."

I know I should listen to him, he's obviously saying something important. But he's just so beautiful. I let my eyes roam over his body, his face, his perfect blond hair . . .

"Tessa?" He waves a hand in front of my face, making me crash-land into reality.

"Wh-what?"

"I wanted to know if you were okay."

"I'm fine," I reply, knowing that a full-blown smile's on my face this very second.

Jay's so cute, caring about me, asking if I'm okay, talking to me even though his girlfriend is vehemently against it.

"Really?" He seems surprised. I wonder why?

"Yeah, totally. I was a little feverish on Sunday, but nothing some good old chicken soup can't help."

"No—I wasn't—" He looks so cute when he's confused!

"What?"

"What?" he repeats, his face scrunched up in adorable confusion.

We take a second to regroup and I pull myself together. Jay squares his shoulders and looks at me sympathetically.

"Look, Tessa, I thought you should know that Cole's coming back. He left a message and he's going to spend his senior year here, at home."

I know all of that, you beautiful creature, because I spend my weekend nights stalking you. But he doesn't really need to know that. Time to put my nonexistent acting skills into play.

"What? Are you serious? I . . . wow, is he really coming back?" I exclaim.

"Yeah, he is." Is it just me, or does Jay look as unhappy about it as I am? "I just wanted to see if you're okay since your relationship with Cole . . ."

"It's not a relationship, Jay, it's tyranny. He's Bush and I'm like his mini Afghanistan."

He laughs, and the cute little dimples appear on his cheeks, making me melt.

"I forgot how funny you were." His blue eyes shine as he grins at me, oh boy.

"Look, if he gives you any trouble, you come to me, okay?" he says seriously and I nod.

"You'll protect me?" I sound sappy to my own ears but to hell with it.

Jay scratches the back of his neck and mutters "yes" as I resist the urge to kiss the life out of him.

"Thank you, Jay, it means a lot to me." There is a faint tinge of pink on his cheeks and it stays there when we walk into the gym together. Thankfully Nicole isn't there, and for that hour I pretend that Jay is mine and that everything is perfect.

CHAPTER TWO
I'm Her Evil Russian Twin, Svetlana

"So, honey, I hear that Cole's back," my father says as we sit together for dinner.

Oh, he isn't back yet. If he was, then I wouldn't be sitting here in one piece, I think as I angrily stab a pea.

"He is? I didn't know," I reply, and my mother snorts in disbelief and chuckles.

"You two always were so adorable together. That boy could just never leave you alone," she reminisces fondly as I struggle to contemplate which part of the misery I had been put through looked "adorable" to my mother.

"I wish he had," I grumble.

"Now Tess, we can't have you on bad terms with the sheriff's son, can we? It's election year and we need all the help we can get," my dad says, and I give him my best "are you kidding me?" look. If he wants me to suck up to my nemesis just to make him win an election, he can kiss his office good-bye.

"Especially since your father was such a disappointment this last term," my mom says sweetly, but making sure that her words sting as much as they can. I can sense the beginnings of a fight, so I finish my dinner in record time. All thoughts of Cole are forgotten and I rush upstairs before someone starts throwing cutlery around.

"Travis, get up!" I shout outside my brother's door, knocking on it loudly three times and stopping when he utters his usual greeting, the F word. This is part of our daily ritual. Alarm clocks don't work for my older brother, so I've taken on the duty of making sure he hasn't slipped into a coma.

It might seem strange that my brother wakes up around dinnertime, but we've all gotten used to his nocturnal nature. My parents understand that

7

they've lost their prodigal son, and I've realized that the best way to deal with new Travis is to keep a safe distance.

See, Travis is now twenty-one and still living at home because he got kicked out of his college. For plagiarizing a paper at that, pretty dumb for a straight-A student. Then the love of his life dumped him and he resorted to alcohol in order to, and I quote, "Deal with this shit."

Ever since last year he's almost always been chronically hungover, and as much as my father wants to, he can't do anything about it. He's the mayor and he can't be airing his dirty laundry in public. When someone asks about Travis, we simply either ignore them or say something along the lines of how he's working on his other "ambitions," such as writing the next great American novel.

In the middle of this dysfunctional family we have me. Unhinged and facing a nuclear attack; others might refer to it as Cole Stone's return.

***

I plop down on my bed and take out the material needed for my homework. I have an essay due tomorrow, which I've written already. Okay, so I outlined and wrote it the day it was assigned, but double-checking never hurts. It's what you do when doing homework is the only thing you have to occupy yourself with. Nicole has made sure that I'm shunned from any sort of activity that might actually involve me being social.

I'm proofreading the essay and adding footnotes when my dad enters my room. His face is flushed and it's because of the screaming match that just ended downstairs.

"Are you free, Tess?" he asks expectantly.

"Well, not exactly, I have this assignment—"

It's like he hasn't even heard what I just said as he thrusts a folder into my hands. "Good, I need you to take these to the sheriff right now. I would've done it myself but I'm going to head out and he needs these right away."

"But Dad . . ."

He wants me to go to the Stones'? Is he out of his mind? Am I that big of a disappointment to him that he's readily sending me to my end? I can't go to the sheriff's house because that sheriff fathered Cole. If Cole's back, then going over to his place is as inviting as poking a beehive. Been there, done that, and it's not pleasant.

"You'll do exactly as I say, Tess, or you'll be grounded," he says smugly.

"Then ground me," I tell him with a huge grin on my face.

8

It's not like I go anywhere except the mall at times with Megan and Beth. Neither of them is a keen shopper so we mostly end up sitting at Starbucks and Beth winds up inside a music store, lost for hours as Megan shares gossip.

He sighs. "Just do it, Tess, and no arguments. I would've sent your brother, but since it's morning according to whatever clock he lives by, he'll either be too drunk to function or too hungover to actually comprehend what I just said."

"But Dad, Cole might be there, and you of all people know how bad he is to me!" I whine, practically willing to fall to his feet and beg him not to make me go.

"Now is not the time for theatrics, sweetheart. Take these papers and go." He pulls me upright and basically pushes me toward the door.

"You're a cruel and heartless parent; you know that, right?" I say as he walks me down the stairs and to the front door, which he oh so graciously opens for me.

"You don't become the mayor by being nice. Now hurry along."

Then he shuts the door in my face.

Bloody brilliant. I wonder how many bones I'd break trying to sneak back into my room.

***

I wish I could say that the Stone residence is miles and miles away. If that were the case, I could say that I experienced severe dehydration, fainted, and ended up at the local hospital. The image of my father apologizing profusely for being such a dictator is surprisingly pleasant.

Sadly for me, the universe never fails to deliver, and it only takes about five minutes before I end up outside their mammoth three-story house. Farrow Hill is a town filled with people who have old money. Houses are more like estates, and the residents tend to be obscenely rich. Sheriff Stone may not be making millions but he comes from money and it shows. It's the same for my own parents, which means that I've long stopped being intimidated by the grandeur.

My hand lingers on the bell as I imagine all the possible scenarios that might occur if Cole actually is inside. Most of them end up with me in the local hospital with a lot of broken bones and a badly bruised ego. While Cole has never physically hurt me, many of his pranks have been designed to target my obvious lack of coordination, and somehow I always end up in a cast. Now, even though I haven't been there for nearly four years, it's not like I exactly miss the place and the wonderful smell of disinfectant. I'd

9

rather not visit old Martha, who's my favorite nurse, anytime soon.

I squeeze my eyes shut and press the damned buzzer twice. After waiting five minutes, I decide to turn the doorknob. Maybe I'm lucky and no one's home. That way I can drop off the papers without human interaction.

The sheriff often spends long hours at the police station, and his second wife, Jay's mom Cassandra, is a doctor who works late-night shifts at the hospital. Jay could be out, too, I think grudgingly. He could be canoodling with Nicole, and the thought makes me clench my fists.

Luckily, I turn the knob and the door opens. Saying a quick thank-you prayer, I stick my head inside to find the entrance room empty. A single light illuminates the path to the kitchen, which is mostly dark. From memory I recall that the boys' rooms are upstairs while Sheriff Stone's is down here. I step in lightly, just so that I don't make a sound. I was told to deliver the papers to a person and not just leave them lying around, but I could always tell my dad that no one was home. I walk farther into the house clutching the file in my hands, treading lightly. I leave the folder on a small desk that holds some other important-looking documents.

"Think fast, Tessie!" comes a voice that sends chills up my spine, and my head shoots up instinctively. A rookie mistake after all these years.

The moment I look up I see the bucket in his hands but as usual am too slow to respond. Cole stands half hidden behind the banisters and spills the contents of said bucket directly onto me, and in a matter of seconds I am completely drenched in a mixture of ice-cold water and green food coloring.

While the shock settles in, I hear the burst of evil laughter that erupts from the monster's mouth. I stand there open-mouthed and soaked, the fact that I'd just been pranked not settling in.

He basically skips down the stairs, still laughing, as I stand rooted to my spot.

"Ah, Tessie, how I've missed you." He chuckles when he nears me but the amusement in his face dies when he sees me. "You're not Tessie." He frowns, standing right in front of me.

Ladies and gentlemen, meet Cole Stone. An entire six feet one of pure evilness, he could fool the world with his shaggy brown hair and baby blue eyes, but not me. On first seeing him, any other person would see a devastatingly gorgeous, runway model God, but I'd call that person a fool. I see him for exactly who he is, and that's the devil incarnate. He's a jerk, a complete dickleweed filled and, and he's . . .

Checking me out. Gosh darn it! I need him to stop staring at me while I look like a drenched green Smurfette.

"But you're still an immature nincompoop," I seethe as I pull my soaked T-shirt away from me and push away the hair that's stuck to my mouth. Attractive, Tessa, attractive.

"You called me a nincompoop and you're in my house when Tessie's father said she'd be here. Who are you and what have you done to my shortcake?" he exclaims, gripping my shoulders and pushing me forward.

I slap his chest and push away. "Firstly, I'm five seven, so calling me 'shortcake' doesn't make sense, and second, don't touch me ever again, Stone, or I will castrate you."

"Seriously, the only girl who could want harm to come to my balls would be Tessie, but you aren't her . . ."

"No, I'm her evil Russian twin, Svetlana, and I'm here to kill you in your sleep," I growl at him.

"The sarcasm, the threat to my balls, and calling me nincompoop when you want to curse so badly. You really are Tessie, aren't you?" he says like he's in shock.

In his defense, the last time he saw me I weighed as much as two sumo wrestlers and proudly sported a double chin. My hair had always been stuck in the unfashionable bob while now it reached my waist. It's soaked and frizzing at the speed of sound, but it's still long.

"Oh, I'm so grateful that you believe me, now get out of my way."

"Tessie, you look different," he says, still looking slightly dazed, turning a deaf ear to all the profanities coming out of my mouth as I realize that my teeth are chattering.

I try not to blush when under his attention, but he's basically the first guy to notice me and my cheeks can't help but heat up. I cannot seriously be blushing because of something Cole Stone said. That's sacrilege.

But he's here. He's actually here, in the flesh, and I'm blushing, for crying out loud.

"Well, that's more than what I can say for you; you're still as ugly as ever." I stick my tongue out at him and he smirks, bloody conceited jerk.

"That doesn't seem to be a popular opinion. In fact, the women I know have referred to me as a god on multiple occasions." He wiggles his eyebrows and I feel my dinner coming back up.

"Okay, all right, way too much information. You're making me sick, and I should leave before I throw up."

"Like you did in third grade during your memorable performance as Snow White?" he says innocently and I glare at him.

"You! You gave me that rancid cupcake; I did not throw up because of nerves."

Although chances are that the cupcake was perfectly fine and I did throw up

11

because of nerves, but I will never admit that to him.

"Whatever you want to believe, sweetheart."

I groan and push past him, heading for the door. But it just so happens to open before I can get to it, and with my luck being as brilliant as it is, Jay walks inside. Of course he looks edible in his jeans and muscle tee. I temporarily forget my current state of distress and openly ogle him.

"Tessa?" His eyes widen as he takes in my appearance. Great, just great. The one time I run into him without Nicole standing over his shoulder, I look like a dog that's just been hosed and then dipped in green Jell-O. Oh, the joys of being Tessa O'Connell.

"Hi, Jay," I say stupidly and give him a small smile. He smiles back awkwardly and we stand in silence just staring at each other. It's the perfect silence, the kind that is in all the romance novels I read. It's the kind that is only interrupted when the guy kisses the girl and everything becomes magical.

However, this one ends because Cole starts making fake gagging sounds.

This is my version of a romance novel, and it would make the makers of Harlequin shed tears of blood.

"You guys are pathetic." He pretends to choke, and I wish he really would. Jay glares at him and strides past me to hit him on the back of his head.

"I thought I told you to leave her alone," he growls, but Cole just rolls his eyes.

"You're jealous, aren't you? Christ, what's wrong with you?" he says to his stepbrother, who averts his gaze shamefully.

"Why would I be jealous?"

I immediately wince at the lack of care in Jay's voice, but try not to show the hurt.

"You would care or wouldn't be nearly this blind if you could escape the leash your girlfriend's got you on."

"You don't know what you're talking about." I see Jay's temper rising but the conversation has stopped making sense to me.

"I know enough, bro." Cole pats Jay's shoulder in fake sympathy.

"Come on, shortcake, let me get you some dry clothes before you become a human Popsicle." He says this without taking his eyes off his brother. Both seem to be involved in some sort of staring contest, but it's Jay who gives up first and turns to face me.

"You can come with me. I'll get you a towel and maybe a different set of clothes," he says kindly, and I nod eagerly before Cole snorts and destroys the moment once again.

"I don't think that's a good idea, Jay Jay. What will your girlfriend say when she finds out you've been spending time with Tessie here?"

I'm about to tell him off and say that Jay isn't afraid of Nicole and that he can be friends with me without thinking about how Nicole would react. But the hesitation that comes across his face is like a punch to the stomach as I realize that Cole's hit the nail right on the head. Jay pulls away from me like there's some sort of invisible force field between us.

A force field named Nicole Andrea Bishop.

Before I know it, Cole's tugging me by the hand and guiding me up to his room. I keep my eyes on Jay even though he's trying to look anywhere but at me. I'm in love with the guy but sometimes I wish he was stronger than this.

Cole pulls me into his room, or what looks like the framework of one. White sheets cover the bed and the two-seater while boxes are lined up everywhere. A thin film of dust coats every visible surface, and I wrinkle my nose when I notice the pigsty that is his floor. Clothes are strewn all over it and I tiptoe carefully, hoping to avoid coming across his underwear.

Cole is digging into one of the boxes and produces a hoodie. "Catch, shortcake," he says, but with my reflexes, the hoodie smacks me right in the face, nearly blinding me in the process.

"Thanks," I say, my voice muffled by the fabric as I escape into the nearest bathroom to change out of my wet shirt. I turn the faucet on and splash some cold water on my face. I'm feeling a bit dazed, the twilight zone lingers in the periphery. Since when is Cole *nice*? Okay, so he's being nice after turning me into a wet poodle, but I know what I saw in his interaction with Jay. It looked like he was standing up for me. But why?

Scratch that, I'm not analyzing his actions. He belongs in the one confined box in my head, the one for people I severely dislike.

When I come back, Cole is lying down on his bed staring at the ceiling, his hands clasped beneath his head. He smirks slightly as I enter, and props himself up on one elbow.

"This is the part where I say you look sexier in my clothes than I ever did, but the narcissist in me won't let me do that."

"I'd rather you not."

"No, I'm serious, Tessie, you've really changed. And before you start calling me a shallow pig, what I mean is that you just stood up to me and I didn't expect that."

"So the water dumping was some kind of twisted experiment? To see how I would react? You do realize how wrong that sounds, don't you?"

"Okay, so maybe I shouldn't have done that—scratch that, it was a stupid move. Would you believe me if I said that I was nervous?"

13

He sounds serious, and for a moment I let myself believe that he means everything he says. I let myself believe that he might actually have a human side to him. I don't often let myself make excuses for his actions, and before knowing that he would be coming back I had managed to forget about our history. But this moment feels different, he seems different.

"So, what? You want me to believe that I make you nervous?"

At first he seems at a loss for an answer but then he says, "So do math tests, so you shouldn't really conflate that with me actually liking you."

Then again, I'd rather just slap him than have him say nice or crude things to me.

"I would rather pull my teeth out with pliers than ever imagine being someone you liked in any sense, Stone." I cross my arms in front of my chest to look intimidating.

"Oh, but you like me, don't you? After all those years of verbal sparring and pranks, I think your heart may have warmed toward me at some point. I won't blame you, though."

I scoff at his arrogance and realize that I'm just killing brain cells by trying to reason with him, so I decide to make a run for it.

"Well, it's been a pleasure having you back to ruin my life, but I need to go before I strangle you."

"Kinky." He winks at me and I throw my hands in the air, exasperated to a point where the instinct to just put an end to his life is uncannily strong.

"Good-bye, Cole."

I turn on my heel and slam his door shut as he chuckles behind me. I have been in the house for no more than thirty minutes but it feels like I've been going at it with Cole for centuries. A dull ache is spreading through my skull as I realize that today's only the first of many to come and that he's back for good. Any peace and quiet that I had expected in my senior year evaporated the minute He-devil decided to return to our great town. I'd learned to deal with Nicole, albeit in the most cowardly way ever, but we were coexisting and it's been okay. Apparently my carefully constructed habitat is about to be bulldozed by a certain blue-eyed miscreant.

There are no signs of Jay as I'm leaving. His lack of presence is morbidly depressing.

I'm on their driveway when the devil reappears. Cole calls my name as he sticks his head out of his bedroom window. That's how he knew I was in the house when he tipped the bucket over me, sneaky bastard.

"What?" I shout as he grins at me with that devil-may-care smile.

"How about I give you a ride to school tomorrow? We can begin the beautiful journey that is our new, everlasting friendship."

14

"What makes you think I'd even sit in a car with you, let alone go for a twenty-minute drive?"

"Hey, it was just an offer. I know we've got a long way to go but it was worth a shot, right? I figure if I begin trying early, you might warm up to the idea eventually."

"You're crazy!"

"No, Tessie, but I am fond of the 'so crazy it just might work approach.'"

The entire conversation consists of us yelling sentences to each other, and it isn't long before a woman with graying hair comes out of the adjacent house. She's tugging her robe tighter around herself and yelling at us "filthy teenagers" to shut our traps. Cole disappears from my view and I like to think that the old lady scared him, but in a minute or two he's downstairs and out the door, slightly breathless as though he ran. He walks toward me and I feel the need to disappear beneath his mammoth hoodie.

"Now that we have that sorted out," he runs a hand through his hair as though nervous, "I'd like to be friends. What I just did up there with the water? It was stupid. So how about we try another route?"

He extends his hand toward me and I look at it like it's been infected by zombies, contagious zombies. He must have seen the look on my face, as he lets out a laugh.

"I don't have any life-threatening diseases, Tessie. It's just a handshake."

"I'm sorry, but given our history, you might understand why I'm a little skeptical of your newfound desire for friendship."

He nods and an emotion passes across his face that I can't decipher. It couldn't possibly be hurt, right? He withdraws his hand and we stand there awkwardly. I refuse to feel bad about what I've just done and so turn around and begin walking home.

"See you tomorrow, shortcake," he says to my retreating figure and I wince. One more year of him, just one more year, I could totally get through this. Right?

CHAPTER THREE
Death by Spearmint—I'd Revolutionize the World of Crime

I can honestly say that I'm not the lightest of sleepers. In fact, a crane could scoop out the roof of my house and I'd sleep through it because that's just how I am. It's purely genetic. We all cherish sleep a lot more than regular people, and my brother took his love for it the extra mile since all he ever does is sleep; well, get hopelessly drunk and then sleep.

Now, this hereditary love of sleep would explain the amount of hatred I would harbor for any person who wakes me up before I absolutely have to. Anyone and everyone who knows me well enough knows better than to mess with my sleep. You can bully me all you want, you can call me all the names in the world, and you can also so cruelly snatch the love of my life away from me, but you just cannot wake me up when I don't want to be woken up.

Sadly, one person didn't get the memo, and the fact that it's my own mother makes it worse.

"Time to wake up honey, we've got someone waiting for you at breakfast."

I do some mental calculations and lift my head from the most comfortable pillow on earth to take a look at the alarm clock that sits on my bedside table. I'm right, I do have fifteen more precious minutes of sleep that are being rather cruelly snatched from me. I don't care if it's the president waiting to share oatmeal with me, I would rather sleep. That is exactly what I tell my mom.

However, she refuses to take no for an answer, or leave my room for that matter. Having never been the nurturing sort, Mom hasn't woken me up for school in a long time, and I think she's still stuck at a place where I'm six and throwing a tantrum about not wanting to go to school. She rips the covers off me.

16

"It's rude to keep guests waiting, Tessa. Please get dressed and come down."

My early morning now effectively ruined, I grudgingly get ready and stomp downstairs, ready to chew out the person who has upset my morning routine.

Of course it's Cole Stone.

"You!" I seethe, having gotten over the shock of seeing him in my dining room pretty quickly. Luckily, Mom is out of earshot and doesn't hear me be rude to our 'guest'. He's casually helping himself to a generous serving of eggs and bacon while I plot ways to make him choke on his coffee.

"What are you doing here?" I hiss as I stride toward him.

"Your dad asked mine if I could drive you to school today. He said he wouldn't be able to drive you because he had to leave early for work and your mom's car is stuck at the mechanic's. Does this ring a bell at all?"

I shake my head. "No, he never mentioned that last night." How very convenient, well played, Father.

"Dad told me you were waiting for me, uh, that's why I'm here bright and early."

Somehow I find myself believing him, because I know that my dad is capable of doing this. He's had some strange matchmaking fetish for me and one of the Stone boys, and maybe this is him attempting to set me up with Cole. He's the one I'm angry with, not Cole, because it looks like Cole's as clueless as I am. Begrudgingly, I let him eat as I head to the kitchen to grab some food for myself, but the weirdness of him being in my house and us being civil to one another never goes away.

***

The thing about my mom is that she never cooks. Any maternal instinct that might tempt her to want to care for her children enough to feed them is long since gone. I know from experience she's a terrific cook. But somewhere down the line, she stopped being the mom who used to make dinner every night and insist that we all sit together and eat.

Seeing the spread on our table right now, I can't help but feel jealous as I realize that Mom would cook for Cole and not for our family. It's stupid, I know. My family's problems won't be solved by over casserole. But I need a scapegoat for all the resentment I'm feeling, and it now seems to be directed toward Cole. Cole, who seems to be oblivious to all the tension surrounding him and is plowing through his breakfast like a tractor on crack.

"So Cole, what are your plans for college?"

My mom's question takes me by surprise since she has shown negligible interest in *my* future plans. She doesn't even know what classes I'm taking for senior year or that I'm a straight-A student. I sigh internally and try not to drown in self-pity. It makes sense that mom is sucking up to him. He is, after all, the sheriff's son, and the sheriff is a very important man in the world of small-town politics.

Cole stops inhaling his food and disarms my mom with a charming smile.

"I haven't actually planned anything. I might not even go to college this year, you know. I'm thinking about taking a year off. Maybe go backpacking through Europe, see the world."

I snort in disbelief. "Backpacking through Europe? Only people who don't have the grades to get into college use that excuse."

My mother gives me an admonishing look and I realize she's warning me to back off. I pout like a stubborn child and cross my arms over my chest, matching her stare. I've told her before that I will not under any circumstances suck up to Cole Stone. There's nothing on the planet that could make me be nice to the one guy who's taken it upon himself to make every waking hour of my life difficult. If my mom thinks I'm going to become Cole's best buddy, then she is obviously delusional.

"Tess, sweetie, about that car you wanted for your birthday . . ." She trails off, on purpose, no doubt, but her words have the desired effect. I freeze, my fork stopping halfway in the air as my mother smirks at me from across the table.

She wouldn't . . .

All year long I'd been saving up for the most beautiful Range Rover Sport. My dream car is also why I've let myself be driven to school right up until my senior year. It's not that my parents couldn't get me a car, but I want *the* car and so I still get rides to school at eighteen. I practiced driving with my parents' cars regularly just so that when I finally owned my Range Rover, I wouldn't let that beauty down. However, in the end my savings had been somewhat meager and my parents stepped in to stop me from sinking into depression. They promised me that I could have the car for my birthday, no strings attached. I'd been floating on cloud nine, dreaming of me and my car cruising down the highway with the wind blowing in my hair and Maroon 5 blasting from the radio . . .

But as the words leave her mouth, the image shatters into thousands of bite-sized pieces because I know where this is going.

"What about my car?" I ask carefully as her smirk widens.

"I was thinking maybe we'd get it next year. You can have Travis's old one this year since you're still a little shaky with parking."

Oh no she didn't! I could park better than she could, and she had admitted it to my face. I know what she's doing. She's blackmailing me into being Cole's lapdog and threatening me by taking away the one thing she knows I could never live without. I really need that car. When you're as plagued by self-esteem issues as I am, the last thing you need is being driven to and from school by your father.

I gulp as I realize the predicament I'm in. The only option I have left is to surrender my pride and take this punishment with a pinch of salt. One day I will, parents, I will get back at you.

"Don't worry, Mommy; I'll work on my parking." I smile until my cheeks ache, but the message has been delivered. When decoded my words meant this: "You win, Mother, I won't be bringing my wrath down upon Cole, at least not today."

"Wonderful, dear," she replies cheerfully, and turns back to her breakfast.

***

"So I think we need to tell our parents that we're not interested in spending time with one another. I think you should be the one to do it though, since I don't think my parents understand most of what I say. There's clearly a communication gap," I tell him, having practiced this speech over and over in my head during our drive. I don't want to be excessively rude to him but also need to get this point across.

"I thought we agreed to be friends last night." Cole pouts but keeps his eyes on the road. I study his profile and notice the stiffness of his jaw, and the tightness around his mouth. Wait, did I just hurt his feelings again? I squeeze my eyes shut and push the thought aside. I did not agree to be his friend and never would.

"We did not agree on anything last night, and I think it's best if we went our separate ways, don't you think? The past is the past, I'll do my thing and you do yours. This does not need to get ugly." I try to reason with him because if I'm stuck in an enclosed space with Cole Stone and cannot get out without risking death, then I might as well use it to my advantage. Stupidly enough, I'd convinced myself that he wouldn't pull one of his stunts on me while we're driving, but given how his face falls as I keep talking, I realize that I might be proven wrong. Why is he reacting this way?

"Do you really think it's that big of an impossibility? Us being friends?" His seriousness is unexpected and I don't know how to answer him.

"I . . . I . . . just think it would be best if we went our separate ways."

"But what if . . . Christ, Tessie, what if I want to try to make it right this time around?"

Noting the look of absolute shock on my face, he retreats from saying more things that are making the foundations of my world shake. "Okay then, before we give you a panic attack bright and early this morning, let's leave this open for discussion, okay?

I don't think I respond.

"Did they put you through a brain transplant at military school?"

"You and that imagination of yours, shortcake. I'm perfectly capable of being nice." He chuckles.

I bet my imagination can think of a thousand different ways to kill him using that pack of gum lying atop the dashboard. Whoever this version of Cole is, I'm even more unsure of how to deal with him than I was with the evil version of him. The sooner I get rid of him, the better it is for my sanity. Death by spearmint—I'd revolutionize the world of crime. They should give me my own episode of *Criminal Minds*.

When we finally make it to the parking lot of ALHS, I feel like I'm a war veteran; shell-shocked is the right phrase to describe my current state of mind. Unaffected by the fact that I almost had a panic attack, Cole eases his Volvo between two parking spaces. My legs feel wobbly as I throw myself out of the car, far away from Lucifer. In my haste to get away from him, I stumble into a cheerleader and prepare myself for an earful.

But it never comes.

Said cheerleader is nearly drooling as she watches Cole. Not only her; as I look around, everyone seems to be frozen on the spot and staring at him.

Figures. Cole's return is a pretty big deal. He's this unforgettable legend to the entire student population. At ALHS, he's hero-worshipped for the many pranks he's pulled throughout the years. Everyone knows who he is, even though he's been gone for three years, and it seems like his celebrity status hasn't diminished even a little bit.

Joy.

He purposely embellishes his exit out of the car. Why can't he do what normal people do and get out without the dramatic flair? It's like watching a really bad episode of *Baywatch* as he swings one leg out and then the other in slow motion. When His Highness finally gets his sorry ass out of the car, he takes off his leather jacket and swings it around his shoulder. He makes a big show of taking off his aviators and inserting them in the back pocket of his jeans. Then he stretches and pretends to yawn so

20

that his taut muscles stretch and ripple as his shirt does nothing to hide how fit he really is.

I can practically hear each and every member of the female population sigh in barely concealed lust as he runs a hand through his hair. It makes it look even better, dang it. He then does the unthinkable and winks at me, and I'm sure that everyone caught the little moment.

I narrow my eyes at him and scowl. "Who do you think you are? David Hasselhoff?"

This wipes the smirk right off his face and I mentally congratulate myself for the little victory.

"Please—if the ladies saw this," he points toward his body, "half naked, all wet and glistening, running on the beach, they wouldn't know what to do with themselves," he says cockily, and I nod in agreement, surprising him.

"You're right; it'd be a hard choice between clawing out their own eyes or taking rat poison."

With that I march right past him knowing that every set of eyes is on me and that sooner or later this will so come back to bite me in the butt.

***

Megan is nearly hysterical in homeroom. I can tell she's just itching to know if I really did show up with Cole and if I did indeed, how come I'm still in one piece. It is the ideal class to spill my guts since Miss Sanchez's head currently rests on her desk and drool is visibly escaping from her mouth. I shudder at the sight and focus my attention on my best friend, who is practically whimpering with the need to know what is going on. I also have Beth, who's pretending to not listen in on our conversation, but I know she's interested. She's been stuck on the same page of her assigned reading book for the past fifteen minutes and it's not because she's suddenly forgotten how to read.

I tell them everything, starting from how I was forced to go to the Stone residence the previous night to how Cole became my ride to school this morning and by the time I finish venting, Megan's eyes have turned the size of watermelons as she gapes at me. Beth simply looks amused.

"Doomed, Tessa, you're doomed," Megan wails, and I slump in my seat, hitting my head against my desk repeatedly.

"There, there." She pats my head sympathetically and I glare at her.

"I don't see what the problem is." Beth's gravelly voice interrupts the silence for the first time. I squint in disbelief. She doesn't think I have a problem? Has listening to all those Led Zeppelin albums finally damaged her brain?

She rolls her eyes as Megan and I give her incredulous looks. "Look, the way I see it, it's a win-win situation for you. Now that he's taken the role of resident bully, Nicole won't come near you, and Jay will realize that there are other guys who are interested. He might actually grow a pair and be the friend you've always wanted him to be."

I splutter in disbelief as I try to make sense of her logic. The words "guy" and "interested" stand out and seem so alien, especially when applied to me, that I think my friend's gone for a ride on the cray-cray train.

"Beth, which part of him being Hannibal Lecter do you not get?"

"I get it, trust me, but what I get the most is that this guy likes you, and he showed it the best way he could. He's obviously trying to make amends and maybe you should let him. So maybe his method isn't the most original, but it's a classic boy manoeuvre," she states like she's discussing the weather, and Megan and I exchange looks, both thinking the same thing. "Sane" Beth isn't with us today.

"Yes, it's a classic boy manoeuvre for when you're in kindergarten. If there is even the smallest possibility that he likes me, he wouldn't torture me like he does," I explain patiently, like I'm talking to a child with learning problems.

"Think what you want; I know I can't convince you otherwise." She shrugs but adds, "I just feel that him being here isn't necessarily a bad thing."

For the rest of the day I cannot stop thinking about Cole's and Beth's words. For the time being I'm able to tuck them away in a corner of my mind, but I realize that sooner or later, I'll have to think about them.

***

She, however, couldn't be more wrong. As the day passes, I realize that people are looking at me with more interest than ever. The last time I was this popular was when I'd been Nicole's fat sidekick. These people had pushed and prodded until she'd dumped me, so it's not surprising if I seem somewhat skeptical about what they are up to today.

I stand outside the door of my economics class. It's a class I have with Jay and Nicole, and I have dreaded attending ever since school started. Nicole does what she can to make it the worst fifty minutes of the day, and I do what I can to protect my poor heart. It feels like someone's taken a butchering knife to it each time I see Jay and Nicole discreetly or not so discreetly touch each other.

I walk in about five minutes early and the happy couple is already seated at their joint table. We have a partner system in this class and it's self-evident that I sit alone. Nicole seems to have warned people against changing my status as a social outcast. I try not looking at them as I walk past them to take my seat right at the back, a seat that I hate since I need to have superhuman eyesight to see the whiteboard. But c'est la vie, you do what you gotta do.

"It's okay, Tessie, I'm sure you'll grow some boobs when you're like thirty; no need to stuff your bra," Nicole snickers.

Ugh, so close! I'd almost escaped her this time. But she's struck a low blow. She knows that my chest area is a major source of embarrassment for me and yet she chooses to pick on it, especially when Jay's with her. He must be comparing his curvaceous and voluptuous girlfriend to flat-chested me and thinking how he got the better end of the deal.

"Or she could get fake ones like you did, but she's not that desperate."

For a second, my heart soars. I freeze halfway and think that Jay's finally defending me and that he's finally seen how rotten his girlfriend is on the inside. Any moment now he's going to kiss me right in front of her, telling me that I have always been the one for him. I snap my head back so fast that I almost pull a muscle, but to my utter disappointment, Jay sits in his seat squirming and another person has joined in on the discussion about my boobs—fantastic.

Cole leans over Nicole and Jay's desk and I can see he's testing Nicole. He wants to know if she has the guts to talk back to him. See, before Cole left, Nicole wasn't much of a queen bee or even a worker bee. In fact, she was happy being the outcast bee with me. That's not even the best part; Nicole also had the biggest crush on Cole. I recall all the times we squealed over the Stone brothers and imagined our joint wedding, after which we'd end up being sisters. Though I did point out that her future husband might not let me live to actually wed.

Obviously, things didn't work out.

Now, it's priceless seeing her face drop as Cole has so blatantly insulted her. Her mouth flops open and shut like a fish's. She struggles to come up with the biting remarks she's used on me all these years. It's nice to see her be the one being bullied for a change; I almost feel a sense of gratitude toward Cole—almost.

"Back off, man." Jay comes to the defense of his girlfriend. It's a little too late, but it still hurts to know that he's got her back and not mine.

"Then tell your girlfriend to stop being a bitch," he says smoothly, and I swear I see Nicole's face reddening in embarrassment.

"Cole," Jay warns, his hands balling up into fists and his jaw clenching.

"Jay Jay," he retorts, clearly enjoying the whole ordeal.

Before either of them can go any further, the bell rings and the teacher, balding Mr. Spruce, walks in clutching his briefcase. Everyone settles into their seats including me. Imagine my surprise when the chair next to me gets pulled up for the first time ever and Cole Stone, of all people, sits down next to me.

He makes nothing of it as I openly stare at him. "You can't sit here!" I exclaim, yet try to keep my voice down as Mr. Spruce starts taking roll call.

"If it won't kill me or endanger my sex drive in any way, then of course I can."

I wrinkle my nose at his indecency and he chuckles at my discomfort.

"No, you seriously can't. No one sits here!"

"Do you have some sort of contagious disease?"

"No!" I say, looking around and making sure that no one's listening in on our conversation, especially not the people sitting two tables in front of us.

"Do you have a foot fetish?"

"Ew no."

"Do you plan on using whatever information you can get from me in this class and use your mob connections to put a price on my head?"

I almost laugh at this one but hold it in and shake my head.

"Then I can sit here. I want to sit here."

"You'll end up at the bottom of the proverbial food chain, then—your call," I say dryly, flipping my textbook open and turning to the chapter we are currently studying. I can feel Cole's gaze burning the side of my head but I cannot look him in the eyes just yet. I might have said the words with nonchalance, but it does hurt that just by association with me, a person would be labeled a loser for eternity. It feels like I'm some sort of disease-carrying rodent that you should warn the public to run from.

"Don't let her get to you, Tessie," he says softly, so softly that I cannot believe that the words have come out of his mouth. It goes against his very nature to be nice to me. Since when does Cole Stone behave like an actual human being around me?

"It's not exactly easy to do that," I say, avoiding eye contact, but I hear him sigh and drop his head on the table.

"You let her walk all over you, but that's got to stop." He sounds determined and I whirl my head around to look at him. There's genuine concern in his eyes, and my mind involuntarily goes back to what Beth said earlier this morning—did Cole like me? Or is he just trying to get rid of his guilt for the way he'd treated me all those years? If that's the case, I can't let

24

myself be a charity case and so I confront him.

Even thinking about it is absurd and I shake the thoughts out of my head. "Why do you care? How are you any different from her?" I ask, and I see something akin to pain flash in his eyes, but just for a second. He shrugs before flashing me his devil-may-care smile.

"Let's just say I don't like sharing. You're my Tessie and I feel like the two of us are secure enough in this relationship without needing an amateur like Bishop. Wouldn't you agree?"

I roll my eyes and realize that he could never be serious for longer than a nanosecond. Who am I kidding, there's no way that his feelings for me go deeper than his preference to constantly pop up in my life, whether I want him to or not. Still, there's lingering gratitude toward him inside of me because it's been a long time since I had someone stand up for me; but I would never let him see that.

"I feel so lucky to have you as my personal bully."

"The pleasure is all mine." He winks and opens his own textbook.

Sometimes I really do wish I could see what it is that's going on inside that head of his. But then I think better of it as I realize it probably holds more conniving thoughts about making my life a living hell. Cole Stone's head is dangerous territory, but I have an inkling that I'm about to become Dora the Explorer sooner rather than later.

CHAPTER FOUR
In the Name of Your Pea-Sized Balls, I Say Unhand Me!

Let's get one thing very clear, especially now that the plague called Cole Stone is fast spreading through my life. I am not an attention seeker, I never was and never will be an attention seeker. I'm the kind of girl who likes to blend into the background so much so that a chameleon would be jealous of my mad skills. See, my ability to socialize is something way past terrible. I'm downright pathetic when it comes to trying to talk to someone new. Evidence of my lack of prowess in this particular department is that I only had one friend from the age of five till the age of fifteen. When she ditched me for a higher calling, it took me months to find a new friend—Megan. In fact, I have to hand it to the girl for tolerating my one-word stuttered responses and the awkwardness that comes as naturally as breathing to me.

The purpose of this explanation is to highlight how frustrating it has become for me to be constantly watched. The eyes follow me everywhere I go, be it my classes, the cafeteria, the bathroom. The beady little suckers even followed me to my shift at Rusty's Diner. It is unnerving to say the least, and most of the time I tolerate this unwarranted attention by telling myself that they are doing what humans are prone to do, and that's not minding their own business. Had I been in their place, maybe I too would've started stalking the girl who seems to be constantly accompanied by the resident bad boy himself.

***

We're sitting at a table in the cafeteria and once again, miraculously, the table isn't the one nearest to the overflowing trashcans. Cole, of all people, threatened a group of soccer players who had scattered comically fast from their designated table. Now once again the feeling of being watched is

26

growing to a point where it's making me paranoid. It's eerily similar to the dream where you're naked in school.

"You're going to eat that?" Cole asks as he eyes my pizza slice, which I gladly push toward him.

Cole's sitting beside me whereas Megan and Beth are sitting opposite both of us. Megan's tray remains untouched as she ogles Cole. Apparently she's never been in such close proximity to, as she calls him, "The Cole Stone," and it's robbed her of her appetite. Beth remains much more composed about the situation and is munching away on her apple with only a hint of amusement on her face.

At some point during all of this I will have a panic attack about how absurd this scene is, but I'll save it for later.

"So do you ladies have plans for the weekend?" Cole asks. It's an innocent question, but I can sense it's more to do with ending the uncomfortable, hostile (mostly from me) silence. He's been sitting with the three of us for a week now, much to the chagrin of the popular crowd, especially Nicole. Her horrific glares are getting harder to ignore. I get it—she's mad. I've somehow gotten myself under the protection of the one bully who could out-mean her and she's probably suffering from going cold turkey from her addiction. It's been a whole week since she's targeted me. Call it pessimistic but I can't help but feel a little frightened, thinking of the quietness on Nicole's front as the calm before the thunderstorm that is my former best friend.

"We might go to the mall or something," I tell him, then mentally slap myself knowing that I've given away my possible location over the weekend. I'd been hoping that the girls and I could go out and do something fun without Cole shadowing us. Now that seems somehow impossible.

"On a Saturday night? Does the mall stay open that late?" He raises an eyebrow and I shrug.

"It's not like we have a lot of options. We're not exactly swamped with party invites." I hope that didn't sound as mournful to him as it did to me. He studies me for a while and before I know what he's doing, he stands up on his seat, turns around, and hollers at someone called Jared across the cafeteria.

"Hey man, you still up for the party on Saturday?"

The person called Jared is sitting at Nicole's table. He's probably a jock since he's wearing the jersey. He yells yes and Cole tells him that he's in.

"Awesome." Jared grins and everyone at his table is immediately buzzing, discussing the all-important issue. Who's going to bring the booze?

Cole sits back down on his seat and grins at me. "That guy's been begging me all week to throw a welcome home party. I didn't want one since you know he's a tool but you're welcome."

I stare at him, trying to comprehend what it is that he's trying to imply. Why would I be thanking him? So someone's throwing a party for him, big whoop. Why should it matter to me? Always the smarter one, Megan squeals in delight and jumps in her seat. That's before she starts clapping her hands like a two-year-old on a sugar rush.

"What?" I look between the two of them wondering what it is that I'm missing.

"We now have plans for the weekend."

I scowl and turn in my seat so that I'm facing him.

"Who says I'll go?" I say determinedly.

He chuckles. "It would be the polite thing to do, besides, it'll be fun." I shake my head furiously. "No! I will not, I cannot, and frankly, I should not for the sake of my own well-being go to this party."

He turns in confusion toward Megan since I'm still mumbling incoherently under my breath, having gone into shock because of what he's just asked me today.

"What's with her?" he asks Megan, like I'm not even there.

Megan is caught off guard, not expecting Cole to directly address her. Her SAT vocabulary flies out the window and she's stuttering through random phrases as she tries to piece together an actual sentence. I call it being Stoned, with a capital S, of course.

"I-She . . . her . . . I mean that . . ."

Beth snorts and takes off her earphones. "What she's trying to so eloquently say is that we're social pariahs. If Nicole sees us at a party, she'll go nuclear. Honestly, I don't give a shit about her royal bitchness; these two are too scared to actually face her."

Cole looks impressed at her response as she puts the Skull Candy earphones in her ears and goes back to ignoring us. Though the impressed look on Cole's face is soon replaced by something I can only classify as anger as he clenches his fists.

"How long has she been doing this?" he asks with barely restrained fury, and I'm taken aback by his reaction. Shouldn't he be happy that in his absence someone's been thoughtful enough to continue his legacy?

"It doesn't matter," I say, trying to calm him down. We're starting to attract attention and the unsettling feeling in the pit of my stomach is coming back. I really wish more than ever to be someone, anyone, else, even a child named North West. However, it seems like Cole's piercing eyes are holding me captive. They keep me rooted to the spot as they burn so fiercely into mine. He's searching for answers I'm not sure he even wants to know.

28

"How long?" he repeats and this time he makes it clear that I'm supposed to give him an answer. I slump in my seat and avoid looking at him. What's he going to do when he finds out that my life is actually a lot worse than it was when he was here? Will he pity me? Will he feel even more guilty for relentlessly bullying me throughout my childhood until the age of fifteen? For some reason I don't want that. He's already going out of his way to insert himself into my life due to some unfathomable desire to make things right. I'm not his pet project and I don't want to give him more to fix. My life, the way it is right now, isn't the best, but I don't think I could deal with him turning it all upside down.

"Like I said, it doesn't matter; I'm handling it," I say, aware that my best friends are watching me intently.

"Oh you are?" he says mockingly. "Because from what I've been seeing for a whole week, your idea of handling is letting her stomp all over you with her giant-ass feet."

I burst into giggles at the last line, surprising everyone. "She does have huge feet, doesn't she?"

Cole groans at my obvious changing of the topic but he can't help but laugh.

"I saw her toes once up close and they're freakishly long," Megan adds, finally finding the courage to speak up. Cole grins at her and she beams with pride knowing that she's made Cole Stone laugh.

"This doesn't mean that I've forgotten what this conversation is about," he says seriously, and we look at him like he's going to start questioning us about Nicole again, but then his face breaks into the most gorgeous of smiles as he says, "I honestly think it's a good idea that the three of you go to this party with me. You can't keep letting Nicole get away with this. We'll all go, we'll have fun and there's nothing that anyone can do about it."

Should I be constantly wary and suspicious of his motives? Yes, I should, but sadly that just joins a long list of things that dabble between the "should" and "could." As I listen to him, I begin to think of all the ways I've let Nicole dictate my life and choices. My friends and I have no social life but how much of that is because I'm too afraid to face Nicole? Maybe a lot of it, and as I take in my best friends' excited faces, I find myself giving in.

"Fine, I'll go."

***

Cole drives me home like he's been doing all week. My father and his car are conveniently missing when I need a ride, and so Cole and I have become

29

reluctant carpool buddies. By now I'm tired of waiting for him to strike. Ever since he's come back, he hasn't done any serious damage and I'm tempted to stop being on my guard so much.

He parks the car in the driveway, which I'm not expecting. Usually he just drops me off and leaves, yet today as he kills the engine I realize that he's planning something else.

"So I was thinking," he begins as he notices me looking at him pointedly, "since we're spending all this time together . . ."

"Involuntarily," I mumble under my breath, but of course he catches it.

"Right." He grips the steering wheel tightly. "I know I'm still not your favorite person and odds are that I never will be, but what about a peace offering? How about I make you lunch and we talk?"

The word 'talk' sounds ominous and I fear for what's to come, but right on cue my stomach growls. The sound is especially loud in the confines of the car and the smug idiot hears it. My cheeks redden with embarrassment but the idea of a home-cooked meal sounds heavenly. I don't get to have a lot of those. I would therefore like to clarify that I invited the devil into my home because of food.

He gets out of the car and I follow him.

"So what is it that you want to talk about?"

The back of his head shakes slightly, and I would bet my right hand that he's smirking. He knows that the conversation looming in front of me is enough to send me running for the hills. I avoid heart-to-hearts and confrontations like it's my day job.

He pauses on the porch and turns around. "Relax, shortcake. I'm not suddenly going to declare my undying love and devotion toward you. If we're going to be friends, I thought it'd be nice if we spent a little more time together, actually talking and not arguing."

"I didn't think you were capable of that kind of emotional maturity."

"Usually I'm not but hey, I'm willing to give it the good old college try if you are."

"And why would I want to do that? Try with you, I mean."

"When life gives you lemons and all that jazz, shortcake." He chuckles. "The thing is, you're stuck here with me for at least a year. You could either choose to ignore me or we could try and build something great. I vote for the latter."

I'm still thinking about his words when he unlocks the door to my house. Wait, it is MY house. "Why do you have a key?" I ask, because there is no possible reason for him to have an all-access pass to my living space.

Unless, of course . . .

30

"Your mom gave me one the other day." He grins. "She told me to make myself right at home."

"Excuse me?" My voice is so high pitched it hurts my own ears.

"Well, she said you have a tendency to forget your keys, and since both your dad and her might not be home to let you in, I was entrusted with the responsibility. I take it you're not so happy about that?"

That is most definitely an understatement, but worse! Oh God, my parents were Cole Stone fangirls!

***

After Cole makes us both lunch, he takes to lounging around in my room, taking up all the space on my bed due to his tall frame. I sulk in a corner trying to do my homework, still unsure of how to deal with his constant presence. He fiddles around with his phone, no doubt arranging his next tryst. I cannot fathom why he's still around, but I'm wary of asking him that. Lately his answers have left me feeling stumped, unsure of what is going on with us, so I let things be.

"Hey Tessie?" he asks and I look up from my notebook to find him leaning on his elbow and staring at me. It's comical watching someone as tall as him on my bed with its floral bedspread and my Build-A-Bear collection. His feet dangle off the end when he stretches; I'm worried, or rather hope, that he might fall face-first on the floor.

"Yes?" I say, pretending to look annoyed.

"Would you mind if I asked you something?"

"You've never really cared about what I thought before. Why are you asking now?"

He doesn't answer me immediately and the fact that it takes him so long to make his point has me on my guard. I'm sure that I won't like whatever it is that he's going to say to me.

"What is it? You can't just say that and then not even ask me your question."

"Look, this might totally not be my place. Actually, I'm pretty sure I'm way out of line asking you this but . . . is there a reason why you barely touch your meals?"

His question takes time to have the right effect. I start off by becoming confused then shocked and then scared. He couldn't possibly know, could he? He's only been here for a week, not nearly enough time to pick up on my eating pattern. However, with the seriousness on his face, I realize that I'm in deep trouble.

31

"W-what do you mean?" My voice comes out shaky and I hate it because it goes against my plan of keeping him at bay regarding the issue.

"Look, just tell me if I'm imagining things," his voice trembles a little before continuing, "but even at school you pick at your food. Whenever I eat with your family, you take a bite or two and then leave thinking that your parents don't notice. We've been back from school for two hours and you didn't even eat half of what I made. Please tell me that I'm wrong, that I'm seeing something that's not there. I . . . I know it's not my place to bring this up, but Tessa, I'm just worried."

My heart's beating faster than normal as I listen to him and think how accurate his assessment is. I realize that he's caught me when no one else has.

"Maybe it's because you repulse me and I can't stomach food when you're around," I bite back, my words coming out defensive.

He doesn't miss a beat.

"I'm not joking, Tessa. If there really is a problem then I want you to be able to talk about it, to someone you trust if not me. I don't know what to do here, maybe I'm just making a huge idiot of myself, but I want you know that I care and that if you ever need someone to talk to . . ."

This kind of attention and concern are foreign to me and have been for so long. No one has really talked to me like they care, especially when it came to taking care of my health. My parents are too busy trying to deal with their messed-up relationship and my brother, well, he's . . . my brother.

"Mind your own business," I say scathingly, wondering where all my witty comebacks were vacationing or where they hide whenever Cole's around.

"You are my business, Tessie." He tries to joke about it but there's something haunting about the expression on his face. Why? Why does he suddenly care so much about me now? I'm a hair's breadth away from having a full-blown temper tantrum and it's all because I've been spending so much time with Cole. He's this incredibly frustrating person who's more cryptic and confusing than any Nicki Minaj song I've heard to date. It's like he's exposed the rawest, most vulnerable part of me and put it on public display. I'm unsure of where to go from here. He knows, he knows my weakness but rather than using that weakness to make me feel worse about myself, he's being surprisingly supportive. I take a deep breath.

"How about we come to a mutual agreement to talk about this on a day when I'm ready, and you've not literally come at me with it out of nowhere?"

"Oh, okay." He looks surprised. "Will you be willing to do that then? Talk?"

"I might as well, since you've somehow made it your job to worm yourself into every possible area of my life."

I grunt in exasperation but really I'd rather just talk to him, someone who is more a stranger to me than my friends or family.

"You might want to tone down the grunts, Venus, or your brother might think we're playing the kinky kind of tennis." He wiggles his eyebrows and I give up any hope of trying to have a decent conversation with him since he's dirtier than the underside of Travis's bed.

***

On Friday I'm taking out some books from my locker when I feel a presence behind me. Seeing as how Beth and Megan are both in their home economics class there could only be one person who'd come stalking me. Hello, Stalker Stone.

"Go away, Cole," I say as I scrape off a piece of gum someone, probably Nicole's minion, has stuck outside my locker.

"Uh, it's not Cole."

I whirl around fast enough to cramp my neck but it doesn't matter, not when it comes to Jay. He's standing before me looking somewhat hurt yet adorable at the same time. He's wearing his baseball jersey and the deep red in it makes him look really good. His mesmerizing eyes are a swirl of color as they shift from blue to green, and I struggle to stop a sigh from escaping.

"Jay," I exclaim as I shoot him an apologetic smile. I wave my hand, dismissing the mistake, "I'm sorry, I thought you were . . ."

"Cole. I get it," he says through a clenched jaw, which surprises me. He's never been like this around me. Usually whenever Nicole's far, far away he's super nice and friendly to me. I wonder what's wrong with him. Maybe that moron he calls his stepbrother did something yet again.

"W-what's wrong?" He seems to have not heard me the first time so I repeat myself. "Jay? What's wrong?"

He shakes his head and it seems like he's finally remembered what he came to me for.

"I've heard you're coming to Jared's party tomorrow." He doesn't sound pleased and I try to remember if I know any Jared. Then like a lightbulb switching on inside my head I realize that he's the jock who's throwing the party for Cole. The party I'm reluctantly coming to terms with attending.

"I guess I am," I say hesitantly and I see the disapproval clearly on his face.

"Why, Tessa? You've never come to any party before—why now?"

33

he asks sourly, and I recoil in hurt. Barely restraining myself from shouting that it's because of his psychotic girlfriend, I take a deep, calming breath and remind myself that this is Jay. He's probably only doing this out of concern. Of course it might appear strange to him that a girl like me would go to a party, and he's just checking if something's off. I want to tell him about how my best friends are actually looking forward to going, about how my baby Range Rover is in danger, but we're not exactly close; it would be a little awkward to rant in front of him. God forbid he starts thinking of me as a bigger lunatic than I already am.

"I don't know. I feel like I'm missing out on an essential part of the high school experience," is what I tell him instead.

He frowns at me for a second and I know it's because he wasn't expecting me to sound so sarcastic. It's partially my fault since every time Jay tries talking to me, I end up sounding like my mom when she accidentally took too many painkillers after she bruised her ribs. Suffice it to say I sound like a flower-crown-wearing hippie.

"Is Cole forcing you to go?"

"No!" I laugh nervously and tug at the sleeves of my sweater. When I look up again, Jay's still there looking extremely unconvinced.

"I'm going to this party because I want to. There's only so much homework you can do on Saturday night."

There's a sad smile on his face as I say this and . . . guilt? I try understanding why he's looking so forlorn at my pathetic social life but come up empty.

He opens his mouth to say something but stops as he looks at something in his line of vision. Before I can see what or who it is that's made him quiet, an arm is slung across my shoulders and I'm pulled to a very well-muscled side of a body.

"There you are, Tessie, I've been looking for you everywhere," Cole says as he ruffles my hair. I elbow him and pull away, fixing the mess he's made of my hair. He pretends to wipe away a tear and coos, "Ah shortcake, always so affectionate." He returns his arm to around my shoulder.

I will not think about the fact that the weight of it around me actually feels good.

"Let go of me, you oaf!" I struggle in his grasp, refusing to be assaulted by his scent and to feel any kind of attraction to him. He's only doing this to annoy Jay, and while I'm enjoying the look of utter shock on Jay's face, I think we're taking it a bit too far.

"In the name of your pea-sized balls, I say unhand me!" I say and stomp on his foot. He gasps and pulls away but I suspect my feeble attempt at hitting him has made little difference.

"I'll let you know that my balls are not pea sized!"

"Whatever makes you sleep at night." I glare at him but before he lunges at me, someone clears their throat. I then feel the overwhelming urge to hit my head against my locker. Jay's standing there with his nostrils flaring and fists clenched as he glares at the two of us. I've never seen him so angry and I can't figure out why he's reacting so intensely.

"Don't you have a class, Jay Jay?" Cole asks like he's annoyed about his brother's presence, and I feel like hitting him again for testing Jay when he's obviously in a bad mood. I swear this boy brings out my violent streak like nobody's business.

"I do. Actually, Tessa and I have the same one so I was hoping we could walk together." He offers me a small smile but before I can say yes Cole answers for me.

"No can do. She's coming with me."

"I am?"

"She is?" Jay and I ask at the same time and Cole nods at both of us.

"I know you didn't get to do your homework last night because of me so I got us out of class by charming the principal's secretary into letting us do stupid volunteer work in the AV room."

Okay, that's surprisingly nice for someone who could possibly be part demon. It's true though—he kept annoying me last night, refusing to leave my room once he'd dropped me off. I think he mostly felt guilty about opening up a particular can of worms and wanted to make sure I wasn't too emotionally vulnerable. A part of me, the part that didn't want to be alone following a revelation like that, was glad for his company at the time. My father had been downstairs watching the game but I suspect he'd been secretly throwing around confetti because of Cole's presence.

By the time he'd left I felt so tired that I crashed immediately and woke up only due to the ringing of my alarm for school. I'd been complaining about it at lunch knowing that my history teacher would no doubt give me a detention for the assignment I hadn't done. Cole's just saved me, thank you, baby Jesus!

"You two were together last night?" Jay asks. He sounds so crestfallen that I feel like giving him a hug, but the fear of Nicole keeps me rooted to the spot.

Cole shrugs. "We were, and now we really need to go. We have DVDs to organize and wires to untangle." He steers me around so that I'm no longer facing his stepbrother and pushes me in the direction of the AV room. I can't help but turn around and catch one last glimpse of Jay, still standing at the same spot. A familiar tug at my heartstrings occurs and the crush that I've had on him since forever rears its ugly head.

"He's not worth it," Cole says quietly as he's now walking beside me. I don't have it in me to ask questions or deny my feelings for Jay. Everyone knows I like him, right down to the lunch lady. It's not exactly a big secret since I've been pining after him for what seems like eons.

Cole gives my shoulder a little squeeze before he opens his big mouth and so appropriately consoles me.

"Trust you to fall for the uglier brother. I can bet he has a smaller pe—"

I slap a hand on his mouth at this point and his voice is muffled by my fingers. "Stop talking, or I will throw up on those three-hundred-dollar high-tops of yours."

That certainly shut him up.

CHAPTER FIVE
If You Wanted Me To Play Sexy Doctor You Could've Just Asked

Saturday evening around six o'clock I lie slumped on my bedroom floor with my back pressed against the foot of my bed. My thumbs twitch to type out a text on the cell phone I hold in my hand; however, my brain just isn't cooperating. Like Beth and Megan would ever be stupid enough to believe that I'd contracted malaria in a space of twenty-four hours. Last I checked, my town isn't suffering from a mosquito epidemic.

Okay then, malaria definitely needs to be crossed off the list of possible excuses. I try thinking harder but for someone with a 4.0 GPA it seems pitiful that I cannot come up with anything worthwhile. After I've racked my brain thoroughly I decide to hell with it and switch on my laptop, going to the holy shrine where all questions come to be answered—Google.

I type in "Most Commonly Contracted Diseases" in the search bar and my page is immediately flooded with an onslaught of information relating to STDs. I wrinkle my nose at some of the images I see and turn my face away from the screen in disgust. I quickly skip the pages that mention STDs, finding it somewhat outrageous that my friends would believe that I've not only managed to lose my virtue in a day but on top of that have also been unlucky enough to actually end up with a "problem" afterwards. I shudder before carefully studying my other options. I quickly select food poisoning as my favorite and after doing a bit of research I decide that it is highly realistic that no one's going to want to be around me when I make the epic reveal. I could just blame it on something I drank or ate, and it is a serious enough excuse to skip Jared the Jock's party.

Grinning, I take out my phone and write a text to both Megan and Beth explaining how I'm camped out in the bathroom. Adding just enough gross details about my condition, I gleefully begin to press Send. In an afterthought I add that I've seen a doctor and he says I'll be fine by Monday, seeing how I can't afford to skip school.

Before sending the text I pause and quickly add Cole as a recipient. The last thing I need is for him to butt in and somehow ruin my master plan. I hope that he doesn't see through my lie and for once in his life leaves me alone.

I snuggle down in my bed satisfied with what I've achieved and decide to take a quick nap. I hardly slept the night before worrying about what I could do to get out of going to the party. Cole doesn't understand why I can't go, and my best friends seem to be recovering from partial amnesia. They faked aloofness over my claim that Nicole would turn us into little lamb chops if we dare show our faces at any social gathering, even Stacy Miller's sobriety party. I remember her threats with extreme clarity and in no way do I wish to incur her wrath.

I'm just about to slip into the most peaceful sleep I've gotten all week when my door bursts open. I know almost immediately that I most certainly won't be napping this evening, and it is a well-known fact that a lack of sleep makes me cranky. So whoever is at my door better watch out.

Of course it's him.

"What is wrong with you?" I half yell at Cole, who's standing in my doorway smirking at me.

"I could ask you the same question, Tessie, aren't you supposed to be dying?"

Oh, right.

He doesn't give me the opportunity to speak up; instead he walks forward swinging a picnic basket behind him, which causes me to become somewhat anxious.

"See, I got your text and I realized how serious your condition is." He takes a seat at the foot of my bed. "Obviously I got worried; I mean, food poisoning is nasty business. Lucky Cassandra was around so I went up to her and asked her what I could possibly do to make you feel better."

I gulp; Cassandra is Jay's mom and Cole's stepmother . . . and a doctor.

"She sends her best wishes, by the way, and suggested that I bring these to you—apparently they work wonders."

I'm too scared to look as he opens the basket and first produces a small container containing a very disturbing green-colored liquid.

"This, shortcake, is called the mean green juice. It's good for cleansing the system." He grins, patting his stomach. I shrink back into my sheets, pulling the comforter around me so tightly that it hides half my face. I cannot let him see the dread and obvious disgust on my face due to that abomination in his hands.

Mean Green? That sounds like a Marvel comics villain. Why would anyone ever drink something that looks so funky?

"Aww, don't be like that, shortcake. You need to drink this. What will I do with myself if you're hunched over the toilet all weekend? Let's not be selfish here—drink up." He coos like he's talking to a three-year-old. I scrunch my face in pure revulsion as he pours a good portion of the juice into a glass and brings it near my face.

"Open wide," he sings and I can feel the bile rise up my throat. The idea of that slimy, bitter liquid going down my throat has me sweating and I am positive that my heart's palpitating. Before I know it I push the covers aside and jump out of bed.

"Get that away from me!" I say in a shaky voice, still eyeing the glass like its contents might come to life and attack me.

"Well, would you look at that!" Cole slaps his knee in amazement and gives me a mock wide-eyed stare. "You're all better already. See, I told you it would work."

"Cut the crap, Stone! You win—just get that thing away from me," I say sourly, still just a little afraid that he might actually make me drink the dang juice. He holds my gaze for about a minute before bursting out laughing; he rolls over in my bed clutching his stomach as his laughter resonates in my room. He continues doing so for about five minutes until tears are streaming down his face and he's sort of panting because apparently he's forgotten that he needs oxygen.

I'm mortified and stand in a corner red-faced. Perhaps faking sickness hasn't been my brightest idea.

"Oh God, Tessie," he gasps between another bout of laughter. I glare at him; this is embarrassing enough without him being here to antagonize me.

He's still laughing five minutes later but I guess he sees how red my face is becoming and his laughter fades. There's still a hint of a smile at the corner of his mouth but he's doing his best to keep quiet and that little gesture seems to warm me up on the inside.

Until he opens his big mouth and ruins it all.

"If you wanted me to roleplay Sexy Doctor and his misbehaving patient you could've just asked." He winks and I groan in exasperation, which only leads to his further amusement. He gets up from my bed and walks until we're face-to-face; placing his hands on my shoulders he whirls me around in the direction of my attached bathroom and pushes me until we reach the door.

"I can picture it right now. You could call me McSexy and be my Bambi."

I cringe at the thought as he continues picking my possible hooker names until I can't stomach it anymore. "Oh my God, shut up, Cole!"

He grins. "Have I grossed you out enough?" I nod vehemently and he seems pleased. "Good, now go shower—everyone's waiting for you," he says as he deposits me in the bathroom.

"I don't want to go, Cole." It's time to play the pity card. I might just add in a dash of tears and it'll be a home run. No guy, even Cole, could say no to a crying girl.

"Not working with me, Tessie. Use the puppy dog eyes for someone who hasn't known you your entire life," he says without even looking at me.

I stomp my foot in fury and whine, "But Cole."

He blows out a breath and walks toward me again, placing both his hands on my shoulders, looking like he's ready to give me the pep talk of my life.

"I know this is way out of your comfort zone and I know the idea of being surrounded by a bunch of people who haven't treated you well doesn't sound all that appealing but I promise you, I won't let anything bad happen okay? Do this and show everyone out there what the real Tessie is about. Don't let Nicole dictate your life, please, just for today.

There must be something about his words that affects me because I find myself agreeing.

***

Wrapping a towel around myself I peep through the door to see if Cole's still here. When the search comes up empty I tiptoe back in. Solely for the purpose of this party, I head into the part of my wardrobe that's filled with the things my mom bought me. I think she had tears in her eyes when she could finally go out and buy me skimpy dresses and bikinis. She went a little overboard and I think it's because shopping for me is her way of being a good parent. What she lacks in motherly instincts she makes up for in her taste for Stella McCartney. Lots of clothes still have tags on them, seeing how I only use the jeans and some tops. Most of my clothes still come from the same stores as Fatty Tessie's did, but now they're just five sizes smaller. I pick out a cropped sleeveless red silk blouse and a pair of high-waisted jeans that fit me like a glove. I finish the outfit with my favorite leather jacket and biker boats. I feel like my outfit needs to scream that I'm not to be messed with and I keep that in mind as I do my makeup, slightly heavier than what I would normally go for. When I've done my hair and am ready to go out, I unlock my door and come face-to-face with Cole.

"Would it be inappropriate to tell you that you look hot?" That's the first thing that leaves his mouth and I think we're both a little dazed by the comment. My cheeks flood with heat and even he looks a little flushed.

"Perhaps, but now that you've said it, I suppose I should say thank you."

He nods, still looking a little flustered as he takes in my appearance.

"Well then, now that we've got that out of the way, shall we?" I gesture toward the stairs. If I'm going, then I'd rather be done with it sooner than later.

As we head downstairs, I discover that he's ordered some pizzas for us and my stomach growls in approval. The smell of it fills the living room and I'm instantly drawn toward the cheesy goodness. It warms my heart a little that there's one pizza with extra mushrooms, extra jalapeños and corn, which is just how I like it. The fact that he's paid attention to little things, like how I like my pizza, is endearing. But I'm afraid that he's done it more so because of how little I've eaten today. He hasn't approached that topic again, thank god, but it does make me question all the little things he does for me. But of course, I can't let this moment get too poignant.

"You do realize that you've crossed a certain boundary when you start ordering food at my house, right?"

"I'm creepy but not that creepy, shortcake. This is for both of us." He shrugs but I need to know more; I need to know why he's so nice to me, why he cares.

"At least let me pay for some of it," I offer, and am about to reach for my wallet when he shakes his head.

"Think of it as a peace offering. I know this party isn't how you planned on spending your night, but thank you for giving it a shot anyway." He shrugs.

I have the urge to ask more questions, the ones that would make sense of this strange new relationship that Cole and I seem to be developing. But of course, the doorbell rings and I open it to have Beth and Megan barge in looking absolutely stunning. Megan goes into a state of absolute shock as she sees Cole, and Beth smirks at us like she's caught us doing something wrong.

"Well, you certainly got better," Beth says dryly and once again I feel like hitting my head against a wall for that moment of stupidity.

"It was my mean green." Cole grins proudly and I nearly snarl at him.

Turning back to my friends, I gush, "You guys look amazing!"

We hardly get the opportunity to dress up so seeing them like this is pretty rare. Megan's wearing a burgundy sleeveless top with black lace detailing and skinny jeans. Her red hair's cascading down in thick waves to one side, giving her the old Hollywood look. Beth's gone the opposite way

41

with her figure-hugging little black dress that rests two inches above her knees. She's paired it with black leather boots and her frenzied, raven-colored hair is twisted into a sleek ponytail.

"You think?" Megan squeals and twirls in front of my full-length mirror. I can tell she's excited and I feel really guilty for taking this aspect of high school out of her life. Had she and Beth not been friends with me, they'd be pretty popular since they were both stunning inside and out.

"I agree, and I think the occasion calls for some pizza!" Cole says and gets up to head to the kitchen to get us some plates. "You two look amazing." He smiles as he leaves and I can practically see them melt, even tough Beth whose breathing falters just a little bit. Megan looks like she's about to collapse there and then or have a full-blown panic attack. He comes back and literally serves all of us food.

"I've got to walk home for a little while, there's some kind of a kitchen emergency and they need my help. I'll be right back though." He winks at me and leaves.

"Oh my God." Megan plops down on the couch after Cole exits and stares dreamy-eyed at the ceiling. I can tell she's swooning and I feel an emotion I can't quite place. It's strange seeing her react to Cole like that; it feels like our roles have been reversed . . . odd.

"How haven't you gotten with that guy by now?" Beth sounds incredulous and I can see it from her perspective. She wasn't around for much of my and Cole's earlier animosity and it would all seem strange to her that I'm so opposed to giving him a chance.

"Easy—he's the devil," I say and she shakes her head.

"He likes you, he really likes you, Tessa," she tells me with way too much conviction.

I roll my eyes and snort, "We are not having this conversation again."

"I just can't believe that you don't see it. I mean, I know your observation skills need serious help but this is just so obvious."

I'm about to respond when Megan decides to help me out. "You can't blame her though, Beth. Everyone saw how Cole was always picking on her and most of the time she ended up crying because of his pranks."

I open my mouth to protest that I did not cry all the time!

"That was then; something must have changed, but the way he treats you, it's hard to think he could ever be mean to you. What he does now are harmless pranks he pulls to get your attention. It's all the guy can do since most of the time you're in la-la land thinking about Jay and your two-point-five children."

"I do not!" I exclaim.

"Oh please," Megan and Beth say at the same time and I hang my head in shame. I really should stop dreaming about those two-point-five kids and the house with the picket fence. I'd run a successful publishing company and Jay would be a famous baseball player. More importantly, we'd hire Nicole as our nanny after she ends up working behind the counter at KFC after high school.

***

By the time we've eaten and I've mentally prepared myself for this party, it's eight o'clock. The house is eerily silent except for the sound of the television coming from the living room. My parents are at a benefit that raises money for Dad's campaign and Travis is obviously at some random bar getting drunk once again.

Cole's been gone for about half an hour now and I have a feeling that there is no emergency at home. I think he wanted me to have this time with my friends so that I could calm down. I don't know if I'd ever say this to his face but I'm glad that he did that for me. So when he comes back, I try not to look too eager to see him. As he escorts us to his car, he tells me yet again that I look nice.

"Thanks," I say shyly, and an awkward silence follows until Beth coughs and nudges me with a smug look on her face.

I glare at her and she smirks at me, wiggling her eyebrows. Does she really think that Cole might be interested in me like that? It's obvious the only reason he's acting like this is because he's only ever seen me as Fatty Tessie or the Tessa that never wears any makeup or flattering clothes. He's just a little surprised and taken aback, feeling out of place. It's perfectly understandable.

"So should we go?" Beth asks a very flustered-looking Cole. I catch him staring at me and he realizes that I'm watching. He shakes his head a couple of times like he's getting water out of his ear and gives Beth a thumbs-up. "All systems are go!"

The three of us give him a confused look and he groans, rubbing his forehead. "I meant let's go."

"Oh," we three say in unison and follow him out to his car. Like the backstabbing friends they are, Megan and Beth take up the entire backseat of the Volvo leaving me with only one choice, shotgun.

Glaring at the two of them I take the seat next to Cole, who's adjusting the rearview mirror, and he can't help the narcissistic urge to grin at his image in the mirror. Conceited baboon.

He starts up the car but then looks at me suddenly and I feel conscious of his gaze on me. My hand reaches to my face wondering if I've managed to smear my makeup already.

"What?" I ask as he keeps looking.

"Open the glove compartment, will you?" He points toward it and I eye it warily.

"What's in it? Is it a rat or a spider, because I can deal with those two, but let me warn you, if there's a cockroach in there, you should say good-bye to your little friend," I say pointedly.

He rolls his eyes. "While your concern for little Cole overwhelms me with happiness, shortcake, this conversation isn't about him. Now open the glove compartment, it's perfectly safe."

I inhale and exhale slowly, my hand lingering on the clasp of the glove compartment. He wouldn't do anything potentially life-threatening while he himself is in the car with me, plus he seems to like my friends, so he won't kill them, either.

Reluctantly I open it and nothing springs at me like I expect, threatening to claw my eyes out.

"There." Cole leans over and points to a corner of the space inside but all I'm aware of is how close he is.

"What am I looking for exactly?" I ask in confusion and he sighs and leans in further, making me press my body to my seat. Megan pops her head in between the gap of the two seats and looks on excitedly.

"This, come on Tessie, sharpen up." He pulls out a small black pouch and places it in my hand. I tentatively tug at the drawstring that opens it, holding my breath.

"It's not poison ivy in there, Tessa, show us!" Megan squeals.

Hands shaking, I reach in and pull out a long-chain silver necklace with a snowflake pendant. I gasp as I hold it in my palm.

"Whoa, that's beautiful, put it on," Beth suggests and, ignoring Cole's gaze, which is burning a hole in my side, I do so. Immediately I love the dainty piece of jewelry. It's beautiful and delicate and . . . it's a gift from Cole?

"Is this for me?" I ask, still averting my eyes. He nods, cheeks slightly flushing. "I just . . . I don't know; it looks good on you."

"I, uh, thanks." I'm aware of how my best friends are watching him with rapt attention. Slipping on the necklace, I turn to the two and they grin deviously.

"Beautiful." They're not the ones saying that.

I catch Cole's eye and blush.

"It looks perfect with her outfit. You've got quite the taste, Stone," Beth says.

"What can I say? I'm good with the ladies." He winks, and when he notices the color my face is turning, bursts out laughing along with my best friends.

They keep laughing as we drive off to the party and somewhere along the way I fight a smile coming onto my face too as I see Cole chatting with Beth and Megan. He's so good with them; he's put Megan at ease and even managed to chip into Beth's tough exterior. I watch them fondly from the corner of my eye and somehow feel a little proud that Cole could bring happiness to these two.

CHAPTER SIX
My Life's One Big Spanish Soap Opera, Let's Call It
Ugly Tessie

"Maybe we should slap her?"

"No, Megan, that only works in the movies," Beth explains.

"We could cut off the seatbelt?"

"Don't you dare talk about my baby like that!" Cole scolds her and perhaps it's because Megan realizes that she wouldn't be having any bright ideas tonight she shuts up for good.

Then there's me and the fact that I've involuntarily started singing "Call Me Maybe."

"What is she doing?" Cole asks Beth, and I think he's looking a little scared.

"Oh this? It's nothing to be worried about, whenever she gets really nervous or scared she starts singing crappy pop songs." Beth waves her hand over to me, nearly slapping me in the eye.

"Right." Cole stretches the word but I can tell he's still not convinced that I'm completely sane.

I stutter, chanting the chorus over and over again to stop my body from trembling. I clutch my seatbelt tightly, the silver clasp digging into my skin as I stare off into the distance. Jared the Jock's house is enormous and currently packed to capacity. If I'd come here on my own I would've run away from the gates seeing the number of cars but since I'm being held hostage, I need to do everything that my kidnappers deem appropriate. Running away yelling "I'm a fatty, get me out of here!" might not be their most desired way to make an entrance. At first I was foolish enough to think we wouldn't find a parking spot and Cole, being the moody, sometimes inconsiderate, and almost always stubborn jerk that he is would get mad and leave the party. Imagine my surprise when he eased the car into a space that had a sign with his name on it.

Now I'm sitting in the car because I froze the second everyone got out. I could try to let my embarrassment over singing Carly Rae Jepsen overrule my fear of being amid large crowds; however, that is not happening. My body's gone into shutdown mode and I'm glued to my seat with my knees knocking together and my arms shaking due to sheer terror.

"Look, why don't you girls go inside and I'll bring her when she's ready," Cole says after some time to my friends, who shoot me worried glances. They're all outside of the car already and standing by my door. I can see that they're debating whether or not it's a wise decision to leave me with Cole, especially when I'm in this state, but I give a little nod as a go-ahead. I don't want to spoil this for them.

"Are you sure, Tessa?" Beth asks seriously and there's concern all over her face. I feel so guilty that I'm ruining the night for her because of a silly panic attack. "I'm fine. I just need a minute—you guys go ahead."

The fact that I say this sounding like Alvin the Chipmunk doesn't really go in my favor. They eye me skeptically but it's Cole who convinces them at last.

"You two look hot, okay? Just go in and have fun. I made you guys come here so she's my responsibility, okay? I'll see what I can do." He winks and this seems to convince them.

When they leave Cole comes by my side again. The car door is open and the slight chill in the air causes goose bumps to rise on my skin. I don't know how long I can sit like this before freezing to death and sooner or later I'll have to make a decision because frankly now I'm just feeling stupid.

"Why aren't you saying something?" I'm still looking straight ahead and not at Cole. From the corner of my eye I can see that he's got his arms folded across his chest and his eyes are studying me curiously. By this time I expect him to be mocking me or to be laughing at me but his silence is scarier.

"I'm just checking," he replies after a while and I furrow my eyebrows, my eyes still avoiding looking at him.

"Checking what?"

"How much you need to let someone in and see the real you."

I'm just trying to decode his words when I feel a strong pair of arms slip beneath my knees and pick me up. I squeal in surprise, my arms instinctively wrapping around Cole's neck as he starts to lift me.

"What are you doing?" Before I can stop him, he wraps one arm around my waist and uses his free hand to unhook my seatbelt. Once I'm free from the restraint he picks me up completely and hauls me out of his car.

"Letting myself in," he says decisively as he holds me in midair,

47

eyes boring into mine. I expect him to break out laughing any second or say something to demean me but it doesn't come. Instead his eyes hold mine for the longest time and my skin begins to prickle in the strangest way. I can't place the emotion I feel when he's looking at me like this, but I realize that I don't like it and that I don't want to feel more of it.

"Put me down," I say, breaking the spell of silence and the eye contact at the same time. Something flickers in his eyes, a foreign emotion of his own before he covers it up with mischief.

"And here I was thinking we'd end this romantic moment with a hot, passionate kiss." He winks but still doesn't put me down.

His unashamed flirting makes my skin break out into goosebumps. The fact that I'm actually enjoying his crude attempts to hit on me is evidence enough that I'm not in the right frame of mind.

"Please—I wouldn't even touch those lips if you were dying and needed CPR." My response is childish and my voice comes out a little breathy at the lack of space between us. It's all I'm capable of at the moment. I think Cole pities my flustered state and puts me down. I stumble slightly when my feet touch the ground and Cole's arm immediately reaches out to steady me, placing a hand at the small of my back.

"Famous last words, Tessie." He smirks and I elbow him in the side.

"Never happening."

"Relax Tessie, I'm joking. But would it be so bad for you to want this?" He jokingly gestures toward his body. I'm momentarily distracted because damn it, the man is good looking and he knows it. I can just never let him know that I find him remotely good looking.

"Want you? Of course I do." I smile sweetly and then grimace at the end of the sentence.

Cole fans his face. "Sexual tension, it's just getting too much."

I should lighten up, he's only joking but something about my own feelings annoys me. I'm so all over the place when it comes to him.

"Do you want me to knee you in the crotch?" I growl and he just shakes his head in amusement. I just don't understand why he's being so annoying right now since the way he was in the car with Megan and Beth made me think that he might have a human side to him after all. I just wish I could tell him to stop using his stupid one-liners on me because it just eats away at me that I want to hear these words, just from someone else. Does this make me a bad person? I hang out with one brother but am in love with the other, and he's in love with my former best friend turned Medusa.

Wow, my life's one big Spanish soap opera; let's call it *Ugly Tessie*.

"I can't promise I won't hit on you anymore, but I'll stop for the night because we're here." He sounds smug and as I end my little internal monologue I realize that I've got one foot inside the house and the other's just resting on the threshold. My eyes widen as I take in the jam-packed space with the music blasting so loud that the glass windows are vibrating. I also see dozens of red Solo cups everywhere, lining the floor, in people's hands, and on the head of an expensive-looking mermaid statue.

That's when it sinks in. I'm at a high school party and it's as cheap and tacky as any party I've seen on *Jersey Shore*. This is awesome!

"I take it you like it?" Cole sounds amused as we walk around, dodging grabby couples. I shudder and realize that what I've been missing for most of my life is a bunch of really horny teenagers getting drunk and dry-humping in the middle of the dance floor.

"No, actually, I'm happy that this is as horrible as I've always imagined it to be." I beam at him and he looks at me like I've managed to lose yet another brain cell.

"You're weird, Tessie," he says simply and I shrug.

"And you're a pain in my ass. What's your point?"

I don't know where the sudden bravery's coming from. I haven't even touched the alcohol yet and I still experience this exhilarating rush that makes me want to do headstands and pirouettes at the same time. I blame it on the pulsating music. My foot's tapping incessantly, and this need to just let go and have fun is surging through me. Consequences be damned, I just want to enjoy myself!

"Hey Tessie?" Cole cocks his head to the side and is watching me with an amused smile on his face.

"Hmm?" I ask distractedly, looking around for a corner I can dissolve in unnoticed and dance my heart out.

"You like this, don't you?"

I don't know what gave it away, maybe the big fat grin on my face or the fact that I've started swaying my body, but whatever it is, I don't try to hide it. I nod my head vigorously. "I do. This is sure as heck better than staying in my room and studying." I grin at him and he grins back.

Uh-oh, my skin's prickling again.

"Come on, let's give you a night you'll never forget."

Cole grabs my hand and we pass through the crowd. I can sense a lull in the commotion wherever we pass through. People are staring and I'm not surprised that they are. This party is for Cole and it doesn't make sense for the main attraction to be hanging out with the outcast.

I get past the curious onlookers and the girls whose faces remind me of the time my mom let me use my paints to draw on her face. Yeah, I think what I achieved was far superior. There's one girl, though, that I don't want to run into tonight and even the thought of seeing her has me rushing for the door. Nicole will not be too pleased to see me so blatantly disregard her laws, but Queen Bitch can drown in the ocean for all I care tonight.

I see Megan dancing with someone but I can't make out who he is since his back is toward me, but he's tall and has blond, closely cropped hair, and whoever he is, he looks like he's making Megan happy. Her cheeks are flushed, her green eyes shining like emeralds, and I can just see her falling for this guy even though she probably just met him.

My mouth waters at the sight of all the junk food, which is placed on a long community table that is obviously rented. My feet gravitate toward all the food like we're the opposite poles of a magnet. I reach for the bowl of Cheetos, dying to taste the cheesy goodness, but my hand is swatted away before I can get to them.

"Oh no, the first rule of any party is to not eat the food if it's openly accessible." Cole warns.

"But I . . ." I whimper at the sight of all the food. "Just one Cheeto, please!"

"You do realize that this bowl has more germs than a communal toilet?"

I scrunch my face in disgust as he begins explaining how different hands have been in the bowl and where those hands could have possibly been.

Let's just say I'm never eating at a party ever again.

"I got you these, though." He offers me a bag of gummy worms and I all but jump at them, grabbing the bag right out of his hands and opening them at the speed of light. I pick out all the red ones and eat them greedily. Gummy bears are my weakness; only KitKats exceed the love I have for them. You put a pack of those chewy delights in front of me and I'm as good as gone.

Cole knows this. He used to steal the ones I'd bring to school all the time. It hurt so much. Now he just stands there as I oh so gracefully devour red worms. I feel like I need to act a little ladylike in front of him but right now I'm channeling my inner lumberjack.

Once I'm done devouring the candy, he grabs my hand once more. He takes us to a corner that isn't as cramped as the rest of the space and the moment I hear the first words leading to "Starships," I jump in happiness. I feel exhilarated and giddy as the people around me start dancing to the one song I've rocked out to in the privacy of my room way too much.

Cole laughs as I begin my routine, one that I have perfected for this very song, and starts dancing with me. I don't protest when he places his hands on my waist and begins moving at the same pace as me. I've always known that he's a good dancer, a quality that sadly Jay doesn't share. I try not thinking about him as I place my hands on his shoulders as we both allow the catchy beat to guide our steps, singing along to the song in the most hilarious way possible.

It's surreal really, an out-of-body experience as I watch our bodies moving in sync and realize that Cole and I are having a good time, no, scratch that, a great time together. We can't seem to stop laughing as we bring out the crazy, embarrassing moves. He lets go of me only to twirl me around and then press my back into his chest as he wraps his arms around my waist, swaying us to the sound of the music. I feel like I'm all on cloud nine as I dance my heart out with Cole by my side.

The song ends and it takes a few seconds for the next one to start but that is enough for two things to happen almost simultaneously. The first being that I realize that I'm pressed way too tightly against Cole, and our chests are heaving up and down almost at the same rate. My back's facing him so I can't see his face but with the way he's holding me I realize that maybe he's enjoying this a bit too much.

The second thing, which is by far the more important one, is that in the same instant as I'm practically glued to his brother, I lock gazes with Jay. He's got Nicole in his arms and she's facing away from me. I'm eternally grateful to whomever is looking out for me up there for the fact that she can't see the murderous, almost hurt, look on her boyfriend's face as he glares at Cole and me.

I let go of Cole immediately, letting my arms fall to the side and struggling out of his grasp. He realizes this and releases me. I can feel his presence behind me and I'm sure he sees what I see, which is a very angry Jason Stone.

I don't understand why he's looking at me like this or what I could've done to make him so mad. He's been distant ever since Cole started sitting by me in our economics class and I can't help but think that he doesn't like the fact that I'm spending time with his brother.

Nicole probably realizes the change in her boyfriend's mood and lifts her head from his chest. She turns around to see the source of his displeasure and when her eyes land on me I pretty much want to be buried six feet under already.

I see her grinding her teeth and unleashing the full wrath of her terrorizing gaze on me. There's so much hatred in her eyes that I can feel it seep through my skin and make me feel nauseous. This is not going to end well and I know it. Her eyes practically turn into slits as Cole places a hand on my shoulder and while he's probably doing this to comfort me, it's the last thing I need in this situation. I do not need to show Nicole that the guy she crushed on for years is by my side.

51

"We should go," I say shakily, still not removing my eyes from where Jay and Nicole stand, both now looking at us like they wished we'd vanish with a poof.

"It's their problem, not ours; we don't need to go."

"Cole, you don't understand. When Nicole gets angry she . . ."

"Don't worry about her. I told you I'll fix it, please trust me."

I'm about to ask him what he means by fixing it but I freeze in my spot as a sly gleam glitters purposefully in Nicole's eyes. This is when she's going to do something that will make me regret ever coming here. She turns in Jay's arms and grabs both sides of his face, and before either he can react or I can pull her off him by her hair, she attacks his lips with hers and kisses him so roughly that it looks almost painful. Although Jay might not be in so much pain, seeing as how he wraps his arms around her and begins kissing her back with equally matched urgency. My heart feels like a freight train's running over it again and again and again. Tears, which I always try so hard to keep at bay, sting my eyes and a vicious wave of nausea passes over me, making me want to throw up on the spot.

They don't come up for air and I'm pretty sure they've started grinding against each other but all I can do is watch, watch as my heart is ripped out of my chest and stomped on by Nicole's size-eleven feet.

"Tessa . . ." I almost forgot that Cole's been standing there the entire time and I can't face him, I can't let him see me like this weak, pathetic girl who pines over his stepbrother. If I do then he might start treating me like he used to treat Fatty Tessie, the weak and vulnerable, unconfident blubbering idiot of a girl he left behind.

I push past him and past all the people dancing, laughing, and having fun in the vast room. I don't see Megan or Beth as I run and I am grateful. The last thing I need to do is wreck their night. Once I'm in the clear I head down a long, winding hallway trying to find some peace and quiet. As if having my wish fulfilled, a guy stumbles out of a room that could only be the bathroom. I pinch my nose and enter hesitantly; when I don't see any puke or anything too disturbing I allow myself to breathe and close the door behind me. Once all alone I slump against the cool wall of the tub and draw my knees up to my chest.

How could I believe that I could make it through this night unscathed? Nicole always gets what she wants, and when you get in her way she burns you. It's as simple as that. Seeing her kiss Jay was so painful that the intensity of the hurt I felt in that very moment takes me by surprise. The two have been going steady for three years now; I'd accepted it and lived with it, so why did tonight make such a difference?

Because you want to be the one to kiss him like that, the voice in the

52

back of my mind says.

I rest my head on my knees waiting for the overwhelming need to be sick to pass. If all goes well, I'm never going to another party ever again—it's just not worth it. Yet when I remember dancing with Cole I ache for the chance to be able to do it all over again, to be free and not imprisoned by Nicole. Is that too much to ask?

I'm pondering this very question when the door bursts open and I hit my head against the tub due to the fact that I jump in fright. My heartbeat goes into overdrive as I take in the intruder, and now my skin crawls once again, but for the worst of reasons.

There's a guy wearing a white muscle T-shirt that emphasizes his burly muscles and wide shoulders; he's tall, like six two, and bulky in a way only gym rats are. His hair is a dirty blond mess and when I notice his glazed-over eyes, my heart drops to the pit of my stomach. He's drunk. I'm alone with him in a bathroom and he's drunk, oh God.

I press myself further into a corner as he closes the door behind him and sneers at me. I don't know why I feel so immobile and helpless. I know that I should probably make a run for it, scream, do anything to get out of here, but I feel paralyzed and that's not the greatest thing to happen in a situation like this.

"Hey, blondie," he slurs and approaches me. The bathroom is small and its grandeur compared to the rest of the house is quite lacking. It takes him all but a minute to come and tower over me. I shake, still pressed tightly in my corner.

"Aww, has the little girly been crying?" he coos and uses his rough, slimy hands to touch my face; he kneels down so that our faces are level and catches a tear on his thumb, which he puts into his mouth and licks in a sickening way. I push his arm away and he laughs at my feeble attempt.

"Don't touch me!" I squeak and it sounds weak and pathetic to my own ears. He makes nothing of my protests as he grabs me by the arm and pulls me flush against his hard chest. He pulls us both up so that we're standing. I feel dirty and sick; to me he reeks of beer and I cover my mouth with my hand to stop myself from puking on him.

"I saw you dancing with Stone." His voice makes the hair on the back of my neck stand up; his hand travels up from my hips slowly to my neck as he feels me up. Suddenly I feel violated beyond measure and having all this skin on display has me begging for comfy sweatshirts.

"You looked sexy. Why don't you show me the moves you've got?" I squeeze my eyes shut as he places his lips at the hollow beneath my throat and licks it.

I push and writhe in his grasp but he grabs my wrists and slams me against the bathroom wall. My head starts pounding immediately from the force and I know that there's going be a bump forming already.

"Please don't hurt me." I squeeze my eyes shut knowing full well that I'll have to resort to begging since he's left me completely bound. One of his hands holds my wrists in an iron grasp, his body is pressing into mine nearly cutting of my circulation, and his other hand rests on my neck below my head so that I can't look away.

"It's not going to hurt, babe, in fact you're going to be screaming in pleasure." His eyes darken with lust as his hand moves to sensually roam my back.

I feel sick, I feel so so sick and disgusted and the only screams that would be coming out of my mouth would be cries of help.

"No . . . please . . . don't." He simply laughs at my pathetic responses and his free hand moves to the bottom of my shirt in order to lift it up while his lips are glued to my collarbone. I want to cry, I want to scream and yell and hit him till there's not a single breath left in his body, but I don't know how. In my mind I conjure up all these scenarios of ripping his head off but the truth is that he's heavier, stronger, and drunk.

"That'll be enough, Hank."

My eyes fly open as I hear that voice and I don't know whether to be relieved or scared to death. The piece of shit called Hank doesn't seem like he's in the mood to let me go, especially if the large bulge in his pants is anything to judge by. I whimper as he continues to lick my neck like the dog that he is and shoot a pleading look at the only other person present in the room with us.

"Please tell him to stop," I beg, and Nicole gives me a bone-chilling smile.

"I don't know; I'm enjoying seeing you like this, so willing to fall at my feet."

"Nicole, please." His lips are everywhere and so are his hands; my shoulders are heaving in silent sobs.

"For what you did today, showing up when I've told you so many times to not show me your fat ass more than I already have to see, don't you deserve to be punished, Tessie?"

I can't believe that I ever used to be friends with someone like her, someone so vile, so hell-bent on getting their way that they resort to the most vicious of things. I taste bile at the back of my throat as Hank's assault continues, his chapped lips now sucking on my earlobe.

I swallow my pride. "I'm sorry. I promise I won't do it ever again, please just ask him to stop."

She watches me writhe for about two more minutes, clearly

enjoying my pain, before she grabs Hank by the top of his hair and drags him away from me.

"Good boy, now leave before anyone sees you. Remember, not a word about this to anyone," she instructs and my mouth falls open when she kisses him square on the mouth, tongue and all, until he's ready to faint. He looks dazed and wide-eyed as he finally leaves the bathroom scratching the back of his head, making me let out the breath I'd been holding for so long.

I need to go, I need to go and shower for the rest of my life to get his germs off of me. I feel so filthy and used that I just want to burst into tears.

He could've gone further, he could've done worse, I remind myself to stop the sobs. I try to push past Nicole in order to leave but she wraps her fingers around my upper arm and yanks me back.

"This was nothing, Tessa. If you ever go against me again, I'll make sure your punishment's even worse," she seethes, shoving me away once she's made her threat. I stand there letting her words sink in as she exits, slamming the door behind her.

***

I stand in front of the sink trying to identify the stranger in the mirror. My makeup is now running down my face, the mascara creating tear tracks as it flows down. My lipstick is smeared, the blush now considerably unnoticeable above my red splotchy cheeks. My hair is tangled and sticking out in all directions with a bump pulsing painfully on my head. My shirt's ridden up and slightly torn at the ends, all in all I look like the kind of girl who went for a quickie in the bathroom stall. Splashing my face a couple of times with cold water I use a towel to wipe away the garish makeup but the thought of Hank's hands all over me has me feeling dirtier than ever.

I rush outside, trying not to run into someone I might know. I don't want to run into someone or explain why I look like Courtney Love on a bad day. The party's still going in full swing and it's the perfect setup to escape without being noticed.

Until . . .

"Tessa? Are you okay?" Jay grabs my arm and I flinch, still a little afraid of being touched. He's standing right in front of me looking worried. I can't find it in myself to look him in the eye, seeing as how his girlfriend just had me assaulted.

"I'm . . . fine, just let me go," I say softly and pull my arm away from him. He backs up just a bit but still doesn't make room to let me go.

"No, you're not, what happened?"

55

"Look, I just, I just really need to go home." My voice is cracking up and I'm seconds away from crying in front of everyone from school.

"No, Tessa, it—"

"Tessie?"

I hear the second voice and something inside of me snaps. It's Cole, he's standing a few feet away from Jay and me but it's obvious he knows something's wrong. He strides toward us pushing and shoving past people; our gazes are locked onto each other and I forget that Jay's here with me too.

He runs a hand through his hair in relief as he nears me, putting both hands on my shoulders. "Where did you go? I looked for you everywhere. I . . . lost track of you and no one knew where you went. Are you okay?" His voice which had been filled with panic earlier, grows softer with each word. It may have something to do with how devastated I look that he takes pity on me but I feel nothing but anger toward him right now. I need someone to blame for tonight and he's the lucky winner.

I stare at him as he looks at me expecting me to answer his damn question, expecting me to apologize for making His Highness worry about me as I was being attacked in a bathroom. I feel fury and anger and rage all directed toward him. He did this; he brought me here even when I told him it would be a horrible idea. He didn't listen to me because he thinks he's so darn smart. All of a sudden the dam bursts.

I hit him. I hit him repeatedly, pounding on his chest as his eyes widen in shock.

"You! You did this! You brought me, I told you again and again that I shouldn't come, you should've listened to me, and you shouldn't have made me come here! I hate you, I hate you, I hate you so much!" I'm sobbing hysterically and the hitting loses its zeal. I clutch the fabric of his shirt in one hand and he pulls me close to him.

"Shh, Tessie, it's okay, I'm here," He sounds lost, like has no idea what's going on but he's still doing his best to comfort me. I bury my head into his chest and wrap my arms tightly around his waist.

"Why didn't you listen to me?" I choke out and he rubs my back, rests his chin on top of my head, and whispers, "I'm sorry, Tessie, I'm so sorry."

I hold on to him even tighter because it feels like if I let him go I might lose my safety blanket and Hank might come back. I don't want Hank to come back. I cry and I cry as Cole continues rubbing his hand up and down my back.

"What happened to her?" I hear a voice ask and it reminds me that Jay's still here. There's nothing more I want to do in this moment than tell him about what Nicole did. I want to hurt her and cut her as deep as she cut me. But now I've been well acquainted with the consequences of going against her and so I know that I need to keep my mouth shut.

"Call it a wild guess but I'm pretty sure your girlfriend has something to do with it," Cole spits angrily and since I'm so close to him I can feel his muscles tense up.

"Don't start with that, Cole, she isn't even—"

"Shut up, Jason, just shut up."

With me still clinging on to him for life he begins leading us away from all the noise. We might be leaving the house but I don't know since I don't lift my head from where it's resting on his chest. It's when the cool, fresh air hits me that I know for sure that we're outside. Cole lets go of me and I feel like hitting him again for doing so but quickly shut up when he takes off his leather jacket and wraps it around me. The material provides instant warmth but also swallows me up due to its massive size; it also smells like him and I once again feel secure.

Cole cups my cheek and makes me look up from where I'm inhaling the scent of his jacket.

"Are you okay, Tessie?" His thumb wipes away a tear that's still lingering on my cheek; the action reminds me of Hank but it doesn't repulse me like his did. It makes me feel warm on the inside.

He isn't asking me to tell him what happened, he's only asking me if I'm okay and I couldn't be more grateful to him for understanding how I feel right now. Just thinking about what almost happened has the tears threatening to spill over again.

I nod just a little bit and he sighs, wrapping his arm around me and hugging me tightly. I'm aware that we're in the parking area and no one's around; just the two of us and it feels good. I hug him back not knowing why out of all the people that can comfort me right now it's Cole who's actually making me feel better.

Not my best friends and certainly not Jay; it's Cole, and I just don't know why.

CHAPTER SEVEN
It's Spoon Lifting, Not Grand Theft Auto!

"I'm not signing that."

"It's not like you actually have a choice—sign it."

"No!"

"Yes."

"How do I know you're not going to use my signature to, I don't know, take away all my life savings?"

"Yes, because working at Rusty's has made you quite the billionaire." He rolls his eyes.

"I will let you know that I have a respectable amount in my bank account."

"Whatever makes you happy, sweetheart, now just sign this."

I shake my head vigorously and once again push the napkin toward Cole. We've been going at it for about twenty minutes and by this point I'm pretty sure that the waitresses are under the impression that they're witnessing an illicit drug deal. It would be understandable, though, since it's about 11 p.m. on a Saturday night with the two of us sitting in a corner booth arguing over a contract that sounds highly suspicious.

"Okay, okay how about this, if you sign this napkin I'll join your Range Rover crusade. Your parents love me already so if I were to drop hints here and there, it could speed up the process."

I lean forward on the table, suddenly very interested in this deal. "Would you really do that?"

"We can talk about how amazing I am some other day, Tessie, we've got a very important napkin waiting to be signed." He grins and I give him my best withering stare.

I groan in defeat and slide the napkin toward me, sign my name with the borrowed Sharpie and then slide it back toward Cole, who's looking so smug that I want to wash that expression right off his face.

With the acid our cleaner sometimes uses to clean the toilets. "There, now was that so hard?"

I am this close to dumping my strawberry ice cream over his head but honestly, I could never do that to my precious, precious ice cream. It deserves so much better than to be wasted on a douche doodle like him.

Right, of course explanations are in order as one might get confused because of our conversation. Let's rewind and go back to the party, even though that's probably the last thing I ever want to do, but for the sake of storytelling it must be done. See, after my knight in shining armor or in this case, my fool riding his much-too-expensive Volvo, rescued me and after we had our little moment, things got awkward. It's almost painful to remember him passing me tissue after tissue and me bawling like the weakling I am.

I haven't told him though. I haven't said a word about why I'd flooded his car faster than the Titanic and he hasn't asked though I know he's dying to. Maybe it's the tapping foot or the fingers drumming consistently on the table but I just know that he wants me to spill my guts.

Maybe that's why he's brought me to Rocco's twenty-four-hour diner, to bribe me with the one weakness I have left from my Fatty Tessie days, well, apart from KitKats. I'm currently on my third serving of the delectable ice cream and with the way I'm inhaling it, I have a feeling that I'll soon be sharing, pouring my heart out to him just so he buys me more ice cream.

Now the contract, or rather the ratty napkin, that's getting a little worse for wear because of us tugging at it endlessly, the napkin is meant to seal a deal between us. By signing it, I will be admitting that I lied about Cole being the reason I once broke my arm in middle school. The reason that actually happened was that I'd followed Jay to the skating rink, lovesick idiot that I was. Given my utter lack of coordination, things had not ended well but the silver lining was that I'd been able to pin the blame on Cole and one of his pranks—heck, Jay even helped corroborate it. Both sets of parents believed me as opposed to him and let's just say he got in a lot of trouble. Now Cole's trying to clear his name and even as we fight, I realize that he's only trying to distract me and I'm relieved to know that it's kind of working.

I shake my head as if physically trying to remove memories of the incident from my mind and spoon some more ice cream into my mouth since it's the only thing that's keeping me relatively close to sanity. The night obviously hasn't gone according to plan and my first attempt at entering the party circuit led to me being assaulted in a bathroom. I shudder as I remember the vicious look Nicole gave me as she left; it was like she suddenly decided to experiment with cannibalism and I would be her first meal. I don't know what I've done to make her hate me so vehemently. No one hates another person so much without a solid reason, and the Nicole I used to know never did anything without a motive.

I feel someone kick me beneath the table and I drop my spoon to the floor in surprise. I gape at Cole, who's snickering in his seat. He doesn't realize how serious this is! The staff at Rocco's is horrible, especially the ones on the night shift. Most of them lock themselves up in the supply room and do God knows what in there until the morning shift. Now where would I get a new spoon from and how on earth would I finish my poor ice cream?

"What is wrong with you?" I growl as I get out of my seat and head toward the counter. Working at a rival diner I've learned a few things so I know the right places to look if I need extra cutlery. Usually they'd keep it in drawers near the cash register so that the limited number of workers wouldn't have to run back and forth. I jump over the counter and sure enough the telltale chest of drawers is there; the only thing that could possible work against me now is if the drawer is . . .

Locked. The darn drawer is locked!

"Are you planning on robbing the place?" Cole sounds like he's standing right behind me and sure enough as I twist my body slightly and crane my neck, he's standing there smirking at me.

"I'm trying, Stone, to find myself a spoon so that I can eat my ice cream." I pull the handles a couple of times but it's useless. They're locked and the manager has the key. From the way he'd been winking at our waitress, one could only guess what the two were up to.

"You're really attached to that stuff, aren't you?" He's still standing there being completely useless and annoying. It's because of him that I'm going to have to steal cutlery or possibly break into the supply room.

"It would be really nice of you if you stopped talking and try figuring out a way to help me."

He snorts and pushes me aside with ease. Taking my place in front of the drawers he tells me, "Watch and learn, rookie."

He takes out a screwdriver from his back pocket and in a move that is surprisingly normal to me he begins picking the lock.

"Of course I forgot, I'm hanging with a delinquent," I say dryly and he winks at me.

"Only for you, babe."

"Gross! Don't ever call me that again."

He bursts out laughing at that point, the top drawer swinging open as he backs away, doubling over. I look at him like he's finally become the lunatic that he's been threatening to become since the day I met him. But all of a sudden the sound of his laughter begins to ring merrily in my ear and not shrilly; all of a sudden I just want to stand there and watch him laugh, my heart flip-flopping inside my chest.

"I was referring to the pig, shortcake."

Well, this is uncomfortable.

After the criminal and I have stolen, no, borrowed the spoon, I finish my ice cream in peace and make a run for it. I can't help but look over my shoulder fearing Betsy the waitress will come running after us and throw her lethal skates at us.

Oh snap out of it, Tessa, its spoon-lifting not grand theft auto!

We escape with great stealth, especially on my part, and Cole heads toward my house. I know he's barely holding in laughter because of my actions, but I'm not a seasoned delinquent like him and even if it was a spoon, I did steal it. He's turning me into a criminal, too! I really need to stop letting him hang around me so much. In fact, when he drops me off I'm going to ask him to stop blackmailing me into spending time with him. I need to stand up for myself and show him that he can't just walk all over me.

"Tessie?" he asks, breaking the spell of the thoughts I'm currently having, ones which consist of me chasing him out of my house with a gigantic baseball bat in my hand. He's staring at the road ahead but with the way his knuckles are tightening around the steering wheel I can tell that his mind is somewhere else and he's not exactly thinking positive thoughts.

"Yeah?" I ask a little hesitantly since I know where this conversation is going. I don't know if I'm ready to answer his questions, especially since I'm already trying to block the memory of Hank and his filthy hands from my mind forever.

"Have you been hurt?"

His words hang in the air and at the same time it feels like they're weighing me down, some kind of anchor dragging me down with it as it sinks. I ponder his question as we drive down the quiet road. I'm not hurt— well, not physically at least, but mentally it's an entirely different ballgame. I'm terrified, feeling like every visible part of my skin is covered in filth and that any moment Hank could show up to finish what he started. Add to that the painful bump on my head acting as a constant reminder of what happened, I could honestly admit that yes, I'm hurt, even if it's not visible.

"No."

I never said I could honestly admit it to Cole, though.

We're both quiet as my words hang in the air.

"If you hate me right now, I understand. I said that I'd take care of you and I failed. But please just . . . tell me what happened. You looked so hurt, so scared. I don't think I'll ever be able to forget the look on your face.

61

Whoever did that deserves the worst kind of hell." He grits his teeth.

My lips start to wobble and I almost give in, almost. He's right to assume that I'm angry at him. Of course he's not Nicole and neither is he Hank but pinning this on him gives my anger an immediate outlet. I almost tell him about what happened but I know he has a history of violence so the probability of him going off the deep end is very high. I don't need things to escalate and what I really should do is nip this thing in the bud while I've got the chance.

"I don't want to talk about it."

"Maybe you talk about it and what I really . . ." He pushes and I groan.

"I just don't want to."

"Will you ever want to?"

"I'm not sure." I wring my hands looking down at my lap.

He doesn't push me again but the silence that falls is just as nerve-wracking. My heart starts to race and my stomach clenches uncomfortably as Cole drives down the road. The need to tell someone, especially Cole makes me taste bile because saying the necessary words make me want to throw up.

"I need some time," I tell him and from the corner of my eye I see him flinch. It has to be bad enough that I can't even talk about it and watching the realization hit him is painful.

"Right." He swallows heavily. "Whenever you're ready.'

The car comes to a stop outside my house and I rush out, greedily breathing in the fresh air like I'd just been underwater. Hoping to get as far away from Cole as possible before I end up saying too much, I rush inside and then curse inwardly when I realize that I've forgotten my house keys, again. I hear Cole come up behind me and I turn away from him as he unlocks the door and lets me go in first.

***

I can hear footsteps behind me as I walk into my living room; I'm still shaking just a little not knowing if it's because of Cole's proximity or the aftereffects of the party. I know it's him, of course it's him, and he's turning out to be as opposed to giving me some space as a kangaroo is to its newborn.

"Tessie, wait—"

"No, okay, no. I'm done, I'm just done with everything. I told you I need some time and space and you still follow me in here. What do you want from me?" I cry out, facing him, and he clenches his jaw, his eyes ablaze with what I'm expecting to be fury but it's not, it's something else entirely.

"I just want to make sure you're okay." His voice is soft as he approaches me like I'm a wounded animal.

"Why? After everything you've ever put me through, do you honestly expect me to share my deepest darkest secrets with you? Was that your master plan, Cole, because if it was, then I have to say military school sure as hell destroyed you."

He looks winded as though I've struck him and maybe that was what I intended, a verbal slap to the face. I'm lashing out, I need someone to take all my anger out on and he's the nearest target.

"I'm the last person who'd ever want to hurt you. I know I've done some stupid things in the past but . . ." he struggles to find words, "I would never intentionally do anything now that could hurt you even a little."

"How can you expect me to believe that? You think you can just waltz back into my life and try to, what, fix it? Have you ever thought about the fact that there's a reason I don't try to do something about it all? I don't want to get myself involved in something I can't handle!"

His face softens and he takes a few steps so that he's now closer to where I'm breathing rather heavily. I'm still angry but I know now that it's not him that my anger is directed toward.

"You're strong, Tessie, you're so strong and I know that more than anyone else."

"Is it because I still haven't kicked the bucket despite all your attempts?" I say dryly. It's a desperate attempt to end our argument. I just don't feel comfortable whenever things get confusing between us. It needs to be either black or white, he either needs to be relentlessly bullying me or ignoring me. I don't like it when we lose sight of what the nature of our relationship is actually like.

"Oh please, I couldn't hurt a fly. Beneath this hot, sexy, rugged exterior there's a heart of gold." Cole, I think, wants us to stop talking about feelings just as much as I do. We come to a silent acceptance to raise the white flag, for now.

"I think you meant stone, Stone." I push past him and toward the refrigerator. Taking out a bottle of water I unscrew the cap and gulp greedily. Between all the crying and screaming one sure does get thirsty. Beside me, Cole takes a minute to cool down and I see him tapping away on his phone. I bet he's taking care of all that needs to be taken care of because he's good at that. And despite our argument, I'm glad he's here because if I were alone, I'd probably be a crying heap on the floor.

63

***

"Aren't your parents coming back?" Cole asks as he leans against my vanity table while I'm changing into my pajamas in the bathroom.

"They've gone to see my grandparents so they'll be away for the weekend," I shout out as I start brushing my teeth. My mom's dad was the mayor before my own father and now with the elections so close, my dad's realized that he's desperately in need of help. It's kind of obvious that my mom was thrilled seeing her husband so readily begging for her help.

"What about Travis?"

"I don't really know where he goes at night or what he does."

"I'm not saying that I have the most normal family, especially with Jay for a brother, but don't you think there's something wrong with this picture?"

"Which part? The part about my absentee parents or my depressed brother?" I finally come out after having showered thoroughly, scrubbing every inch of my skin until it's raw. I feel much better after having convinced myself that no traces of Hank remain on me and I almost feel normal again, almost normal but just not quite there.

"All of it, Tessie. What the hell happened in these three years?"

He's watching me as I towel-dry my hair but it's as if he knows that at the moment, anything that is remotely sexually suggestive would freak me out so he averts his gaze. I've intentionally gotten out my baggiest clothes for the night. The full-sleeved red shirt has a picture of Snoopy on it and the striped pajama bottoms are so long that I had to roll them three times to keep myself from tripping.

"All the bad stuff. My dad became mayor, my brother lost everything, and my best friend decided that I wasn't good enough for her. In more recent news, you decided to come back."

"Ah, your love for me just overwhelms me, Tessie."

"Glad I could make your day." Sarcasm drips from my voice as I settle on the little stool placed in front of my vanity table and face him.

" Ah yes, you're such a ray of sunshine, shortcake." He places a hand over his heart. "What did I ever do to deserve a friend like you?"

"Friend? In your dreams maybe." I don't look at him and start brushing out my hair.

"At least you're okay with me dreaming about you. I thought I was going to have to deal with a blanket-ban situation. Note to self, it's okay to dream about Tessie."

"Stop flirting with me, it's nauseating!" The effect of my command is subdued by the huge yawn that I let out while I say this. All my muscles ache and my head feels like it weighs a ton, my eyes are drooping and I feel like if I get up from the little stool I'm sitting on I'll just end up falling face-first on the floor.

"You've made your point, Sleepy, now come on get into bed." Cole helps me up and guides me to bed. Because the events of the night have taken their toll on me, I don't think twice about snuggling into bed and pulling the covers over me. It's when I register that Cole's still in my room looking a little uncomfortable that I lift my head from the pillow.

"You don't happen to have a spare mattress I can crash on, do you?"

We have an entire spare room but I don't think I want to tell him that.

"Why would you do that? You literally live five minutes away."

"Look, I can't leave you alone in this place, not after tonight."

I open my mouth to correct him and tell him that I don't need him to babysit me but he continues talking.

"I know you hate the idea, I get it but I've seen you looking over your shoulder every other minute since we left that damn party so I know you're scared. It'll give me some peace of mind if you're not here by yourself."

"If you really want to, you can crash in the living room," I mutter under my breath and he exhales, as if relieved that I'm letting him stay. I close my eyes and pretend to sleep when I hear him walk away.

Half an hour later I'm cowering in my bedroom and pull the covers tighter around myself so that they surround me like a cocoon. My eyes keep darting toward the locked door and the shut windows as if expecting someone to jump right out of them.

Expecting Hank to break them open is more like it.

I try to sleep but as soon as I close my eyes, I start remembering and seeing everything that happened and it makes me feel sick. I don't know what to do anymore, nothing's helping. No amount of deep breathing or super crappy pop songs. All I can do is overthink and reach the point of hyperventilation as I think about Nicole's threat, Jay's expression, and most of all Hank's hands all over my body. I sniffle and shoot out of my bed as the need for a distraction is driving me crazy. I need to be annoyed the crap out of, if I want to stop thinking about the night and of course there is only one person whose services are available twenty-four-seven.

I find myself going downstairs and the very first thing I notice is that Cole is shirtless! He's shirtless and lying on the pullout couch, wrapped up in a throw blanket. He's got my copy of *The Alchemist* in his hands and he seems to be pretty engrossed in it so I don't think he'll notice if I sneak by him and curl up next to him. But it's as if he senses my presence in the room

65

and lifts himself up, putting the book aside.

"Are you okay?"

I abandon my ninja-like plans and just stand there feeling embarrassed. I mean I basically told him that I didn't need him to worry about me and here I am acting like the weakling I truly am.

"I couldn't sleep," I admit and then find myself explaining it to him. "I was scared and the nightmares kept waking me up."

He looks a little dumbfounded and I'm just about to run back up to the room, pretending that I never cracked like this but the way he treats me is surprisingly gentle. It's as if he knows exactly how to make sure that I don't break down and shut him out.

"This pullout bed is big enough for two people . . ." he suggests and I'm shaking my head before he can finish the sentence.

". . . or how about you go back to bed and I can crash on the floor. That might help with you being afraid," he tells me softly.

Eyeing both the couch and thinking of my bed upstairs, I realize that he's right. Much as I hate to admit it, I just might need him by my side.

"Just don't even attempt to touch me and we'll be fine. You will stay on the floor." I warn him as he starts to sit up. I immediately avert my gaze from his naked chest.

"Relax, shortcake, I promise to be a complete gentleman. No touching, I promise."

I think we both find ourselves thinking of the promises he'd made earlier and the debacle that was my first party. I shudder at the thought.

"Perfect, thanks. Also let's try not mentioning this to anyone, okay? It's just a one-time thing. I . . . I don't usually ask boys to sleep in my room. This is a one-off, have I said that already?" I find myself rambling and his brows furrow in confusion as I rush up the stairs, comforted by the sound of Cole's footsteps following me. I freeze at the threshold to my room.

"Tessie," he says carefully, "what happened?"

"I'm too tired right now, I'll explain tomorrow, I promise." I don't want him to hear the panic in my voice but it's there and it's apparent. He sighs but says nothing else as we work together to create a makeshift bed for him on my floor and I realize that he won't be asking me any more questions, not tonight, at least.

***

I wake up gasping in the middle of the night after a very horrible and a very vivid nightmare.

Someone's calling out my name and shaking me. The idea of

someone touching me makes ice settle in my veins. I open my mouth to scream when I hear his voice.

"Shh Tessie, it's just me. It's Cole, you're okay, I got you."

My bedroom is pitch black but the moonlight from the window illuminates his face. I lift myself to sit up straight as Cole gets me some water. Utterly embarrassed, I start worrying about how I'd explain this to Cole. He obviously knows that something bad happened to me but bad enough to give me nightmares? Yeah his imagination must be going wild.

I start to panic and it starts getting harder to breathe. I'm almost about to ask for a paper bag when Cole sits down next to me and slowly, tentatively rubs soothing circles across my back. He's hesitant as though not sure how I will react but the circular motion feels so comforting, I almost purr.

"You're okay," he repeats.

I breathe in and out and let myself calm down. The nightmare is still lingering in my mind but knowing that Cole's here and that I'm safe within my house makes it easy to push thoughts of the party aside. I lean into Cole, as if seeking more of his warmth and rest my head on shoulder, his very naked shoulder.

Now my heartbeat's skyrocketing for an entirely different reason. Despite all my attempts to keep him out of my space, out of my bed, that's exactly where he's ended up and I . . . I actually don't mind. Clearly I'm conflicted because even as I try to shift and put some distance between us, I miss the heat of his palm against my back. Cole's not trying to make a move, he just sits there with me and holds me. His face is mere centimeters away from mine and I can see every single line and contour of his face clearly. He's gorgeous, of course he is, I won't deny that any further but he's also . . .

Mean.

Yet he took care of you today, says a nagging voice in my head.

Arrogant.

He's been sitting with you in all your classes and at lunch since the day he showed up. He obviously isn't worried about his image, the voice scolds.

Conceited.

With a face like that who wouldn't be?

I shake the thoughts out of my head before that stupid voice can defend Cole some more. It's annoying, and I don't like that any part of me, however small it is, is starting to accept him, faults and all. I do owe him for today but he owes me ten years' worth of humiliating memories.

Though that's not what I think when I shift just a little closer to him,

67

seeking his warmth. His breath fans my face and boy, does he smell good. It's such an addictive scent making me want to move closer and closer to him. Taking me by surprise, his arm tightens around me and pulls me closer so that I'm now pressed up against his chest.

I would question his motives but there's nothing sexual about how he's holding me, he's simply trying to comfort me when I badly need it. So even though my breath hitches and my skin tingles I don't move away from him. I just feel his heart beating against my own and somehow it relaxes me. I stare at his face for some time trying to understand this boy with his delinquent instincts and his irreparable habit of constantly shaking up my life and realize that he's changed.

He's changed; he isn't the guy who left me four years ago with a stink bomb in my locker as a farewell present. Something's happened that has made him change his attitude toward me. That something that is stopping him from teaming up with Nicole and joining her quest to make my life a living hell.

So as I'm having my first-ever sleepover with Cole Stone, I try to think of a reason as to why he's acting the way he is and honest to God, I'm just too terrified to find out.

CHAPTER EIGHT
You're Smiling Like a Horny Guy on a Dodgy Street Corner

I wake up the next morning due to the annoying morning light that seems to be so annoyingly streaming through my window. I groan and roll onto my side so that my face presses into the sheets and mentally curse myself for not drawing the curtains before going to bed. I pull my fluffy purple blanket over my head and try going back to sleep.

However, even as I'm trying to slip into a deep slumber I can sense that something's different and it's irking me. I'm still too warm and comfortable in my bed to actually get up and see why it is that sleeping in—an experience that I cherish more than life itself at times—is getting so bothersome. Then I sense it, the reason why my stupid brain refuses to shut down and let me get some sleep, I know what the difference is.

My sheets don't smell like the peach-blossom-scented detergent our cleaner uses. It's like the scent has been overwhelmed by something stronger, something much more delectable and inviting. Before I allow myself to greedily inhale more of the delicious scent my brain goes into overdrive and warning bells sound in my head. This smell does not belong to me, this smell cannot be associated with any of my family members because there's only one person that I know who could leave traces of such a scent, and I really don't want to think about the hows and the whys regarding that particular situation.

Sleep abandons me immediately when I realize that I'm no longer sleeping but just lying down and acting like an obsessed stalker while smelling my sheets. Getting up quickly, I groan and grunt, stomping my feet on the ground, cranky because I really could do with more sleep. I yawn, opening my mouth widely, and run my hand through the tangled mess that is my hair.

"Good morning to you too, Tessie."

69

My eyes are still encrusted by the remnants of sleep so I have to squint and focus to make out the person who has the nerve to bug me when I'm feeling like a cavewoman. Of course it's him, who else could it possibly be? Cole leans against the door, looking ridiculously good for whatever god darn time it is. I could say that I've forgotten about him holding me last night, I could say that seeing him doesn't have my jaw dropping or my eyes bulging out of their sockets, but that would be a lie.

"Not in the mood," I mutter grouchily and lock myself in my bathroom, though I can still hear him laughing outside.

Even though I took a shower before going to bed last night, I still feel grimy and hence allow myself to be assaulted by the hot water as it rouses me out of my zombie-like state. Once I'm as shiny and new as a baby's bottom I brush my teeth and pull on my robe. Afterward, I lock my door and walk toward my closet.

Usually it takes me about two minutes to pick an outfit but somehow today I don't want to wear my ratty old sweatshirt and jeans. It's like my hand gets repelled when I try taking something out from my everyday clothes and I frown. It's the weekend, the perfect opportunity to dress down, but I just don't want to.

Sighing, I go to the very back of the walk-in closet and try not to flinch at the amount of pink in there. I like pink, don't get me wrong, but then there's only so much of it that you can have in your closet before it starts looking like something the Pink Panther threw up.

I pick out a fitted long-sleeved gray top with some distressed jeans. Since we're at home, I slip into a cute pair of sandals. Once dressed I tie up my hair into a messy bun and put on some gloss. Then I bounce downstairs, suddenly finding myself in a good mood.

I find Cole busy in my kitchen. There are blenders whizzing and pots and pans on the stovetop. He's got a chopping board in front of him and is going at the vegetables like a pro. For a second I just stand there fixated by his skill and feel slightly embarrassed by the fact the only time I tried to cook I ended up blowing up the oven.

"Done drooling, shortcake?"

I stop staring as I register his words and manage to put some bite behind my words even though I'm not really up for an argument with him at the moment.

"I'm sorry but I don't bat for your team, Martha Stewart."

His smirk drops and he glares at me. "Now you're just being sexist."

"You're wearing my mom's old apron; you should've seen that coming." I chuckle and take a seat opposite the kitchen counter.

"This," he points to his T-shirt, "is new and cost me fifty bucks; I don't care if I look like one of the Real Housewives of New Jersey as long as I don't get pancake mix on it."

I notice that he's changed too; maybe he left at some point to go home.

"You sound more and more like a girl each day."

He gasps audibly and before I know it he's thrown a fistful of flour at me. "Take that back," he says and I just sit there in shock while grimacing at the bitter, powdery taste in my mouth.

"You idiot! I just showered," I whine as I try dusting off the flour from my face, my hair, and my brand-new top.

"You questioned my masculinity, bad move, Tessie."

"You're so, so . . . !" In frustration and mostly annoyance at how he's turned my good bright sunny day into one where I'm possibly in the mood for murder, I grab my glass of orange juice and throw it at his face.

Though when I realize what I've done I gasp in shock and cover my mouth with my hands.

I'm not an impulsive person; I always think something over a billion times before I actually go through with it. In fact, I don't just think, I overthink. I am the queen of the land of the overthinkers, so for me to have done what I just did is just completely out of character. I have somehow managed to pour orange juice all over the guy who's known better for his ability to keep a grudge than his sexcapades, basically hitting the motherlode of impulsive mistakes.

"I'm so sorry! I didn't, I mean you were there and I got angry and I'm so sorry." My voice is muffled as I cover my face with my hands and peek through my fingers to see if he's breathing fire and if I should start reciting my last will and testament but to my surprise he looks . . . amused?

"What?" I ask him as I finally uncover my face and he, in all his OJ-drenched glory, smiles at me. I wonder if he's suffered any serious brain damage between the hours that I slept.

"You splashed juice all over my face," he muses, still smiling.

"Yes, Einstein, I did, but that doesn't explain why you're smiling like a horny guy on a dodgy street corner."

He bursts out laughing at that and his laughter is infectious and I find myself joining in though I still don't know why he isn't choking me with his bare hands.

When he stops laughing, Cole takes a dish towel and wipes his face clean. The shirt he tried so hard to protect is now stained so obviously he does what he considers the most rational move.

He takes it off.

My eyes widen and my breathing falters as he slowly shrugs out of

71

the now-sticky material. It's like watching an Abercrombie & Fitch commercial only better because his body is so much more sinful than any of their Photoshopped models. I withhold a sigh as he uses the towel to wipe off his stomach and I nearly faint when I see the eight-pack. Holy cow, eight freaking pack.

"Try not to burn the house down while I put these in the laundry." He chuckles, leaving the kitchen with me standing there feeling absolutely starstruck. I know I saw him shirtless last night but it was nighttime and we were in bed. It kind of made sense to be half naked then but now in broad daylight my heart and brain just can't handle it as they're both going into overdrive. I stare at his broad, smooth-skinned back and the indentations of his muscles as he walks away from me and to the laundry room.

I'm vaguely aware of shutting down the blender and trying to flip a pancake perfectly but narrowly missing the floor when I try.

"The key is in the wrist." I jump as arms shoot out from behind my waist and take a hold of my hand that holds the spatula. All of a sudden I'm surrounded by the same scent that I was intoxicated by in the morning and there's no hint of a doubt as to who it is behind me. The sound of his voice tells me that he's closer than I want him to be and the fact that his arms are around me is seriously destroying my resolve. I don't want him to know that his nearness is having the effect that it is so I straighten up my spine and nod like I'm listening to his instructions. His fingers are gentle as they clasp on my wrist and help me flick a pancake perfectly in the air before it lands perfectly in the center of the pan.

"I did it." Smiling to myself I try to move to face him but at the same time as I turn my head and before I can register the situation, Cole grabs the bowl full of pancake batter and pours it all over my head.

I squeal as the cool, thick liquid travels from the top of my head, slipping gradually inside my sweater, making me squirm. I splutter and choke as Cole clutches his stomach cackling like the slimy hyena he is.

"That was," he can't stop his laughter and I see his eyes water because of it, "epic!" He gasps like he could use a tank full of oxygen at this point. I lean against the counter and angrily wipe at every reachable corner on my face but it dawns on me that nothing is salvageable at the moment and I'm going to need another shower.

"You!" I lunge for Cole, who's trying to catch his breath but failing miserably. Grabbing a bowl of whisked eggs I take advantage of his distracted state and nearly smash the bowl over his head so that the gooey liquid is smeared all over his gorgeous hair.

Dye my hair red and call me Brave—eat your heart out, Disney!

"You didn't!" He growls and stalks toward me. I smile sweetly.

"Aww, is the widdle baby hurt?" I coo and pinch his cheeks and apparently that's what it takes to set off Cole Stone's fuse since he grabs me by the waist and throws me over his shoulder in a move as fast as lightning.

"Oh, you're going down," he says, his voice dripping with promise and pure evil.

I really do hate to admit it but I don't mind the view I'm getting right now. His still-naked back is fully on view, and the fact that he's walking causes the muscles to flex. His jeans are slung low and I do have to admit that he has a fine, fine backside.

"Oh no, oh no, please don't do what I think you're going to do," I beg as he jogs lightly in the direction of the pool.

"You should've thought about that before." The mischief in his voice has a shiver run down my back and I increase the pounding on his back.

"Let me down, Stone!" I try to put some power behind my words but all he does is chuckle in response; I can tell because his shoulders are shaking. The blood's rushing to my head as I hang upside down and from behind the curtain of my hair I see us approach the edge of the pool, and Cole's hold on my waist loosens. I squeeze my eyes and brace myself for the fall.

"Take a deep breath, Tessie!" he shouts and I prepare myself for the fall but to my surprise he jumps along with me as we both fall into the pool with a gigantic splash. I'm swallowed by the water and Cole finally releases me, and even underwater I can see the fat grin on his face. Placing my hands on his shoulders I push him downward as I propel myself out of the water. Turns out this isn't the greatest move since he wraps his own arms around my waist and pulls me flush against him.

He resurfaces looking every bit the male model he could be and smirks at me. I hate seeing how he's not at all breathless or flustered like me. In fact, his gleeful expression is confusing me so much. I don't know what we are anymore; there's no defined relationship and our compromising position isn't really helping it. We're pressed together, his shirtless chest with my soaked top is no match for the water.

I should've done something, in hindsight. I mean there were so many options to choose from. I could've used one of the many witty remarks stored in my arsenal. I could've kneed him in the crotch or broken his nose with one quick punch, taught courtesy of a lucid Travis. But I don't do any of that.

In fact, as I see him looking at me like he is with his blue eyes shining and the corner of his mouth pulling up into what looks like a genuine smile, I can't help but want to be closer to him. It's all so foreign to me, all of this. Every single touch, every look, every smile is new to me

73

since at eighteen years old I've never been kissed nor have I ever dated. When you have a falling out with the girl who has the reins to the entire school in her manicured paws, guys don't really want to be around you.

No guy, except Cole.

I shiver as his hands travel from my waist, skimming lightly up the skin of my sides until his hand's cupping the side of my neck, angling my head toward him. I know he's waiting for a reaction, any sign that I want him to stop but I don't think I'm really in the mood to go all ninja on him right now. It's like he senses this and a heartwarming smile lights up his face, one which has my heart doing Olympic-winning flips. I rest my hands on his shoulders, needing the support to just be upright. There are a lot of things that are wrong with this situation, the first and foremost being that I'm in the arms of the boy who's done nothing but make my life a living hell for as long as I've known him. Does the fact that he's currently suffering from the guardian angel syndrome necessarily have to change everything? Should I trust him knowing what our history is like? Should I . . .

"Stop overthinking, Tessie, just enjoy the moment." He winks and dips his head so that our foreheads are pressed together intimately along with our bodies.

"What . . ." I start but he places a finger over my lips.

"Enjoy the moment," he repeats.

I do listen to him this time. Cole doesn't move his face even an inch because if he did, then our lips would definitely brush up and the idea terrifies me, almost as much as it strangely seems to exhilarate me. I look into his eyes trying to work out what secrets lie in their sapphire-like depths. The distance between us is becoming almost imaginary and there's a thin line we need to cross before everything changes.

"Cole, is that you?"

Or we could just be interrupted.

I freeze, dropping my hands from Cole's shoulders instantaneously. In response his eyes harden as they look into the distance. He can see the person who just called out, and whoever it is is the one responsible for his mood's one-eighty-degree turn. Even though he backs up a bit so that our faces aren't touching, his hand still cups my neck and it seems like he's not willing to drop it. I feel like he's challenging the person watching us.

It's sad, though, that I know from just from the sound of his voice who the person is. Having that particular piece of information, I just wish I could drown in the five feet of water we are currently standing in.

"You always did have the worst timing, Jay Jay."

I untangle myself from Cole who, realizing that I feel extremely uncomfortable, lets me go. Swimming toward the large rectangular steps that lead out of the pool, I begin to climb out. Fully aware that I have two pairs of eyes watching me and the fact that my clothes are soaked and dripping wet, I wrap my arms around myself and head inside the house, scurrying past Jay, who to his credit isn't even looking at me.

I rush to my room and quickly shrug out of my clothes, throwing them to one side. I dry myself and pull on a different shirt and jeans. My sandals are floating somewhere in the pool so I trade them for flip flops. My big blond mess of hair makes me look like Cousin It so I let it down over my shoulders, running a brush through it to get the tangles out.

I don't even care what I look like as I take two steps at a time hoping that the Stone brothers haven't drawn each other's blood yet. I find them in my living room standing across from each other. Cole with his hands stuffed in his pockets and Jay with his arms crossed over his chest. While the former looks arrogant as always, the latter has a deep frown set on his face, which reduces considerably when he sees me coming. I halt at the very unlikely scene before me; never could I have imagined that Jay would be in my house.

"Tessa." He smiles but it looks forced. Cole turns his head and then averts his gaze after giving me a single glance.

"What're you doing here?" I skip the pleasantries knowing that the atmosphere doesn't really call for them.

"I think she means 'how the hell did you get in my house?'" Cole adds.

"You seemed pretty upset last night." Jay ignores Cole and addresses me. I wince recalling the memory but he doesn't notice. "So I thought I'd check up on you. I rang the bell a couple of times but you never answered. I got worried and asked your neighbor if she had a spare key. She knew who I was and let me in," he explains, still not looking at Cole.

As much as I want to swoon over his words, it just doesn't seem right. It's been nearly four years since he's come over and trust me, there have been plenty of occasions during said four years when I could've used a friend. I'm not mad at him but I'm pretty okay with the arrangement we have going on here. I pine away for him in the distance and he remains unreachable and untouchable—that works perfectly.

"You've seen her, she's standing in one piece, so I think it's time to say good-bye." Cole sounds biting, harsh, and it's like I can almost feel the waves of jealousy radiating off him, but that's just me, right?

"I don't think it's any of your business, Cole. Back off," Jay says with barely restrained anger. I don't think I help the situation when I finally walk over to them and stand next to Cole. It's like he senses that I've picked a side.

75

"Like hell I will, you've done enough to her, man. If you can't help her, then don't make things worse for her."

"What the hell do you mean?" Jay growls and marches forward looking quite intimidating. I realize that this could lead to something that could get out of hand so I position myself in front of Cole and place a hand on Jay's chest as he approaches us.

"Calm down, Jay." My attempts at soothing him seem to fly right out the window when a flicker of hurt and disappointment comes across his face.

"He's the one who's hurt you and you're defending him? What does he have over you, Tessa? Why are you spending so much time with him? I thought you hated him."

Yeah, well, you and me both.

"It's a long story and not easy to explain so just let it go, please."

"So what, you guys are buddies now, is that it? All those years he put you through hell and I'd be the one to step up and help you, but now that he shows a little interest, you switch sides."

I back away from him like he's slapped me and fall right into Cole's chest. He steadies me and wraps an arm around me, pressing me to one side where I lean on him.

"You need to stop talking before I break your face," Cole growls threateningly and Jay's face falls a little when he meets my eyes. I know he realizes that he's hurt me and that his attack was uncalled for. In this very moment I don't recognize who he is. His eyes aren't the warm ones I get lost in every day and there's no smile threatening to break out over his face. He looks cold, worn out, dejected and lost, and I have no idea who he is.

"Tessa, I'm so sorry, that came out all wrong, I shouldn't have . . ."

"You're the one who picked someone else, Jay. I was always your friend," I say through the choking feeling in my throat. I'm not going to cry in front of these two; they won't have a repeat of last night's show since I'm so much better than that.

He looks dumbfounded for a while before hanging his head in shame; he knows what, or rather who, I'm talking about. Cole's arm tightens around me but that's not what I need right now. I need some space from both of them. These two bring unnecessary commotion into my life and I just need to get away from them.

"I think you guys should leave," I say quietly before removing Cole's hand from around me and stepping back.

With that I run back into my room and fall down into my bed. Life's a lot of things, I ponder. It's tough, cruel, unfair, unpredictable, and whatnot, but it most certainly isn't all about Cole and Jay Stone. Before either tries to make amends with me, they need to sort out their own demons, they really do.

CHAPTER NINE
Well At Least The Kidnappers Are Keeping It Classy These Days

Discretion and stealth are not what some may call my strong suits. When you spend a better part of your life severely overweight, you tend to become a klutz and in relation to all that excess weight you also become noticeable. In the hallway you can always pick out the fat girl over and above everyone else. It's always the fat girl who gets picked on in the lunch line and it's always the fat girl who thinks surviving gym is tougher than going into battle. I was that fat girl three years ago.

Now since I fit society's description of an acceptable high school girl, I've managed to lose a ton of those disadvantages. People for the most part tend to leave me alone. However, what I haven't managed to lose is my lack of subtlety, which is why the moment I creep into school I'm ambushed by one of Nicole's cronies. Even though I have my hood up and my face is hardly showing, they still somehow recognize me and one of them, Marcy, shoves into me hard enough so that all the contents of my bag spill over the floor. Sighing, I bend down to collect all the flyaway notes and important pieces of paper. It figures that they choose today to attack, seeing it's the first time in nearly two weeks that I've come on my own and have not been driven by Cole.

Cole.

Another despondent sigh escapes me as I think about him and how things went the last time I'd seen him. After the two of them left I switched off my cell phone and laptop and spent the rest of the day just wandering around the house listening to sad Shania Twain songs and reading depressing Edgar Allen Poe stories.

Before I can reach for my notebook someone else has already picked it up and as my eyes travel from her skull-and-bones-patterned Converse to her ripped tights, warmth and a sense of relief is finally starting to fill my chest. Being tossed around by a bunch of minions isn't the best way to kick-start your Monday mornings, now is it?

"Hey." Beth smiles as I get up from the floor. She hands me the notebook, her hands shaking slightly as she glares into the distance, no doubt at Thing One and Thing Two.

"One of these days I'm going to rip their fake bottle-blond hair out and you won't be able to stop me." She's still fuming as we walk to homeroom.

I understand why she reacts so strongly to these things. In her old school she'd been the bully she once told me, and it'd taken one near-death experience to make her realize that you just can play with people's emotions so much. Beth looks quite intimidating but inside she's a big softie and seeing people being taken advantage of brings back that side of her. If I were Nicole I'd tread with care because no one knows when my friend here will reach the point of saturation when it comes to bullying.

"You don't need that on your permanent record, okay? Remember Berklee, your big dream school, I doubt they'll take ax murderers."

"At least I'll rid the world of those brainless Barbies."

"Hey! I like Barbies. You should see my collection sometime, well at least what's left of it. Cole tended to feed their heads to his dog," I tell her solemnly.

She chuckles and shakes her head as we enter our homeroom. Miss Sanchez is hiding her face behind a copy of *Macbeth* but we all know she's asleep. There's an essay topic written on the board, one which no one will bother to write. Well, no one except Megan, who's already in her seat and scribbling away like crazy. As we take our seats, me behind her and Beth next to her, she doesn't even look up.

"What happened to her?" I ask while taking out my own notebook and pretending to copy down the topic.

"She's been grounded because she came back home absolutely smashed and threw up in mom's most expensive French vase." Beth tries to hold her laughter back and so do I. What I wouldn't have given to see the expression on Mrs. Sharp's face when that happened.

"How come I didn't know?" I ask quizzically.

"Well, if you actually switched on your phone you'd realize that this weekend didn't go according to our little Meg's plans." She smirks and I see the girl in question pause, like she's about to say something but she thinks better of it and continues scribbling away.

I feel a little guilty and eye my phone lying at the bottom of my bag. It made sense at the time to switch it off since I needed to get some space from both Cole and Jay but I didn't think about the fact that my friends would try to contact me. After all I did desert them at a practical stranger's house, left them hanging for a ride, and then avoided all their calls and messages after leaving.

"Speaking of the weekend, Cole said you needed some time before you'd want to tell us about it but seriously, Tessa, we were freaking out when we couldn't find you. Then Jay started acting all weird, apparently he punched a wall or something and Nicole was extra nasty. Does this have anything to do with your disappearance?"

I duck my face to avoid any eye contact since my blinking would be a dead giveaway regarding the lie I'm going to tell them. I want to tell someone about Hank, I really do, but whenever I try to get the right words out of my mouth, my throat constricts and my knees begin to tremble. I get terrible flashes of his hands all over me and his lust-filled gaze and all I want to do is lock those memories up in the deepest recesses of my mind.

"No, of course it doesn't," I say in my too-high-pitched squeaky voice, "I just asked Cole to take me home because I wasn't feeling so good. I think someone spiked my drink so I was feeling pretty out of it."

Beth gazes at me for a few seconds like she's trying to call my bluff but thinks better of it.

"Yeah, he texted us after you guys left and told us his friend would give us a ride back. I tried asking him what was wrong with you but he sounded a little pissed off."

"We had a fight," I murmur and doodle on my notebook. I try to place his unasked-for fury but to think he acted the way he did for my sake just baffles me. Since when does he care so much? Usually it's him that's making me cry and for him to get so mad at the idea of my getting hurt is pretty absurd.

"Like that's a surprise," snorts Beth, "but he took care of you, didn't he? I talked to him yesterday and he said that you were much better."

"Since when are you two so friendly?" I hope and pray that in reality that question didn't sound as pathetic and laced with jealousy as it did in my head.

"Careful there Tessa, or we might start thinking you actually care about him." She raises a pierced eyebrow and I turn red at what she's trying to insinuate. I'm not jealous! I don't care who he talks to in his spare time. I'd actually be so relieved if he finds another girl he can torment all the time. I couldn't care less.

Except Beth's just the kind of girl someone like Cole could fall for; she's tough, adventurous, thrill-seeking, a bad girl out and out. The bad boy and the bad girl, they could live happily ever after. Why does this image make me want to gouge my eyes out with a blunt pencil?

"I don't care; I just don't want you getting hurt. Cole's not exactly the kind of guy you want to get romantically involved with. He's slept with half the school's female population, you know," I try saying nonchalantly, hoping that it's enough to put her off him for life.

"Whoa there, hold your blond-haired Barbie-loving horses, I'm not into him like that," she exclaims. "You have dibs on that boy, Tessa. He's all yours even if you don't want him to be."

Why are they under the impression that I have some sort of twisted claim on Cole? I don't. Our relationship is more like . . . well, I really don't know anymore.

"Oh no, we're not talking about this again. Cole and I aren't like that. He's the super villain in my life. You know the kind with a creepy white cat in their lap, who wears an eye patch," I say animatedly, but it appears that she's not buying my theory, seeing how she's rolling her eyes at me.

"That's not what Alex said." Megan speaks up for the first time and I can see that her ears are turning red.

"Of course we've just got to believe what Alex says since he knows everything about anything." Beth snorts and I stare at the two of them curiously.

"Am I missing something?"

"No, it's nothing. I was just being silly as usual," she chirps and goes back to working on her essay.

"Megan's got a crush and she's being too stubborn to do something about it," Beth says easily and then checks her nails. "They met at the party and he's the one who gave us a ride home. You should've seen the way he was flirting with her."

"He was not flirting!" she says determinedly, finally abandoning her attempts to complete her homework at school. "We were just talking and he seems like a really nice guy."

"He called you beautiful about eight times; I know, I counted."

"It doesn't matter." She's blushing profusely and now I'm just itching to know more. Megan's the kind of girl who's always been too busy to fall in love. When she's not aiming for a straight-A transcript, she's volunteering at the homeless shelter and the orphanage and the Red Cross and the old age home . . .

"It does! He likes you and he's cute, so why don't you just answer his texts?"

"Wait, is he the guy you were dancing with?"

"No . . . I—I . . . he asked me and I didn't want to say no. It didn't mean anything."

"But you looked like you were having a lot of fun."

"Just drop it, guys, we're not discussing this." With her fiery red hair and gleaming green eyes, she's quite the picture when she's angry so we decide to not prod her further on the topic. It's obvious that she feels uncomfortable discussing boys since she's always been taught that education and college are her priorities.

"So where is Cole, anyway?" Megan changes the topic but I can sense that she's sorry for snapping at us like that.

"I don't know really, usually he picks me up around seven thirty but he was late today and I had to ask my dad to drive me. I thought he'd be here but . . ."

"Could this have something to do with the fight?" Beth asks earnestly and I shrug. It may have something to do with a fight but not the one they're talking about. I don't know why I can't tell them about me almost kissing Cole or Jay showing up and then the argument that followed. I want to, but somehow it just seems so personal. I'm such a horrible friend!

"Well don't worry, he'll probably show up, he can't stay away from you for that long." Beth winks and takes out her song book, signaling the end of her presence in this particular conversation.

"Yeah, what she said, just find him later and talk things out." Megan smiles warmly and I nod.

"Yeah I'll do that, I'll find him later."

***

I can't find Cole.

I should be jumping for joy and running around like I've won the lottery, but all I feel is a stupid sense of despair building up in the pit of my stomach as I scan the hallways for him. Ever since he's arrived back in town he's been by my side, even when I've threatened to make voodoo dolls using his hair and prick them with sharp pointy needles every night before I go to bed. If the promise of dark magic couldn't keep him at bay, then why is it that one little spat has made him vanish from the face of the earth? He's not present in any of our morning classes but Jay is and he's been sneaking glances in my direction when Nicole isn't paying attention. While usually this thrills me, today I just feel depressed. He's so confusing with his mixed signals and I'm almost tired of waiting for him to realize that he can do so much better than his vicious pit viper of a girlfriend.
He's sorry, I can see that, but it's not so much his words that keep me away from him but the clear warning that's written all over Nicole's face. Now that Cole's not around she's been making up for lost time and adding in extra

perks just for me. For example, since morning I've been called out for my fat hips at least ten times. I've got a nasty purplish bruise forming on my forehead from where she "accidentally" hit me too hard with a dodgeball and somehow I've managed to "misplace" the file in which I keep all my homework assignments; therefore, I didn't hand in a single one today, which in turn has earned me detention.

This is my logical explanation for why I feel deprived of Cole's company today. It's not because I miss him or am thinking about our almost kiss—I haven't thought about it since it happened. It's not like I spent the better half of my Sunday replaying the scene over and over again in my mind and thinking about what could've happened had Jay not shown up in time. I miss him because he saves me from all this hassle and while I should feel insulted that I need a man's help to get through the day, I just want my inner feminist to suck it for the time being.

I'm on my way to the other side of the school for my economics class; the hallways are now more or less deserted since I'm running late because of my hunt for Cole. If I don't see him today, then that'll be that. It's his choice if he doesn't want to be around me anymore and I'm not going to beg him for his company.

With this optimistic thought in mind I skip to my class, feeling as though I've made a firm decision like the mature adult that I am. I'll be the bigger person, I'll be the one who gets to hold her head up high in the end, I'll be . . .

I don't get to finish the thought because think of the devil and he definitely does appear. Cole comes out of nowhere and veers me the opposite direction of where I'm supposed to go for class. I dig in my heels to try and stop or at least get an explanation out of him. He ditched me this morning and if he thinks that he can come up to me now and make me a partner in whatever crazy thing he's up to then he's wrong.

"Where are we going? I'm not missing class." I stand my ground.

He whirls around and I'm hit with the force of his blue eyes for the first time today. It takes me back to our moment in the pool and my skin breaks out into goosebumps.

"If you checked your email you'd realize that class got cancelled today." He hands me his own phone so that I can double check and there it is, our teacher is sick in bed and they couldn't find a substitute in time.

"Okay so I have a free period, I'll go catch up on some homework."

"Or you could work with me here, please."

"But where do you want me to go?"

"Do you trust me?"

We're in the middle of the school hallway and attracting attention. I can feel so many eyes on the two of us but at that moment, I only see him and the sincerity in his gaze. He wants me to believe him desperately and in that moment, given the way things have changed for us recently, I do believe him.

"I do."

***

He takes me to one of the supply closets near the girls' bathroom. Well at least the kidnappers are keeping it classy these days, or maybe not. I feel like I'm in a cheaply budgeted Hollywood thriller as he guides me into the darkened room. A single lightbulb flickers dimly above us and I'm pretty sure I see something crawling up the wall that I'd rather pretend I didn't see. I'm about to tear into him when he flicks a switch and the small room is illuminated.

"Is this where you're going to kill me, Stone? I have to admit, I'm a little disappointed. Where's the theatre?"

He rolls his eyes and checks his watch impatiently.

"Would you believe me if I told you that no, I wasn't planning on murdering you here?"

"Well, you could have fooled me. This is the ideal setting."

I press myself against the wall and study him closely. He's tense, his body rigid as if ready for a fight. I didn't pick it up earlier but there's this quiet energy around him that screams of barely restrained fury. What the heck happened?

"Cole, this is a little creepy. Will you please tell me why we're here? And why do you keep checking your watch? Are we waiting for someone?"

He hesitates and I'm pretty sure I won't like where this conversation is headed.

"There's a rumor going around and I wanted to be the one you heard it from." He takes a tentative step toward me.

"What kind of rumor? Would you just say it already? This place is nasty and you're starting to freak me out."

"Some of the guys heard Hank Kelly saying some things after the party."

My face drains of color and I start to tremble. Cole obviously doesn't miss the change because he inches closer. He studies my face and his fingers lightly caress the back of my hand.

"I'm not going to repeat the things he said but I know that he's lying. If he put his hands on you then . . ." he swallows, " I have to believe that you didn't consent to it. "

My breath gets stuck in my throat and I inhale sharply through my nose. Goose bumps rise all over my skin, my heart's hammering inside chest wildly.

"You don't know what you're talking about," I gulp.

I now have a full name to place with my attacker's face. He's a person, a very real person who wanders these very hallways. I could run into him at any moment and that makes me want to lock myself inside my room and never leave.

Cole's voice is gravelly. "If he did something to you, if he hurt you or put his hands on you, you need to tell me."

"It's none of your business. I don't owe you anything." The line would have sounded better if I wasn't stuttering like crazy. I sound like I'm in the midst of having a seizure or that I have some sort of tongue paralysis. It's no surprise that he keeps pushing.

"I'm not asking you to tell me because I think you owe me an explanation. I want to know because it's not fair nor is it safe that a scumbag like that is wandering these halls without so much as a scratch on him. Predators like that deserve to rot in prison."

He doesn't get it, if I admit to the attack then it becomes real. I've spent most of the past two days trying to forget whatever it was that happened at that party. I'd rather not relive it but on the other hand . . . the idea of Hank out there and still being able to prey on other girls sickens me.

"I need to go,." I tell him. I don't think I can breathe.

Pushing past him, I open the door and run straight into someone. It's a girl, young-looking, probably a freshman, with red-rimmed eyes. She's startled to see me and jumps back. I feel Cole come up behind me.

"Annie, hey we were just waiting for you."

She looks like a scared animal that Cole has to coax into speaking. First things first, I find us a better spot than the supply closet. Since it's a free period for Cole and I, the halls are deserted with most people in their classes. I lead the two to a bench near the central courtyard of the school. Annie sits on the bench, her hands clasped in her lap while Cole and I stand leaning against opposite pillars.

"Annie, would you please tell Tessa what you told me?"

She looks scared but not of the two of us. It's as if she thinks someone might be watching her so Cole kneels down before her and assures her. "She's not here and even if she was, we're not going to let her do anything to you. Just repeat what you heard."

"I . . ." she begins and casts me a pitying look. "I was at the party and I overheard Nicole and Hank." She swallows. "I just got into the dance squad and Nicole had an initiation ritual for me, that's why I kept following her at the party. I didn't expect to walk in on . . ."

She couldn't have . . . we were alone in that bathroom so she couldn't have witnessed it but she knows.

"I overheard them talking about what they did to you and this morning he was around her again. They were coming up with all these lies that would destroy your reputation. I couldn't . . . I couldn't let them do that."

You know how they say if looks could kill? Well, if Cole's face is anything to go by, I know that the possibility of Hank leaving school premises in one piece today is not very high. I hadn't anticipated a witness, I wanted this to go away quietly but that hasn't happened.

Why? Why can't I for once in my life be fortunate to have something work out in my favor? Why am I cursed with this horrible luck— I mean my mom's half-Irish, does that not count for anything? Where's my little leprechaun and that shining pot of gold at the end of the darn rainbow?

Annie scurries away as the bell rings and I don't blame her. Nicole is the she-devil disguised in a dancer's body. My hatred for her has soared this past weekend and maybe that's what gives me the courage to open up to Cole.

I tell him everything and guess what?

Yeah, Hank wasn't going to be among us living for very long now.

CHAPTER TEN
Discussing Who The Peeping Tom Creeper Likes More?

"Do you have a two?"

"Go fish," I say, feeling smug, and he narrows his eyes at me.

"You've said that the last three times, shortcake, are you bluffing?"

I squawk at his accusation and throw my cards on the floor.

"I don't play dirty, unlike you, Stone, and I would appreciate it if you stop accusing me of cheating!"

"Okay, okay, I'm sorry; how about we start again?"

"I'm not playing with you again." I turn my head away from him and cross my arms stubbornly over my chest. I can hear him apologizing repeatedly but still it's fun to give him a tough time. Let's see how it goes for him without having someone to talk to or take his mind off the fact that he's
. . .

"Shut it down, you pipsqueaks; don't make me come all the way down there!"

I roll my eyes, "all the way down there" simply means down the hallway. But for good old Detective Greene it would mean taking his feet off his desk and stop munching on the box of donuts that currently rests on his beer belly. He gives us a reprimanding glare before going back to his truckload of jelly-filled goodness.

"Sorry, detective," I yell back before going back to ignoring Cole, who's starting to look worse for the wear.

Confused? Okay, then please allow me to explain.

Currently I'm sitting cross-legged on a grimy floor outside a single prison cell. Cole is mimicking my position, sitting opposite me, but the difference between us is that he's behind the bars and I'm not. It took a lot of begging and pleading on my part to let Detective Greene allow me to sit here and wait until someone shows up to bail him out. It's been two hours, two hours filled with abandoned card games, trips to the donut shop, and bickering, of course bickering.

"Tessie, come on, talk to me. I'm this close to starting to mark my time here on the walls." He groans and I fight back a smile. He's quite the image, sitting there wearing only a thin wife-beater and jeans. His hair's more messy than how he usually keeps it and his bottom lip is split. Usually I'm not the type to appreciate the whole scruffy look, I like them well-kept and free of criminal convictions.

However, there's something about seeing him like this that's just so appealing.

"It's only been two hours, man up."

"You try coming in here if it's so easy. Hey, detective!"

Slipping my hand through the bars I shove his chest. "Shut up! If we don't stop annoying him he'll lock you up with that other guy."

I shudder as I catch a glimpse of the prisoner whose cell is opposite Cole's. Apparently he'd installed hidden cameras in the changing rooms of the shop he worked in. The toothy grin he's been giving me the entire time I've been here makes me feel paranoid, like I'm one of the people he's got on tape. Even though Detective Greene's assured me that he's from the next town over, my faith in the changing rooms of the world cannot be restored.

"The one's whose been eyeing me like I'm a piece of meat. I'm starting to feel pretty violated if you ask me." He shivers and once again I find myself rolling my eyes at him.

"Hey don't get all cocky, mister, I'm the one he's been staring at!"

"Are you blind? It's obvious that he's been drooling over me, can you blame the guy?"

"Are you for real? Haven't you seen the way he's been smiling at me all this time?"

"More like death glaring, he obviously doesn't like you being this close to me," he retorts, his face contorting into that of the arrogant prick that I've known my entire life.

"You conceited, big-headed, narcissistic . . ."

"Where is he?" I hear Mrs. Stone before I see her and promptly shut up. Cole's face has gone pale as his eyes dart in the direction of the voice. He clutches the bars to his cell and whispers, "If she kills me in the slammer, tell the guys at school it was an ax murderer who finished me off."

"Nothing more masculine than being high-heeled to death, is there, Coley Woley?" I grin evilly and rub my hands together as the telltale clicking of high heels become less distant. Watching Cole's face fall as he waits for the unmatchable fury of Cassandra Stone is priceless. There aren't many occasions when you see him like this. A big fat grin lights my face as I get a whiff of Cassandra's designer perfume.

"Cole Grayson Stone, what the hell are you doing in prison?"

I chuckle and get up from the floor, giving her full room to yell at him as much as she wants. I'm dying for some popcorn right about now. Maybe Detective Greene will lend me some of his donuts . . .

"Discussing who the Peeping Tom creeper likes more?"

"Tessa, dear, how are you?" She gives me a warm smile when she catches my eye and I simply give her a thumbs-up in return, something tells me I shouldn't be talking right now.

"Don't give me all that nonsense! Do you realize how worrying it is to come out of surgery to find that your son's been arrested for assault?" she yells, but due to her gentle, almost caressing, voice, it doesn't have the kind of impact she wants.

Cole looks at her sheepishly. "Sorry, Mom." I see her anger melt the second he calls her that, and you can see that she's practically already forgiven him. That's the thing I've always loved about Jay's mom. Ever since she married Cole's dad when both boys were six, she's treated Cole like her own flesh and blood. I know for a fact that Cole loves her just as much even though he tries not to show it. Cassandra is a wonderful woman and gorgeous as all hell; tall, blond, and absolutely stunning—it's not really difficult to tell where Jay gets his good looks from.

"No, the mom thing isn't going to work unless you tell me why you're here."

He groans and scratches the back of his neck. "Can't you just bail me out first? I don't think I can stand that guy staring at me for another second."

"Oh for the love of God, he isn't staring at you."

"You're just jealous."

I'm this close to strangling him; if he opens his mouth one more time I swear to all that is pure and good I'm going to . . .

"Are you two really having this conversation?" Cassandra asks and it looks like she's holding back a laugh. My cheeks heat up in embarrassment as I realize that we just started arguing in front of his mother.

"Tessie's a little different, Mom," he whispers theatrically, "her parents haven't told her about the time she got dropped accidentally and rolled down two flights of stairs."

"Oh, I'll give you brain damage." I'm about to lunge for him, prison bars or no bars, but once again Cassandra's subtle coughing makes me realize that I cannot attack him while we're at a police station. That would be pretty ironic, though, wouldn't it?

"You two always were so adorable together." Her eyes twinkle with amusement as she looks between her stepson and me. Cole gives me an annoying smirk and it's scary how I know immediately what it means. He's celebrating the fact that we've distracted Cassandra and is giving me a virtual high-five. She then shakes her head lightly and turns back to Cole, placing her hands on her hips and giving him her best "bad cop" look. He squirms under her gaze and refuses to meet her eye.

"Well, I'm waiting; would you tell me why you hit that kid?"

Kid? Hank isn't a kid! He's a monster that deserves to go back to the gutter he crawled out from.

"*Hit* would be putting it mildly, Mrs. Stone. Your boy here went to town with his fists. Luckily someone managed to break up the fight or the other one wouldn't have been able to recover."

I look up to see the new addition to our little party and find that it's Detective Greene with a bunch of papers in his hands. Cassandra scans them thoroughly before signing them. While she's busy Cole gives me a victorious smile and I smile back, feeling warm all over. I haven't thought about Hank at all since we arrived at the station but it really is wondrous that his injuries still don't allow him to go home. Frankly I feel really good about that.

"Please call me Cassandra, John, and will this be all? Can I take my delinquent home?"

For someone's who has just had to bail her son out of jail, she's surprisingly okay with it. It makes me think that maybe incidents like this happen often. Then again, I feel as though Cassandra needs to play the good cop given how Sheriff Stone has the tendency to go overboard with his parenting.

"You sure can, but try to keep a leash on him for me, will you, or the next time I'm calling up the sheriff. You realize that the only reason he isn't facing charges is because of whose kid he is and that the other guy flat out refused to press them. I don't know what you said to the principal either because I haven't gotten any calls from the school again, but he got very lucky if you ask me."

I don't miss the hint of panic on Cole's face as his father is mentioned and neither does Cassandra, she positively beams at Detective Greene and pats his arm. "I'm sure my husband doesn't need to be bothered by some childish spat at school. Isn't he investigating the Carson homicide? He doesn't need the distraction, John, so we'll keep this between us, right?"

He seems to be absolutely enchanted by Cassandra and all the poor guy can manage is a hardly noticeable nod. When his deputy comes and unlocks Cole's cell, the man's still in a trance. Cole pinches his cheeks. "It was a pleasure to be here, John, maybe I'll come visit soon."

90

This earns him a slap on the back of his head by his stepmother, who to his utter humiliation grabs him by the ear and drags him outside, yelping and all. I follow suit since she's my ride and scurry behind them as she thanks the various officers. I quickly take my place in the backseat of her Ford but don't miss the argument she's having with Cole once all the cops have left. I feel guilty. I feel so incredibly guilty for all of this, but things just got so out of control and I just couldn't have seen this coming.

Things spiraled out of control after I told Cole about the party incident. The moment school ended Cole tracked down Hank. The one-sided fight that ensued in the parking lot will definitely go down in history as the shortest and bloodiest.

For all his talk and rather intimidating, ape-like appearance, Hank was more like a little kitten when it came to combat. One punch and the waste of space was writhing on the ground begging for mercy. I shiver as I remember the almost-possessed look on Cole's face as he threw punch after punch until Hank's face was a bloody mess. He'd stopped not due to my incessant yelling but because the principal had shown up. I suspect he'd only called the cops to make a point and not exactly press charges against Cole. It's a well-known fact that money and power rule at our school, which is why this whole situation feels like a joke. Cole's not here because he risks facing a sentence but because the principal had to show some kind of authority to save face.

Which is how we'd ended up at the police station. I'd gotten a ride from Megan and after promising to tell them the full story later on, I forced them to leave. Megan's parents wouldn't take too kindly to their daughter spending time in a jail.

The slamming shut of doors snaps me out of my thoughts. Cole's taken the front seat next to Mrs. Stone and is trying to explain to her why he had to beat Hank to a pulp. I wish he could tell her the truth but he wouldn't. He doesn't want to embarrass me or drag me into this. That's just the kind of guy he's turning out to be.

"Fine, if you want to keep this a big secret then you'll have to suffer the consequences. You're grounded for a month. That means no TV, no Internet, and no Xbox. You will also be taking over all of Jay's chore nights, which means washing the dishes, taking out the trash, and cleaning the toilets."

He doesn't protest.

"Mrs. Stone," I start, and Cole whirls his head around to give me a wide-eyed stare. I think he's assuming that I'm going to come clean and tell her about the party. But the last thing I want is for an adult to get involved, especially one as caring and protective as Cassandra.

91

I ignore his warning looks and continue after taking a deep breath, "Please don't be so harsh on him, he was only trying to help me."

She looks at my image in the rearview mirror, her brows furrowing in confusion. "What do you mean, sweetie?"

"Hank, you know, the guy he beat up, he was bullying me and it was getting a little out of hand." Cole scoffs at my use of the word *little* but I carry on, tugging at the sleeves of my sweater. "He only hit him because he was picking on me."

Cassandra gasps looking aghast. "Bullying? Why didn't you tell me this before? Have you told the principal? How long has this been going on, Tessa?"

The bullying? About four years.

"It's very recent. What Hank did, it was the first time I've ever experienced it," I say earnestly and I can almost feel Cole rolling his eyes at that one.

"Still, you should've told me the second I walked into the station. Never mind now, I'll talk to your principal first thing in the morning."

"No, seriously, Mrs. Stone, there's no need. I'm pretty sure Hank won't do it again," I plead, not wanting this to turn into something bigger than it's already become. Cole's not getting suspended for the fighting, though, since a very bloody Hank lying on his stretcher had told the principal that he provoked Cole and that it was his fault. But I have a feeling that the Stones would be donating heavily to the school. I'd been there with Travis, I know what money is capable of and in this case, it's a miracle that Cole isn't facing suspension or worse, expulsion.

"You don't know that for sure, maybe all he needs is a little talk with an authority figure and he'll never pull such a stunt again."

"With all due respect, I think what Cole did to him was more than enough," I say quietly and to my utter surprise both mother and son start chuckling at my words, Cassandra even looking at Cole fondly like she's proud of him.

"Well, this sure changes things, but you're still being punished, Cole, violence is not the answer to these problems. I'll let you off with two weeks of grounding and you can watch TV for an hour, but that's it."

He grins at her, looking pretty smug. "I'll take it." In other words, I'll sneak out of the house when you're sleeping, Mommy.

Cassandra drops us at her house since she has to rush back to the hospital. I glance at my watch and almost scream when I see that it's nearly nine, long past the time I needed to be home. The blood drains from my face; I'm going to have to come up with a good explanation.

"You look like Casper, only whiter and blonder." This is Cole's brilliant observation as we stand on the front porch. I'm panicking slightly, digging through my satchel to find my phone, which I'd completely forgotten about in all the panic. I unlock the screen only to find that there are no calls or texts from my parents. Should I be happy or depressed about this? Decisions, decisions.

There is, however, a text from Beth saying that she called my mom and told her that I was at her house working on a project. I make a mental note to buy her that The Doors T-shirt she's been eyeing for so long for what she's done.

Then I turn to Cole.

"Thank you, for what you did today. You shouldn't have gone to all that trouble, I—I was going to do something about it, I was, but then you know you . . ."

I surprise us both by hugging him. The kind of gratitude I'm feeling can't be expressed by words. He needs to know what it is that he's done for me. The fact that he went out of his way to ensure my safety and to get me the justice I needed, I'm absolutely floored.

His smell swarms my senses as my face is buried in his shoulder and his in the crook of my neck. Before I know what I'm doing I take one big whiff of his neck since I'm addicted to his scent. His arms are tight around me and with the way we're pressed together, the only things providing some distance are his too-thin wife-beater and my light knit sweater. I can feel the furious beating of his heart. It thrills me to know that it could be for me.

I breathe slowly through my nose and very gently and carefully guide my hands over his back until they rest on his shoulder blades, gripping fistfuls of his shirt. I don't miss the slight shiver that passes through his body at my touch and once again I feel confused. Am I the one doing this to him? I try not overthinking for once, dismissing his reaction to the chill in the air and my freezing hands; yes, that explains it.

We stand there holding on to each other for what seems at the same time like centuries and seconds. Slowly I begin to pull away, untangling our bodies, but that still doesn't provide enough space. Our faces are centimeters apart and I can feel his minty fresh breath fan my face. Consciously I reach for the hair that's falling all over my eyes but, lightning fast, Cole's hand reaches them before mine could. He tucks the stray strands behind my ear and smiles at me warmly. It feels like the best part of my day.

***

To no one's surprise Cole decides to walk me home even though he's bruised and battered. Also to no one's surprise, my darling mother invites him in for dinner the moment she sees us standing on the doorstep. Nerves filled my stomach and were acting up despite things being less chaotic now. I ate as much as I could muster and then excused myself, leaving my mother chatting animatedly to Cole. Desperate for a shower, I let the hot water ease the day's damage done to my muscles and lather and rinse and scrub thoroughly, wanting to get all the grime off of me. Changing into the sweats hanging behind my bathroom door, I walk into my room feeling extremely tired.

And there he is, rocking back and forth on his heels as he stands outside my door.

"If you've come this far Cole, you might as well come in."

I stifle a yawn and settle down in bed. "Weren't you leaving?" I roll onto my side facing him. He eyes are cast downward. When he doesn't answer I call out to him again.

It's as if he's gone into shock and the events of the day are catching up with him. I get out of bed, genuinely concerned about him. He's had his eyes on me all day, making sure I was okay but who was looking out for him?

"What's going on? Did you want to say something?"

After a few minutes of painful silence, he exhales like it's painful for him to breathe.

"You shouldn't feel the need to hide something like that, Tessie. I keep thinking about what would have happened if Annie hadn't come to me."

I flinch since I didn't expect the conversation to head this way.

"Why are we even having this conversation? It's all in the past right? What's done is done. I'm never going to see Hank again so let's just not talk about it."

My heart's racing under the scrutiny of his blue-eyed gaze. There's fire in them and I want to look away but it's like I'm trapped.

"You never mentioned it to your best friends or your parents. Tessie . . . please let people in. It couldn't have been easy for you and to have to go through it alone." He growls, "I can't imagine the pain you were in. I can't believe Nicole could sink so low."

I'm twisting my hands feeling highly uncomfortable, wanting nothing more than to get out of this situation but Cole's eyes pierce mine with so much intensity that I just want to duck under my blanket and hide before he finds out all my secrets. Knowing that he's so attuned to my feelings is heartwarming but the more he cares, the more difficult it is for me to define our relationship. Feelings are getting mixed up, the lines are blurring. I can't just slot him into one category now and I don't know how to deal with it.

"Please don't kill Nicole." I blurt out the first thing I can think of and watch his face scrunch in confusion.

"I know she's horrible and mean and sometimes you just want to run her over with a tank, but you can't murder her! You'll get into so much trouble. I mean I know your father's the sheriff and mine's the mayor and maybe they could pull some strings to get you out, but I've seen the show! It'll probably mean some poor guy named Stan will be arrested instead and he'll get a life sentence. He'll probably have a wife and kid at home, if you . . ."

It's a desperate attempt to change the topic and I know Cole sees right through it but he humors me anyway. My rambling's stopped when Cole slaps a hand over my mouth. He looks at me strangely for a few seconds before he starts laughing so hard that tears spring to his eyes. His hand's still firmly placed over my mouth but then he crumples on the floor clutching his stomach and laughing his useless backside off. His laughter is infectious and maybe it's just the kind of day that I've had that's hitting me but I start laughing as well, nearly hysterical. I fall on my bed and laugh till tears stream down my face. His laughter dies as he wipes his eyes and stands up.

"Where do you get that stuff from?" He sounds a little breathless and raspy from all that laughing.

"You don't have to rub it in, you know." I'm finding it difficult to catch my own breath.

"Oh come on, Tessie, I was just . . ."

"Being a jerk?"

"Being human. That was some serious gibberish you were spouting there."

"You could've been less mean about it." I'm pouting but he can't see.

"Okay, I'm sorry, I promise the next time you get verbal diarrhea I'll slap you before it gets too bad."

"How can I ever thank you?" I say dryly and snuggle down into my pillow, making it obvious that I'm done talking to him. I switch off the lamp on my bedside table and we're shrouded in darkness. I feel his weight settling next to me. "Hey, shortcake," he whispers into the darkness. I debate for a few seconds whether to reply or not then decide that I want to hear whatever he has to say.

"Yeah?" I murmur just as softly.

"I'm here for you, always. I know it's hard to believe but anytime you feel like you need a friend, I hope you think of me. And if you need my help getting rid of Nicole's body, I have my resources."

I can't help but laugh.

It's strange how I almost had no one to look after me for a long time. I'm not really used to someone having my back. More unnerving is the fact that this person is Cole. Had someone told me this when I was fifteen I would have laughed at them, probably called them delusional and then laughed some more.

"Whatever you want, Stone."

Then I kick him out and crash immediately.

CHAPTER ELEVEN
I Think Cole is a Sex God

I am not a violent person; in fact, I pride myself on my ability to calmly accept any acts of oppression that Nicole and her minions might feel like bestowing upon me for the day. My Irish grandfather tells me that I'm a disappointment to the family, that I skipped the famous fiery temperament that my maternal side possesses. But sometimes, good lord, sometimes it really does come out and that sometime would be now.

"Shortcake." Poke.

I ignore him and spoon some spaghetti into my mouth.

"Hey, shortcake." Poke again.

I swirl my fork in the spaghetti with a bored expression on my face and cup my chin, with my elbow resting on the lunch table. Letting out a long and dramatically exaggerated sigh I turn to Beth, who's sitting at my side.

"Did you get started on that history assignment? I've been trying to jot down some points for my essay but it's all so confusing."

I never talk to Beth about homework, mostly because she's not a big fan of it. She's the girl who leaves it to the absolute last minute and most of the time it's a mad dash by the three of us to get her assignments completed on time. Why then, you may wonder, am I talking about an essay which doesn't even exist? I've decided to go down the old-fashioned route and am giving Cole the much-needed silent treatment. He literally had me ambushed by our calculus teacher, Mr. Goodwin, today to get me to tutor him for an upcoming test. I know for a fact that he's probably smarter than me, so his motives for depriving me of any free time I might possibly have seem questionable.

Beth looks at me uncertainly and then her eyes flick toward Cole, who's frowning at me. She seems unsure of what to say since there's no essay, but I am thankful for the day she stepped into my life since she catches on pretty quick.

"Err yeah, the essay, umm, I'm working on it too and it's hard, I can't help you, sorry?" She poses this as a question and I realize that she's as bad of a liar as I am. Cole is a professional and he will not buy what we're trying to sell.

"Shortcake, come on, why are you mad?" He leans forward on the table and rests his arms on it. I avoid looking at him and turn to Megan, who's sitting on my other side. It's no use talking to her since she's got her physics textbook out and is prepping for a quiz we have after lunch. She already knows everything and she's been studying for it every day since our teacher announced the quiz. Plus it looks like I'm not the only person who's a little agitated due to her studiousness. I find the next person I can't chat to and blatantly ignore Cole in front of me.

"So, Alex, how was your summer?"

He looks a bit uncomfortable and gazes at me like I've lost my mind. I don't blame the guy, I have never spoken to him in my entire life even though I've known him for as long as I've known Cole. When Megan and Beth told me about an Alex, I couldn't have imagined it to be him. He's Alex Hastings, the only close friend and non-lackey that Cole has. They're partners in crime and I cannot count the number of times the two of them have teamed up to pull some prank on me. He's started to sit with us fairly recently, seeing how he just got back from Europe.

Now he seems besotted with my redheaded best friend.

"It was pretty good, Tessa, umm, how was yours?"

"It was fun, Beth here had to go to live at her aunt's, but Megan and I did a lot of crazy stuff, didn't we?" I nudge her slightly to make her look up from her book but all she graces us with is a slight nod of the head.

"What do you like to do for fun?" Alex asks but I know he wants my clueless friend to answer his question. I nudge her harder this time and kick her from under the table until she drops her book with a yelp. Glaring at me she picks up the enormous textbook, but I grab it from her before she can bury herself in it again. I give her a pointed look that screams, "Stop ignoring the cute guy who's into you!" and she turns red.

Alex is still looking our way and to my dismay so is Cole, but the slightly amused expression on his face is scaring me.

"I'm sorry, what was your question?" Megan asks politely but she sounds both breathless and flustered.

She likes him! Hallelujah. Beth and I share a victorious look and return to watching how this plays out.

Alex seems taken aback by the fact that the girl who's been ignoring him all week is suddenly paying attention. At first he seems equally nervous but then he flashes her his trademark smile and Megan just seems to come under his spell. We watch in silence as he flirts shamelessly with her and she utters one-worded starstruck responses. It's all so cute to watch, I just want to pinch their cheeks and then get them married.

Cole's hypnotizing blue eyes zoom in on me as the bell rings, signaling the end of lunch. Alex walks Megan to class and Beth heads out to the other side of campus for her own. I try to make my escape before he catches me since I plan on fully ignoring him for a bit longer but he's like a predator circling me and just waiting to pounce.

"So you're not going to talk to me?" He stands in front of me. The lunch room is slowly starting to empty as people rush to their classes.

I try to move past Cole but he stands his ground. A finger placed beneath my chin tilts my head up so that I'm looking him right in the eye and boy, is my view fantastic. He's got the most amazing eyes I've ever seen, the blue in them almost radiates this mind-numbing power that turns you to jelly the moment you look into them.

"You're going to just stand there and let me do this?" He doesn't take his eyes away from mine as he places his hand on my waist, his thumb brushing against the small strip of skin on my stomach that is visible due to my tank top. The cafeteria is nearly empty but I can see people glancing at us curiously as they leave.

Well, *glancing* is a bit of an understatement. I see jaws dropping and eyes coming out of their sockets as people openly stare at the two of us. Most of them just stand rooted to their spots for a few minutes but then have the decency to move once they realize that no one's getting naked anytime soon. Then I realize what's actually happening and freeze. Shiver after shiver passes through my body as his hands never leave their teasing movements. I should stop this. I don't care about the darn silent treatment, I should really stop this.

But I just don't want to.

I watch him lean into me, placing his lips next to my ear.

"If I do will you tell me to stop?" He lightly nibbles at my ear and an involuntary gasp escapes my mouth. His thumb's rubbing dizzying circles at the side of my waist and his lips are too close. I can feel his warm breath all over my face but the thing is, he never stops looking at me.

"Speak up, Tessie, tell me what you want."

I don't want you to stop, but I can't say that to you.

"You should really ask me to end this," he murmurs huskily and I just about lose it. His lips hover over mine, his hand's pushed up my top just the slightest bit, and his fingers are gently skimming over the sensitive skin, making me feel like firecrackers are exploding inside of me. His touch is light as he pushes his hands beneath my top, his cold fingers tickling my skin. They brush up my stomach gently toward my ribcage, if he goes any further . . .

"Cole!" He drops his hands and backs away just a little. He's staring at me as I lean against the table, pressing my hands on top of it so that I don't collapse. The words haven't come out of my mouth since the sensible part of me has packed up and decided to vacate the premises.

Cole's looking at me intently and I think he thinks that I am the one who spoke up. Then he realizes that I'm too dazed to actually form a coherent sentence so turns his back toward me and I wish he hadn't.

I see her before he does and I notice the expression on her face before she masks it for Cole's sake. Nicole's mad and she really wants me to know it. Her eye is twitching, her mouth is pulled up into a vicious sneer, and she's tapping her fake Louboutin-clad foot furiously on the ground. If she had laser vision I'd be obliterated by now.

"Nicole?" Cole asks as he turns to her, hiding me behind his back in what I can only assume is a protective gesture, one I'm extremely grateful for.

"W-what are you two doing here?" she asks in a sickly sweet voice that makes me want to vomit. Clearly Ms. Bishop has an agenda, an agenda that involves being so fake that she could possibly have been manufactured in China.

"I don't see how that's any of your business," Cole replies surlily and I subtly squeeze his arm in warning. He cannot let Nicole know that he's aware of what she tried to do to me. If she figures out that I squealed I'm surely as good as dead.

"The principal just called for a special assembly for us seniors and since I'm class president I'm supposed to get everyone together." Her voice is still dripping with pretense and the way she's batting her eyelashes at Cole is sickening.

Doesn't she have a boyfriend?

"Thanks for the concern, we'll be right there." His voice is tight as he answers her and I know Nicole isn't too pleased with how things are working out at the moment. She's never been denied a guy's attention. Even Jay, the one guy I thought wouldn't go for looks, fell for her and shoved me into a corner.

He's basically asked her to get the hell out but it looks like she's a bit slow on the uptake. When Cole turns back to me, she takes the opportunity to glare at me some more before twirling around, flipping her hair over her shoulder and stomping away. I bite back a laugh realizing that not only is she majorly ticked off but she still has a crush on Cole. After all this time she still likes him and he still couldn't care less.

"That was awesome!" I grin at him and he gives a genuine dimpled smile in return before it turns into his signature smirk.

"Oh, now you want to talk to me? You didn't look too eager before."

I blush, realizing what he's referring to, and don't know why I never stopped his hands from roaming my body. Right now I cannot think of one witty thing to say to him because the truth is that that I liked it.

Silly, right?

***

After school, Cole drives me back to his house for some "tutoring." I'm trying to figure out what game he's playing since he doesn't need my help.

I shudder at the over-the-top theories as Cole parks in his driveway and opens my door for me. He looks far too enthusiastic for my liking and by the time we enter his house and head for his room, I'm growing a little wary. Since it's about four in the afternoon, Sheriff Stone is at the station and Cassandra is at the hospital. The only other person that could be here with us is Jay but thank God I don't see him as we pass by his room.

Cole's unpacked his boxes and his room looks somewhat normal now; the space is much cleaner and homier. I take a seat on the leather couch he's placed opposite his bed and beneath the windowsill. He's gone downstairs to make us something to eat and since I don't want to cause an explosion I've decided to stay away from the kitchen. Taking out my books from my bag, I decide to start working on my homework but something's off, I feel too distracted. My mind keeps reeling back to and playing those few moments when Cole and I were nearer than we should have been. It's not right, not right that I like having him so close to me. I can't like him like that, especially when I'm so hung up over his brother. It's just physical attraction, that's it. However grudgingly I do admit that he's hot and those eyes of his . . .

I shake my head to get rid of my wayward thoughts. If I allow myself to come to terms with my attraction toward him, then I'll also end up admitting that he's not the Cole that left our town three years ago. Ever since he's come back he's made my life so much easier. He might annoy me, get on my nerves and frustrate me, but in the end I don't really hate the fact that he's back.

"Why are you so quiet?" Cole notices my silence over two bowls of scrumptious tomato soup and plates of grilled cheese.

101

I don't want to tell him that it's getting really awkward sitting here with him when all my mind is in the mood for is replaying that moment in the cafeteria. Like the girl I am, I'm overthinking and it's probably showing on my face.

Would he have kissed me?

I remember what happened at the pool and once again I question what could've happened if Jay hadn't showed up. Would we have kissed? Would I have let him?

"Tessie?" Cole's hand on my shoulder allows me to realize that I've zoned out. He's looking at me worriedly and I see concern in his eyes, something I'm still not used to.

"What?" I try to be inconspicuous about the fact that I clearly haven't been listening to a word he's said so far.

"Are you okay?"

"Why wouldn't I be?"

"Well, you look a little dazed. That must have been some daydream." He winks.

"Trust me when I say you didn't star in it." I say dryly and go back to my food. We're sitting cross-legged on his bedroom floor with textbooks and notes scattered all around us. I've tried asking him why he's purposely failing calculus but he seems intent on lying. Though even when I did give up and offer to teach him something, he wouldn't look at his book. Instead I'd catch him staring at me and my stomach would erupt with butterflies.

"So now that you're done daydreaming about me, have you thought more about what you want to do to Nicole?"

"I was daydreaming!"

"You were looking at me with hearts in your eyes; I'd say you came pretty close to it."

I nearly snarl in protest even though he's nearly hit the nail on the head.

"Please, like I'd ever be interested in you."

He moves his dishes to the side and scoots closer to me. As he nears me there's a mischievous glint in his eyes.

"You want to try saying that again?"

He's so near once again and my heart's just going crazy. I need to get away from him before I have a heart attack.

"I . . . I—I—"

"Think Cole is a sex god." He smirks and moves away, just giving me enough space to let out the breath I've been holding for so long.

"You don't need to say something for me to hear it, Tessie. I got you, we've got that mind reading thing down pat."

I nod stupidly before realizing that he's a pompous imbecile!

I lunge for him as he sprawls on the floor cackling. I move over him and try kicking him, hitting him, doing anything that would retract my stupid nod but the damage is already done. He keeps laughing as I sweep all my things into my bag and give him one parting glance. He straightens up once he sees I'm leaving and tries returning to sobriety but he can only hold in his laughter for so long.

"Come on, shortcake; don't get mad, I was kidding." He then places his fist against his mouth, I presume to hold in the laughter. I narrow my eyes at him one last time, swing my bag over my shoulder and walk right out his door. His footsteps alert me that he's following, much like the stalker he is. However, it's not him that causes me to halt in my tracks, it's something else entirely.

I pause at the top of the stairs, causing Cole to run into my back. He opens his mouth to curse but I place my hand over his lips and give a pointed look at Jay, who's on the phone with someone. I don't want to run by him since I haven't actually prepared myself to face him. After our argument, he's made many subtle attempts to try to speak to me but I keep ignoring him. His words still sting and whenever I remember that day, I still feel a twinge of anger and hurt.

"Yeah, man, I'm really going to have to work to get that scholarship. The last thing I need is to end up a fucking loser like Travis O'Connell."

His words resonate around me like he's screaming them. I don't know what exactly it is that I'm feeling right now. I feel hurt; that's the easiest emotion to pinpoint. The best thing to do would be to stop listening and run away while I can, but a bigger part of me wants to stay here and listen to what else he has to say.

"Tessie," Cole starts, his eyes once again full of concern but I shoot him a warning look, telling him to butt out of this, man.

"That guy's a total screwup. He had everything and he lost it because he was too stupid to write a paper."

He listens to what the other person has to say before a smirk crosses his face. "I wonder if Jenny's still single. She's just a couple of years older and man, she used to be so hot."

I feel sick, I feel so sick listening to him talk about all the things he'd like to do to my brother's ex, the bitch that broke his heart and then stomped all over it.

"Tessie, come on; let's get you out of here," Cole whispers but it's like I can't move. I look at Jay and I see someone I've never met before. He's a completely new person, an ugly person, a person who is rude and mean and insensitive.

Cole tugs at my arm again and this time succeeds in pulling me away from Jay before I attack him with a cleaver; no one insults my brother but me, no one.

Not even Jason Stone.

I hide out in Cole's room waiting till the coast is clear and I can leave. Like I said before, I'm not a violent person but right now I want to punch Jay in the face so bad.

"He crossed a line; he shouldn't have said all that. I'm sorry, shortcake."

Cole's kneeling down in front of me, holding my hands in his and rubbing his calloused thumbs over my knuckles. It's surprising how he's the one comforting me and that it's working. I can feel myself calm down and my murderous thoughts are dwindling to plain old anger.

I let out a bitter laugh. "I know a lot of people think that Travis is a loser, but I never thought Jay would be one of them."

He sighs and now places both of my hands in both of his, interlacing our fingers. "You think you know him but he's not Mr. Perfect, Tessie. He's a good guy but he's got flaws too, flaws you don't want to see."

I agree with him but don't voice it out loud. He's right; all my life I've placed Jay on such a high pedestal that finding out he's not all that great is hard to stomach. It's the shattering of a decade-old image and it hurts like hell.

"Come, I'll take you home." He gives me a tentative smile, one which I return even though my heart's not quite up to it.

Maybe I've been obsessed with the wrong Stone brother all this time.

CHAPTER TWELVE
I'm Not the Love Child of Edward Cullen and Tinker Bell

"Travis!" I bang rather loudly on my brother's door.

Nothing—there's no response. It's around seven in the evening and he's passed out, drunk as ever. It's been the same for so long that I cannot remember a day when I have had the opportunity to have a decent conversation with him. We used to have a very good relationship, right from the beginning. He wasn't the kind of brother who liked to pick on me or annoy me; I had Cole for that. Travis was someone I looked up to; he was someone who took care of me whenever my parents forgot to. He was the single reason why I'd never been bullied throughout much of my school life. No one messed with Travis O'Connell's little sister, but I guess that novelty only lasts till you lose your brother to the bottle.

"Travis," I yell again and pound at his door even more furiously. Jay's words ring in my head as I try to keep my rage at bay. Whatever I may feel for Jay does not in any way allow me to ignore the fact that he basically trashed my brother and blew whatever dignity he had left into smithereens. It's the most difficult thing ever to come to the realization that the boy who I thought could do no wrong would actually have such an ugly side to him.

Cole is right; while I never expected myself to ever admit this, I do realize that he has a very valid and fair point. I put Jay on a pedestal, I considered him flawless and I let myself think that he was perfect. Guess I should've realized that anyone who dates Nicole couldn't possibly be completely right in the head. Her ugliness is the kind that seeps into whomever is close enough.

"What!" My brother screams in my face as he throws his door open.

He looks angry, annoyed, and, above all, hungover. His eyes have huge bags beneath them, his breath stinks of alcohol, and he has two days' worth of stubble on his face. My twenty-one-year-old brother looks far older

105

than that. There's no light in his eyes, it's not been there for nearly two years now and suddenly I miss him.

I miss the old Travis and I need to get him back. I need to show people like Jay that my brother's not a lost cause.

In what I suppose is an intimidating manner I place my hands on my hips and glare at my six-two sibling who's rubbing the sleep from his eyes. He's still wearing the clothes he must have put on before heading out last night; it's a miracle he didn't sleep with his shoes on.

"What do you want?" he grumbles before stumbling back into his bedroom, which is in the dark due to all the lights being off. Pizza boxes are scattered all across the wooden floor and beer bottles litter the remaining visible space.

"I want you to clean up and then meet me in the kitchen," I order with authority in my voice but he flops back down into his bed and pulls the covers over his head in an attempt to drive me away. I narrow my eyes at him and tug at the duvet until it falls to the floor.

"What the hell is your problem, Tess?" He grabs a pillow and throws it in my direction, I duck and for the first time in my life my hand-eye coordination doesn't fail me.

"My problem is that I'm sick of seeing you like this, Trav; please just hear me out once. Take a shower or whatever; I need to talk to you when you're sober."

He's taken by surprise and honestly so am I. In the past couple of years we've drifted apart. We went from having the perfect brother-sister relationship to hardly acknowledging each other even though we live in the same house. He stopped looking out for me so I became an easy target and I stopped caring about him so he's been destroying his liver.

"Is everything okay?" He's still slurring his words and his eyes are drooping. Disappointment shoots through me as I realize that this is the person he's become. From having everything one minute to being reduced to nothing the next has taken its toll on Travis. Seeing him like this further strengthens my resolve to get his life back on track.

In a sudden display of affection, I sit by his side on the bed and ruffle his blond hair so like mine; his gray eyes concentrate on my face as I smile sadly at him.

"I just need my big brother right now."

***

My mother's spoon slips from her fingers and clatters to the ground. My father is forced to put down his glass of wine and I smile widely as Travis pulls up a chair next to me and sits down at the dining table.

Shock. The single emotion is plastered onto both their faces as they watch their son sit and eat with them for the first time in years. Mom's mouth hangs open in the most unladylike of ways and Dad looks like he's going to start choking on the wine he just put down. It's priceless, seeing them like this and knowing that I somehow have a part in all this. It's been three days since I confronted Travis and our talk went really well. I'd been able to get through to him by reminding him that this family needed him, that he needed to come back to us.

"Travis?" My mother finally manages to croak as she stares at him like he's a foreign creature and not her son.

"Hey, Mom." He disarms her with a single crooked grin and her eyes widen. I can relate to how she's feeling since it's been a really long time since we've seen Travis in good spirits. The fact that he's smiling and being so nonchalant about all of this is kind of creepy but I'm not complaining. At least I'm going to get my brother back this way.

He's helping himself to some lasagna and Dad still hasn't said a word. He's just staring at him, much like our mother, but even she's managed to get herself under control.

"Can I help you with something, Dad?" Travis asks with an edge to his voice.

I start to panic just a little. My brother and father don't exactly have the best relationship. Dad didn't take well to Travis's little crash-and-burn experience. He practically disowned him and my brother's never quite gotten over the desertion. Now watching them having a stare-down I realize that it might take some time to fix this.

"Just surprised to see you leave the bottle." His snide remark has me wanting to pour my glass of Coke all over his head. This is not the time for settling old scores; we need to show Travis that we love him and support him and the way my father's looking at him you can't really see the rainbows and unicorns. Instead I see the steely cold and calculating gaze which I've become accustomed to in the past three, nearly four, years.

"Dad," I begin in a warning tone and Mom darts her eyes nervously between the three of us. She looks a little panicked, never one for confrontations. This must be taking its toll on her nerves.

He raises his palms defensively and looks at me innocently. "I'm only stating the obvious, honey."

"You haven't changed a bit, have you, Dad," Travis says through gritted teeth and I can see his anger rising, the famous Irish temperament that I didn't inherit is rising to the surface.

"Well, we all can't stop living our normal lives and become

alcoholics, can we now?" he says calmly before returning to his food.

Okay, that's it. One more word from him and he's going to be drenched in fizzy goodness.

"You know what, screw this." Travis shoots up from his seat, throwing his napkin on the floor. Before I can say or do anything to stop him, he stomps out of the room without glancing back. I know I need to let him cool off before the next round of our family feud.

"I don't believe you! Why would you do that, Dad?" I ask him, my voice full of disbelief, exasperation, and a thinly veiled urge to throw something at him.

"Now, now, don't make this about me. Your brother had that coming."

"Oh for the love of God, Branson, get off your high horse and apologize to your son."

My mom looks like Mama Bear with her claws out as she glares murderously at Papa Jerk Face Bear.

"I have nothing to apologize for, Susan, he deserved it," Dad replies tersely and I grunt in aggravation. I may or may not love him but if he says one more word against Travis he's going to suffer.

"If you don't go up to his room right now, you can forget about my father supporting you in the elections. We all know how fond he is of his grandson and if he hears about this, sweetheart, well I'm sure you know what's going to happen."

I give my mom a virtual high-five. Never before have I been so proud of her and at this very second I do feel something akin to love swelling in my heart for her.

"Are you threatening me?"

Sometimes, Dad, you can be as dumb as a post, maybe worse.

"Consider it more of a promise. Now go, and remember, be nice. I've got your ticket to victory on speed-dial."

I will never forget the sight of watching him scurry up the stairs with panic and terror written all over his face. Mom winks at me and begins sipping her wine. It will need a lot of time and effort to get things with Travis back to normal; today's a start but things are going to get a little crazy in order to patch our family back up.

Oh well, at least I have one big-headed, arrogant, narcissistic moron looking after me in all this.

***

I'm about to go to bed after completing my homework and arguing with Cole over texts about how it would not be the best idea to egg Jay's car. It's shallow and vindictive, plus he drives the most gorgeous Hummer and marring its beauty would be a crime against nature. I don't really know if I want to retaliate, I mean Jay wasn't exactly lying when he labeled Travis a loser. It hurt, it did, but I can't stop him from having an opinion, now can I?

Cole sure feels differently about the situation. I'm actually feeling extremely afraid for Jay; if I were him I'd flee the continent.

"Tessa, honey, are you free?" I put my iPod away as my mother walks into the room, grinning and holding a garment bag in her hands. My eyebrows pull together as she lays it carefully on the bed and looks at it like it's her third child.

"Mom, what's this?" I begin warily. It's never a good thing when her eyes sparkle like this or when she looks this happy about something.

"This is your dress for our annual charity gala," she gushes as she begins to unzip the bag. "I wore this when I was eighteen and I won Ms. Farrow Hills in this."

I stare at the taffeta abomination she pulls out. It's the kind of dress I have nightmares about, the one I think I'll end with by wearing it on my wedding day after Nicole's destroyed the original. It's ghastly neon pink with sequins all over the bodice and a big puffy skirt that seems endless.

Oh fudge pops.

"Isn't it lovely?" she gushes as she places it against her body and looks at herself in my full-length mirror. In what world is that thing considered lovely?

"Mom, I'm not sure I even want to go to the gala, let alone enter the competition."

"Nonsense! You're the mayor's daughter, you have to be there and I'm the chair of the Ms. Farrow Hills committee. What will people think if they see that my own flesh and blood didn't bother entering it?"

"I'm sure we can convince Travis to give it a shot," I joke but she flinches like she's been physically hurt.

"I've been planning for the event all year, Tessa. Why are you acting like this?"

I roll my eyes at her theatrics. "No need to be dramatic, Mom. I just don't see the point. Nicole's been preparing her whole life to win this thing. Why would I want to go up against her?"

She clicks her tongue and settles down on the bed, putting the monstrosity she calls a dress on the side. Pushing my bangs aside, she ruffles my hair and gives me the first motherly smile I've seen in ages. I bet it's all because she wants me to enter her stupid competition.

"That girl is not what a Ms. Farrow Hills is supposed to represent. We're looking for someone who's beautiful inside and out and that's you, sweetie. I know you don't see it but you're growing up to become such a wonderful young woman, I'm so proud of you."

Okay, who is she and what has she done to my snarky, antidepressant-popping mother?

"Mom, I . . . didn't realize this means so much to you."

"I know we haven't had the best relationship these last couple of years but what you did today for your brother, it . . ." Tears spring to her eyes and I just sit there in amazement. I've never seen her cry or get emotional in front of me. Usually she has such hard walls all around her that it's almost impossible to penetrate them but right now she's displaying a very foreign vulnerability.

"It just reminded me how lucky I am to have you as my daughter."

My throat feels thick as I try to get some words out but I cannot. To be honest, I'm not miraculously feeling an outburst of love for the woman who's been neglecting me for as long as I can remember. When things became difficult she decided to leave me on my own and used prescription drugs as a refuge. It's not exactly easy for me to welcome her back with open arms.

"Thanks, Mom."

She looks disappointed with my answer but doesn't push it. Instead she asks me to try on her dress and while I'd rather light myself on fire than do just that, I feel like we've reached some sort of breakthrough in our relationship tonight and I can't let my fear of pinky poof destroy that.

When I come out of my bathroom, I immediately cringe at the sight of myself in the mirror. The dress clashes horribly with my pale skin and the fitting is horrible. I don't have the chest to fill it out nor do my legs go on for days, so it ends up pooling by my feet. The puffed sleeves make me look like a hunchback and the sequins prick my skin, making me squirm.

"Oh wow, Tess, you look . . ."

I can see her reflection in the mirror and shake my head at her. "Don't, Mom, don't."

"You look wonderful, honey; we might need to fix it up a little but . . ."

"I look like a cross between Pippi Longstocking and Grandma Judith."

"Well, that's exaggerating it, it just needs a little work and . . ."

I turn around and breathe deeply. Fatty Tessie the pushover would have allowed her to get away with this just to please her and get her attention. However, shortcake here has been spending a bit too much time

110

with the town's bad boy and isn't about to back down.

"Mother," I begin patiently and she looks at me expectantly, "I promise I will participate in the competition and try my best to win, but you have to let me pick out my own dress, please."

She looks taken aback by my request and I'm not surprised. Usually I just let her have her own way with me and try to keep any arguments at bay. She's not really used to me expressing an opinion or, well, doing anything that might hint at the fact that I do have a mind of my own.

"Oh, okay, then that's perfectly understandable. I'll tell your partner about the change, I think the poor boy will be glad that he doesn't have to wear a pink tie."

My heart sinks at the very mention of the word.

"What partner?"

***

"Hey, partner." Cole nudges my shoulder and I glare at him.

"Don't look so smug, I did not choose to be here."

"When life gives you lemons, Tessie . . ." He trails off and starts his car, pulling away from his garage.

"You squeeze the life out of them and then throw them in the trash, genius," I scoff.

From the corner of my eye I can see him grinning with amusement all over his face. I fight back a smile myself and turn my head so that I'm looking out the window.

"So are you okay?" he asks and I guess he's referring to the incident with Jay. I suppose that it's all worked out for the better. Travis is struggling to change his routine and going back to normal but at least he's making an effort now. I've talked him into registering for a couple of online courses and starting to work on his degree again. The alcohol consumption is still a problem but it's hard for anyone to go cold turkey to an addiction.

"I'm better than okay, actually. For the first time it feels like my family is actually making progress." I smile warmly at him and he seems a bit dazed at first, not responding but just staring at me.

"What?" I ask, feeling a little flustered.

"Nothing." He shakes his head and then gives me that disarming smile that I'd been looking for.

"Nothing," he repeats, "you should just smile more often."

I melt a little at his words and don't even notice when he pulls on the highway, taking us out of town. We're going to a mall two towns over to look for a dress for me. While I argued that I am perfectly capable of finding

111

a dress for myself, he simply rolled his eyes at me and convinced me that if I wanted to win I needed his expert opinion. Winning isn't that important to me, I'm just participating for my mom's sake, but then he reminded me about our plan. Our plan to take Nicole down and make her regret the way she's treated me all these years.

"Well I guess even when the prodigal son screws up, something good comes out of it. He truly can do no wrong, can he?"

I'm surprised at how bitter he sounds. I can see why they're not exactly best friends, both are too different for that to happen, but they've also grown up together and know each other better than anyone else. Why is it that ever since he's come back, Cole's treated Jay with nothing but hostility?

"It still doesn't make it right, Cole; he shouldn't have said all that about Travis and Jenny."
He looks surprised and takes his eyes off the road to study me. "You haven't forgiven him by now?"

"It's not exactly easy. I've always thought that he was a different person and that somehow Nicole was tricking him into being with her but now . . ."

"You've realized that they might not be that different?"

I nod before I realize what I'm doing. It hurts to acknowledge the truth, to find out that the person you've obsessed over for as long as you can remember is closer to being someone you hate.

"We're going to kick butt at the competition, Tessie, and when we win I promise I'll let you bash my brother's head in with the trophy."

I chuckle at his enthusiasm and shake my head. "It's not a wrestling match, Stone, it's a beauty pageant, and my trophy will most likely be a plastic tiara."

"Well don't those things have sharp pointy combs? You can dig them into his eye or something."

"You have a really twisted mind, you know that?"

"Thank you, shortcake." He smiles that boyish smile of his like I've given him the biggest compliment of his life and warmth spreads through my chest. He looks so happy and carefree, it's infectious.

***

The rest of the ride I try not to look at him or focus on the hand that's resting on the stick shift, dangerously close to my thigh. Once or twice his fingers accidentally brush across it and jolts of electricity pass through my body.

Trouble, this is going to cause so much trouble for me. Why on earth did my mother ask him to be my partner and what on earth possessed him to agree? He loathes formal occasions and wearing tuxes. He calls them penguin suits and mocks anyone who dares to wear them. Then I remember his saying that together the two of us were guaranteed to win due to his, and I quote, "Killer sexy godlike looks, and my 'meh,' good genes."

We arrive at the mall to find it bustling with shoppers. Cole grabs my hand, startling me as he pushes us through the throngs of people. He makes nothing of the action but my heart rate has spiked, a traitorous blush colors my cheek, and I'm starting to sweat through the thin cardigan I have on. Once in a space we can actually breathe in, he lets go of my hand and then places his at the small of my back as he guides us.

"So where do you want to go first?" he asks but I can't make heads or tails of whatever's come out of his mouth. I am way too aware of where his hand's rubbing my back slightly. He slept in the same bed as me and that didn't freak me out as much as this is. It's not normal for this to happen, I cannot be blushing because of Cole Stone, it's so absurd!

"Tessie?" He sounds a little worried as we walk up to where the escalators are. I cannot let him see that he's affecting me the way he is. I'll be just another girl who falls under his spell and then once he sees that he'll leave me alone. I like being special and I don't want him to leave me alone. Not just yet.

"Oh, sorry, I guess I just spaced out a bit."

He grins, a satisfied gleam in his eye as he bends down and whispers in my ear, "I bet you did."

***

We've been to about eight different stores and I cannot find a dress that doesn't make me want to throw up. Why must society force us to wear that amount of glitter or pink? Seriously people, I'm not the love child of Edward Cullen and Tinker Bell, just a whiny teenager.

"Okay, that's it, shortcake, I need a break," Cole pants as he falls behind. He's being so dramatic; we haven't even been through half of this floor. Well, technically this is the fourth floor we've been on but the guy needs to get a grip.

"Come on, don't be a wuss, Stone. Let's just see what shops they have here and then we'll go to the food court."

He bends, resting his hands on his knees and shakes his head furiously. "No more dresses, I beg you, Tessie. If I hear one more thing about a built-in bra bodice, I'll keel over."

I sigh in defeat and decide to have pity on the poor guy. He's not

113

used to walking around malls all day and I've perfected the art. Since my friends and I don't go to parties or do other recreational things, we shop on a regular basis so it's not as tiresome for me.

"Look, how about you go sit in that café over there and I'll meet up with you once I look through Shirley's Boutique?" I point at the shop a few feet away from us.

"Amen," he says and walks away without questioning my decision. I smile at his retreating back and realize that we've actually been having a good day. He hasn't been crude, well, not too much. He's only tried to hit on me once or twice and hasn't directly insulted me, definitely progress.

I walk over to the boutique and am immediately nauseated by the smell of perfume. It's pungent and making my eyes water. I fight back the coughing fit that's threatening to arise and rush out of the store before colliding into someone.

"Tessa?" the person I've knocked into questions and I stop apologizing long enough to look into the ocean-blue eyes of the boy I've been smitten by since I was eight.

"Jay?" I ask incredulously.

Seriously, oh you fickle thing called fate? Am I like the butt of every joke they plan up there? This is really starting to get annoying.

"What are . . ." we begin in unison and then stop awkwardly. The stars that sparkle in front of my eyes whenever I'm around him are surprisingly absent. All I can do right now is think back to the words he said about my brother.

"I umm, I came here to find a dress, what about you?" I mutter, staring at my shoes.

"I just started working here as a salesman on some weekends. It's good money."

"That's nice." I tug at the sleeve of my cardigan and shuffle my feet. Well, this is uncomfortable.

"Did you drive all the way here alone? It's not safe, Tessa." He sounds stern with just a hint of possessiveness to his voice. I don't want to feel giddy at the thought but I do. It's nice to know that he cares.

"No, I got a ride."

"With whom?"

"Listen, it was nice seeing you but I have to go," I say hastily before he finds who I'm here with exactly.

"Wait up," he calls and I know he's following me as I scurry away. It's not long before he catches up and pulls me back by the arm. His fingers curl around my forearm as he looks at me with confusion written all over his face. I refuse to meet his eyes and bite back my tongue. I do not trust myself to stay quiet and not yell at him or tell him how he's hurt me.

"What's wrong? Why aren't you talking to me?"

I open my mouth but he cuts me off. "Is it because of what I said about you and Cole? Look, I'm sorry about that, really sorry. I saw you guys in the pool and I don't know why I just exploded."

"Jay, I . . ."

"I'm so sorry, Tessa. I'm an idiot, I know that. Can we just start over?"

"You got the idiot part right."

Cole's lazy drawl has the hair on the back of my neck standing up. I know he's right behind me because I can feel his breath fanning the nape of my neck.

Jay's face hardens as he looks at his stepbrother but he stays where he is, close to me. His fingers tighten around my arm to the extent that it hurts, making me wince.

"So you two are here together."

"And you're an oblivious prick. Now that we're done stating the obvious, you can let go of her." I get chills just from listening to his voice.

"You don't own her, stop acting like her damn father."

I look at Jay like he's grown a second head. Whoa, when on earth did he become so brash?

Cole scoffs, "Trust me, right now she might just prefer my fatherly behavior to your face."

Jay's eyes dart to mine as if waiting for me to deny Cole's words but I can't bring myself to do it. His face falls in disappointment as I remain silent. It hurts to know that I'm causing Jay Stone pain but he shouldn't have insulted my brother like that or stood by silently for years letting his girlfriend walk all over me.

"I get it. I'm sorry for interrupting whatever you two are up to."

"It's not . . ." I begin but he's not listening to me but is instead glaring at Cole. I'm let out of his grip and Cole brings me to his side, an arm wrapping around me protectively.

"You don't have to explain. I know when I'm not needed, you have him now."

Why is he making it sound like I'm the bad guy here? Why does he care so much? He raises his hands defensively and backs away from us.

"Remember, Tessa, when he screws up and ends up hurting you, I'll still be there."

He turns on his feet and walks away from us, leaving me standing there absolutely baffled. What just happened?

"Forget about him, he really is an idiot."

115

Cole grabs my hand and takes me to the other stores I wanted to go to but all I can think about are Jay's parting words. Is there any truth to them?

CHAPTER THIRTEEN
Is That a Rhetorical Question?

Beth is a lot of things. She's tough; she's confident, outgoing, unapologetic, and a little too punk rock. What I haven't pegged her as is someone who's as interested in my love life as the rest of the town is at the moment. Beth, yes, my perfectly-sane-if-just-a-little-out-there friend is starting to freak me out with her constant look of absolute amazement on her face. It's somewhat uncomfortable to have her liner-rimmed eyes on me like this, especially in response to what I've told her.

"You're going to the charity gala?"

"Yes."

"You're participating in that demeaning competition?"

I cringe at her words but nevertheless repeat what I've previously said.

"Cole's your partner?"

I nod my head and she sighs. "I knew I'd lose you to the establishment one day. Megan I could imagine pulling this on me but you, Tessa? I'm just disappointed."

"Oh come on, there's no establishment. My mom's blackmailed me into entering the pageant and I have to go to the gala, my dad's the mayor."

"Details, details." She dismisses my rebuttal with a flick of the wrist and collects her books from her locker. We walk side-by-side to homeroom and yet another hour of watching Miss Sanchez being attacked by spitballs.

"But I've always gone to the gala, ever since I was a kid. Why are you getting mad?"

"I'm not mad," she sighs again. "It's just that for the last two years you've been the only person I can trash the stupid tradition with. Remember how we always snuck out halfway through your dad's speech?"

I smile, remembering good times.

117

"It's different this year. I feel like my family's finally getting it together and I want it to work," I reply, clutching my books to my chest as I'm shoved into by someone who closely resembles one of Nicole's minions.

"Watch it, you bimbo," Beth yells over her shoulder and then shakes her head. "I have a bad feeling about all of this. Nicole's not going to be happy about you entering; God knows how desperate she is to win this thing."

"Though," she continues without me having added a word to ease her concern, "if you beat her it could change everything."

I listen to her talk about the new world order and the possibilities of world domination. She sounds a lot like Cole right now. Both are under the impression that winning a beauty contest would ultimately help me dethrone Nicole and take her place as the new Queen Bee. I don't want that, nor have I ever wanted that, but to see her lose what she cherishes most . . . well, it would be quite a sight. That's the plan, taking away all that she treasures most and, being as shallow as she is, that mostly means her popularity.

***

I don't see Cole in any of our classes and nor do I see Jay. At first I begin to worry that the encounter at the mall might have led to something more, but then Beth points out that all the jocks are missing. Cole has joined the football team and not surprisingly he's been made the varsity quarterback. As the first half of the day progresses into lunch I learn that the boys are volunteering to set up for the gala. A kind of fear creeps into me as I walk into the cafeteria to find that my safety blanket isn't there. If it's not Cole then one of his teammates from the football team would watch out for us, keeping the bullying to a minimum. We also got to sit at the table Cole had claimed on his very first day but today Beth and I are confused as to what will happen.

Cautiously I take a seat at said table and take a look around the room. Sure enough Nicole's glaring at me from where she's sitting but as time ticks by and she does nothing to inflict humiliation on me, I begin feeling relieved.

Someone taps my shoulder and I immediately start conjuring vicious scenarios in my head. This is it, Tessa, this is where Nicole unleashes her wrath on you. It's all been too good to be true.

"Why is that plankton at our table?" My friend's staring at whomever is behind me and I let out a breath when it's obvious that it isn't the "Let's make Tessa's life miserable" squad. I crane my neck to find a burly freshman boy smiling widely at the both of us. Typically, we stick to the food chain in this school and don't fraternize with those below us. They in turn stay away from the big bad world of eighteen-year-olds. Which is why I'm confused as to why he and his friend, a few feet behind him, are looking at us expectantly.

"Can we help you?" I ask as politely as I can manage.

"Actually, we wanted to know if we could help you. Cole told us you don't like cafeteria food so do you want us to get you something off-campus?"

Beth and I look at the two boys thinking that they've obviously lost their minds. Why would these strangers whom we treat like scum half the time want to spare us the torture that is mystery meat Tuesday?

"Why would you want to do that?" I ask.

"Because it's part of our job requirement. If he finds out we've been slacking, he'll kick our . . ." the freckled freshman with a head of brown floppy hair pauses to think of a more ladylike word, "butts. We have to make sure that you're taken care of," he says with a serious nod of his head. The two stand so tall and proud, it's like they've been entrusted with national defense.

"Wait, let me get this straight. Cole's got you guys watching over us?" Beth asks with barely hidden amusement as she makes air quotes over the words "watching over."

"Everyone but the freshman players from all the teams are helping out with the charity gala so he told the two of us," he gestures between him and his olive-skinned friend, "to make sure that no one bothers you guys today."

I don't know whether to feel giddy that he cares so much or worried that he has the power to "employ" freshmen as bodyguards. This explains why we've been left alone the entire day, why no one's tried to attack us or take advantage of the fact that Cole's not here.

It's all because even though he's not here, he's still taking care of me.

"In that case, boys," Beth is disarming the boys, who stand no chance when it comes to resistance. Giving them her best flirty smile and twirling a strand of her hair around her finger, she says, "Can you get me a cheeseburger?"

***

"Should we go check up on Megan?" I ask Beth as she's driving me back home. Her mother's finally given in and let her buy a car. It's a little old and needs work but Beth might as well have given birth to it seeing how much she loves it already.

"Her text said that whatever she has is probably contagious so we should stay away." She frowns as she turns into my street. Megan missing a day of school is pretty rare so it's believable that she's sick, but something doesn't feel right about this.

"I know what you're thinking. Let's give her a day before barging into her room, okay?" I nod as I realize it's probably best to give Megan the space she needs. Things have been a little difficult for her, what with Alex relentlessly pursuing her and her mother's insistence that she lives a nun-like life until she's thirty.

"I just hope she survives spending all that time with her mom." I shudder at the thought as I get out of the car. I would invite Beth in but she has to get to work so we say our good-byes for the day and I go inside.

I'm in the process of pouring myself a bowl of Cocoa Puffs when my phone buzzes in my back pocket. Surprisingly it's a text from Cole. It's about four in the afternoon so it's possible that he's done for the day.

Cole: Dress warm, we're going out. Pick you up in ten.

The old me would like to argue with him, to tell him that I have better things to do on a Friday night but the new me has other plans. The new me actually wants to spend time with Cole Stone and is excited at the prospect of "going out" with him.

Me: Okay.

In five minutes I race upstairs and try to salvage something of my appearance. I spring my hair free from the messy top bun I made in a hurry this morning and run a brush through it. Taking off my oversized sweatshirt I slip on a soft pink top with lacy scalloped edges over my dark-wash jeans. I decide to stick with my white Converse and race downstairs. Peeping out the kitchen window, there's no sign of Cole's Volvo. It gives me time to put on some of the makeup stashed in my purse and spritz on some perfume.

The doorbell rings as I'm trying to calm my nerves. It's just Cole, the guy who's made me cry more times than I can count. There's no need to feel all light-headed.

"You should remember that I only ring the bell out of courtesy. I still have my key."
He saunters in wearing his black leather jacket over a snug white T-shirt and jeans, rendering me speechless.

"Are you done checking me out, Tessie?" he says smugly, making me realize that I need to do damage control. I cannot let him think that I like him like that.

Or like him, period.

"Are you not aware that you have grease all over your face?"

120

Actually it's just a smudge on his forehead but hey, I'm not Tessa O'Connell if I don't exaggerate.

"What? I thought I washed all the damn stuff off." He groans and walks over to the kitchen sinks and starts splashing water all over his face.

Oh no, this is way worse.

The water's soaking his shirt and trickling down his throat muscles, which flex as he swallows.

I must not stare. I must not stare at the gorgeous human standing a few feet away from me.

Averting my gaze I look for minuscule tasks around the house. I pick up a cleaning cloth and begin rubbing at a spot on the counter even though it's already gleaming.

"You ready?" he asks once he's drying himself using a whole wad of paper towel. I don't look at him but just nod, grabbing my purse.

He tugs at my arm and pulls me back before I walk over to the door. Turning me around he grabs ahold of both my shoulders then tilts my chin to look him. His eyes penetrate into mine like they're trying to figure something out.

"Are you okay?" He's scanning my face and visible parts of my body for I don't know what.

"Why wouldn't I be?" I detest sounding so breathless but he doesn't make a big deal out of it. It's very un-Cole-like and goes to show that our relationship is changing. I don't know if I want that to happen. While it's nice that he isn't terrorizing the living daylights out of me, it's even more unnerving to have this sudden tension between us.

"You're acting a little weird. Did something happen in school? I'm going to kill those . . ."

I roll my eyes as he threatens his freshmen lackeys. "Calm down, Butch, I'm fine. Don't we have somewhere to go?"

Getting out of his grip, I turn my back on him and take a few deep breaths. It's getting easier to lie to him but I would never profess to be a professional. It's hard to believe that the guy whose sight I once couldn't stand has started causing all these strange feelings to explode inside of me.

"Every day, Tessie, every day you get weirder."

Turns out he didn't drive his car to my house, which is why we end up walking up to the park after getting some pizza. I still don't understand what we're doing; at this point he seems so animated and happy that I don't want to ask him to stop. He's talking a mile a minute about how we're going to crush Nicole in the pageant. If I wanted to rain on his parade I would tell him that winning doesn't mean much to me and that I'm only doing it for my mom. Strangely, though, I want him to think that I'm just as excited about this as he is.

We settle near the lake, thankfully the grass isn't wet so we don't need a blanket.

"What I wouldn't pay to know what goes on in that head of yours." He chuckles as he passes me a napkin and a slice of pizza.

"Usually nightmares about how you pushed me from this very tree when we were nine. I broke my arm, had to wear a cast for three weeks, and missed my piano recital."

"It wasn't this tree," he says defensively, pointing to the weeping willow behind us. I shake my head and smile at the sudden embarrassment on his face. Is he feeling bad?

"I think I would remember, thank you very much."

"I didn't think you'd actually fall," he says softly, picking on the blades of grass. His bottom lip is sticking out, looking incredibly pink and way more attractive than I want it to look. Cole's made me have a lip fetish apparently.

"It's okay, it's been nine years, and I think I'm over it by now." I chuckle and he laughs with me. Much as I used to want to, I don't like making him feel guilty anymore. It's apparent that he feels bad for all the times he's bullied me in the past.

"So did you pick a song?" he asks as we finish eating. I lean back on my elbows and look up at the starry night sky. I don't want to talk about the silly competition right now. Here, in my own bubble, I just want to relax and not think about all the problems plaguing my life. I'd stopped coming to our town park a long time ago. Nicole and her posse would almost always be here and she was almost always making out with Jay. In hindsight I think she kissed Jay to drive me away, not because she actually wanted to.

"What song?" I ask looking at him, only to find him staring at me with a wide-eyed gaze. Immediately I sit up straight, wrapping my arms around myself. That look of his, his intense piercing gaze, has my heart doing a dance of its own inside my chest. No dancing, heart! Not over a potential heartbreaker like Cole Stone.

He scratches the back of his neck and avoids looking at me. Once again I feel like a douche for making him uncomfortable. I don't want him to think that he creeps me out. It's the opposite, in fact, I like the way he's been looking at me way more than I should.

"You know, the one we're supposed to dance to?"

Oh, right, the dance. The dance every couple taking part in the competition has to perform, the one if you nail it, it means that you've won the title. Cole wants to wrench it right from Nicole's grasp and give me the one thing she's worked for for so long. Her popularity is all she cares about and watching someone else take it away from her would destroy her in more ways than one. I'm not sure I want to do this to her. I'm not sure that I'm even capable of dethroning her. Though whenever I say such a thing, I receive a huge lecture on self-esteem from my unwanted spiritual coach, Cole, and am forced to suck it.

"I didn't think you'd be interested. You said slow dancing was for pansy pants."

"It is for pansy pants, shortcake, but we need it to win; besides, I'll be dancing with you. That makes all the difference."

He winks at me and like a fool I gape at him. He's flirting with you, Tessa, say something, do something. Stop looking at him like you want to jump his bones. Tell him how much he repulses you; tell him you're not interested. Just do something!

"I got new curtains for my room," I blurt out.

What in the name of fudgesicles is wrong with me? Curtains? Why, Tessa, Why?

"Do I make you nervous?" He sounds so smug that I want to hit him. It's not nice that he wants to take advantage of my idiocy. I have to work on not letting myself get tongue-tied in front of him or he'll think I'm just like every other girl in town. Though I can see now why they're as attracted to him as they are. He's gorgeous and he's extremely aware of it.

"No, spending so much time with you is killing my brain cells, Stone."

"That's obviously because of all the time you spend staring at my airhead brother." He gets up, making me think that he's mad at me or something or that I've said the wrong thing. However, when he reaches for my purse, lying on the ground, I realize he's up to something else entirely.

"You have your iPod in here?"

I get up and snatch my bag away from him.

"Haven't you been told never to look through a lady's purse?" I cringe at the sort of things he would find in here, my tampons being the worst.

"Where's the lady?"

I kick his leg. "Just don't touch my bag again," I growl and hug the bag tightly to my side.

"Here." I place my iPod on his waiting palm. He grins at me before wrapping his free arm around me and pulling me to his chest. The small action knocks the breath out of me and if he hadn't been holding me I would have melted into a puddle on the ground.

"W-what are you doing?" I stumble a little as I cough out the words. His hooded eyes twinkle as he places the iPod in the front pocket of my jeans. One piece of the earphones goes in my ear and the other in his. I watch, absolutely hypnotized as he guides my arm to rest on his shoulder and interlinks our free hands so that they're hovering in the air.

"I'm dancing with you, Tessie."

Soft music begins to play as I fear the song that will follow it. I share my iPod with Megan since her mother won't let her go near technology before college. Let's just say my friend and I have starkly different tastes in music.

"Follow my lead," Cole whispers as we begin to sway.

As the first verse starts I try my best to not focus on the lyrics. It's a song I've listened to an embarrassingly high number of times. It's about a guy telling her that he loves her because and not despite of her imperfections. Lyrics have meanings, words have power, and I can let myself be overwhelmed by all this.

"Loosen up, you're too tense. "I nod at his instructions and copy his movements without ever looking into his eyes.

The words of the chorus hit home and my bottom lip begins to quiver. He's holding me so close and so tight like he'd never let me go. Just when I'm thinking about letting go of him and running for my life, he removes our interlinked hands for the briefest of times. Tilting my chin up, his eyes bore into mine.

"You need to look at me." His voice is husky and causes tremors to rock through me. "The judges need to buy what we're trying to sell."

Right, of course. We're putting on an act because we need to win. I let out a deep breath, not as close to death by hyperventilation as I was minutes before. This is all about beating Nicole, nothing more.

"Now let's try again and this time look at me, okay?"

His hand inches up from the small of my back, up my spine. It's slow and sensual enough to make me squeeze my eyes shut. The stupid song isn't helping; I need to tell Megan to stop putting all these sappy songs on my iPod!

"I'm going to lift you now, okay?"

"Please don't throw me in the lake," I say weakly.

He lets out a laugh before pulling me even more tightly against his chest.

"Don't you trust me, Tessie?"

"Is that a rhetorical question?"

He rolls his eyes at that one. "I'm going to lift you anyway. You're just going to have to learn to trust me."

I snort at his claim. "Easier said than done, buddy. You tormented me for most of my life. I wouldn't put killing me past your bucket list."

He mutters something under his breath and I'm pretty sure it's along the lines of "drama queen." This is good, this is normal. Bickering, arguing, wanting to rip each other's hair out is what we do best. Any lingering feelings might disrupt our awesome dynamic.

The second verse begins and without warning he hoists me up by the waist and in a matter of seconds my legs are dangling in the air as Cole moves us. The words that we hear in our individual earbuds now resonate all around us. With the way Cole's looking at me and with the singer's soft caressing voice, it's just the most magical thing to have ever happened to me.

As he brings me down, slowly his hands move so as to grip my hips. The space between us is as much as the width of a hair. As my feet touch the ground, I find myself completely tangled in Cole. His arms around me, one leg in between mine, my hands gripping his shoulders fiercely, it's surprising that there's any space left between us.

His eyes zero in on my lips and I can't even make sense of the way my heart is threatening to crash out of my chest. Every single part of me is aware of how close he is, this is it.
Something that's going to happen right this moment will change my life forever.

"Tessie," Cole whispers as he leans into me. I find myself inching my face closer and closer . . .

A shrill buzzing sound ruins the peaceful silence of the night, making me feel like I've been drenched by ice-cold water. Cole curses silently and untangles us as I stumble away from him, nearly falling on my butt. My cell phone continues to ring and vibrate as I take it out from my back pocket with trembling hands.

"Hello?" I sound breathless, my voice is cracking and I feel like driving a nine-inch nail through the skull of whoever just called.

"Tessa, oh thank God. You need to come up to Megan's right away, she's having a meltdown and I don't know what to do."

Beth keeps on talking about how she's worried about our friend or how she thinks Mrs. Sharp has finally pushed her daughter over the edge with her controlling behavior. I'm only half listening to her; my eyes linger on Cole's back as he tosses pebbles into the water. From his tense posture I can tell he's angry, or irritated at the very least.

We were going to kiss, that I was certain of. Had Beth not called, would we have finally done it?

"You there? Can you hear me?"

"Yeah, I'll be there soon."

I end the call and walk toward Cole, who notices my approaching footsteps and turns to face me. His expression gives nothing away; he seems like he always does; carefree, happy, and a tad bit crazy.

"Everything okay?"

I wave my hand dismissively. "Apparently Megan has an emergency. Can you drive me there?" Hopefully the drive from his house to Megan's would give us a chance to talk.

We almost kissed, again. This demands some kind of serious attention, right? Isn't that what grown-ups do, talk about stuff?

We walk in silence to his house with an awkward distance between us. It's nerve-wracking to not have him babbling away or making fun of me. I want him to tell me that I dress funny or that my teeth are too big, anything insulting or outrageous would do. Anything but this terrible quietness. The time it takes us to get there is enough for my brain to go into hyperdrive, to analyze and then overanalyze. If I don't stop thinking about the what-ifs, I'll surely end up with the mother of all headaches. So I force myself to think about something mundane until we reach his house and get into his car. Cole has remained quiet beside me but I can almost feel the nervous energy bouncing off of him.

I strap myself into his Volvo as he revs the engine. Thinking of safe topics for conversation I begin by something which obviously can do no wrong—boosting his ego.

"So where'd you learn to dance like that?"

"Cassandra taught us when her sister was getting married. Jay and I must've been about ten." He smiles at the memory and I can imagine a ten-year-old Cole with his gangly frame, learning how to slow dance.

"Obviously Jay wasn't a very good learner." We both chuckle thinking about how bad of a dancer the other Stone is. Nicole's yelps are heard throughout the gym whenever there's a dance.

"Cassandra gave up trying to teach him after she got blisters all over her feet. Let's just say, my brother might be many things but he's definitely not a good dancer."

"You got that right." I snort and he grins at me. All at once the awkwardness vanishes and we go back to being ourselves. All it takes is dissing Jay a little and honestly, I don't even mind that right now.

We park outside Megan's house smack-dab in boring old suburbia. "Thanks for the ride, I'd ask you to come in but I fear what Mrs. Sharp could do to you."

I remove my seatbelt and climb out of the car. I'm halfway up their porch when I hear footsteps behind me and not surprisingly Cole right behind me. The only difference is that he's holding a large gift box with a silver ribbon on it.

"What's this?" I ask nervously and watch him once again scratch the back of his neck.

"Look, I don't want you to think I'm forcing you or anything but . . ."

"What is it? Why do you sound so scared?" My laugh sounds fake to my own ears as I eye the box warily.

"I know you were having trouble finding a dress and since you don't want to look like a disco ball wearing your mom's, I got you this." He thrusts the box toward me shyly, like a little boy offering his teacher an apple on the first day of kindergarten. Though if I remember correctly, poor Mrs. Grisham got a whole jar full of earthworms from her least favorite pupil that fateful day.

"You bought me a dress?" I gasp as I grab hold of the heavy box. How much did the thing weigh?

"Technically Cassandra helped me pick it out but I think you'll like it. If you don't you can always return it. I mean I'm not going to force you to wear it, it's not like I know a lot about dresses. Cassandra said you would like it and I thought it would look good on you. I swear it's not important that you . . ."

He's rambling. Oh gosh, he looks so cute when he's all caught up and nervous and rambling.
I've never ever seen him lose his calm like this and boy, is it adorable.
Without thinking I place my hand over his mouth.

"Shut up, Cole."

When I'm sure he's not going to start talking again, I stand on my tiptoes and press my lips to his cheek. Applying the slightest pressure, I let them linger there for about five seconds before moving away. The dazed and starstruck look on Cole's face is worth braving my fears.

"Thank you, I'm sure I'll love it," I whisper before backing off and walking away.

"You're welcome, shortcake! Though I do accept Swedish massages as tokens of affection," he yells as I'm nearly in the house.

"Only in your dreams, Stone," I whisper yell, not wanting to scandalize Mrs. Sharp.
He winks at me before going back into his car. Before driving away he blows me a kiss and I stand there watching him leave thinking about how much he's changed, how much we've changed. The difference is staggering.

CHAPTER FOURTEEN
I'm As Smooth As Chunky Peanut Butter

The last time I'd been asked to act was in the seventh grade. We were putting on a performance of *Romeo and Juliet* and I was asked to play the Nurse. It made sense at the time, with my weight and my Lane Bryant clothes I was the perfect fit. However, my fifteen minutes of fame came crashing down when I took one look at the crowd. My parents were sitting in the front row, my mom had been waving more than enthusiastically at me, my dad had an encouraging expression on his face while my brother made funny faces.

Glory never came to me, though, and you wouldn't have been able to unfreeze me with a blowtorch. The girl playing Juliet had tried her best to work around me. She'd made up random gibberish, dialogues Shakespeare would never claim to be his own, but it had worked. I'd stumbled off stage earning a death glare from my drama teacher and all the Montagues and Capulets. It took a while for it to hit me and then came the embarrassment, a whole lot of it. I was so terribly afraid of the reactions that I knew would come that I hid in the costume closet for the rest of the show.

However, when I came out, things were even more chaotic than when I'd left. Turns out, our Romeo had decided to add his own twist to the tale and had refused to kiss Juliet, claiming that her braces grossed him out. He'd then proceeded to grab Marsha White, the cutest girl in our grade, who was playing Juliet's mother and kissed her smack on the lips. It caused quite the uproar.

Cole had been Romeo.

Now when I think about it, I wonder if he did it to take away the attention from me. It wouldn't be surprising, not with the way our relationship has done a one-eighty. If I start thinking about it, I'm sure I'll find a valid reason behind everything he's done so far. Though it's not something I'm ready to do right now.

"They're here." Cole sticks his head through the door of the supply

128

room at Rusty's. He's excited, with eyes like an open book, it's not that hard to tell. I can tell that he is in his element, scheming and plotting. This is what he does best and he's finally getting his chance to do it. All at once the three of us spring into action as his head disappears. I straighten my apron and grab the bread basket.

"Time for action, ladies; remember, Megan, you can't come out. No matter what happens, your parents shouldn't find out that you were here." Beth has sprung into manager mode. She knows the two of us are hopeless when it comes to anything that involves an extended amount of lying. I've asked Rusty to let her work some shifts this week, just so that she could help us today.

"Okay," she agrees in a meek voice but I can see how badly she's shaking. She's nervous, we all are, but this is what she wants but is too weak to actually ask for it herself.

I take a deep breath and get ready to put on a performance of a lifetime. Beth is already out the door, seating Mr. and Mrs. Sharp. Cole must already be schmoozing the life out of them and Alex . . . poor, poor Alex.

"You think this is going to work?" the anxiety-ridden redhead asks me and I put on my most reassuring smile.

"Of course it will."

On the inside I keep going back to the thirteen-year-old girl who choked and choked badly.

Mr. and Mrs. Sharp are the epitome of white-collar douches, no offense to my best friend. They're both lawyers and are partners at a prestigious firm. In their books, if you're not rich or powerful then you might as well be dead. Suffice it to say, they love me. It sickens me to have them gushing over me, ignoring their own daughter in the process, but today that's about to be mighty useful.

See, when I raced to Megan's house a couple of nights ago, I found her a sobbing mess. Beth and I spent hours coaxing her into telling us what was wrong. A sleepover, an Audrey Hepburn movie marathon and two boxes of KitKats later, she told us everything. Apparently Alex had asked her if she wanted to go to the gala with him. They had reached the point where they were friends but both wanted something more. When Alex posed the question, she ran. She ran until she locked herself up in her room and tried to find some way around this. Her parents flat-out refused to let her go with a date and they weren't budging. On the other side, Alex had been terrified that he'd scared Megan off. Bombarding her with calls and texts, Cole told us later that his best friend had been a mess.

It was a disaster of epic proportions and so we needed to fix it and sew our friends' hearts back together. For that to happen we needed a master plan and who better to concoct one than the master of manipulation himself?

Beth has set the mood; I notice this as I walk out with the menus and bread basket. She's seated them at our cleanest booth and as promised the rest of Rusty's is empty. It took a while to convince my boss but after we promised him a lifetime supply of Farrow Hill's special tomatoes, courtesy of my father, he agreed.

I walk out smiling like I'd been taught during my training. Holding back laughter as I take in Cole's attire I appear at the table placing the basket in the middle of their table and watch Mrs. Sharp's eyes light up.

"Tessa, dear, we didn't know you would be working today," she exclaims, and it takes every facial muscle I've got to not let my smile disappear. I hate this woman; I really, really hate this woman.

"Good afternoon Mr. Sharp, Mrs. Sharp. I'm glad I could be of service. Here are your menus. Let me know when you guys are ready to order," I say politely before setting the newly laminated menus in front of them and backing away.

"Well, we've never been to a place like this." She looks toward her husband, who's swiping his finger against the tabletop, no doubt checking for dust. Thank God I scrubbed and cleaned their booth thoroughly a few hours ago. He's short and more or less bald. Megan inherited her good looks from her maternal grandmother and it's no secret.

"Well, in that case, how about I bring you the house special?" There is no house special. We've bought some lobster dishes from a fancy restaurant and are hoping that they fall for it. Immediately Mr. Sharp looks interested and stops scrubbing at the singular spot before him.

"Special? Is it the most expensive thing you have here?"

Before I grab the pitcher of water placed on the table and pour its contents over him, Cole intervenes. He looks . . . different in his baby-blue button-down and khaki slacks. He's actually managed to tame his hair, which is combed and gelled back so that none of it is falling into his eyes. I'm not a big fan of the look but Megan's parents are eating it all up. He's the one who went to talk to them and invited them here. He convinced Mrs. Sharp to let their daughter go to the gala and that he'll even find them a boy they would approve of.

That boy would be Alex, or Alexander, as he's been calling him all the time. They're here to meet, or rather give him the third degree, and I'm certain the poor guy is sweating bullets in his truck.

"It's the best dish on the menu; my parents have it all the time."

At the mention of Sheriff and Doctor Stone, their ears perk up and they immediately place their order. Beth is behind the counter, wiping the imaginary dust off it. She winks at me as I go to the kitchen. Even though we've already got the food plated, Megan and I wait a little before I go back. By this point she's chewed her fingernails to the point where you'd almost see skin.

"What if this doesn't work? What if they figure out . . . I'll be in so much trouble! I can't believe I'm making Alex do this. He must hate me; he must think he was an idiot to ask me out."

I listen to her rant, as we wait. It's good for her to get rid of the stress. When she's done, she lets out a huff of air and her shoulders slump in defeat.

"Listen to me, and I'm only going to say this once. The person behind this whole operation is Cole. He's been manipulating and scheming since the day I met him. The guy's a genius. There's no way he's going to fail. Also, Alex is crazy about you, like crazy-cat-lady crazy. He's doing all this to spend one day with you, Megs, don't you think that's proof enough?"

She seems to calm down a little after my lecture. I briefly consider becoming a motivational speaker.

I peek out of the kitchen door and see Cole chatting up Mr. and Mrs. Sharp, looking so positively perfect, but he's so much more than that. He's not the golden boy, the prodigal son or whoever he's pretending to be. In the past I've held his imperfections against him but today his flaws are helping my best friend out and all that does is endear them to me.

Placing the dishes on a tray I walk back into the diner, to find that Alex has joined the party. Only, he doesn't look like Alex at all. Instead of wearing his usual band T-shirts and ripped jeans, he's taken a page out of Cole's book and gone down a more conventional route. A white button-down shirt, with a sweater vest on top paired with tan slacks.

He looks like my grandfather, almost exactly. His short, almost cropped, hair has been brushed back but that's not the most apparent change. My eyes zero in on his nerd glasses and I stifle a laugh, or more like the loudest snort on the planet. I try to keep a straight face as I catch Beth's eye over the counter and notice that she's trying just as hard to not double over.

Placing their food in front of them, I smile once more at the couple who are eating every word that comes out of Alex's mouth. He's discussing some high-profile murder case that's been in the papers a lot. Mrs. Sharp has her attention focused solely on him and is yapping away at record speed. Mr. Sharp is, on the other hand, trying to catch up with their fast-paced conversation.

"Tessa, you never told us you three were friends with Alexander Hastings." She emphasizes his last name and I realize that the boys have told her. Alex's father owns a chain of high-end restaurants up in New York plus his mother has a lot of old family money. I can practically see the dollar signs glimmering in her eyes as she drinks him up.

"Well, I thought Megan would have mentioned him." She waves her hand dismissively. "The silly girl told me about a boy, but I had no idea he was Alexander."

"Well then, I'll leave you guys to it; nice to see you Cole, Alexander." I nod at them before walking away.

***

About an hour later, the five of us are sitting in the empty diner laughing our butts off. They bought it; Megan's parents bought and paid full price for the Alexander Hart show. They believed him to be the good boy; he definitely isn't. They don't even know that his father's threatening to disinherit him or that he wants to drop out of high school.

"If you had stayed with her for one more minute, I think Mom would've proposed to you." Megan chuckles.

"What can I say; no one can resist *the* Alexander Hastings." He emphasizes his name just like Mrs. Sharp did and we all start laughing once more.

I study Cole, who's leaning back in his seat and shaking his head at something Alex is telling him. We haven't really had the time to talk today, in fact we haven't been alone since the day he got me the dress. The dress which is still sitting packed neatly in my room. I haven't had the guts to open it. Something's scaring me and it's not one of his pranks. It's knowing that I never suspected him of being up to his usual tricks. Not once did I consider that he might be tricking me by coating the dress in itching powder or something. Have I really put down all my guards, when it comes to Cole Stone?

"Penny for your thoughts, shortcake?" He's grinning at me and I snap out of my deep, life-questioning dilemma. As if knowing the reaction it would cause, he touches the beer bottle in his hands to his lips and takes a sip. Once more my eyes can't help but be fascinated by his throat muscles. Watching them flex is as fixating for me as delinquency is for Cole—I just can't stop.

"You're ogling." Beth elbows me, smirking like she's clearly enjoying this. I squirm under both hers and Cole's gazes. He's cocked his head to one side, a crooked smile on his lips.

"I was just thinking about . . ."

"Jumping Cole?" Beth offers discreetly so that I'm the only one who can hear her. Alex and Megan are too lost in their own little bubble of happiness by this point.

132

"I was thinking," I pause to give Beth a pointed look," about how crazy today was."

"Everyone needs to have a little crazy in their lives, Tessie; I don't know how you guys got on without me."

This normal, cocky Cole is acceptable. It's when he's heart-achingly sweet that I have palpitations.

"We didn't." Beth grabs a beer of her own and takes a long sip. "We used to hide out and allow that single-brain-celled ho to walk all over us."

"Beth," I hiss and she rolls her eyes at me. I don't need her to remind Cole about the things Nicole has done in the past. He was mad enough when it came to the Hank situation. Reminders like these would cause him to completely blow his top and that wouldn't be pretty, for anyone. "Well, it's going to change, all of it," he says simply, but the viselike grip he has on the bottle in his hand tells me this is affecting him more than he lets on.

***

Beth goes to work some time later, claiming she doesn't want to be the third wheel. I argue that while Megan and Alex were skirting around the edges of a relationship, Cole and I were far from it. She shook her head, at my lunacy, perhaps, and then left. Alex took Megan shortly after; they needed some time to talk about all their issues, specifically her parents.

Cole and I are sitting in his car and he's driving me home. My parents are out meeting my grandparents. Dad has some serious schmoozing to do before the gala if he wants Grandpa to attend, and they'll probably stay the weekend. While some other time this might have scared me, the thought of being in a house all by myself isn't all that intimidating anymore. Travis is home more often than not these days. When he's not trying to avoid Dad, he spends time with me and Mom. I've helped him look for some online courses he can apply for and I think he's looking for a job, too.

Things are turning around and not all change is scaring the life out of me.

"You sure you'll be okay? I have this family dinner Dad wants me to go to but I can come check on you later," Cole offers and I shake my head, smiling to myself.

Concerned and worried Cole is one that I definitely want to get used to.

"I'll be fine, I have Travis now. It's so sweet though that you're worried about me," I coo and I see, just for a second, a reddish tinge color his cheeks.

"Sweet? I'm not sweet; I was just looking for an excuse to spend the night in your bed."

I gasp and hit his knee. "Pervert."

"Hasn't anyone ever told you to never hit the driver?"

"I'm sorry; I've never had the misfortune of driving with a sex-crazed egomaniac."

"Hey, you're the one who brought up sex. I just really liked your silk sheets."

My face reddens almost at once and he laughs at my discomfort—typical. How do I continue making myself look like an utter idiot in front of him all the time? He needs someone who knows how to flirt back and be all coy and smooth. I'm as smooth as chunky peanut butter.

He doesn't bring up the dress, nor do I but I feel like I should. It's only polite; after all if he actually went through the effort to look for one I should say something.

"About the dress . . ."

He groans and hits his head against the back of his seat before I finish the sentence. "You hate it, don't you? I knew it! I'm sorry, Tessie, I was being stupid. The only thing I know about dresses is how to take them off."

I blush once again at the insinuation. Is taking dresses off something he's done a lot of?

"No—I didn't mean it like that," he corrects himself but obviously it's too late.

"It's okay, your lifestyle isn't exactly the biggest secret, is it?" I work really hard to keep the irritation and anger out of my voice. After all why should I even feel that way? What Cole does in his spare time is none of my business. He's a hot guy; he must have girls throwing themselves at him all the time, and if he sleeps with them then . . . I want to pull their fake blond extensions out with my bare hands.

"Tessie, come on. It's not what it sounded like."

"You don't need to explain yourself, Cole, I'm not your girlfriend or anything." I laugh nervously, fidgeting with the hem of my shirt. "I just wanted to tell you that I haven't seen the dress yet, I don't know why but I haven't."

"I swear I haven't put a dead frog in the box, you can ask my mom if you want to," he says pleadingly and I can't help but notice how cute he looks. The little boy in him, desperate for approval, is too darn irresistible.

"I have a semi-sober brother now, Stone, so if you have done that tell me now," I say mock seriously and his eyes widen in panic.

"I forgot about Travis, dammit. He's going to kill me."

"Why would he do that?" Any conversation about dead, rotting amphibians and busty fake blondes is forgotten.

"Because he told me he'd beat me to a pulp if I ever came near you."

"When was this?"

"Right before I left town. I'd dropped by your house to say good-bye to you but I found Travis first and well, that guy scares the shit out of me."

His answer leaves me speechless. Cole had come to say good-bye? All those years ago, he'd actually wanted to come see me before he left for good? Maybe back then I would've started happy dancing right in front of him but knowing this now, my heart can't help but hurt a little.

"I'm sure he was kidding. He's not that bad."

"I don't think he wants you to know why he never let me see you that day. I'm not sure I want you to know."

"What does that mean?"

He's being shady and cryptic, not the arrogantly honest Cole I've come to expect. This is news to me, the fact that my brother threatened him in some way. Well, it's not that surprising. The old Travis used to do that a lot; he was fiercely and sometimes insufferably protective. The Travis I have now is only a shadow of his past self but I know and belief that he'll be back.

We arrive at my house before I get answers. The light is on, which means that Travis is home and can probably see us from the kitchen window. Since I want to avoid watching the live version of *Fight Club* in my front yard, I let my questions go.

"See you tomorrow," I say as I climb out of his Volvo. He acknowledges it with a nod and starts the car again. He realizes that I have questions but he's also smart enough to know that he needs to protect that pretty-boy face of his. For someone who claims to not be attracted to him, I sure as heck compliment him a lot.

"Open the box, Tessie, I have a feeling you'll like what's inside," he yells as he drives away.

***

Inside the house I find Travis sitting at the kitchen island with a bowl of Lucky Charms. He isn't wearing his usual ratty old shorts and torn T-shirt, which means he hasn't just gotten up.

A good omen, perhaps?

I give him a smile and make an attempt to scurry past him so that he doesn't question me but alas I fail.

"Was that Cole Stone that dropped you off?"

He sounds like himself again, his old self. Well, if getting in trouble means I'll get to see glimpses of my big brother, then why not? It's not like he'll go all raging bull and red cloth on me. Things are different now; I'm not his fragile little sister anymore. For two years I've faced the big bad world all on my own, I've learned things and I've been in situations he never wanted me to be in.

He'll need to understand.

"Yeah, it was." I rock myself on the balls of my feet as he slurps down his cereal.

"You got into that car willingly?" He raises an eyebrow, which is all I can see since the bowl is covering half his face.

"Pretty much. He's been giving me rides to school and back for like a month and I'm still alive."

"He hasn't tried something on you? He hasn't tried to hurt you?"

"Nope."

"Well, it's about damn time," he mutters under his breath, making me strain my ears to hear him.

"He's doing what I knew he would; I'm surprised he didn't come back sooner."

What is it with the men in my life going all fortune cookie on me today?

"Trav, what—"

"Forget it, forget I said a thing. So I met a girl today." He grins and just like that I forget all about the conversation we're having. It's a huge deal, the hugest, in fact. Travis hasn't been in a relationship since Jenny broke up with him two years ago. He was in love with her; he wanted to marry that gold digger. I never liked her, not even when she was sucking up to me and letting me sit with her cheerleading friends in school. That conniving thing knew that the only way to get to my brother was through me. As soon as she had him where she wanted him, she went back to pretending I didn't exist. He had been happy with her but if she wasn't my brother's girlfriend I would've done something unimaginably cruel to her. In my dreams, of course.

Knowing that he's finally met a girl he's interested in has me both ecstatic and frightened. I can't have him relapsing because of his poor taste in women. This time around, I need to protect my brother.

"Oh? When did this happen?" Walking on over to the island, I grab a stool and sit opposite him.

"I went to the music store downtown and ran into her in the Indie section."

"That alone was enough for you, wasn't it?" I smirk; knowing my brother he probably thinks he's met his soul mate.

"Kind of, I mean she didn't look at me like I'd just run away from rehab. She didn't know who I was, Tess; she didn't know I was Travis O'Connell."

"Most of the world doesn't," I point out and he rolls his eyes.

"Everyone in this town looks at me like I'm a monumental fuckup. This girl, she didn't have pity in her eyes and she wasn't staring at me like I'd grown a second head. In fact, she went ahead and called me a dick! Can you believe it?" he asks, looking frighteningly happy for someone who'd been insulted.

"Is that a good thing?"

"It's the best; at least I know she doesn't want me."

"Again, is that a good thing?"

"Oh, come on. It means that she isn't using me. She's hot as hell and she hates me, it's like the perfect combination."

"Let me understand, her hating you is perfect because . . ."

"You of all people, little sis, should know that there's a very thin line between love and hate." He chuckles before getting off the kitchen stool and walking away.

Stupid fortune cookie of a brother.

***

At school all anyone can talk about is the charity gala and suddenly I'm everyone's best friend. Word's gotten out that I'm going with Cole and now girls want to talk to me about hair, makeup, and the travesty that is having huge pores.

I smile politely at all those who come up. I smile at the dance team who once dedicated a whole routine to my excess fat. I smile at the jocks who've concussed me with their various sports balls more than once, and last but not least, I smile at Nicole.

Though that's only because she looks so miserable sitting at a table all on her own while people push and shove to sit with us. Obviously she's got Jay and her minions with her, but with the way he keeps glancing in my direction, it appears he's ready to make a run for it too.

"They make quite the pair, don't they?" Cole laughs bitterly as we both notice the stares coming from the table opposite ours. His brother and the girl who's still obsessed with him are both unrelenting in their desire to burn holes in the sides of our respective heads.

It doesn't hurt one bit when I say, "Yeah, they do."

***

137

I'm in the ladies' room at school and it's only a couple of minutes till lunch is over. Megan has decided that she needs to fix her makeup after every two classes. While part of me wants to tell her that Alex likes her, tangled hair and unglossed lips included, I decide to let her live in the honeymoon phase while she can. They haven't even kissed yet but with the way her green eyes light up at his name, that time isn't far.

"Do you think he'll like Raspberry Blush or Strawberry Ripe more?" she asks, holding out two lip glosses which honestly look exactly the same. However, since the strawberry one reminds me of the ice cream I'm craving so bad, I tell her to go with that one.

She's just about done with her routine when the door opens and the last people I want to see walk in. Nicole's followed closely by her minions. Their ponytails swish from side to side and their heels click on the tiles as the leader stalks powerfully toward us. I'm reminded of one of those grizzly bears on the National Geographic Channel, ticked off and hungry grizzly bears.

"Well, if it isn't Prude and Pruder," she chides as the minions snicker.

I think something along the lines of, "Slut, sluttier, and sluttiest," but think better of it. She's angry; she's probably having withdrawals from all the bullying she's had to forgo.

"We were just leaving," Megan stutters and begins collecting the cosmetics that are sprawled all over the counter. Before she manages to do that, Marcy, Nicole's right hand, takes the tiny perfume bottle Megan always keeps and lets it slip from her fingers. It crashes to the floor and the bottle shatters. The glass vial means a lot to her; her grandparents send her a bottle from France every year on her birthday.

"Oops," she says, but it would be obvious to a blind man that she's anything but sorry. Rage starts building up in me as I see my best friend's bottom lip quivering and my former best friend's vicious smile.

"Don't," I warn as I step in front of Megan. Surprise crosses Nicole's face for a second before she replaces it with a sneer.

"Or what, Tessie? Will you run to Cole and cry? Are you that thick-headed that you can't see how tired he is of you? Everyone knows he thought you were an easy lay but obviously he's not getting any."

"Stop it, Nicole."

"Maybe I'm wrong, maybe he is getting laid. Is that why he hasn't gotten rid of you yet? Have you learned some new tricks?"

"But why would he want to sleep with her?" the other minion, Kenna, spits in her nasally tone. "She's as attractive as my sixty-year-old housekeeper. Flat chest, gigantic ass, and stumpy legs, yup, she's just like her."

My eyes begin to prick but Megan places a soothing hand on my shoulder. I know what she's saying; she doesn't want me to react. She's worried I might do something reckless and get myself into trouble. Cautious, that's all I ever am, aren't I?

Blinking away the tears, I straighten my shoulders and look Nicole right in the eye.

"You might want your lapdog to shut up right now." Once again she's taken aback. I enjoy seeing the shock on her face; it's good to know that she doesn't know me as well as she thinks she does.

"Why is that? Are we hurting your feelings?" She chuckles, placing a hand on her hip and refusing to back down.

I smile politely at them, like I've been doing for about a week or so now. "Not mine, I couldn't care less. But see, my mom's a little protective when it comes to her children and hers might get hurt."

All three start snickering and look at me like I'm the dirt stuck to the bottom of their designer shoes.

"Is that the best you've got? You're going to tell Mommy, Tessie?" She closes in on me until we're nose to nose. "Don't play this game with me, you won't win."

"Funny how you brought up winning," I say, appearing least affected. "My mommy, Nicole, is the chairman of the gala's committee and that includes the pageant. I hope you haven't forgotten that."

Her entire body stiffens at my words and this time I feel like laughing but I hold it back. "So if you try to pull a stunt like this one more time, you can kiss your chances of participating in it good-bye."

With that I grab Megan by the hand and push past Nicole and her minions. The latter look like they're about to start foaming at the mouth while their leader just looks . . . stunned. Mission accomplished.

I wait until we're out of earshot and stop walking. Megan and I look at each other before she starts squealing and jumping up and down.

"That was awesome! Oh My God, Tessa. Did you see her face? I repeat, did you see her face?"

"It looked like she smelled cow dung." I try to stifle my laughter because of all the curious onlookers but this just feels so good. Adrenaline is coursing through my veins and I want to skip and dance and sing at the top of my lungs, all while shoving as many KitKats as I can down my throat.

We keep laughing all the way to class, where I take my seat next to Cole. He takes one look at me and gives me that half-moon-like smile.

"What's with you?"

"I just feel awesome." I shrug and he shakes his head.

"You're weird."

"You're a sick pervert."

"But you want me."

"Shut up."

"See, you're blushing. You so want me, Tessie."

"Mr. Stone, Ms. O'Connell, if you two would please stop your shameless flirting, I would like to start class." The teacher glares at us and I duck my head out of embarrassment. Everyone's laughing and with the way my desk is shaking, so is Cole.

CHAPTER FIFTEEN, PART ONE
He's Searching My Body Like It's a Map to Atlantis

I'm going to puke, that's it. I clutch my stomach which is churning heavily and stare at the pristine floor of Town Hall. To think so much effort has been put into making the floor gleam like Ryan Seacrest's teeth saddens me as I'm obviously going to hurl all over it.

"Sit still," Beth orders but I can't. I need to be ready to run in case I can't hold it in anymore. Why would I agree to put myself through this? What possessed me to agree to putting on a pageant gown and parade in front of people who have nothing better to do with their evenings?

Voodoo, that explains it. My mom must have found another pastime now that her book club has ended. Dark magic might possibly be the only reason that I find myself in such a situation. Sitting in front of a large mirror, all I have on is a shocking pink—definitely picked by my mom—robe with Beth hovering over me.

"Look, I get it, you're nervous, but looking like a Crayola-gangbanged clown won't help."

She's right, of course she is. I should be grateful that it's her and not her mother, Marie, who's doing my makeup. Marie owns a small salon in town and has been hired by the planning committee to do the hair and makeup of the contestants. Beth is just as skilled as her mom and so I asked her if she could do it instead. I refuse to let her go near my face with the amount of makeup and hair weaves at her disposal today.

"Do you think I can actually do it?" *Apprehension* and *anxiety* are weak words to describe what I'm feeling. This is bad, just really bad, and I've got this ominous feeling in my gut telling me I should hitchhike a ride to the middle of nowhere.

She tsks before answering. "As you know, I'm not the biggest fan of beauty pageants. I think it's demeaning to women to have them make a spectacle of themselves just for the sake of entertainment. Do you think when we were fighting to get the vote, this was the future we had in mind? These competitions are a vain, self-absorbed, demeaning show of how materialistic human nature is . . ."

"Your point, Beth, what is your point?"

"Oh, yeah that. All that being said, I think you'll kick ass." She grins at me before squirting foundation onto a sponge and lathering it all over my face. It's sticky, itchy, and uncomfortable, but apparently if I don't want to look like a vampire under the spotlights I need to wear it.

There's a knock on the door and shortly afterward Megan lets herself in. It's still early in the day so she isn't wearing her dress yet, just jeans and a T-shirt. She isn't taking part in the competition but is coming not only to support me but for her first date with Alex. We're in one of the rooms at Town Hall, which was originally a mansion for a previous mayor, back in the 1800s. Since then it's been converted into a tourist attraction and a place to host events such as these.

"I just came to make sure she doesn't turn you into Morticia." She giggles as she takes a seat at the foot of the bed.

"Oh har har, I swear you guys are tempting me to actually do just that."

"Please don't. It's bad enough I have to do this, I don't want to horrify the judges."

She purses her lip in a mock attempt to give me a disapproving glare but it doesn't hold for too long. She grins at me and pats my shoulder.

"When I'm done with you, you're not going to horrify, honey, you'll stun them. You're gorgeous, even if you don't know that, and with the right makeup you're going to take the bitch down."

Oh, Nicole. This is all about her, beating her, humiliating her, and taking her place.

"I saw her when I was coming up." Megan adds, "She was shouting at her poor mom. Apparently the back of her dress isn't backless enough."

Her dress would be something extreme. If not spectacular, it'd be one to shock. Surprisingly I still haven't seen my own. Honestly, a part of me is too scared to even imagine what's inside the box. The Cole I knew before military school would probably have something akin to a gag gift in there. The Cole I know now . . . well, I don't really know what he'll do. It's stupid of me; hours before the pageant starts I haven't even looked at the only dress I have.

Turns out I'm not the only person who is having these thoughts.

"Speaking of dresses, when are you planning on looking at yours?" Megan asks as the three of us look at the large box resting on the bed. It's like the thing is a ticking time bomb and the moment we touch it, it'll blow us to smithereens.

"I don't want to. Ever," I admit as both look at me incredulously.

"Then do you have a backup dress? I'm all for being risqué, but going in naked doesn't seem like the best idea."

"I don't need your sarcasm right now, Beth. The problem is that . . ." I don't really know how to explain it to them. No one understands how big of a deal it is for me to trust Cole. It's like I know opening the box will cement the relationship we currently have, albeit a very unpredictable one. If it turns out that there's something like a skimpy bikini or lingerie in there then I'll know that nothing's changed. I like to think that it has, I like to think that we've come a long way. He's done so much to prove that he isn't the same Cole, and I'm so close to not rethinking all his actions.

"You're being silly, Tessa; he said his mom was with him when he got it. How bad can it be?" I warily eye the mascara wand and hope Beth won't poke my eye out with it.

"She's right." Megan gets up and walks over to where the box is placed. Picking it up, she brings it toward me and settles it on the cluttered dressing table.

"Open it," she says with determination in her green eyes.

I have no other choice, obviously. If I don't want to go out in my birthday suit I might as well get this over with. If all else fails, I could try to fashion a dress from the horribly frilly curtains in the room. A Disney Princess, though, I am definitely not.

Sighing heavily, I get to work. The ribbon comes off first and then the wrapping paper. When all I have to do is lift the top off, I hold my breath and do it. The moment I remove the lid, I'm blinded by white light. Megan and Beth gasp at whatever they see but I'm unable to since my hand's covering my eyes. The light from the chandelier overhead is hitting whatever reflective object is there and I get visions of more disco-ball-like dresses.

"It's . . . gorgeous, Tessa! Oh My God, open your eyes and look," Megan squeals and my dread begins to go away. As long as it's not pink and sparkly I'll be fine.

My eyes open to find a bedazzling bodice. Gingerly lifting the dress so that I can see it fully, I become momentarily stunned. It takes a long time for my eyes to get used to the shining jewels and when they do, that's when I fall in love.

It is gorgeous. No, gorgeous would be the understatement of the century. Looking at it, I know the feeling is mutual. It's like someone's bottled moonlight and sprinkled it all over this exquisite fabric. A delicate shimmery silver lace covers the sleeveless top half. Like the wings of an exotic bird, it spreads down, curling around the waist. The cinched waist gives way to a silver fitted mermaid-like skirt which flares out toward the bottom. The material ripples beneath my touch and I'm almost afraid that wearing it would destroy the intricate work.

I stand there stunned. I can't believe that Cole Stone is capable of being so unconditionally thoughtful and kind and . . . amazing.

We gush about it endlessly as I try it on. It fits perfectly and accentuates whatever curves I have and emphasizes my now-thin waist. Fatty Tessie would never have been able to wear something as beautiful as this and I feel euphoric at what I've achieved.

Megan leaves since she needs to get dressed. The event coordinator tells us that we have ten minutes before I have to go to the main hall to meet the rest of the contestants and have a dress rehearsal. The thought frightens me as I think about being in enclosed spaces with the kind of girls I know I'll meet. They'll all be the kind born and bred to win pageants. Lord knows they'll faint when they see the state of my nails.

"Go get 'em, tiger." Beth squeezes my shoulder in support before leaving. In a frightening turn of events, she's the DJ tonight. I wonder how much Mom had drunk when she hired her. Does she have any idea what kind of music Beth likes to listen to? I'm not sure it's the type she'd want the snooty old ladies of our town to hear.

Oh well, I can assure you that Beth wouldn't let us be bored.

A large dressing room leads to the transformed main hall. I pass it to reach the dual staircases which lead down to it. The hall has been transformed, filled to the brim with stunning flower arrangements.

In the dressing room I'm very much aware of all the girls who I'll have to compete with. They stop dead in their tracks as I walk in, making me feel extremely uncomfortable.

"Where'd you get that?" a brunette asks harshly as she points toward me. I furrow my brows, confused that most of them are looking at me the same way. They look stunned, shocked, awed, and a bit angry all at once.

"Get what?" I ask meekly, feeling a little overwhelmed.

"That dress, where'd you get it?"

How do I tell them that a boy, whom I have no idea means exactly what to me, bought it for me? I have a feeling that the second I say Cole's name I'll be greeted with something akin to the stampede in *The Lion King*. Right, it's best if I exhibit my awesome lying skills here.

"I bought it."

The brunette who's interrogating me doesn't buy it. I've seen her around school, she's on the cheerleading squad and isn't a big fan of Nicole's. That itself made me respect her but right now she's seriously

144

freaking me out.

"That's not possible. The designer hasn't put it up for sale yet and I would know. I've been on the waitlist for weeks and they still aren't replying."

She says this in an accusatory tone like it's my fault I have the dress and she doesn't. I didn't
know that it was a designer dress that I have on, let alone know that it has a waiting list. Who has a waiting list for dresses?

"I-I . . ." I'm at a loss at what to tell them. It's not clear what the fuss is about. All of them are wearing gorgeous dresses of their own, though I realize mine looks a lot more expensive. How much had the idiot spent on me?

"Well?" She places her hand on her hip and taps her manicured fingers impatiently.

"Let it go, Celia, you're being pathetic." A voice breaks through the silence and my eyes shoot to the source. Lauren Philips, head cheerleader, is walking toward us with a frown on her face. It's like she's got "Celia" here on some kind of command-control program. The moment Lauren orders her, she backs away.

"I'm sorry about her; she tends to get a little intense at times."

Lauren is a gorgeous girl with the perfect body. She's blond just like me but her hair is like spun silk, all shiny and smooth. It's in loose curls now, styled for the evening, framing her face and reaching her waist. All the cheerleading and gymnastics have given her the most toned body I've ever seen. Her gold, floor-length shimmering dress clings to her like a second skin without looking obscene. Her high heels make her already long legs look endless.

My ego has just taken a huge hit. She's breathtakingly beautiful and she's nice.

"That's okay, thanks for intervening. I . . . I better go."

"Wait," she calls as I spin on my heels and prepare to flee.

She's smiling warmly at me as I face her. I've known her since kindergarten and she's never once acknowledged my existence. The fact that I never seemed to want a friend other than Nicole might also possibly explain why we've never really talked.

"Where are you going? Your vanity is this way." She points toward a row of dressing tables with huge mirrors. Oh, right.

"I just, uh, I need to get some air."

She shakes her head. "You can't let them get to you. I can tell you're new to the world of beauty competitions. They're sharks, all of them. They'll smell your fear from a mile away so try not to look too intimidated."

"I don't see how that's possible. I don't even know most of them and they're looking at me like they wouldn't mind having me for dinner."

She waves her hand dismissively. "That's because they're scared of Nicole. She doesn't like it when they try to talk to you or your friends."

I know that, I've known that for a very long time but it still hurts. I've never done anything to Nicole, ever. I stepped out of her way when I was starting to become a liability. I didn't cling to her like the Saran Wrap she is around Jay. So it's kind of a mystery as to why she hates me so much.

"Oh, and the fact that you've got Cole Stone wrapped around your finger doesn't help things either," she says in a hushed tone as we both sit at our dressing tables.

The statement knocks the breath out of me temporarily. Is that the impression they get when they see Cole and me together?

"It's not like that. We have a . . . complicated relationship." I unzip my makeup bag and add the finishing touches like Beth instructed. She's done most of the work. My hair's twisted into a stylish chignon at the base of my neck and my makeup is already done. I try not to be taken aback by the difference it has made. I look . . . older, less like the twelve-year-old everyone mistakes me for.

Maybe Cole will notice that too.

"That's not what it looks like," Lauren says as she reapplies her lipstick.

I try to convince her that there's nothing going on between me and Cole. Perhaps if she's convinced then all her followers will stop giving me the death glare.

Speaking of death glares, I can see Nicole's face reflected in my mirror and she doesn't seem too happy. Although she's left me alone for the most part, I can see the barely-there restraint on her face. She's itching to do something; at this point I almost welcome an attack. It's better if she just goes ahead and does what she wants right now rather than coming up with a master plan when I'm strutting around on stage.

The girls and I spend another thirty minutes or so before the host comes back again. This time he tells us that guests will start arriving soon and that we better have a dress rehearsal now. I fear tripping and breaking my neck as I struggle to balance myself in the six-inch heels Megan had forced me into. She said I needed every inch I could get to compete with the "Amazon-sized gorillas" I would be going against.

She's right. Most of these girls have the perfect supermodel height and I welcome the height my heels give me, even though they're a walking deathtrap. My dress is still earning me glares as we practice. It's a fairly simple process. As our names are called, we walk out from the dressing room and take our place at one of the staircases. With five on each one, we introduce ourselves to the crowd and judges. One by one, we walk down to our partners who lead us to the dance floor. Each pair has their own five minutes to dance and impress. Then contestants merge into the crowd and take the floor by talking and charming the pants off old people. This is where judges mark you for your personality. You can dance with anyone you want but the pressure of being judged remains.

The escorts will arrive once the show starts so we have our dress rehearsal without them. My stomach is twisted into knots as I think about seeing Cole. A part of me wants to throw something at him for spending so much money on me. Another part wants to hide behind him and just vanish into our bubble. When I'm with him, all I can concentrate on is either arguing with him or trying to keep up with his crude remarks. I kind of miss his unending attempts to flirt with me right now.

"Tessa, sweetie, is that you?"

Cassandra pops her head inside the dressing room, where we've all come back to. She looks ravishing as usual in a cream-colored lace dress. Her hair's in a bun just like mine but obviously she pulls it off much better.

I'm extremely aware of Nicole stiffening as her boyfriend's mother walks in and takes the empty seat next to mine. As much as I love Cassandra, I wish she'd just look in Nicole's direction to appease her.

"Your mother told me I'd find you here. You look beautiful, honey, and I knew the dress would look wonderful on you," she gushes and I blush. I'm trying to avert my gaze from Nicole's piercing one.

"Thank you," I say meekly, hoping she'd pick up on my lack of enthusiasm. I'd given Nicole a big reason to pounce on me, what with the bathroom incident; I didn't need to instigate her further.

"You have no idea how hard Cole made us look for it. I canceled all my appointments just so we could go shop but nothing was good enough for him." She shakes her head, reminiscing fondly.

Whoa there heart, stop melting.

"After two days of finding nothing, I called in a favor. One of my friends works with this famous designer; I'd operated on his daughter once and he was very grateful. I took Cole to see him and with the way my son fussed, I thought the poor guy would have a heart attack. Nothing we saw made him think that you'd like it."

Does he think I'm fussy? Does he think I'm an obnoxious brat who wouldn't settle for anything less than a dress costing thousands of dollars?

"Don't be mad at him, Tessa. I know Cole pretends to be this bad boy and I've seen enough of them when I was your age, but when it comes to you he's a big softie." She places her hand over mine and gives me a smile that warms my insides.

"I honestly thought he'd stick to his routine of being with a different girl every week but when I see him with you, it gives me hope. Jay's my son, my flesh and blood, but he really is an idiot for not knowing what he had."

I gape at her. Wait, did everyone know that I liked Jay? Had I had a sign plastered on my forehead all these years?

"I don't . . . I mean I don't like him, we're friends . . . I, I don't," I stutter but she laughs gently and pats my hand.

"I'm not judging you. I love my sons equally but I'm glad one of them had the balls to fight for what they want." She winks at me as I sit there, utterly flabbergasted.

"Right, okay, no more scandalizing the contestant. I just came by to wish you luck and give you this." She places a gift bag in my lap and looks at me expectantly. I dig inside and the first thing I touch is a smooth wrapper. Pulling it out, to my delight I see a huge bar of a chunky KitKat.

"That's from Cole." Cassandra grins and I match her expression. He sent me KitKats! How am I supposed to fight with that? I dig around the bag for a second time and my fingers curl around a velvet box. Pulling it out, I'm stunned to see a maroon Cartier box.

"This is from me, open it," she urges and I cautiously follow her instructions. Inside I find the most stunning pair of diamond teardrop earrings that I've ever seen. They gleam brightly, reminding me of how much they must have cost.

"Cassandra, I-I can't accept this, it's too . . ."

"Nonsense, I've had these for ages but never got around to wearing them. They'll look lovely with your dress."

"So can I give them back to you after the pageant?"

She shakes her head and pushes the box into my hand, making me fist it in my palm.

"I want you to have them."

Cassandra leaves then and I'm a mess. Did I actually have this conversation with Cassandra Stone and did it actually mean that Cole's interested in me?

But the worst thing that happened is the fact that she blatantly ignored Nicole. It's like she didn't even notice her sitting there. That's bound to have consequences.

Trying not to hyperventilate, I take deep breaths and prepare myself for the show. Guests are arriving; we can hear the polite yet totally nonsensical conversations taking place downstairs. Any moment now we'll be herded outside and made to parade around these people.

"Ten minutes, girls." The turkey sub I had for lunch threatens to come up. Deep breaths, Tessa, that's it, just take deep breaths and you'll survive this. After that you can take off your six-inch heels and clobber Cole with them.

"Try not to choke, fatty," Nicole sneers as she pushes past me to take her place in the line.

The one-shouldered crimson silk dress she wears flows behind her as she walks away. She's playing her best asset, her more-than-ample chest and her boobs are mostly on show. The back of her dress is more or less nonexistent with a singular strap connecting the top of the dress to the small of her back. She looks every bit as stunningly fierce as she is and I'm scared for my life right now.

My head's spinning by the time they call my name and I have to go take my place at the stairs. A large crowd is watching us and it's apparent that everyone in town is here. My mother stands at her podium calling off our names. The partners line the elevated dance floor in the middle of the room. My heart skips a beat as I see Cole's eyes on me. They never leave me as I walk and take my place.

He looks so good, so perfect, that I shiver slightly. He's wearing a suit just like the rest of the boys but he seems to look just so much . . . sexier, I blush at the word, than the rest. He's wearing a steel-gray tie to match my dress over a plain white shirt and it brings out his eyes beautifully. He winks at me when he catches me watching and I hold back a giggle.

I mouth "thank you" to him and I hope he understands that it's for the dress. Then I realize that he can't actually see how I look since I'm obscured by the girl in front of me and she's a good five feet nine inches tall. Oh well, he'll see me when we walk down.

One by one the ten of us introduce ourselves to the crowd. I see my father standing amid everyone else but Travis is nowhere to be found. He's tall enough so I'd know if he was here but he isn't.

Disappointment courses through me. He'd promised to come and support me, after he'd stopped choking on pizza, that is. I get that he wanted to avoid all the judgmental stares, but if I was going to do this, I needed people here who wouldn't make fun of me if and when I choked. Travis was one of those people.

Soft music plays as one by one the escorts guides participants to stand at the edge of the dance floor. My heart's practically ready to tear itself out of my chest by the time I reach Cole. My breathing's heavy and I'm feeling so faint that I could just fall to the ground any second. With a trembling hand I reach for Cole, who's staring at me wide-eyed at the bottom of the stairs.

It's something that only happens in the cheesiest of chick flicks and for that moment I feel exactly like those girls. Time seems to stop and the only people in the room seem to be this bad boy with the heart of gold and me—the awkward girl he likes spending time with.

My skin tingles with excitement as he interlaces our fingers and helps me step down. His eyes unapologetically roam my face and body and I don't try to hide. It's his dress I'm wearing, if he wants to look then he'll look. It doesn't matter that he's searching my body like it's a map to Atlantis. I'm doing this for him, this entire charade is for him, and it's about time I admit it. I feel an immense amount of gratitude toward him, for everything he's done for me so far. I'd like to thank him in whatever way works best.

"You look beautiful," he says as our Lifetime Movie moment ends and I become aware of people applauding all around us. I even see Megan jumping up and down at her spot, squealing and waving at me frantically. I laugh at her excitement as poor Alex looks clueless as to what to do with her. Waving back, I let my eyes scan the room looking for more familiar faces. Beth grins at me as I catch her eye behind the DJ booth. She looks professional and at home with her headphones and a complicated-looking contraption in front of her.

My eyes continue wandering as Cole walks us to the raised platform. They zero in on Jay, who's standing at the sidelines and I frown. What is he doing there? Isn't he supposed to be escorting Nicole? Immediately I look toward Nicole, who's on the arm of the deputy sheriff's son, Henry.

The nerve of the evil bitch. I know what she's done, I know the second I see Jay's downtrodden expression. She's ditched him for Henry because everyone knows Jay can't dance. Obviously someone who's so set on winning won't choose a guy with two left feet to be her partner, but still he's her boyfriend! They've been dating for three years. He must be so embarrassed right now. Especially seeing as Henry's kind of groping Nicole's butt and she's doing nothing to stop him.

"Why are you frowning?" Cole asks as we take our place and I crane my neck to look at Jay. Yes, after everything he's said and done I still feel horrible for him. Standing there with his hands stuffed in his pockets and shoulders slumped, he looks so . . . sad. I want that sadness to go away. I want to kill Nicole for treating him like this.

"Nicole didn't choose Jay to be her partner," I mutter angrily and Cole sighs.

"Trust me, Tessie, he doesn't care. That's not why he looks

miserable." He clutches my hand so tightly that it verges on being painful. I don't understand what he's saying but the dangerous clenching of his sharp jaw tells me that I need to steer in another direction.

"This dress . . . it's absolutely gorgeous, Cole. Thank you; I don't know what to say."

He chuckles slightly and shakes his head. "Since when do you have a lack of things to say to me? Did you finish *Great Comebacks for Dummies* already?"

I give his hand a hard squeeze. "Be serious for once, I really do appreciate it, you know."

"No big, we didn't have to look much. I found it at some vintage store Mom took me to."

Thinking about Cassandra's words and Cole's contradictory statement has me smiling to myself. I know he's the one who's lying. What I'm wearing doesn't seem likely to belong at a vintage clothing store. I might be fashionably challenged but I know an expensive dress when I see one.

If he wants to just shrug off his kind gesture then that's his choice. If he feels uncomfortable telling me about the effort he made for me then I'll leave him alone. I like teasing him, I love getting under his skin, but this time I'll let it go.

One by one each couple goes to the middle of the floor and dances. Whenever we practiced, Cole always told me to maintain eye contact and now I can see why. Apart from Laura and her boyfriend, Mike, none of the others have chemistry. Their routine looks robotic, practiced, and, frankly, boring. It's especially entertaining to watch Mr. Golden Boy. Henry Riley drops Nicole on the floor when he attempts to dip her. It's hilarious but I literally have to stuff my fist in my mouth to stop from cackling like an idiot. It didn't help things when Beth accidentally played Kanye's "Gold Digger" just as they were about to leave the floor. She apologized, looking sheepish, and I was reminded why we'd become friends in the first place.

When our turn arrives, my entire body freezes. Cole tugs at my hand to lead me forward but I'm this close to passing out. He watches me with concern on his perfect face before bending down slightly so that our faces are level.

"Freaking out?"

I nod.

He tucks a lose tendril behind my ear and his fingers brush my cheek, making my skin blaze. "Look at it this way, if you fail, I fail, and I hate failing. We've got this, I've got you, Tessie," he promises.

"You said that when you asked me to jump down from your tree house. I ended up in the emergency room with a broken ankle."

151

He scratches the back of his neck, wincing slightly. "I thought you'd aim for the trampoline. But in any case, this is different. I-I'm not that stupid kid anymore. I promise no more trips to the emergency room."

"You sure?" I ask, already feeling much better.

"Cross my heart and hope to die, shortcake."

Grinning at him, I loop my arm through his elbow and together we take center stage.

CHAPTER FIFTEEN, PART TWO
Ripping Jay's Bieber-Sized Ego into Shreds

The beginning chords of the song I'd heard way too many times as a little girl startle me. But even Edwin McCain's "I'll Be" can't distract me. I'm fully aware of all the eyes that are focusing on Cole and me. Some are smiling, warm faces full of encouragement, while others, mostly my escort's relentless admirers, are scowling fiercely. The tension is palpable; no one is talking as the only voice that resonates around us is that of the singer.

"Hey, don't look at them. Look at me, just me, like we practiced," he whispers gently and I find myself staring deeply into his eyes. Seriously, how can they be this blue?

Steadying myself, I place one hand on his shoulder and interlink the other with his. Even though we've been rehearsing for days, the novelty of the experience never wears off. My skin still tingles, little bolts of electricity still dart through the length of my arm, and my waist, where his free hand is placed, feels like it's been seared.

People, mostly women from my mother's gardening club, gush all around us as we sway on the dance floor. Ballroom dancing isn't the most exciting form of the activity but it's so very beautiful to experience that I have a newfound love for it. It's intricate, delicate, and just so . . . romantic. There's no overbearing music, no wild dance moves, just two people moving in sync.

I blush when I think of another activity that sounds similar.

"Ready for our big move?" he whispers in my ear and I stop a whimper from escaping my lips. I nod, feeling completely dazed. He's never struck me as the type who'd be good at something like slow dancing. The way I used to think about him always portrayed him as someone who wasn't ashamed to grind the house down at some club. I've always known he's a skilled dancer and even the part of me that was terrorized by him wanted to be that girl who gets swept off her feet when the music played.

The music picks up its tempo as Cole lifts me off the ground by the waist and twirls me around. Gone are the fears of being dropped that I had for a very long time. Now I smile widely as people gush all around us. I forget about the watching eyes as I concentrate on the person holding me. I realize that after all this time, after fifteen years of knowing this boy, I finally trust him. Even if he's a narcissistic pig.

Our dance hasn't even ended but people are already clapping and hollering for us. I recognize Megan's voice cutting the crowd's. She's probably yelling her lungs off since this is her fantasy being played out. She's always wanted a moment like this and for Alex's sake I hope he knows how to dance as well as his best friend.

Cole's eyes never leave mine as he lowers me to the ground. I'm taken aback when I notice he's mouthing the words, which just doubles the effect. My knees start to buckle and it would be darn embarrassing to fall on my butt in front of all these people. He notices my trembling and places both hands on my waist as I twine my arms around his neck.

"Good?" he simply asks as he presses his forehead against mine.

I close my eyes and swallow deeply. This jittering, this shaking, this urge to want everyone else in the room to suddenly vanish is as foreign as it is strong. I'm not completely crazy when it comes to these feelings, I had them for Jay for as long as I can remember, but somehow these seem . . . stronger. Cole, of all the people who could cause my heart to do these Olympic-gold-medal-worthy somersaults, it's Cole.

"Perfect," I whisper, opening my eyes.

Suddenly he lets go of my waist and places his hand on my lower back and straightens up. He interlinks our hands and begins lowering me to the ground. Having seen Nicole just being dropped, my fears are stronger than ever. However, he doesn't even give me a chance to stop him before I am inches from the floor. He lets me stay that way for about five seconds before pulling me back up and twirling me around with one hand.

When everyone starts cheering and clapping again he lets go of my body only to hold my hand. We take a bow as he can't help but yell over the thunderous applause. "And that, ladies and gentlemen, is how you do a dip." He winks at a scowling Henry and a red-faced Nicole.

I could honestly say that that moment alone made my night.

Still holding my hand, he leads me off the dance floor. Since we're the last couple of the competition to perform, all the contestants can now disperse and do whatever the heck they want. I for one want at least a gallon of water since my throat feels drier than the Sahara. Rushing to the drinks table, I gulp down large amounts of the only thing available to drink—a funny-looking fruit punch.

"What did I tell you about eating at parties?" Cole questions, trying to snatch my paper cup from me. I smack his hand away, needing the cool liquid to flow down my throat.

"You know that thing's probably been spiked, right?"

I almost cough out said punch as I realize that he probably is right, but not before gulping down a good few mouthfuls.

"Is not!" I retaliate oh so maturely but throw my cup away just in case. If the questionable alcohol hasn't already entered my system, I don't want to improve my chances.

"Don't worry; they won't use the strong stuff. Kids these days are too worried about authority." He rolls his eyes like he's disappointed that someone hadn't emptied a whole bottle of Jack Daniel's into the punch.

"Well you certainly never had a problem like that, did you, Stone?"

That's not my sarcastic comment. I realize this just in time to see Travis walking over toward us, ignoring the curious looks he's getting from all the nosy lowlifes around us. The heavily Botox-injected women begin whispering among themselves. Just showing up at an event like this is difficult enough for him; he doesn't need the gossiping hags adding to his troubles.

"Travis," I squeal, running past Cole, who'd suddenly backed away, and hug my brother. He's dressed up after God knows how long. Even though his suit's a little looser than it used to be two years ago, he still looks immaculate and I know every pair of female eyes is glued to him right now.

"I thought you ditched me," I say, pulling away and he chuckles.

"You thought I'd let you go through this on your own?" He looks pointedly in the direction of our parents.

"Mom was going to change your song, you know."

I tilt my head to the side, confused. "What?"

"She thought you'd impress the judges more if you used something more current. I had to talk her out of doing that. Then Dad thought it was a good idea to chat up Dartmouth's dean of admissions for you. Don't worry though, I handled that too."

He winks at me and the tight knot of worry that had formed in my stomach after hearing the word *Dartmouth* quickly disappeared. My father is a Dartmouth graduate and is more loyal to his school than he's ever been to his wife. We've avoided talking about the topic for long but it's senior year and I need to tell him that I want to go to Brown.

I hug him again, thankful now more than ever that old Travis is back. "You're the best brother ever."

"You can thank me with a dance." He tugs at my hand, leading me toward the now-crowded dance floor. I look over my shoulder, to see Cole drinking Coke from a can he's obviously brought with him. He winks at me and I smile back. Though the smile disappears when Travis notices the look we're sharing and glares at Cole. For a minute, the two are involved in an intense staring match but it's Cole who gives up first and walks away, an angry look on his face.

"What was that about?" I ask Travis as we begin dancing. People are now unashamedly rooted to their spots and staring at us like we're prancing around naked. My brother is obviously uncomfortable; they need to learn to mind their own business before I teach them how to.

"Nothing."

"No, not nothing. Why were you guys looking at each like that?"

"Just because." He grits his teeth and looks everywhere but at me. His eyes seem to lock onto something, making his eyes widen comically but before I can see what or who has caught his attention, he looks away and moves us away from the spot.

"Come on, Trav, I thought you were okay with him now."

I think about his behavior the night Cole had dropped me off, the same night he'd met his mystery girl. He hadn't seemed too opposed to the idea of my spending time with my ex-tormenter. He actually seemed pleased about the fact that we were getting along, so what is with the mood swing?

"He needs to start thinking about what he's getting you into. You think I don't know the shit Nicole puts you through?"

"I don't understand." I lower my voice and am hoping he does too before my mom has a heart attack.

"Look, if it were up to me then I'd say that you were better off without either of the Stone brothers. One has no balls and the other's just going to get you into trouble."

"I know what I'm getting myself into," I say, a little more harshly than I'd intended. "He has his fangirls and probably some criminal charges but he's been the best friend I could ever ask for. It's weird, I get it, but I want to make this work."

He tips his head to the side, studying me. Looking at me seriously for a while, his face breaks out into a huge grin, which takes me by surprise. What is with his erratic behavior today? Did he just walk into the event after downing a whole bottle?

"Hear that, Jason, best friends. Now you can stop following her like a sick puppy."

Oh My God. No, he did not just say that to whom I think he just said that to. Too horrified to move a muscle, I stand there allowing my brother to walk right past me, no doubt shoving into Jay in the process.

"Wow, he really hates me, doesn't he?" Jay asks as he steps in to take Travis's place. I look at my feet, shuffling them, not very successfully though in my deathtrap heels.

In situations like these I do what I do best. This time it's a Britney Spears throwback. I mutter the lyrics about doing it again through my teeth, hoping he doesn't hear me. I don't need to embarrass myself even further in front of him.

"What?" He strains his ear as he takes a step closer.

I laugh nervously before shrugging. "Don't take Travis seriously, he's just being his stupid, overprotective self."

Placing one of my hands on his shoulder, Jay guides the other to clasp into his. I look around for either Cole or Nicole, not knowing who would react worse. Even though I've dreamt about dancing with him for as long as I've known him, this is quite awkward. The anger I had toward him for demeaning my brother has faded into disappointment. I know I should be more forgiving but I couldn't do that; had it been anyone else but Travis I would be kinder, but he chose the wrong person.

"He thinks I'm a coward who hurt you. I don't blame him because it's true." He laughs bitterly as we sway together.

"Jay, no . . . It's not like that."

"I'm an idiot, the biggest asshole on the planet. I had no right to say all those things about Cole to you; clearly it's none of my business anymore." The bitterness never leaves his voice as his eyes bore into mine.

"What are you trying to say?"

"I strung you along for too long. I knew about your crush and shouldn't have encouraged you. I'm sorry that I broke your heart."

Wait just a minute. The little piece of donkey poop, is he feeling sorry for me? Does he think that I've been shattered and broken because he chose my slut of an ex-best friend over me? Well, maybe that had been the case a month ago but now . . .

The most magical thing happens next. The calm ballroom music changes and instead Gloria Gaynor's breakup anthem blasts around the room. It's so appropriate for the moment and the look on Jay's face is priceless. I barely hold back a laugh and my eye catches Beth's and I see her glaring at the back of Jay's head. I think, in this very moment I've found someone who's as furious at him as I am.

Patting his chest, I smile serenely at him. "You did," I sigh theatrically as we move onto the middle of the floor. If I'm going to do this, I might as well put out a show right in front of his girlfriend.

The rather prophetic lyrics of "I Will Survive" give me the strength I need to nip this right in the bud. Jay's still looking at me like he's afraid I'll have a meltdown any second. Oh, there is going to be a meltdown, just not mine.

"But then I realized something. I realized that I knew this really hot guy, the hottest I've ever seen, and instead of going after him I was wasting my time over you. Frankly, and I really don't mean to offend you, but you're not that good looking." His eyes widen but he doesn't do anything that might attract attention. We're smack-dab in the middle of the crowded building and he'd need to watch his step.

The song is so spot-on; it's actually freaking me out. Is this how Beth spends her time, making a playlist for my life? Anyway, getting back to ripping Jay's Bieber-sized ego into shreds.

"I think I'm better off now. Of course, I understand your concern, Cole is well, he's Cole, but there's something so undeniably sexy about bad boys, don't you think? Who can resist them?"

His jaw drops to the floor, his eyes threaten to bulge out as I push him away. I don't know where this courage or the urge to be provocative is coming from but I'm relishing it. Perhaps the punch really was spiked, oh well, who cares.

"Tessa, are you . . . are you drunk?" he asks in utter astonishment.

I place a finger on my lip and pretend to think. "Mayyybe," I giggle. This is so much fun, why haven't I gotten drunk before? It feels like I have this visa to say or do anything I want without fearing the consequences.

"Holy . . ." He runs a hand through his hair and looks around, as if for help. He's being so silly. I don't need help. I'm perfectly fine, just feeling a little more brave than usual.

I skip past him and go to where Cole's standing with a bunch of cackling hyenas around him, of the female variety. I frown at the sight; he's looking way too friendly for my liking as he is allowing one of them to run her hand up and down his arm suggestively. He is not flirting with someone else while he's my partner. That must violate the laws of beauty pageants everywhere.

I stalk toward him, pushing through the scantily clad STD poster child women until we're face-to-face. Amusement is written all over his face as he takes another swig from his flask.

"What, did you get bored of Jay Jay already?" His eyes may have humor in them but his voice is so icy that I'm surprised I haven't gotten frostbite by now. What's his problem now?

"He was being an idiot; I put him in his place," I mutter, feeling a little hurt that he talked to me like that in front of his groupies. They must think I'm as pathetic as they are.

He looks taken aback by my response and snatches his arm away from the girl who'd nearly been dry-humping it.

"You two had a fight?" He seems interested now.

"Yes, I told him I thought he was ugly. Does that make you happy?"

His face lights up in an instant and I feel at ease. I don't like it when he's mad at me, it just feels wrong and too painful to handle these days.

"Absolutely." He grabs my hand and pulls me to his side. The groupies are glaring now but beginning to disperse since they've noticed that they've lost his attention. Together, we walk to the middle of the stage where my mom's calling out for all the participants. Apparently it's time to deliver the verdict. I roll my eyes at my fellow contestants, who've started to hyperventilate. For Christ's sake, it's not Miss Universe we've got going on in here, calm the fudge down.

Feeling a little woozy as we line up in front of the judge's podium, I grab Cole's hand for support. Nicole is on the verge of hysteria from what I can see and Henry looks like he's in pain. Poor guy, Nicole must be digging her nails into his flesh. I've sat by her through enough horror films to know what she does when she's scared or nervous.

Mom starts to drone on and on about the importance of being a responsible citizen. My eyes are drooping and I feel like I need to curl up in my bed and sleep through the next century. Resting my head on Cole's shoulder, I try making myself comfortable and am nearly successful before being shaken thoroughly.

"Get up, shortcake, you won!"

Huh? What does winning have to do with the double cheeseburger I'm inhaling at Rusty's? Why is Cole even here? Doesn't he have practice?

"Come on, wake up."

I moan at his persistence before lifting my eyelids. The gala, yes the stupid gala, is still going on. I'm being led by Cole as people clap around us. Megan intercepts us on the way and traps me into a big hug.

"I knew it! I knew you'd win." Alex pulls her away as I give her a lazy smile in return. Yup, I am so drunk. Stumbling I walk after Cole, who makes sure I don't fall face-first. Seeing the stern look on my mother's face is a little sobering. I think she suspects and I hope I don't reek of alcohol. I'm not even sure what is it that I drank but it sure wasn't something light.

"Miss Farrow Hills for the year 2014 is Tessa O'Connell," she says loudly and I try to think of what sober Tessa would do right now. Right, she'd blush because of all the attention and then shrug her way into the background, letting someone else steal her thunder. Well not today.

As they put a sparkling tiara, which I know is a fake, on my head I grin widely and start waving at the people. I stumble just a little, before grabbing the mike from my mom's hand.

Clearing my throat, I approach the podium and address the people of my land.

"I would like to take this opportunity to thank my family, my parents," I gesture to where they're standing on stage, "my lovely brother," Travis hollers as I mention him and the crowd bursts out laughing. "I would like to thank my friends, Beth, you're the best DJ we've ever had. Seriously, the last one played music that shouldn't have survived past the Middle Ages." People chuckle again and so do I. "Megan, you're the best. You're like my personal cheerleader. Alexander, take care of her or I'll go all Jackie Chan on your butt."

He shouts something which sounds like, "I will," but I've already started talking again. "Cassandra, I love you, you are such a cool person," I gush and the lady in question, who is present on stage, kisses my cheek, laughing too.

"Lastly, I want to thank Cole, my buddy, my pal. He's so awesome and he's a fantastic dancer, ladies. If you want his number . . ."

"Okay, that's enough, Tessie." I pout as Cole pries the mike from my hand and gives it to my mother. She announces the end of the evening but people are allowed to stay for an hour or so to enjoy the music and the food.

"Is my daughter drunk?" she hisses once we're safely away from the crowd.

Cole looks a little embarrassed as I tug at his hair and say, "Pretty."

"It was the first batch of punch you served. She nearly drank the entire bowl and I'm pretty sure it was spiked."

"I'm going to kill him," she seethes, all thoughts of my drunken behavior forgotten, and marches off to where a boy roughly my age is collecting plates from around the room. She snatches him by the ear and marches out, with the poor guy yelping in pain behind her.

Cole laughs loudly, making the corners of his eyes crinkle and the dimples in his cheek deeper. I'm tempted to dig my finger into the indentations but he halts the thought in my mind as he holds my hands in both of his and begins walking backward.

"Where are we going?" I half chuckle, half hiccup as he grins deviously.

"I'm going to take advantage of your newfound bravery and we're going to do something which will make you feel awesome."

***

"I'm cold," I complain as we make our way through the parking lot. Still in my slightly backless and completely sleeveless gown I shiver as we go past

160

car after car. Then coming to a rest near a very familiar-looking Jeep, Cole grins and fishes out a pocket knife from his trouser pockets.

"You carry a knife in your suit?" I ask, not completely shocked.

"Yes," he says like it's no big deal.

It's not until he hands me said knife that I begin to freak out. What does he want me to do that requires me wielding a weapon?

"Slash his tires," Cole urges and I shake my head vigorously.

"This is a bad idea, this is a very bad idea, and even drunk me knows that. Let's go inside, Cole," I say patiently. He doesn't seem to want to comply. In fact as we speak, he pulls out yet another small knife. Crap.

"You said so yourself he was being an idiot. Well, this is payback, let's slit the damn tires," he says excitedly. I think back to the rather insulting things Jay said about my brother and the pitiful way he looked at me tonight.

I don't need his pity.

"Okay, let's get to work."

***

An hour later, we stumble into my room. The house is quiet as per usual; my parents are out for drinks with the people who sponsored the gala. Travis is likely searching for his music store girl.

"Go and change, Tessie, you look like you're about to drop dead." Cole chuckles as he sits at the foot of my bed and begins taking his shoes off. The tie follows, and then he pushes up the sleeves of his dress shirt, before unbuttoning its top three buttons.

Yum.

Grabbing one of Travis's old T-shirts from the closet, I carefully undress myself in the bathroom, knowing that what I'm wearing costs more than my entire wardrobe. Once the dress from the heavens above is safely put away I let out a breath and stumble back into my room.

"I'm beat," I mutter, falling onto my bed with a loud thump. When I don't hear a response, I open my eyes to see Cole standing a couple of feet away from me, looking rather pale.

"What's wrong?" I ask, yawning and stretching my sore muscles. Heels and I are never going to develop a close relationship.

"You're not wearing anything but the shirt," he stutters and I furrow my brow—so what?

"People can sleep without pants, Stone. S'no big deal." Another yawn escapes me as I bury my head in my pillow and snuggle up to it.

"Uh no, you need to cover up."

161

"I don't want to," I say stubbornly, hating that he's keeping me from slipping into the best sleep I've had in months.

He's quiet and I hope he won't push the topic anymore. That's when a blanket is pulled over me and I'm tucked into bed. I sigh at the pleasant warmth and pull the covers tightly around myself. Hmm, this feels nice.

"Hey, Cole," I say as I hear my door creak open.

"Yeah?" he asks in an unusually throaty voice.

"Please stay," I murmur into my pillow.

Even in the state of being half asleep, I hear the lock on my door click into place after about five minutes. Whatever internal debate he's having seems to have settled as he lifts the covers and slips underneath.

"Goodnight, Tessie," he whispers, as we lay side by side with a good amount of space between us.

"Goodnight," I reply before drifting back into sleep.

CHAPTER SIXTEEN
Victory for the Socially Inept of the World

Around the time of my ninth birthday, my mom had another one of her "brilliant" ideas. She's had a lot more since then but that one took the cake, no pun intended. Half of my class was invited for a birthday sleepover. She hired a party planner and everything. Her goal was for me to extend my circle of friends beyond Nicole.

Maybe she'd had an epiphany about what a major witch my BFF would turn out to be.
Anyway, imagine my shock, disgust, and body-paralyzing, brain-freezing fear when both the Stone boys showed up at my doorstep that day. Everyone always saw them as brothers, a pair even though they had different parents. I was the only one who saw how stark the difference between them was. One was an angel, the other Lucifer.

I threw a tantrum, I wanted Cole gone but it wasn't what a "well-brought-up young lady" would do. He stayed the night and in the end the damage wasn't as bad as I'd expected. I only had a severe rash from the itching powder he'd sprinkled all over my sleeping bag. I only had an allergic reaction to the white roses he'd brought me and my hair only turned a mild shade of green when I used my shampoo the day after.

For him, this was tame. I think he went easy on me because of my birthday.

These are the thoughts passing through my mind when I wake up the next day. Well that and the fact that I feel like I have hundreds of thousands of Oompa Loompas doing Zumba inside my head. My skull feels like it weighs a ton and has been mistaken for a set of drums. Someone needs to stop hitting me! This realization is quickly followed by another one. I can't breathe, like I literally can't. My lungs feel like they're being compressed by a ton of weight. It hurts to inhale and I start to panic. Quickly springing into panic mode, I wrench my eyes open and try to wriggle out

163

from beneath the weight, all the while battling the headache from hell.

Someone grunts near me and I freeze. My hands stop shoving something that feels like a wall of steel and I scoot closer to the edge of the bed. What on earth?

"Is that how you wake people up in this family?" Cole groans next to me, finally removing his arm from over my torso.

Cole. Arm. Torso. Bed. My Bed.

Being as smooth as I always am, I let out a shriek as soon as all the jumbled words come together.

"You forgot I was here, didn't you?" A very shirtless Cole yawns and stretches. My eyes are pivoted to his extremely shirtless body, fixating over his rippling muscles and defined stomach.

"Yeah, I think that's it." Struggling to breathe, I look away. The bed creaks, telling me that he's gotten up.

"You can look now, I'm decent."

He sounds a little too smug for my taste but it's deserved. He knows I'd been checking him out. Heck, every girl he meets must check him out. I'm not blind; I'm a teenage girl with crazy hormones. Hormones which never seemed to make me feel this perverted until Cole came into the picture.

"How much did I drink last night?" I groan, pulling my knees up to my chest, and drop my head to rest on top of them. I have visions of Jay and Gloria Gaynor. Flashes of being up on stage and giving a speech, images of Cole surrounded by a bunch of girls with fake boobs. Okay, so maybe not all of them had fake boobs but they were still desperately all over him. That's just as bad, I think.

"Not enough to not remember everything," he snorts and settles down next to me. He pries my hands away from my face and makes me look at him. All the while, I'm alternating between the urge to puke and battling a surefire heart attack. Being near Cole does weird things to me, I swear.

"I haven't forgotten. I mean what's the point of getting drunk if I can visualize every stupid thing I did under the influence!"

"You didn't do anything stupid. For the first time in your life, Tessie, you were honest and I think that rocks."

I look at the determined expression on his face. Understanding dawns upon me and I realize that yesterday I did things he's always asked me to do. I stood up to a guy whom I've allowed to control me for far too long. I was myself in front of the whole town instead of being shy, quiet, meek Tessa. I did something incredibly selfish, I slashed the tires of Jay's car, but it made me feel good so I let it pass.

"You're right, I did sort of rock yesterday, didn't I?"

He chuckles and gets up to go to the guest bedroom with its own bathroom. I'm not worried about anyone seeing him come out of my room, for the simple reason that no one's home. My parents usually take a break after the gala. This year they're taking a fishing trip with some of their friends. Travis would have made his presence known by now so it's likely that he's not here either.

I go to my own bathroom, ready to shower till I turn into a prune but something makes me freeze.

Shutting my eyes I turn on my heels so that I'm standing right in front of my full-length mirror. It's not my bird-nest hair that's causing me to turn beet red, nor is it the mascara smeared all over my face. I don't even mind the lipstick staining my teeth. Oh no, that is not worrying me, though it should. What is absolutely mortifying is the fact that I'm not wearing any underpants!

I slept in the same bed with Cole Stone and forgot to wear underpants. Someone please fetch the cyanide.

***

After showering and washing all of yesterday's grime off, I decide to dress down for the day. The sparkling tiara resting on my dressing table is the constant reminder of what I achieved yesterday. If I wanted to, I could be like Nicole or one of the more popular girls. The tangible proof is a huge boost to my self-esteem. Finally, even though it might be a little shallow, I know I'm not loser Fatty Tessie anymore. I also know that this guy I'm beginning to possibly develop feelings for and one who is responsible for almost all of my nightmares, is in my house. I eye my tattered, oversized shirt in my hand and throw it into the back of my closet. I could definitely do better. In the end I settle for a look that's both cute and doesn't look like I've spent nearly thirty minutes trying to perfect it. I'm wearing a pair of the designer jean shorts my mom bought me and I pair it with a cute, slouchy, off-the-shoulder white knitted top. Trying to be casual, I throw on my flip-flops, showing off my sparkly toenails, which had been done yesterday.

I find Cole downstairs, whistling as he cooks. It's a familiar sight from not too long ago but the difference is evident. I'm much more aware of him now. I like to look at him and I like to study his profile. I appreciate the athletic grace he possesses as he moves around, flipping, frying, whisking and shaking. I love the way he bites his pinkie when something tastes odd. I love how he frowns when he burns a piece of toast.

Trying to be noiseless, I tiptoe down to him. His back's turned toward me and I can tell he's making coffee. The smell hits me like a freight train but only in the best of ways. My mouth waters and the Oompa Loompas inside me gravitate toward the source.

"How much sugar do you take in this?"

Well, so much for being sneaky.

"One sugar, oh, and creamer too."

When he settles it in front of me, I all but gulp it down in one go. The coffee is an elixir of life for my pounding head. I have no idea why people make such a big deal out of drinking. It is not fun and I'd really rather wake up without a headache.

"Here, you need to take these, but not on an empty stomach."

He pushes two Advil toward me along with water. Even though the thought of food makes me queasy, I manage to eat a hard-boiled egg and some toast. The blander, the better. The medicine kicks in about ten minutes later and the Oompa Loompas return to the chocolate factory.

Beyond embarrassed by the fact that I slept half dressed with him, I can't even look at Cole. He's humming to himself, definitely in a good mood, which shows that he wasn't affected by my lack of clothes at all.

"Why are you so quiet?" He sips his own coffee and raises an eyebrow at me. Trying to look dreadfully casual, I shrug.

"I'm thinking about last night," I say truthfully. I don't mean the gala, or winning a title, but what happened later. We may have slept in the same bed before but something seems different now. He must have felt it too since he was basically wrapped around me when I woke up.

"Yeah, I knew you'd win." He grins. I knew he'd take it the wrong way; I'd been counting on it.

"Nicole will probably be spitting fire right now. I'm almost afraid to run into her." I shudder, but only jokingly. Something changed last night; my inhibitions went away. Speaking to Jay, letting him know how I truly felt about him now and finally admitting that Cole was a better person than him has made me braver. I know I can face Nicole now. She's the same girl who's terrified of ants. She's the same girl who has the most horrible allergic reaction to coriander and she's the same girl who cried for hours on end when Marissa Cooper died on *The O.C.* Yeah, I know the girl like the back of my hand. Knowing that she's as human as I am rationalizes my resolve to end her torment.

Cole doesn't understand that I'm joking. His face hardens, his eyes losing all of their previous humor. I really know how to put my foot in my mouth, don't I?

"We're ending it right here, Tessie. Whatever hold she has on you,

166

it's over. If it were up to me, she wouldn't even be alive after that stunt she pulled with Hank. We're taking her down and you need to stop being so afraid."

"It's not that I'm scared." I break off, gauging his reaction. Cole refuses to look me in the eye as he finishes his breakfast. This has to be done right or his temper will get worse. "I let her get away with things mostly because I really lack in the self-esteem department."

He begins to say something but I stop him. "I get it now, I do. I might not be skinny enough, blond enough, smart enough, but I also don't deserve all the shit she gives me. I allowed her to walk all over me thinking that that's what I deserve, but it's different now."

"Why?" His eyes bore into mine intensely. The atmosphere is charged, a palpable tension surrounding us. I almost miss his crude flirting and teasing, I even miss the bully inside of him.

"Because I met this complete douchebag who made me realize that being a little narcissistic is good for the soul." I place a hand against my heart and sigh dramatically. Finally, the spell of awkwardness breaks and Cole laughs; the sound is like music to my ears.

We laze around for some time. It's not even afternoon yet so I text Megan and Beth, asking if they want to do something today. Both replies are disappointing since Megan can't leave the house after nearly breaking curfew yesterday and Beth is working. She's almost always working, taking odd jobs here and there. Her mom's an aspiring-musician-turned-beautician. She wasn't very frugal with her inheritance, wasting almost all of it when she made a demo and tried to get signed. When she ended up pregnant, she had to give up her dream temporarily, move back to her old town and raise her daughter. No one talks about Beth's father, not even her. It's a taboo topic that no one dares touch. Marie hasn't been the greatest mother; she still spends money like she's best friends with bank robbers. Her dreams of being a singer haven't died but the more rejection she faces, the more she sinks into depression. Beth puts on a brave face and pulls through but I know how much she's struggling to earn enough for college.

We're watching cartoons, Cole's sprawled all over the couch in my living room and I'm snuggled down in my favorite armchair. He's texting someone constantly and even though I don't want to admit it, it's bothering me.

It's bothering me a lot.

What if it's one of the girls from yesterday? They certainly looked friendly enough to give him their numbers. They were all gorgeous; he'd be an idiot to not want to get in touch with them. They're probably better at flirting and witty banter than I am. I bet they would be doing something far more interesting with him than watching *Rugrats* reruns.

When he laughs for what seems like the tenth time, I throw a cushion at him, which he obviously skillfully ducks.

"What did I do?" he asks incredulously and I scowl.

"You're interrupting my cartoons. I can't even hear what they're saying because of your pig-like snorting. Stop texting your groupies or get out!" I huff, crossing my arms over my chest.

His face is blank for a second or so and then he bursts out laughing. That idiot has the nerve to laugh at me, like he's making fun of obvious jealousy. I start feeling uncomfortable pretty fast and sink into my armchair, wanting to completely vanish. Once again, my mouth shoots and scores, victory for the socially inept of the world.

"I was texting my grandmother." Tears start streaming down his face as he buries his face in the back of the couch and thumps his fist against it, his body shaking in laughter. Well, this is awkward.

"I—I, I didn't know. You were just being annoying." I scowl and pull my knees up to my chest. Right now, I just need the earth to open up and swallow me whole. I wouldn't even bat an eyelash if a meteor struck and eliminated the entire human race.

"You were jealous, Tessie, admit it." Even though he's trying to be smug, his eyes sparkle at the idea and I feel all warm and gooey on the inside. He likes that I'm jealous and I like that he likes that I'm jealous. It reinforces the idea that maybe, just maybe, I'm different from all the other girls in his fan club.

For the sake of pretense, I roll my eyes and snort. "You're delusional, Stone."

"But you're jealous," he nags, making my cheeks heat up. He's going to enjoy himself with this one. I need to change the topic before he sees right through me.

"How is Nana Stone? I haven't seen her in ages."

Nana Stone is Sheriff Stone's mother and one of the coolest people I have ever come across. She breaks, no, scratch that, smashes every stereotype you might possibly have for a person above the age of sixty. When we were kids and she used to live in this town with her husband, Cole's grandfather, I used to go to her house every other day since she volunteered to babysit me. I still remember all the eccentric clothes she used to wear. She had all these different colored wigs, which she'd pair with crazy outfits. If one day she wore a neon pink wig and a floor-length gown, the next she'd wear an inky black wig with leather pants, a black T-shirt, and a leather jacket. On top of everything else, she was the only one who didn't let Cole get away with the things he did to me. Once she caught him emptying a tray of ice down the back of my shirt and she punished him by having him clean every toilet in the house. Obviously, I idolize the woman.

When Cole's grandfather died, she sold her house and moved away. I hear stories of her traveling around the world and scuba diving in the Caribbean and I wonder if she's really out there doing all that. I know Cole still sees a lot of her, even when he was states away in military school; he's really close to her even though he tries his very best not to show it. From what I've observed so far, he still goes to see her once every two weeks. For someone who's considered the town bad boy, he sure is a softie when it comes to his Nana.

If he senses the fact that I'm clearly deflecting the jealousy question, he doesn't make anything of it. He just looks warmly toward the cell phone in his hand and shakes his head.

"She's still the craziest old lady I've ever met. She was just telling me about how she let a stink bomb go off during bingo night."

Cole's grandma through and through.

"Do you still see her often?"

He nods. "I try to but she doesn't like me seeing her in the seniors' home a lot. If it were up to her, she'd be off street racing, but my dad put his foot down. She hates that place."

I could understand. For a free spirit like Nana Stone, being confined to an old age home would be a nightmare. It didn't matter how good the care was, the woman wasn't supposed to be kept all caged up.

Cole studies me as I stare out the window, looking into the distance but painfully aware of his gaze on me. My skin's starting to prickle under the scrutiny and I just want him to spit out whatever he's thinking but I'm afraid to open my mouth again. My feelings are starting to become painfully obvious and I need to put my guard up before he sees everything.

"Do you want to go see her with me? You're free, right? We have a Founder's Day long weekend and nothing to do. Do you want to go visit her? She'll love to see you."

I'd love to see Nana Stone too; it's been far too long. But from what Cole tells me she lives about two and a half hours away, the drive isn't that long. I know my parents wouldn't mind; they themselves won't be home till tomorrow. Travis would make a scene but I can take care of him. Besides, he's so obsessed with Mystery Girl at the moment that nothing else matters.

The sad thing is that even though this teeny tiny part of me is questioning all of this, a bigger part is jumping up and down in excitement. Of course I want to go with him.

He's waiting patiently for my answer but there's a sort of apprehension and anxiety surrounding him, like he's testing me. I wonder what would happen if I said no but I guess we're never going to find out since the word yes leaves my mouth before I can overthink anymore.

His entire face lights up and he's grinning like a kid on Christmas. We immediately go into prep mode. I put on some makeup while he goes home to change and get his car. It gives me time to regroup and get my nerves under control.

Now, I'm no fortune-teller, that I can assure you. However, right now I have this feeling in my gut telling me that this trip will define who we are. We've been swinging like a darn pendulum between being frenemies and then something more. Buying dresses, dances, and almost kisses—we are already something more, aren't we?

I start hyperventilating at the thought of all the possibilities that could possibly be. I'm absentmindedly doing the dishes, trying to calm myself down when all of a sudden the hair at the back of my neck stands up. I know it's him, without even questioning myself.

"Ready to go?" he whispers in my ear. I hadn't realized that he was so close. The plastic cup in my hands drops to the floor with a loud clatter.

I whirl around, only to notice that he's caged me in his arms. I'm breathless, panting heavily with my heart crashing wildly against my ribs.

"Don't do that! You could've killed me," I chastise but the effect is dimmed by my breathy voice.

I expect him to tease me, to mock me, and to turn the situation into a humorous one, but the serious look in his eyes takes me aback. His blue eyes are sparkling, his lips slightly parted, cheeks flushed.

"Cole, what's . . . ?"

"You told Jay you thought I was sexy?"

Oh crap.

I want to disappear, I want to be abducted by aliens and I want to be run over by a truck, like yesterday. That big-mouthed, no-good ape! I felt slightly guilty for slashing the tires of his car but now I feel like I let him off easy. I want to grab a baseball bat and wreck his Jeep so badly that even that stupid MTV show won't be able to fix it. How could he . . . why would he even . . . ?

Why do these things keep happening to me?

"I—I didn't exactly . . . he misunderstood and I . . ." I don't know what to say and my pounding heart isn't helping. With all the blood rushing to my head and a whooshing sound in my ears, I don't exactly feel good.

"Do you like me, Tessie?"

I gulp. Is this the part where we finally talk about all the weird tension between us? Do I want to admit that maybe I could have a crush on Cole Stone? The words *crush* and *Cole Stone* in the same sentence just sound so strange. It shouldn't feel right but it does.

He tilts my chin upward to look at him. There's an odd mixture of happiness and fear on his face. It makes answering him all the more difficult. All that hope, all that anxiousness, every conflicted feeling shared between the two of us is now out in the open. I could wreck everything with just one word.

"I don't know."

He cocks his head to the side, a crooked smile on his face. "Well, at least that's better than a no."

"I wouldn't say no, not after everything," I say in a quiet voice, afraid to even look at him again. My heart rate is going haywire; it's not normal. This dizzying effect he has on me is now so overwhelming that I can hardly hear myself over the pounding in my chest.

He cups my cheek, his thumb brushing over my cheekbone. My eyes flutter close and instinctively I lean into his touch. This moment feels so perfect, so earth-shattering and unreal that I almost feel like I'll wake up any second and realize that it is all a fantasy my mind has conjured up.

"Tessie," he says in a voice that says it all. It expresses longing and desire, care and warmth, yearning and . . . something more.

He takes a deep breath, as if preparing himself for something. I'm afraid to let out the breath I've been holding. I have all these thoughts and feelings, emotions I can't put into words. I don't think I'm ready for whatever he's about to say.

"We'll take this slow, as slow as you want." He gulps audibly and I'm relieved to see that he's as nervous and rattled as I am. "Whatever you need, it'll all be on your terms. I just want a chance to show you that I'm not that stupid boy who left four years ago."

You haven't been that boy for a while now; I want to say this out loud. I want to tell him that he's changed my life, quite literally ever since he's come back but I feel numb, incapable of speech. I just nod stupidly and his hand drops from my face. Instead he takes my hand in his and interlinks our fingers.

"I promise, Tessie, I won't let you down."

I squeeze his hand in response, not knowing what else to say. Only someone who's known me for my entire life knows that this means more than words. He knows I'm not the most eloquent person on the planet so he doesn't push me, doesn't try to make me speak. We finish doing the dishes together and that's the only time Cole lets go of my hand.

Later, when I've made sure that the house is safely locked, Cole and I head for his Volvo. We haven't said much aside from mundane instructions and single-word responses. Is this how it's going to be between us now? Will it be awkward, will we both be too shy to behave the way we usually are with each other?

I take shotgun as Cole starts the car. Once we pull out of the driveway, he takes my hand again and smiles at me shyly; I mirror his expression.

"Tessie?" he says after a while and I remove my gaze from outside the window.

"Yeah?" I say quietly, afraid of what's coming next.

"I told Jay slashing the tires was completely your idea." He chuckles and I gape at him.

"You did not!"

I lunge for him over the gap between the two seats but am restrained by my seatbelt. He chuckles at my misery and embarrassment and that's when it hits me. It doesn't matter what we become to each other, in the end the most important part of our relationship is his ability to drive me crazy.

And he's doing a stellar job with that. But I will admit, that when I tug my hand away so that he can drive, I immediately miss the warmth of his skin.

CHAPTER SEVENTEEN
Don't Strip on Top of the Pool Table, Nana

The members of the Stone family are not the kind of people who subject themselves to conformity. Nana Stone was far from being a sweater-knitting, cookie-baking, slobbery-kiss-giving kind of grandmother. Her husband always seemed as if he were the older version of Cole himself. They even looked alike so it wasn't really a surprise that they were like two peas in a pod. When his Grandpa died, Cole lost his partner in crime. I remember my heart breaking for him. I remember the funeral, where he silently shed tears. A thirteen-year-old boy had just lost his best friend and it didn't matter how I felt about him, I still wanted the tears to go away.

I think about our pasts as we drive through an obviously elite beach town. It's kind of like the Hamptons but the glamour is more subdued. It looks like the kind of place where the extremely rich would come to retire. I can see the ocean from the car window and the large Spanish-villa-style houses that line the streets. It's beautiful, of course it is, but everything screams money and it's kind of confusing me.

That's not the only thing that's confusing me right now.

"What do you mean she ran away?"

"I mean exactly that, damn that crazy Nana." Cole slams his fist against the steering wheel and hangs up on whomever he's talking to. He runs a hand through his hair and while I'm all for caring about his escape artist grandmother, I cannot for the life of me concentrate on anything but how weak in the knees I feel when his hair's disheveled like this. Oh boy, we've only just established this thing between us and I'm already turning into the psycho from *Swimfan*.

"So you're saying that she knocked out her caretaker and busted out from the seniors' home after stealing said caretaker's car?"

I find it a little hard to believe that a sixty-five-year-old woman is capable of doing all that. She might be a Stone but even they aren't invincible.

"I told her to wait for me; I would've gotten her a much better car than that beat-up old Mustang."

Ha! He's not mad that his elderly grandmother ran away from a facility which obviously provides excellent care, he's mad that she made a poor choice of car to steal. Who says I know boring people?

"Well then, since you obviously were going to help her you'll know where she went. Problem solved, call your dad and tell him everything's fine."

Sheriff Stone had called us about half an hour ago. Apparently he'd been informed that his mother attacked an employee before busting out, oh and stealing a car. He's fuming and he thinks Cole somehow assisted her. That's where I came in, I told him feeling absolutely mortified that Cole had been with me for the better part of last night and today. Things got really awkward really fast and he dropped the subject. When he found out that we were on our way to meet Nana Stone, in some cruel twist of fate, he asked us to find her and take her back to the retirement home.

Cole, it turns out, has done this a few times. He's a Nana Stone whisperer and whenever she pulls a stunt like this, he's more or less involved in the process. He knows how she thinks, so if she's hitchhiking her way to Texas, we'll find her.

"It's not that simple, shortcake. If she didn't wait for me, then she's obviously planning something big. She knows that in the end I'll tell my dad where she is because we all worry about her. She doesn't want to be found."

He squeezes his eyes shut, tapping his fingers against his forehead as if willing the answers to suddenly come to him. I've known Nana Stone for a long time but even that doesn't qualify me to figure out where on earth she is. It's one thing to help her carry water balloons to the terrace to throw on the mailman but it's another to pinpoint her location after she runs away.

"Well, maybe you should let her be on her own for a while. I mean she obviously wants some space so what's the harm in that? She's more than capable of taking care of herself."

Opening his eyes, he sighs. I can see the worry written all over his face and my heart's aching for him. Whenever he's around me, he does whatever's possible to make me smile. He's never made me aware of his own problems, except maybe the ones he has with Jay. I cannot believe how selfish I've been. I've never once asked about how he's doing. I haven't talked to him about military school, about why he came back, about . . . anything.

Okay, time to change, Tessa. He needs you. He's been your fairy godmother and now you need to return the favor. Obviously this means a lot to him and you need to stick with him through this, no matter what.

"She has asthma, Tessie, and it's bad. She doesn't take it seriously enough. I humor her by letting her run away but I've always got an eye on her. I know where she is, what she's doing, and if she gets sick, I find her and bring her back immediately. Right now I'm scared shitless because I know the woman doesn't give a damn about her health."

The knots begin to form in my stomach. All of this sounds bad, really, really bad. A woman Nana Stone's age, one with asthma and a wild streak, out there all by herself, doing God knows what. Suddenly I feel like I can't breathe. I fear for the boy sitting beside me, who's probably going out of his mind right now. He's lost his grandfather, he can't lose the only other person who understands him and loves him unconditionally.

I scoot closer to him, between the gaps of our seats. He's stopped the car, holding his head in his hands and breathing hard. The need to comfort him is so powerful that it takes me aback. I am not a touchy-feely kind of person, I like my space, but this is something else entirely. I wrap my arms around his waist and rest my head on his shoulder. His breath hitches as he realizes how close I am but it's probably due to surprise.

"It's going to be okay, we'll find her," I mumble into his shirt. His heart's beating so fast that I can feel it. I only have to slide my hand up his chest to rest on the place that's practically pounding to confirm my suspicions but now's probably not the best time to feel him up.

His arms come around me almost instantly, like it's a knee-jerk reaction. If he's shocked by my actions he doesn't show it. He buries his face in the crook of my neck, holding me tightly and just like that we're wrapped all around each other in the middle of a residential parking lot. If one of the Stepford Wives that live here gets a glimpse of us, they'll most probably get the wrong idea since I'm practically straddling him. Something as innocent as a hug suddenly has a whole new meaning. I don't know what to do next. Do I just let go of him? Do I keep sitting right where I am? Somehow the latter seems like the best available option. I can feel his breath on my neck and it sends tingles down my spine. If his hold wasn't so tight, I'd probably shudder in pleasure. I know what it takes to feel this way; I've read my fair share of romance novels. So why is everything I believed to be true, being proven so darn wrong?

"Tessie," he groans into my skin and that one sound basically tears me apart. He sounds so, so . . . seductive. What do I do? Do I kiss him? Do I say something just as exciting? I need an instruction manual right now, please.

He chuckles and I feel the sound reverberating through my own body. Why is he laughing? I pout. Obviously he's amused by my lack of skills. This is the point where he'll tell me that this morning was a mistake and that we were better off being . . . a confused unlabeled pair.

"Remember what I said about not overthinking and enjoying the moment?"

My face heats up rapidly as I remember the pool incident. I thought we'd both boxed up that particular memory and stored it until further use. I guess that would be now.

"Uh-huh."

Where's Shakespeare when you need him? If I were the kind of girl a guy like Cole is meant to be with I'd say something sultry and confident. I'd charm him into thinking that I am the most irresistible woman on the planet, but right now he's probably contemplating ways to end whatever it is between us without breaking my pathetic little heart.

"You really need to work on that."

Despite myself, I laugh. We both know that despite my best attempts I'd never be able to let go in his presence. He winds me up in both the best and worst of ways. If I'm not raging at him, I'm melting at his feet. There is no way that I can ever "enjoy the moment" when he's around and that's what I tell him.

"I don't think I can."

The smug look on his face says it all. He knows what he does to me and he's proud of it.

"Well, we can try; we have a really long time to work on that," he promises.

I don't know if he wants to kill me with his words alone but if that isn't his intent then he's doing a pretty good job of it otherwise. The words *we* and *time* sound sweeter than any of the lyrics of the love songs I've listened to my entire life. He's not even being poetic, he's just being . . . Cole. The impact of the words weighs down on me, as I try to comprehend what this means for us.

I don't get to say much before his phone rings. I shift from his lap and return to my seat, immediately missing his warmth. The relief on his face is more than evident so I realize it must be something to do with Nana Stone. The ringtone he's set for her is a Beatles' song I remember hearing a lot when she babysat me.

"Nana, I told you to wait for me," he groans, clutching the phone to his ear with one shoulder and starting his car with his free hand.

I try to make sense of the conversation but when he casually drops in words like *breaking and entering*, *theft*, and *car chase*, my head starts to spin. What is the woman not capable of doing?

"Wait, what? What did you say you were doing?"

176

He falls back into his seat, hitting his head against it several times. I watch all this with an emotion I can only describe as concern coupled with amusement. If someone could make Cole prematurely gray, it would his grandmother.

"Don't strip on top of the pool table, Nana," he says patiently, like talking to a toddler.

"What? You can't expect me to just leave you? I'm coming to get you right now, tell me where you are."

I can hear her arguing and then the sound of her infectious laughter. Cole grinds his teeth, obviously feeling annoyed and irritated. It seems like Nana Stone is going to get her way since he mutters several "okays" before hanging up.

I quirk an eyebrow, following the strangest one-sided conversation I've ever heard. "I suppose that could've gone better."

"She's staying at some bar with a friend I never knew existed!"

I open my mouth to say something but he continues to ramble. "I can't believe she's doing this. We had a plan, I had a plan for her and now she's going to start flashing drunken idiots. It'll be all over YouTube tomorrow. Great, my grandmother, mayor of Cougar Town."

He's out of breath by the time he stops the rant and I have never found him more adorable than this. I know, it's slightly sadistic of me to enjoy his misery but I cannot help it. Cool, reserved, in-control Cole Stone can lose it too and this trait makes him all the more appealing.

"Cole, calm down. I'm sure she knows what she's doing. The woman is more than capable of taking care of herself."

"But . . ."

"But, nothing. I heard her saying that you can pick her up first thing in the morning and bring her back to the retirement home. Give her one day and then tomorrow you can tie her to the bed if you want."

I am not someone who possesses or might even remotely want to possess leadership qualities. I'm more than happy to take a backseat; you can superglue me to said seat and I will not complain. I think that's why we're both surprised by my authoritative tone. He blinks at me, once, twice and I feel my cheeks beginning to heat up.

Then when a full-fledged grin makes an appearance, I know I'm doomed.

"You're sexy when you get bossy." He winks and blood boils beneath my cheeks. Yes, he's made such remarks before but after the developments this morning, his words take a whole new meaning and I'm sweating buckets. He's flirting with me, right? What do I do? Think, think, think about all the times you've watched *The Hills*! What is it that Megan's always saying? WWLCD? What the heck would Lauren Conrad do?

"Shut up."

No, LC would definitely not do that.

I'm thankful that he doesn't try to further my embarrassment. For some preposterous reason, he's interested in me, lack of social skills and all. I like that, I really like that because I can't change who I am—not for the lack of trying, obviously.

"So what now?" I ask looking at our surroundings. We've driven all the way here for no use. But it seems like such a waste to let go of all the beauty. It would be out of place to suggest that we stay here, especially when the person we'd come to visit was more or less honky-tonking God knows where.

Cole studies my face for a while. It's like he's questioning himself but then seconds later a half-smile lights up his face and it seems like he's reached a decision. He drives us to a nearby restaurant that is right in front of the beach I'd ogled.

Is this a date? I start hyperventilating at the idea. A date with Cole. An opportunity where I could totally and utterly embarrass myself. I need time to adjust to how things have changed between us. I need to commit *Cosmopolitan* to memory, darn it.

"Calm down, we're just eating. I wouldn't let our first date be this . . . unplanned," he decides after pausing, wrinkling his nose. I sink down into my seat as we park. There he is again, giving me heart attacks with simple words.

"Sorry," I mutter feeling embarrassed.

We make our way into a pleasant diner. It's more or less like Rusty's except cleaner. There aren't a lot of people around since it's the middle of the day but a steady service continues from behind the counter. We take our seats at a private booth, my stomach somersaulting throughout the process. For something that isn't a date, this seems extremely date-like.

I look out the window, which gives a clear view of the ocean. Attempting to calm myself down by watching the waves, I don't realize it when Cole's fingers come to rest on top of mine on the table. I jump in surprise but his hand is firm. My breathing and heartbeat both become erratic as I take in the expression on his face.

"You don't mind, do you?" He seems nervous. I remember him acting like this when he gave me the dress. It looks like the two people who can bring out this side of him are his grandmother and me. I don't like it when he thinks twice about what he does or says around me. It's sweet, God it's sweet, but it's also not him.

"I-I . . . don't like it when you have to ask."

He seems surprised by my answer and if you concentrate enough, also a bit flustered. My face reddens immediately following my boldness but oh well, I'm on a roll so might as well continue.

"You shouldn't change, not for me."

"So if I do this," he quickly leans forward and kisses me on the cheek, making my eyes bulge out of their sockets and causing fireworks to erupt inside of me, "without asking, you won't mind?" He gives me a cheeky grin and I all but disintegrate. My hand touches the spot on my cheek where his lips were mere seconds ago and all I can think about is how I want more of it. I stutter some incoherent response and he just laughs. Douchebag.

An elderly waitress comes to take our order before I get to answer him. I order a chicken salad and Cole gets his usual cheeseburger. He goes ahead and orders a strawberry milkshake for me even though I just ask for water. Secretly, I'm jumping for joy since I really do love a strawberry milkshake.

We eat in silence but I'm distracted by how Cole's constantly rubbing circles over the back of my hand. I catch him looking at me once or twice when I am stuffing my face with lettuce, appealing I know. That's how the lunch goes—filled with sneaking glances and coy smiles. It is different but in the best kind of way.

***

Now we're at the beach and Cole's gone to bring some blankets from the trunk of his car. The sun's hanging low in the sky, letting me know that it's time to check in with my people. I take out my phone and send quick texts to Travis and the girls letting them know that my body isn't six feet under.

"How long before you have to get home?" Cole asks, spreading the blankets on the sand. Thank God there are two of them, while I'm all for cuddling, the idea of being so near Cole has me ready for another coronary.

"My curfew's at ten but I should go back earlier. Mom and Dad aren't home but Travis might ask questions."

He nods, as if understanding why my brother might be an issue. I really need to know what it is that's going on between these two. For now, however, I concentrate on his sitting form and how he pats the space next to him, motioning for me to sit down. I sit, leaving plenty of space between us. Drawing my knees up to my chest, I hug them so that my hands are kept busy. If I were to let them free, they'd most probably end up in Cole's hair. I've resisted the urge to run my fingers through the thick silky mess for so long but now that we are on the verge of becoming something more, the limitations and boundaries I set are starting to become hazy.

179

"Sorry about making you come all the way here. If I'd known that she'd be pulling a stunt like this . . ." He shakes his head but I know now that he's starting to see how hilarious the entire situation is.

"That's okay. I'm used to dealing with crazy Stone family members. It's my specialty now." I grin, lightly bumping my shoulder with his. Turns out I'll take any excuse necessary to touch this boy, wonderful.

"That reminds me, I'm sorry Tessie," he says a little gruffly, his voice thick.

I think about what he could possibly be apologizing for. Hard as I try, I don't really come up with something that could make him look so forlorn. He's been so perfect, caring and attentive to me, so I couldn't really fault anything.

"What for?"

"Everything. Take this as a combined apology for fourteen years of making your life miserable."

I'm absolutely stunned and taken aback. He's bringing our past up now? After ignoring it altogether for so long, he's chosen one of the most perfect days of my life to remind me of how things were between us. All of a sudden, my walls go up. I try to convince myself that he means no harm but as a slideshow of our time through the years plays in my head I have so many reasons to run away screaming. Breathe, Tessa, he's not that guy anymore and you haven't had to go to the emergency room in a while, which is always a good sign.

"I was a stupid kid," he continues, ignoring the panic attack I'm currently having. "You were the prettiest girl I'd ever seen and I got your attention the only way I knew."

"By shoving me into a ditch full of mud?" I ask dryly, interrupting his monologue. I'd worn my favorite blue dress that day and my mother had woken me up early so that she could braid my hair with ribbons in it. It was the first day of kindergarten and also the first of many times that Cole would humiliate me.

I watch his face as he winces and messes up his hair. "Yeah, I could've gone about that better. I wanted to be your friend but the other kids, they would've . . ."

"Made fun of you for hanging around a girl?" I remember the unruly kids he used to be friends with in elementary school. They'd been right with him every step of the way but now that I think about it, they themselves never bullied me. I shudder thinking about how much worse those other kids would have been, having seen what they could do in the hallways many times.

"Actually they would've teased you for being friends with the kid whose mom was dead. Later I realized that kindergartners aren't that cruel. Like I said, I was a stupid kid."

My heart aches for him after this revelation. I can picture it so clearly. Cole, the broken little boy filled with insecurities. It takes a second for me to forgive him for everything he'd ever done.
Impulsively I wrap my arms around his waist and bury my face in his neck, comforting that little kid.

"What about when we grew up? Why did you do it then?" I ask softly as I pull away. I couldn't bear to know that he'd been just like the rest of them, that he let my weight dictate how he saw me. "Was it . . . was it my weight?"

His eyes are a stormy dark blue when I look at him. His jaw clenches, nostrils flaring—he is angry at me and I can't think why.

"Is that what you think of me? I would never . . ." He stops himself before groaning and tugging at his hair. I'm half afraid he'll pull it all out with the way he's going at it. He hides his face behind his palms and I hear some distinct curse words.

"I deserved that. You should think the worst about me so I'm not going to complain." He twists his body so that he's facing me, sitting Indian-style. I don't freak out until he's cupping my cheek and rubbing his thumb across it.

"You've always been the most stunning girl I've ever seen. I don't care about your weight, Tessie, never have, never will. You could weigh a hundred pounds or three hundred pounds, it doesn't matter. You'll always be my shortcake. The girl who's gorgeous but doesn't have a clue about it. The girl who's so forgiving and kind, funny and sarcastic as hell."

How exactly do you breathe? I remember reading something about lungs and oxygen but I swear I can't link either of the two together right now.

"You're not afraid to talk back to me, you treat me like the idiot I am and I . . . I was scared. Having those kinds of feelings at eleven wasn't normal. Before, I wanted to only be your friend but I didn't know how to do that. When I started feeling more, you only saw Jay. I was jealous as hell so I took it out on you. I'm sorry."

Huh, would you look at that. I should remember to give Beth a gift card for her favorite music store or something. She'd figured it all out eons before me.

"Cole, I-I . . ."

His thumb brushes my bottom lip and I promise you could've heard how loud my heart is beating.

"Don't. I don't expect you to suddenly feel how I do. I'd be crazy to think that after everything I've done, you still want something to do with me. I took a shot by coming back, but it's the best decision I've ever made. Give me a second chance, Tessie, and I promise I'll do it right this time."

How do you tell a guy who's fighting so hard for you that he's already won your heart? The dreaded four-letter word makes an appearance but I shove it in a corner. Now is not the time, he doesn't need to find out that I'm a bigger freak than everyone takes me to be. We're taking it slow so if he wants to win my heart than that he shall do. I really could use the special treatment.

"Okay," I whisper, not really knowing what else to say. However, his reaction is like he's been given the map to the Holy Grail. From looking absolutely crestfallen he goes straight to elated, his eyes sparkling with the sun's rays, making the impact so much stronger.

"Did you just say okay? Will you go out with me?"

"Yes, Cole. Yes, I'll go out with you." In all honesty, I want more—I want a lot more.

CHAPTER EIGHTEEN
"You're Not Sexting Stone, Are You?"

The next morning all I see around me are baby unicorns and fluorescent rainbows. A goofy smile has been plastered to my face since yesterday and all I can concentrate on is reliving the experience. Cole's coming to pick me up in about two hours and we're going to go lasso Nana Stone right back to the seniors' home. We have a plan, one involving tempting her with double chocolate fudge cake if she protests. I'm trying to convince myself that the reason I'm up at seven in the morning during a long weekend is because I really want to see Nana Stone, but seriously, who am I kidding?

I want to look exceptionally nice. The last thing I want is to come across as someone from the set of *The Walking Dead* when Cole arrives so I made the decision last night. I'd showered and straightened my hair before going to bed. The blond locks fall in soft waves right to my lower back and if I do say so myself, when I twirl they bounce like they belong in a Pantene commercial.

For my outfit, I don't know if I should try hard. I don't want him to think I want to change myself for him. Of course I could wear my short skirt and a tight tank top but who am I kidding? Fatty Tessie would never be able to wear clothes like that and so wouldn't I. It's important that I try to maintain a sense of self while I do whatever it is that we're going to do. Yes, that's it, Tessa, be a strong, independent woman and don't let a boy get to your head.

Well, considering how I'm sacrificing precious hours' worth of peaceful sleep over him, I'd say he's already gotten inside my head and thrown a house party while he's there. Fudge this; I'll just wear the first thing I grab from my closet.

I'm contemplating the merits of such a decision when the doorbell rings and I jump. It's early; it is way too early for Cole to show up. He cannot ambush me while I'm still in my pajamas. I rush to my window from where I can get a pretty good view of whoever's outside. It can't be Cole, now that I think about it. He has his own key, much to my chagrin, and he rubs the fact in my face every time he can.

I pop my head out the window just in time to see a figure sit down on my front porch. I know who it is almost immediately and when the realization hits, I rush downstairs without pausing once to take a breath. Throwing the door open, I find a very tired-looking Beth. Her appearance takes me aback. It's not like the three of us haven't seen each other at our absolute worst; we've had our fair share of sleepovers but this is something else entirely. She looks like she's just thrown on clothes in a hurry, a pair of ratty old jeans with a mismatched T-shirt. Though it's not the clothes that worry me, it's her bloodshot eyes. She looks like she hasn't slept in days and it doesn't help that she's swaying on her feet. Her hair's a mess, like she's been running her fingers through it constantly and if you concentrate hard enough you'll see the tear tracks she's been trying too hard to cover.

"What happened?"

I know, though. I know the answer even before she says it and it makes me feel both sad and ridiculously furious at the same time.

"Marie," she says simply and it's all she needs to say. I let her into the house and she heads into the kitchen, bracing herself against the counter. It's been a while since things have gotten this bad. Marie hasn't done anything too drastic in a while but seeing Beth like this makes me forget all that. It's not fair; it's not. I know I didn't exactly win the lottery when it came to parents but she doesn't deserve the hand she's been dealt.

"Do you want something to eat? I could make you coffee and I'm pretty sure we have some leftover lasagna in the fridge."

She smirks and suddenly all's right in the world. I don't like seeing her like this, so defeated and just . . . broken. It took a long time for Megan and me to break through her nearly impenetrable walls but after lots and lots of trying she finally opened up. Even though she always hesitates about talking to us about her home life, we more or less force it out of her. This would have to be one of those cases.

"You're offering me lasagna at seven in the morning? You really aren't programmed to be up before noon, are you?"

"It's food, you're hungry. I don't get why we as a society need to label foods according to what time it is. If you want to eat lasagna, you should eat lasagna and not care about the dang clock," I finish passionately and she smiles, shaking her head.

"Go to bed, Tessa. You shouldn't be up right now, it's messing with your head. Did I wake you?"

"No, I was already up. I was supposed to meet . . ." I leave the sentence hanging, not sure how to say it. If I said his name, Beth would ask questions. She'd most probably deflect all the attention onto me just because she wouldn't want to talk about what happened at home.

". . . my partner for the history project but we can always reschedule." I hope I sound convincing.

"No, it's okay, go. I just need to catch up on some sleep and I'll be out of here." She yawns in the middle of the sentence and once again I have this overwhelming urge to hit Marie.

"I'll stay here. My parents left us a bunch of chores to do and I bet Travis hasn't done any of his so I should get started on those."

"Chores? Since when do you have chores? Don't you have a cleaning lady and a cook and a gardener?"

Right.

"Mom gave them the week off; you know, Founders' Week. We're big on celebrations."

Liar I am not.

"Well, that sucks." Beth doesn't seem convinced, though. But she's not in a state to question my Tessa-ness.

Once she believes every lie I've fed her, I take her up to the guest room. Giving her one of Travis's T-shirts and a pair of shorts, I decide to give her some alone time to get some sleep. I'll hound her with my questions later when she doesn't look like she'll pass out any second. Changing out of my pajamas into a striped black-and-white tank and jeans, I decide to try my hand at cooking. Yes, it's true I almost burned down my kitchen but there are a few dishes I could manage. Beth will need a home-cooked meal when she gets up; I think she's had her share of pizza nights for a lifetime.

Though there's something else that needs to be done before I decide to play Betty Crocker. Fishing out my cell from beneath a mountain of clothes, I prepare myself for what's to come. What sort of a potential relationship could Cole and I possibly have? We haven't even gone on an official first date and I'm already bailing on him. The thought of hurting him makes my heart sink. I know Cole's looking forward to this, I know I am more than looking forward to this, but I can't bail on my best friend. She's someone who has been there for me, more times than I could remember and the least I could do for her is be there when she needs me.

Me: Hey, I'm sorry but something's come up. I can't go with you today.

I press send and place the phone on the kitchen counter, standing as far away from it as possible. I mean I know it's not like Cole's going to jump right out of it and break my heart but right now, I'm nearing a full-blown panic attack and that rectangular piece of technological terror is the sole reason.

I'm just collecting the necessary ingredients from our pantry when my phone beeps, signaling the arrival of a text. Wow, that was definitely fast; maybe he knew all along that I would be a horrible person to date. Maybe he's relieved that I'm canceling so that he can go out and pick a girl who's more his type. Let's just pretend the thought isn't like someone driving a dagger through my heart.

Reluctantly I open the text, closing one eye as if that will soften the blow.

Cole: Are you okay?? Do you want me to come over? Do you want me to get Cassandra?

Oh. He isn't breaking up with me. I don't know if we can break up since we're not even really together but he isn't abandoning me, he's not angry. I finally let out the breath I've been holding for so long and my chest fills with warmth. Why does he have to be so perfect? Can he just mess up once, just once to show me that he's still the Cole I used to know?

Me: Everything's fine. It's Beth; I should stay with her today. I really am sorry.

The comment about Beth is self-explanatory. He's perceptive enough to know that she has an unstable home life. He asked me about it once and I tried to tell him as much as I could without betraying Beth. She isn't comfortable with people knowing what her life is like; she says she doesn't like the pity. I just wish one day she'd realize that it's not pity we're offering, its empathy.

Cole: Call me if you need anything and I mean it. Promise or else I won't be able to leave. Also, stop apologizing before I make you.

He's so cute but I don't think he realizes it half the time. It's like he doesn't know what his words do to me. Oh and is the last part supposed to be flirting, and am I supposed to flirt back? Uh.

Me: I promise, don't worry about us. Oh and what exactly do you have in mind to stop me from apologizing?

There, flirty, open-ended question with just the right hint of suggestiveness.

Cole: I'd kiss you, simple.

Cue the hyperventilation and all hail the king of flirtatious text messages.

My hands literally shake as the phone nearly drops to the ground. I blink furiously at the screen, reading the text over and over again. Is it getting hot in here or is it just me?

Cole and I kissing. Of course, that's supposed to happen. I agreed to go out with him and kissing is a natural part of the whole deal, so why haven't I thought about it until now? We'd come pretty close to it a couple of times but now it's out there in the open and suddenly all my fantasies stand a chance to become reality.

But of course I can't say that when I reply. If he wants to play with me, I can play right back.

Me: What makes you think I'd let you kiss me?

The reply is instantaneous, like he doesn't need to think twice before coming up with an answer. What if he knows that I take minutes to reply because I'm all over the place with my frazzled nerves?

Cole: I have this feeling you would do it quite willingly Tessie.

I inhale and then exhale loudly, trying to calm myself down, but this conversation is kind of . . . a turn on. He's not so open about things like these when we're together. Sure, he makes crude remarks but most of the time he's just teasing me, trying to embarrass me and rile me up for my virgin ways. However, this isn't teasing. It's just outright intense flirting and I'm totally into it.

Me: Beth needs to talk to me. I have to go, talk to you later?

I'm a huge coward and an epic fail when it comes to intimate conversation but I hope he understands. He knows me so well that I just hope he realizes that I'm nervous and not trying to get rid of him.

Cole: Can't wait to see you, have a good day shortcake.

Me: You too Cole.

"You're not sexting Stone, are you?"

My head whips up from my phone, only to see Travis making his way toward me in the kitchen. I glare at him, the goofy grin disappearing from my face.

"You did not just say that." The words *sexting* and *you* should never come out together in a sentence from your brother's mouth, never, I tell you.

"Hey, you're my baby sister. It's my job to make you so uncomfortable about boys that you decide to join a convent."

"You need to get your head checked," I say, tapping my knuckles against his forehead.

"So since it's obvious you were texting Cole, it's safe to say he isn't the one lounging in our guest room?"

I open the cupboard above the sink and take out a box of Cocoa Puffs, abandoning my efforts to cook an actual meal till later. Both of us liked our cereal with warm milk so I heat some up and then make us both the only breakfast I could safely make. When we're both seated at opposite ends of the island, I answer his question.

"That would be Beth."

His spoon freezes midair. A look of surprise flickers across his face but is gone as fast as it appeared. He chews on his cereal thoughtfully and I follow suit.

"One of your new friends, right? Is she the redhead?"

"They're not new. I've known them for two years and no, not the redhead, that would be Megan. Beth was the DJ at the gala, remember?"

"Oh."

"Is everything okay, with her, I mean, is she all right?"

I gulp, swallowing loudly. Suddenly I don't want to keep it all to myself. I want to talk about it with someone who understands what a dysfunctional family is like, and who better than my brother? If I tell him, maybe he can give me some advice on how to help Beth.

"She tries really hard to pretend that she is. Beth's like that, she never wants anyone to see beneath the surface but I wish she did. I wish she'd tell us more about what's going on in her life before we find out ourselves when something like this happens."

He's frowning into his bowl, concentrating really hard as if trying to unravel the greatest mystery on earth, and that's exactly what Beth is to many—a mystery.

"And what do you mean by something like this?"

"Her mom, basically. Sometimes she forgets who the teenager in the house is. She throws parties that last for days at a time. Beth has to go to the library to get her homework done. She has to sleep with her door locked so drunk strangers won't try to grope her. She works to pay the bills, to keep her mom's business afloat. I know our parents aren't a prize but it seems like she never seems to catch a break and it's all her mom's fault."

I should feel guilty for telling Travis all this but I don't. He'd know what to do, he's my big brother and he always has all the answers. That's how it's been since I was a kid.

I look at him again and now he just seems angry, like seeing-red, ears-flaming kind of angry. I guess the protective instincts are kicking in. My best friend must be like a little sister to him as well and being the person he is he'll want to protect her from all the bad things too.

"Why doesn't she just leave? She's eighteen, right, so why doesn't she use all the money she earns to find a decent place to live?"

Megan and I have had or tried to have the same conversation with Beth several times but to no avail. We even offered that she stay with one of us for the remainder of the school year but she won't budge. She won't leave her mother, not until she has to go away to college. The reasons are a bit vague but I guess family factors into the equation. Even if her parental abilities are more than questionable, Marie is still her mother and Beth still loves her enough to stay.

"That's not the kind of person she is, Trav. She doesn't quit on you, she'll stay right until the end."

He mumbles something under his breath and we finish the rest of our breakfast in silence. He asks me what my plans are for the rest of the day and I tell him that most probably we'll have a girls' day in and then a sleepover. He nods and hands me thirty dollars for food before going back into his room. He makes a reappearance a couple hours later, all dressed for the day. It's still early, around ten, so I'm surprised to see him looking chipper. He's dressed in a white button-down with khakis and Converse. It's the most effort he's made into picking out his clothes in a while, besides the gala.

"Got a date with mystery girl?" I stop scrubbing the kitchen tiles and sit up on my knees, smirking at him.

He sighs, "Don't I wish."

"Still no luck with her? Wow, she's the first girl to ever give you such a hard time. I like her already."

He narrows his eyes at me playfully. "Yeah, the two of you would be best friends, but don't worry, I've got the situation under control."

His tone is cocky, more self-assured now. Whenever we've talked about this "mystery girl" before he's always seemed a little depressed so it's good to see he has a plan. Any girl who's managed to resist him for more than two weeks seems like a keeper to me. Travis has always had it easy and I'm pretty sure no girl's cared that he's been holed up in his room, hugging a bottle of Jack Daniel's to his chest for more time than is acceptable. They swarmed toward him at the gala, he's still the town's golden boy, but this girl's definitely putting him through the wringer.

"Well, best of luck with that. If she does come around, I'd really like to meet her."

"You'll be the first to know, baby sis." He ruffles my hair, making me swat his hand away. Chuckling and seeming in a better mood than ever, he heads out the door. I huff exasperatedly and start cleaning until he pops his head back in.

"Oh and I know about your little chaperone-less trip with your boyfriend and we'll talk about it when I get back."

"By talk, you do mean you'll make everything sound ten times dirtier than it actually was, don't you?"

"You know me so well, young grasshopper."

I glare at him and he leaves and I hear him laughing as he gets into his car.

***

189

Beth's been asleep for more than six hours now. She must really have been tired to be out of it for so long and every second that passes I get angrier at Marie. How could she do this to her own daughter? If she continues to go at the rate she's going, she's going to lose the only person who has ever honestly cared about her. Beth deserves better, so much better than she allows herself to accept, and it's about time she understands that.

I make Beth's favorite salad for when she wakes up, with plenty of lettuce, tomatoes, jalapeños and olives. There's some roasted chicken left over in the fridge so I shred it and toss it in there as well before pouring ranch dressing over the entire thing. Then I make a big jug of iced tea and carry it all upstairs on a tray. She's awake, just lying there staring at the ceiling. It's the kind of mood I'm most afraid of. It's when she's making decisions, big ones, and usually self-destructive ones.

"Lunch is served," I announce, plopping the food down next to her on the bed. She's startled like she didn't even hear me entering and again, I'm worried. This is not good; time for a distraction.

"Did you make this?" She examines everything carefully.

"Well, if you don't want to eat it . . ." I trail off, popping a jalapeño into my mouth knowing it would annoy her the most. She loves those little spicy suckers.

"Hey!" She swats my hand away and hugs the salad bowl to her chest. "No touching my food."

I've already eaten so I leave her to set up a movie in my room. She's opposed to anything remotely defined as a "chick flick" and hence I raid Travis's collection and pick out a Matt Damon one; the girl is obsessed with Matt Damon.

I strip the comforter off the bed and lay it on the floor, throwing plenty of cushions on there too. Then I make a big bowl of popcorn and get out some KitKats from my secret stash.

Beth's showering so I leave a T-shirt and some shorts for her in the room. It surprises me when she comes out wearing the same shirt I lent her this morning, over my shorts. She shrugs. "This is more comfortable."

Halfway through the movie, I try asking her about what happened. We're propped up against the foot of the bed, blankets covering us and cushions forming a cocoon around us, currently experiencing a sugar rush.

"Can I ask what Marie did this time?"

Her eyes never leave the screen and she shrugs. "The usual shit. Party, drugs, strangers getting it on in my bed."

I scrunch my face up in disgust. The last part was a new one.

"She blew whatever she earned at the charity gala by spending it on booze. I told her we needed the money to pay the electricity bill but there's not a dime left. I don't know how many more shifts I can take, my grades are getting low and Berklee won't take a slacker."

I rest my head on her shoulder. "You're a brilliant music producer, they'll take you the minute they hear one of your mixes. Don't worry about that."

"But I still need to have enough for tuition. I can't save much if I'm taking care of her messes all the time."

"So what are you going to do?"

"Right now," she lets out a humorless laugh, "I have no idea. The plan's to take it one day at a time and see where it goes. I'm going to start standing up to my mom. She's gotta end all her crap."

"Well, if you need help with that, you know where to find me."

She rests her head on top of mine and we watch the rest of the movie in silence.

***

We're watching the third Jason Bourne movie when someone knocks on my door. It must be Travis since he's been gone for the better part of the day, so imagine my surprise when I open my door and find the most brilliant deep blue eyes staring back at me.

Cole.

"Hey." He smiles his crooked smile and my thudding heart soars right out of my chest. I just realize how much I missed him. There had been something wrong today, the entire situation with Beth aside. I'd felt incomplete, a little depressed, and now I know why. He hadn't been there with me to make it all okay.

"Hi," I say, my voice coming out a little breathy.

"Hi," he says, the blue orbs shining brightly as both corners of his mouth now pull up into a dazzling smile.

"Hi."

"Are you two planning on going beyond that?"

Beth's voice brings me out of my Cole-induced coma and I turn scarlet. Opening the door wide enough, I move back to let him in. He's holding two Walmart shopping bags and is dressed in a fitted gray long-sleeved shirt and jeans. The conversation we had in the morning immediately comes to mind and if it's possible, I turn redder.

"Hi Beth." He waves at her sheepishly and she rolls her eyes.

"If either of you says the word *hi* one more time I swear I'll pummel you to death."

191

He raises his shopping-bag-laden hands defensively. "No more greetings, copied. Besides, if you killed me I'd take my peace offering with me."

He takes out three different tubs of ice cream and yet again if it's possible, I get more infatuated with him than I already am. How does he know that ice cream is just what I needed right now?

"Strawberries and cream for you." He hands me the biggest-size tub they have in stores and I almost snatch it away from him. "Mint chocolate chip for you." He gives that one to Beth and I'm touched that he knows what her favorite is and lastly he takes out his favorite, cake batter for himself. Just like that he becomes part of our evening. I scoot over on our blanket on the floor so that I'm sitting between him and Beth. The close proximity has my nerves on high alert and I'm extremely aware of the lack of space between us. I wonder if he can hear how loud my heart's beating. I can smell his cologne, mixed with the scent of aftershave and pumpkin spice. If I could bottle the smell up and keep it with me forever I would.

"Hi," he whispers in my ear, low enough so that Beth doesn't hear. She's too engrossed with Mr. Bourne to care anyway.

"Hi," I say, smiling and biting my lip nervously.

He wraps his arm around me and scoots closer so that my entire right side is pressed against his left. I can feel his body heat searing me through our clothes. Goose bumps rise on my skin but it's not at all because of the cold. Momentarily I forget how to breathe but then when the urge to be closer pulses through me, I brace myself.

Taking a deep breath, I rest my head on his shoulder, leaning into him. His breath hitches and I feel this strange sense of satisfaction. I caused this reaction in him; I have some sort of power over him. I'm not the only one who feels so affected.

When his breathing becomes constant, I look up at him and he's staring down at me. His eyes smolder, scorching me to the core with just one look.

"I missed you."

It's not him that says this, it's me, and I take us both by surprise. I'm whispering but it feels like we're in a world of our own, an all-consuming world where Cole's the center of the universe.

His fingers curl around my waist, digging into my skin but not in a painful way. If anything, it's more pleasure than pain.

"I missed you too, so much, shortcake."

I rest my head on his shoulder and we watch the rest of the movie wrapped up in each other. So much for keeping it a secret from Beth, huh?

CHAPTER NINTEEN
I'm Trapped in a Never-Ending Episode of
General Hospital

If I were to make a list of the most excruciatingly painful moments in my life, most would have something to do with Cole. Every embarrassing and public-humiliation-related memory I have has Cole in the foreground. I think the top of the list would be the day he posted flyers all over school announcing that I was having my period that week.

Do not ask how many tampons ended up in my locker after that.

However, something's been able to beat that moment and not very surprisingly it has something to do with him yet again. This time though it isn't horribly embarrassing or physically painful. What he's done now is that he's made me miss him, terribly so. On the plane ride back to our small Connecticut town I think about the couple of days I've spent with my grandparents for anniversary weekend, also known as the family reunion from hell. It had been in the works for a couple of months now and attendance was mandatory. I'd had to take a couple of days off of school because my parents forced me to do so. How many high schoolers can ever truly say that? Although I do realize that I spent most of my time sulking. It's a good thing no one apart from Travis noticed these things or I'd have been called out. He seemed to be in a funk of his own so we left each other alone.

The only reason I survived the separation was because he called me every day like clockwork. We'd talk for hours before I had to go to bed. During the day we'd text each other almost every ten minutes so it felt like he was almost there with me, *almost* being the operative word here. We talked about anything and everything. We were still Cole and Tessa but something had shifted monumentally. It felt like I was suffocating without him being near and I could only hope that he felt the same way.

The day of the party had pretty much been a torture in its own right as most of my grandparents' guests had sons or grandsons they wanted to 'introduce' me to. By the time I called Cole, I had dodged more unwanted advances in two hours than I had in my three nearly four years of high school. My phone had been tightly pressed against my ear as I concentrated on hearing the sound of his breathing to retain some hold on my sanity. We both knew where we'd rather be, what we'd rather be doing. The thought of it made me feel both nervous and euphoric. I knew that I'd be getting my first kiss pretty soon, if the slightly husky tone of Cole's voice was any sign.

The flight's supposed to land any second and I can't keep still for the life of me. My mom throws me a reprimanding look before going back to her book. We're in first class so I have to sit with her and Travis is with Dad. Having the two of them sit together is a recipe for disaster since their relationship hasn't exactly progressed, but Mom insisted that they need to spend some quality time together. But from where I'm sitting, I can clearly see that Travis is watching a movie and Dad's busied himself with a magazine. Oh well, it was worth a try.

By the time we arrive, it's mid-afternoon. Despite our efforts to pack light and mostly have carry-ons, we still spend an hour at baggage claim. The number of people traveling at this time of year is insane so I should've anticipated the delay. It doesn't make my impatience go away though; I'm tapping my foot like crazy and am ready to go strangle someone if our bags don't arrive soon.

"Regretting telling lover boy to not come to the airport?"

There's amusement written all over Travis's face. He seems better already, like being back in our own state has suddenly taken away all his brooding. Mystery girl better give him an answer soon, I don't know if I can go back to his whiplash moods.

"I have no idea what you're talking about," I say sweetly, keeping an eye out for my parents. They're currently getting coffee from the Starbucks a few feet away. I doubt they'll be coming back, though. The number of people fighting for luggage could cause a stampede and God forbid my mom chip a nail or Dad rip a button from his shirt. It's a thin line between being someone's kid and their personal slave, isn't it?

Travis nudges my shoulder with his, nearly making me fall over the conveyer belt. Glaring at him, I spot two of our bags and quickly grab them.

"Two down, two to go," I huff before Travis takes them from me and loads them onto the luggage cart. What on earth did mother dearest pack in these things? Ostrich eggs?

"I didn't realize things were so serious between you guys." He's watching me with those perceptive eyes again. Nothing good can come of it when Travis does this. He's probably seen through all my clever attempts to

194

hide what's going on between Cole and me. Mostly, I don't want my parents to know just yet. If they did, they'd probably book a church and have us married within an hour. I do not need that kind of pressure on me right now. Travis finding out is both a good and bad thing. The good part is that he's my favorite family member and it'd be nice to share this with him. The bad part? He might just go ahead and beat up the boy responsible for my happiness.

"We're just hanging out, Travis. It's casual," I say breezily. To get him to understand the nature of our relationship, I need more time. Travis needs to see with his own eyes that Cole has changed for the best and that when I'm with him I feel happier than I have in ages. We'd do that when we got home. I'll show him how Cole is with me now.

He grabs another bag from the conveyer belt, slinging it across his shoulder since it's his Nike. "You're not that girl, Tess, you're not someone who does casual," he says, making air quotes around the word *casual*. "You're either deeply involved or not at all so don't try to sell me that."

I can't look him in the eye because this conversation seems eerily familiar. I even remember when we had it the last time. I'd come home crying my eyes out because Jay had kissed Missy Reeve at a dance in middle school. I knew he'd be there with her and hadn't wanted to go but our mom had been persistent. She'd wrestled me into a too-tight dress and slipped the most uncomfortable heels on the planet onto my feet. Every second in them had been painful but with Nicole's help I stumbled my way into the gym. Cole had skipped out on the occasion so the night had started on a good note. However, the moment I saw Jay dancing with another girl, holding her close and looking in her eyes, I realized that coming here had been a terrible idea. That was bad enough but when he kissed her, something inside broke. I remember running out of there, calling Travis and asking him to take me home. That's when he'd said similar words. He'd been right then, asking me to get over Jay, to not invest myself too much emotionally, and I'd listened with no intention of obeying him, but this is different; Cole is different.

"I like him," I admit without looking my brother in the eye. "He's not the person we thought he was. Everything he's ever done to me was because . . ."

"He liked you, because he's always liked you," he says like it's the most obvious thing in the world.

I gape at him for a few seconds. "You knew? How long have you known?"

"We all knew, Tess. From the first day in elementary school to now, everyone's known. We just thought we'd let you two figure things out on your own." He shrugs.

"But, I don't . . ."

Travis holds up his hand and looks over my shoulder. "We'll talk about this later. I know why you don't want Mom and Dad to know and trust me, it's better if they don't."

Our parents join us a few seconds later, just in time for the last bag to arrive. Once we have everything, we take a cab for Farrow Hills with my anticipation growing with every inch we move. My phone hasn't rung once nor have I received any texts so I'm a bit worried. What if he's forgotten that I'm returning today? What if he has plans of his own? I shouldn't expect him to be waiting for me with a bouquet of calla lilies and as desperate to see me as I am to see him. Stupid Tessa.

I'm frowning at my phone when we pull up in front of our house. The disappointment is crushing in a way I've never experienced with Jay. Maybe with him I've always expected it and my expectations have always been met. Cole always surprises me, always exceeding expectations so I've become a little used to it. I guess that's what I wanted him to do today, take me by surprise.

"Who's that sitting on our porch?" Dad asks as he's paying the driver.

I look up from my phone immediately and my sunken spirits soar. I know it's him without a doubt. His face isn't visible since he's holding it between his knees but the hair is a dead giveaway. The leather jacket helps too but then it's almost like magic. Theatrical or not, I can sense him when he's near me and it takes every ounce of will power in my body to not jump out of the car and run toward him.

"That's Cole, isn't he, honey, what's he doing here?" My mom sounds equal parts confused and giddy.

Probably not the best idea to say hey Mom, that boy sitting on the porch? Yeah, we sort of have something going on now but I can't tell you since you'll start suggesting flower arrangements and centerpieces on the spot and embarrass me to death. He'll run for the hills and I'll hate you for the rest of my life.

"I have no idea." I almost blind Travis with my elbow as he snickers in response.

"Well don't keep the poor boy waiting, go ask him." She shoos me away as they get our bags out of the trunk. I'm much too happy to oblige. Cole's looking my way now, his expression mirroring mine but I bet my smile is wider. We try to curb our enthusiasm for the sake of my family but as soon as we're within touching distance it's like there's a magnetic pull between us. My arms itch to wrap themselves around him. I have visions of burying my face in his neck and inhaling his scintillating scent. His hand reaches for me, like he's going to touch my face but he thinks better of it. Cole clearly understands my parental unit problems. He sighs in disappointment, pulling his hand back and instead thrusting the bouquet of calla lilies toward me.

"Welcome home," he whispers.

He brought calla lilies. I do a mental happy dance and the urge to touch him is stronger than ever. He's everything I imagined my perfect guy to be and more. Is it possible to die from wish fulfilment?

"Thank you," I say shyly, hugging the flowers to my chest. I can practically feel my mom's gaze boring into my back. Both she and dad will have questions later but unlike my brother, they won't be able to tell what's going on even if it slaps them in the face. Sometimes it's a blessing to have clueless parents.

"You look great." He quickly rakes his eyes over my body and I blush. Trust him to always be the perfect gentleman; I'm well aware of how I look anything but great. We had an early morning flight so I spent a total of ten minutes in the shower. Then Mom hogged the single blow dryer we had so my hair is Medusa-crazy times ten and I don't have a speck of makeup on. There must be T-Rex-sized bags under my eyes and don't even get me started on my clothes. I threw on the first T-shirt I could find, which is a ratty black Garfield one, and paired it with the oldest pair of jeans I have. My mom nearly had an aneurysm when I showed up to breakfast but we were running late and all my clothes were already packed. It didn't help matters when I spilled coffee all over myself while waiting for our flight, hence reeking of Starbucks.

"Yeah right." I roll my eyes but he doesn't look like he's kidding. His eyes never leave mine as he steps closer to me.

"You want to get out of here? I can tell you in detail why I think you're beautiful."

I'm left breathless and feel like I've been knocked over by the force of his words. He can't say things like this when my parents are only a few feet away! I will not be held responsible for my actions when he's like this. The change in him is electrifying and it's making me all sorts of excited. There's an intensity in his eyes that makes my breath hitch and I'd like nothing more than to take him up on his offer.

"Cole, my boy, it's so good to see you." Dad's voice booms from behind us. They do one of those handshakes and man hugs. Mom hugs him too, a little too warmly for my liking. You could almost see the church bells surrounding her head like a halo. Travis acknowledges him with a nod and with that heads into the house, leaving the four of us standing around

awkwardly. After some painful small talk Cole takes the plunge.
"So, Cassandra wanted me to invite Tessa for dinner."

"Ah yes, that might have something to do with how the two of you spent an entire week with each other on the phone." My mom laughs and I cringe. I had been really obvious now that I come to think of it but Cole doesn't seem fazed.

"I agree, I think she's a little curious herself and would love to get to know Tessa a little better. Apparently she really charmed her at the gala."

He winks at me when my parents start gushing about how nice Cassandra is.

"Do I have to go?" I ask them, putting on my best "please don't force me to go" face. If I pretend that I would go anywhere but to the Stones for dinner that's exactly where they would send me.

"Of course! You must; it's very nice of her to invite you." I could hear the slight disappointment in my mom's tone. Obviously Cole hadn't realized that a dinner party invitation by Cassandra Stone is the holy grail of dinner party invitations for my poor mother. She looks a tad bit green but there is no way I'm letting her come with me.

She tries to make more uncomfortable small talk as Dad goes into the house to get something for the sheriff. He comes out with a bottle of wine, the kind that's really old and costs hundreds of dollars. He tells me to give it to the Stones and then they finally let us go. Cole doesn't even let me go into the house to shower or change clothes; what I would give to scrub every inch of visible skin right now.

"I can't go to your house looking like this," I tell him as we round the corner, "I'm wearing a T-shirt with a giant cat on it, for God's . . ." My words are cut off when Cole suddenly stops, spins around and hauls me to his chest. His arms go around my waist and he buries his head into my hair, inhaling it.

Oh my. For a few seconds, I'm in shock. He's doing what I wanted to do the moment I saw him on my porch but didn't have the courage to do but now he's given me such a great opening. Who am I to refuse? Immediately the shock wears off and my arms wrap themselves around his shoulders. I rest my head on his chest and do the same thing he did, inhale. Finally, the knot that's been forming in my stomach for the past two weeks releases and the weight that'd been settled on me lifts. I fill my lungs with his heady scent and allow myself to savor being with him.

We stand like that, tangled each other for what could be a second, an hour, or forever. When we finally let go, there's a tenderness on Cole's face that resembles an emotion I'm scared to death of. My heart skips a beat because of the way he's looking at me. His fingers skim over my face, tracing every feature until they come to rest on my cheek, which is undoubtedly colored red and heated.

"Did I tell you that I missed you?"

I shake my head coyly, watching as amusement flickers across his eyes. "Hmm, I guess I didn't. Can you blame me? If we didn't get out of there soon, I thought your mom would propose."

I burst out laughing at that and so does he. It's amazing how he just knows what I'm thinking or feeling and isn't afraid to call me out on it.

"You better stay away from her then. I don't know how long I'll be able to hold her back. She seems to be slightly obsessed with you. It's creepy."

"What can I say? The O'Connell women can't seem to resist me."

I roll my eyes at his cockiness but a big part of me is relieved that we've moved on to lighter, safer topics. The look on his face mere minutes ago seems to be permanently imprinted on my brain and it's scared the wits out of me. Too soon, it is too soon for me to even imagine those kinds of feelings. I must be getting delusional.

I start walking backward, away from him and in the direction of his house. "Make sure you don't trip on your giant ego on the way, Cassandra and the sheriff might want you home in one piece."

He chuckles and starts walking toward me. It's not long before we're holding hands, fingers interlinked and grinning goofily at each other. I admit, on the plane back home I had been worried. It's common for people to be able to talk comfortably over emails, texts, and phone calls. Being face-to-face makes things awkward and I was half expecting for that to happen between us but thank God it didn't. We catch up on our weeks apart. They'd brought Nana Stone back home and she'd been chastised and grounded by her son. Cole made me laugh heartily when he described his and Nana's combined efforts to sneak out and go to Rusty's. Sheriff Stone caught them while they'd been trying to unlock the front door with a bobby pin.

"I tried to go and see Beth like you asked but her mom said she was away," he tells me and my forehead creases with worry. In the few times we'd managed to talk in the last couple of days, Beth had been distant. She always said she was busy with work and too tired when she got home. We didn't discuss the events of the day she'd shown up at my house and I didn't push it. She's hiding something, that I'm sure of, but what could it be and why couldn't she just tell me?

"Was Marie sober? I can't even imagine her ever stopping to think twice about what she's putting Beth through," I say bitterly, concentrating on the cracks in the pavement. Cole squeezes my hand tightly, realizing how my mood's dropped in an instant. Marie's name always leaves a bitter aftertaste in my mouth and I feel bad for bringing her up now.

"I checked every day, you know. The house was pretty quiet and the driveway empty all week. I saw Beth around town but she was working and it seemed like she wanted to . . ."

"Avoid you?" I complete his sentence.

"You too, huh?" he asks and when I nod he pulls me close and tucks my head beneath his chin. I take a few calming breaths and let my head stay where it is. Cole has a calming presence when I let him take the role. Most of the time I'm too aware of him to allow myself to relax but this is nice, this is different.

"At least Megan and Alex are doing well. The guy's whipped," Cole declares and I smile. They're so good for each other. Opposites in each and every way but when they're together they literally are two halves of a whole.

"She feels the same way, I know she does."

"Young love, what a freaking cliché." He snorts and I elbow him, causing him to grunt in pain.

"Don't make fun of them and don't you dare say anything to Alex."

He rubs the spot where I've hit him. "Yes, ma'am." Then he pulls me back to my old position, which just warms me all over.

We walk in silence for the short five-minute trip until we come to a halt outside his house, where extremely conveniently Jay and Nicole are fighting. Ugly, screaming, pushing and shoving kind of fighting.

"Shit," Cole curses next to me and I mentally agree this does not look pretty.

Nicole is in one of her moods, the kind where she uses her hands to illustrate just how angry she is. Right now she's hitting Jay on the chest repeatedly to get her point across. The poor guy seems clueless as to what to do but deflect her vicious attacks. Over the years I've seen Nicole get into fights with a lot of the boys she's dated and she's merciless with them. When she decides to pick a fight, even when they've done nothing wrong, she will go to extreme lengths to get the job done.

The irony of the situation doesn't fail to hit me. I've always wanted to see the perfect couple finally realize that they're not so perfect for each other. But now I don't even care. If anything I feel a little sorry for Jay for what he's going through. If anyone can tell how cruel Nicole can be, it's me.

"Come on, we can get in through the back." Cole grabs my hand and starts pulling me toward the yard. Clueless to our presence, Nicole and Jay keep shouting at each other. I strain my ears to catch a few explanatory words but all I can hear is Nicole swearing like a sailor and Jay asking her to calm down.

We try sneaking around them, walking stealthily like it's *Mission: Impossible* out here but as soon as we cross the small wooden door that opens up to the backyard I hear my name being called. I suggest Tom Cruise be kept for his role.

"Keep walking, you don't need to hear this." Cole places his hand at the small of my back, hunching over me protectively but I want to know what she has to say to me and why she's bringing me up right now. The confrontation doesn't seem so daunting now for some reason.

"No, it's okay. I can handle her now." I smile but his face is grim. There's something he's not telling me and it's scaring me.

Before I can ask him to tell me what it is that's exactly going on, Nicole's all up in my face with Jay trying to keep her at bay. She looks mad, her eyes frenzied, and I'm not completely sure if she's sober right now.

She zeroes in on Cole's hand, which is gripping mine tightly, and her nostrils flare. I haven't seen her like this, ever—not even when she was her brutal best to me. The kind of loathing and hatred for me that I see in her eyes right now takes me aback.

"Ask your girlfriend to back off, Jay," Cole snarls when Nicole takes a step toward us.

"Nic, come on. You don't want to do this right now." Jay tries grabbing her shoulder but she violently shrugs him off.

"Look at you two, fawning over the fat cow." Her cackle is bitter, her words intended to cut me deep but I don't even care anymore. I'm done trying to be good enough for her, done trying to seek her acceptance and sure as hell done wishing our friendship had survived.

"Nicole," Cole warns. The vein in his neck is pulsating, his free hand balled into a fist.

"Don't let her get to you, her words don't matter anymore," I say to him. For her I put on the blankest and coolest expression I can muster and keep my voice remarkably monotonous.

"What's your problem Nicole? What the hell do you want from me?"

Her eyes narrow into slits, hands resting on her hips, her stance appearing as if she's ready to pounce on me. "You little bitch, you're my problem. Why the fuck don't you just get out of my life? Tagging along with my boyfriend's brother, charming his mom with your little innocent act, and hijacking my crown makes you think you can have my life? Guess what, Tessa, you're nothing but a worthless little stalker."

She might as well have slapped me across the face because those words hurt. I blink, once, then again, and then repeatedly. Ten years of friendship and this is what I mean to her? Did she ever consider me a friend, ever?

"Enough!" Cole's voice booms, shattering the silence. I focus on breathing, trying to form an answer. I have no idea what to do when you're verbally attacked like that. In movies, the heroine always has a comeback. She has all these powerful dialogues planned and she puts the Queen Bee into place, but that doesn't happen in real life. I'm quite literally speechless.

"Nicole!" It's Jay this time. His eyes are practically bulging out of his skill and his jaw's about to hit the floor. Now it becomes obvious that he's never seen his girlfriend in all her fire-spitting glory. How can someone be this clueless?

"You both are pathetic. Look at her; she's a blubbering mess, for Christ's sake. We'll all be better off without her and her bullshit in our lives."

Don't hit her, Tessa, don't do it. Don't use that right hook Travis taught you, she is not worth it.

"I've been told to never hit a woman but Jay, if you don't get her out of my face in two seconds, I swear I'm not even going to think twice about it."

Cole's voice has been reduced to a steely, grim undertone and this is more dangerous than when he's shouting. It sends shivers up my spine and even causes Nicole to go pale. Jay winces and begins dragging her away knowing that Cole's limits are being tested.

"When we were in the ninth grade, you offered to give our chemistry teacher a blow job if he gave you an A. You wanted to go to dance camp but you needed to pass your classes first." She gapes at me, her face whitens considerably more.

"You lost your virginity to a college guy when we were sixteen. You told your parents you were coming to my house for a sleepover but you snuck into a party in his dorm instead. He kicked you out the next morning and you didn't leave your house for a week afterward."

Jay grows even more flabbergasted than he already is so I assume he too didn't know about the little incident. Cole's just staring at me, I can feel his eyes watching as I do what I've wanted to for ages.

"During the summer before freshman year you told me you were in love with Cole." I glance at him as he winces but I feel particularly nasty right now. "You went to his house and told him that you wanted to sleep with him but he wasn't interested. You cried for days."

"During Jared's party, you basically had Hank molest me. Did you tell your boyfriend that?"
She can't even look me in the eye, there's no need for a confession.

"The point is, Nicole, that I know a lot about you. I haven't even scratched the surface on the things you've done, the things you don't want other people to know. I don't want your life because I know how low you've sunk."

"You little whore." She lunges for me but Cole blocks her path, gripping her shoulders and shoving her away.

"Leave now and don't come near her again if you know what's good for you."

She looks expectantly at Jay like she wants him to defend her but he looks too shell-shocked to move. He's just standing there, his face devoid of color, his figure trembling and at that moment I feel horrible.

He didn't need to know these things, at least not like this. But I can't take back my words and just like that it's like I'm trapped in a never-ending episode of *General Hospital*.

Finally realizing that no one's coming to her defense, Nicole calls me a few more choice names before stomping away and getting in her car. The tires screech as she speeds away, leaving us all behind totally and utterly silent.

***

I don't know how we ended up here but it's happening. I'm lying on Cole's bed, trying to pull his shirt off and he's kissing my neck. He says he won't kiss me on the lips, that he's waiting for a special moment but this is good enough for now.

After Nicole left, he dragged me inside and stomped his way to his bedroom. There I had to listen to him rant about how big of a . . . let's just say he used a very bad word that Nicole was and that I'd done the right thing. I felt guilty as anything and he'd only been trying to make me feel better.

In the process of feeling better, he'd knelt before me as I sat at the foot of his bed. He cupped my cheek, rubbing his thumb over my lower lip, which just leaves me senseless.

"None of the things she said were true. That girl is all kinds of messed up, Tessie, you know that, don't you?"

"I used to think her words had some truth to them. I mean we'd been best friends for so long that I thought she knew me better than anyone else but I couldn't have been more wrong. She's not the person I thought she was."

"When did my shortcake get all Chinese-grandma wise on me?" he mused and I chuckled.

"It's just something you have to learn when your patience gets tested

203

every second by an egomaniac."

Somehow the conversation led to him tickling me, somehow it led to me being sprawled on his bed with him hovering on top. Then when I was panting like crazy, writhing beneath him, trying to get revenge, I slipped my hands beneath his shirt and everything shifted. Desire swept us both up along with a strong sense of awareness. Cole gasped as my fingers traveled over his tight abdominal muscles, giving me incentive to continue. I'd never felt more brave or exhilarated. Something in him snapped too, all his restraint and control getting lost on the way. That's how we ended up where we are right now. He's kissing down my neck, driving me absolutely crazy. His hands are everywhere and I make sounds I don't even know I could make until now.

"Your parents . . ." I gasp as his tongue gently goes over the areas his lips have just been all over.

"It'll still take them half an hour to get home, we have plenty of time," he mumbles distractedly, going back to what he's doing so skillfully.

This is amazing. Why haven't we done this before? His lips feel so good. If all I could do for the rest of my life is make out with Cole, I'd do it. He isn't even kissing me but everything feels amazing.

"Hey guys . . ."

The doorknob turns and we still. My breathing is heavy, I'm panting like crazy, and Cole has crazy hair because I've been running my fingers through it. His shirt is halfway up his torso and he's situated between my knees. This is the sight that greets Jay.

That is probably why he curses rather loudly, slams the door behind him, and runs like a vegetarian vampire in a blood bank.

CHAPTER TWENTY
My Inexperience is as Obvious as *The Scarlet Letter*

"No way."

"Come on, Tessie, you just need to try once. That's all I'm asking."

"It's too soon, I can't do it." My head hangs in defeat and I silently curse myself. Why do I have to be such a coward? It's not like he's asking me to do something completely unheard of. People do it all the time; it's a staple when you're a teenager.

"You don't have to be scared. I'll help you through it and I'll make sure you have fun," he promises, his voice ringing with sincerity. I am tempted now, the idea sounds promising and as time goes on it becomes less and less daunting but there's still a lot of self-doubt and absolute terror stopping me from actually agreeing. I suck at being an almost-girlfriend, really I do.

"I'm sure it'll be fun for you, me I'm not so sure about."

He sighs, knowing I'm trying to pick a fight. Darn his perception, why can he not be as aloof as the rest of the male population?

"Tessie, I wouldn't force you to do this unless I thought it would help us."

"We don't need help, we're fine just the way we are and definitely don't need to do it."

"Everyone does it. It's not a big deal and you don't need to psych yourself out over it. Like I said before, I'll make sure you're as comfortable as possible."

"But . . ."

This is the point where Alex pokes his head in between the two of us. I didn't even realize that he'd moved from his seat next to Megan at the lunch table. So when he says what he does next, I realize that Cole and I haven't really been paying attention to the world around us. Can you blame us though? We were discussing a very taxing topic.

"You guys do realize what your entire conversation sounded like, right?"

Beth chokes on her soda and Megan tries hard to stifle her laughter. It's no use, by the time I've caught up, everyone's given up on pretending that I hadn't just royally embarrassed myself. My cheeks burn as I glare at Cole, who as usual finds amusement in my humiliation. He nudges my shoulder with his once everyone has calmed down.

"Just so you know, I enjoyed that conversation very much."

Now it's not embarrassment that causes me to flush.

The possibility of something like that happening between us seems ludicrous when we haven't even kissed each other yet. We've been "together" for nearly three weeks now, what is he waiting for? Doesn't he want to kiss me as much as I want to kiss him?

"So what's the verdict then? Are we going or not?" Alex asks and I let out a noncommittal response.

"We have to go!" Megan sides with her boyfriend—traitor. She notices me casting an extremely evil look in her direction and begins defending herself.

"Think about it, Tessa. All everyone can talk about is you two. If you guys go to the party together and make an appearance as a couple, people will stop speculating. Weren't you saying you were sick of all that attention?"

The last part is unfortunately true. Returning to school after winter break has been torturous to say the least. The rumor mill was rampant with stories about me and Cole. It didn't matter that most of them were true, I still felt sort of violated and generally creeped out. On top of everything, Nicole had been dethroned in the cruelest of ways. After losing her crown and boyfriend all in the span of weeks, she'd been snubbed to the bottom of the pyramid.

Our roles are now reversed and I couldn't be more miserable about it. Girls who'd never once glanced in my direction seem more than eager to be my best friend. People who'd ridiculed me and stood alongside Nicole in her mission to make my life a living hell now treat me like I'm the long-lost member of the Brangelina clan. Cole's clearly the biggest reason for the change. From the way we've been acting the entire week it's become clear that there's something going on. Whether it's the hand holding or him carrying my books or the not-so-hidden forehead kisses that I'm so in love with—everything's basically screaming that we're together. Would going to a party finally make people see what's been right in front of their eyes all along? If the answer's yes and if they'll stop following me everywhere then maybe this might not be so bad.

"Are you sure it'll work?" My experience with parties hasn't been so great. I've been to one during my time at high school and look how that turned out. Cole places his hand on my leg in acknowledgment of my fears. He's the only one at the table who knows exactly what happened. I can practically feel the anger rolling off him. If Hank hadn't already transferred to a school across town, I'd fear for his life. Or maybe not.

"Yes. Once everyone knows you're together, they'll let you be. You two are like the shiny new toy they're infatuated with. If you act like it's nothing special then maybe they will too."

I shoot Beth a pleading look. "Are you sure you can't come with us?"

Smirking at me, she chews slowly on her French fry. Another traitor, she looks way too overjoyed at the prospect of what I'm going to do there. That said, if she knew what I'd gone through she would volunteer to be my personal bodyguard.

"I'm pretty sure your boyfriend will take care of you."

I'm not sure whether strangling Beth or punching her in the face is more appealing. I sneak a look at Cole and he's busy talking to Alex now so maybe he didn't hear her. While the girls have been extremely supportive of my new relationship, supportive being Megan hyperventilating for a good hour, they're constantly asking me to label what Cole and I are to each other. We shouldn't feel pressured into labeling what we are. I know he likes me, he knows I like him, and that's enough for now, right?

***

Cole drops me off at home; we have a few hours to kill before going to the party, which I reluctantly and very difficultly agreed to go to. He understands this and is being very sweet about the whole thing. I think the real reason he wants to take me is to get rid of my fear of parties. I'd sworn to never attend one ever again and it makes him angry. He doesn't want Hank to have that kind of power over me so this is how he's going to get me to take control over my own life.

"Hey." He stops me halfway to the kitchen with his arm going around my waist. Thanking my lucky stars that my parents are rarely home and Travis is starting to hang out with his old friends again, I let him pull me toward him. Resting his forehead against mine, Cole kisses the top of my head, making my eyes flutter shut.

"I'm sorry if I cornered you into going to this thing. I just . . . I want you to be able to have fun without looking over your shoulder all the time. It's killing me that you feel so scared and I can't do a damn thing about it."

He sounds so anguished and hurt that I immediately begin feeling guilty. I hadn't really thought about it like that before. I understand what he means. Ever since the thing with Hank, I've felt a little wary and nervous about going out, especially loud places with a big crowd. Cole deserves better than that. He needs to be with someone who doesn't want to spend the entire weekend holed up in her bedroom. Although as soon as I picture him with a party girl rivaling the likes of Snooki, jealousy rears its ugly head. Suddenly I'm scared for a completely different reason. I can't lose him because of some silly fear; if he wants me to do this then I'll do it for him. I'd rather spend a few hours sipping horrible warm beer than letting one of his groupies paw all over him.

"You don't have to apologize," I whisper, heart pounding at the closeness. "This phobia, whatever I feel, it's silly and you're right I need to get over it. I want to do this with you."

A smile breaks out on his gorgeous face at my words and he lifts me up in his arms, spinning me around. His enthusiasm is reward enough. I'd do anything to see him so happy and a stupid high school party suddenly doesn't seem like that big of a deal.

"There you go with the double-meaning statements again, Tessie." He laughs once he puts me down, making me smack his arm.

***

In my room, I allow myself to have my mini-freakout before Cole comes back to take me to the party. When he was here I pretended to be a cool and mostly fraudulent cucumber and we had fun cuddling on the couch and watching tacky reality television. Now though, I'm pretty sure what I'm experiencing are the symptoms of a panic attack. It's miraculous that I even managed to get dressed but I've apparently come a long way when it comes to not being a complete fashion victim. Casually throwing together some layered tanks and skinny jeans to form a party outfit became the easiest part of my evening. Makeup was even simpler since Cole prefers that I don't put much on.
Seriously, how am I walking into all these unintentional crude remarks today?

I get myself under control just in time and put the cucumber face back on. Cole always rings the bell before he arrives to take me out. I'd always thought he took way too much satisfaction in knowing that he basically has an all-access pass to my house but when it comes to dates, he's the perfect gentleman. Taking deep calming breaths I run downstairs, not giving myself any more space to contemplate barricading my door. It'll all be good, it'll be worth it. I remind myself that I'm doing this for Cole and that I can't let him feel guilty anymore.

"Did I give you enough time to talk yourself out of doing this?" This is the first question Cole asks when I throw the door open and literally jump onto him. My need to just go ahead and take the plunge is greater than ever and he senses this but I admire him for being so lighthearted about it.

"Oh no mister, I am doing this. We are going to go to the dang party and we're going to enjoy ourselves. I don't care if I end up breathing into a paper bag but we are going to go out like a normal couple and we will have fun. Are you listening to me, Stone? We are going to have fun."
I exhale loudly at the end of my rant and find Cole looking at me with only amusement in his eyes. Good, he doesn't think I'm a loon. Well, the night's still young and I am after all Tessa O'Connell.

"Couple?" He smirks and I roll my eyes.

"Is that the only word you caught on to?"

"It's the only one which mattered to me. I don't care about the stupid party anymore. The fact that you're putting yourself out there is enough, shortcake. Honestly, I was expecting I'd have to break down some doors and drag you out but you're here. I'm so proud of you, baby."

The term of endearment I'd always considered unoriginal and uninspired suddenly starts meaning so much more. It is now my favorite word that Cole's ever said.

He chuckles at my wonderstruck expression and loops an arm around my waist.

"If you don't want to go, just say the word. I'll take you out, we'll get some Chinese, watch a movie, take a stroll in the park, go for a swim, whatever you want."

My feelings for him grow infinitely stronger while listening to him be so considerate. He cares so much about me and the least I can do is try to fit into his world. I don't want there to be this divide between the person he is to the rest of the world and the perfect boy he is with me. If I do this, start hanging out with his friends and their girlfriends, then maybe he'll be able to have the best of both worlds.

"No, I want to go. Let's do this."

***

Ryan Foster's place is more of a bachelor pad than anything else. He lives on his own since his parents travel all over the world as part of the TV show they host and produce. That's the story I'm told by Megan as I step into the minimalist-style condo. It's all granite counters and steel finishes with black accents. This party is a lot more toned down than the one I previously attended, way less crowded, and I find it easier to relax.

Though it could have something to do with the fact that Cole hasn't left my side once since we've arrived. He introduced me to all the guys on his team and I did not miss the stink eye their cheerleader girlfriends gave me. Everyone's been acting a little hostile but Megan says it's only because they're scared. All the girls acted on Nicole's commands and now that she's no longer in the picture they're like lost puppies. To top it off, I'm dating Cole and that to them is the high school equivalent of having mob connections.

Is it bad that I feel a little gleeful? This is so amazing, the way some of the girls literally cowered makes me feel like I'm the Godfather. It is very, very cool if I do say so myself.

"Do you want something to drink?"

I eye the red Solo cups everyone is holding and shake my head. My last drinking experience did not go so well so I'll try to refrain from making a total idiot out of myself in front of these people.

"Nah, I think I'll avoid the alcohol tonight."

Cole pouts jokingly, "Aww man, and here I was looking forward to Drunk Tessie."

"Yes, I hear she's very amusing," I say dryly and his eyes gleam with mischief.

"I think I might be partial to her since she thinks I'm so unbelievably sexy."

Groaning, I hide my face with my hands. He will never, ever let me live that one down. Why did Jay have to go ahead and open his big mouth? I'll have my words hanging over my head for the rest of my life!

"Hey, come on, I'm kidding. I won't bring it up again, promise," he says but there is no way I'm going to believe him. No matter how hard he tries to hide it, what I said that night really matters to him. What matters even more is that I said those words to Jay, and for Cole that signifies the end of a crush that should've ended way earlier.

***

"Hey, guys."

My back stiffens as Cole's arms tighten around me. We were just swaying on the dance floor along with lots of other couples and I was more than happy in my own little Cole bubble. I didn't need to hear that voice again, especially after what had happened at Cole's house.

"You're drunk," Cole notes and I'm too scared to turn around and face the person standing behind me. If anything I shrink further into Cole's chest to seek protection.

"And once again, you look too comfortable with something that didn't belong to you in the first place."

If Cole tightens his grip around me any more, my lungs are more than likely to get crushed. I try squirming out of his ironclad hold but there's no use.

"Go away, Jay, you don't want to do this right now."

"What, you scared I'll show you up in front of your girlfriend? Scared that she'll see you for the no-good loser you are?"

This is not happening. Please, please don't be happening. Is there such a thing as a party god? If yes then please, Mr. Party God, rescue us before one of the Stone brothers ends up in jail for attempted murder and the other in the hospital.

People are starting to stare now, it's like they feel a sick sense of satisfaction watching these two guys, who're basically brothers, treat each other like this. I know that Jay's only acting like this because of the alcohol. Yes, these two aren't so close but they always have each other's backs. Why isn't someone stopping them? Don't they see where this could potentially go?

I realize that Cole's temper is hanging by a very fine thread. One more word out of Jay's mouth and Cole will go for him. Taking advantage of his distraction, I break free of Cole's arms and face Jay. He looks absolutely horrible and for a handsome guy like him that's quite a feat. His eyes are bloodshot; his face sports a two-day stubble, his hair looks scruffy and in need of a cut. Overall he just reeks of alcohol and cigarettes.

He's like the poster child of a bad breakup, but the poor guy has had to face a lot more than just losing Nicole. I feel sorry for him and I feel immense guilt seeing who he's become. I remember the guy who came to me a day or two before Cole came back to town. I remember him volunteering to be there for me and what did I do? I let myself become so obsessed with Cole that I basically forgot all about him. I don't regret a single second I've spent with Cole but maybe I shouldn't have cut Jay so drastically from my life. Even though he's said some things he had no right to say, I've still known him for most of my life and at one point I was convinced I was in love with him. While I now know that what I felt for him was nowhere near love, I did have a crush on him and he deserved better.

"Jay, please, you're drunk. Go home and sleep it off," I plead but his eyes are too glassed over for me to make out any sense of comprehension. He's glaring at Cole, looking like he'd kill him with his bare hands if he could.

"See what you did? All her life, Tessa thought I was her freaking knight in shining armor. I was the one she loved, not you! But you couldn't stand that, could you? You took my mom, my girlfriend, and now her too!" he roared, shoving Cole hard.

Immediately I block Jay's path as he moves to hit Cole. The blow meant for him lands on me instead and it's like all the wind is knocked out of my body. I clutch my side painfully, trying my best to not curl into a fetal position on the ground. All around us I hear gasps but the one that stands out the most is the curse that comes out of Cole's mouth.

"Tessie, are you okay?"

"I'm so sorry, Tessa, I didn't mean to—" Jay's words are cut short as Cole literally plows into him and knocks him down onto the floor. His fist lands on Jay's face and I hear a distinct cracking sound.

"Alex!" I scream, looking around for someone who might be able to stop this. Everything seems to be happening in slow motion. It's like everyone's playing a game of statue and all I can do is stand there and watch Cole beat the life out of his brother, who seems too drunk to fight back. Finally someone begins to pull Cole off and I'm being hugged from the side. Megan is hysterical as she asks me again and again if I'm okay and apologizes for not getting to me in time. I think I tell her that it's not her fault but everything feels like I'm in a bit of a daze. I see Alex pulling Cole off of Jay and restraining him. Some other guys finally grow a pair and rush to help Jay, who looks more than a little battered. His nose is broken, his lip is split, and there's a nasty gash on his cheek.

Cole's chest rises and falls rapidly as his eyes meet mine. I see the sorrow in them, the begging and pleading. I think he's expecting me to blow my top but as bad as it makes me feel, I can't bring myself to feel angry. I don't know what it is that he sees in my eyes but the torment on his face goes away, leaving only remorse behind. That's the thing about Cole; he's an incredibly passionate person. This passion of his makes him do crazy things and once the spell breaks he realizes that the outcome of his actions isn't that great.

"Take him back to your place, Tessa. I'll patch Jay up and make something up for Mr. and Mrs. S."

"I can handle it," Cole protests but Alex shoots him a look which apparently speaks volumes. They're having a silent conversation and whatever it is that Alex is trying to tell him works because the next thing I know Cole's lacing his fingers with mine and tugging me forward. I shoot Megan a small smile and we have a silent conversation of our own. She wants me to text her after everything's over and I promise that I will.

Heeding Alex's advice, I drive Cole's car back to my house. The lights are on in the kitchen and my parents' cars are in the driveway. Great, I hit my head against the steering wheel in frustration. Things are just not going my way today.

"Are you hurt?" Cole's voice breaks the silence and it's then that I remember my aching ribs.

"Yeah, it's nothing a painkiller won't fix." But the way his face flinches tells me that he doesn't believe me.

"I'm so sorry, Tessie, about everything." His voice is filled with remorse. I don't doubt his sincerity. I know he's sorry but it's not him I'm angry at, it's me. Tonight was supposed to be fun, we were supposed to go to a party and hang out but no, the drama has to follow me everywhere.

"I just . . . I don't know what to say, Cole. You shouldn't have hit him but he made the first move. He was drunk and he's your brother . . . you two shouldn't be fighting over me. It's not worth it."

Cole sucks in a breath and I know I've upset him. I peer at him through my lashes and his jaw is flexed, his posture stiff.

"Don't ever say that again. You're worth it, you're worth everything to me."

I blink back tears and try to ignore my constricting throat. The tension between us is palpable, like Cole can sense that I'm self-destructing all around him. I need to get out of this car.

"Tessie . . ."

"You're hurt, let's get you inside," I say quickly, jumping out of his car and he follows suit after briefly glancing at the split skin around his knuckles. The words *my fault* keep ringing in my head and it makes me feel nauseous. Afraid of running into either my mom or dad, I put a neutral expression on my face, or at least I hope it's neutral and not my oh-god-I'm-Yoko-Ono face.

Thankfully, the moment I step into the house I know I'll be left alone today. The neighbors can probably hear my parents' shouting match and when that happens, they usually let me be. The sense of relief is so great that I'm not even embarrassed that Cole's hearing my parents at their worst. Quietly we climb the stairs to my room and neither is willing to break the silence.

I make him sit on my bed and grab the first aid kit from the bathroom. Gulping down some painkillers for my side, I head back for Cole.

One look at his knuckles and my lips begin to wobble. He'd be so much better off without me. If I had any sort of a conscience I'd let him go but right now I'm too invested to even think about it.

"Give me your hand." I sit beside him and begin working. When I apply the antiseptic he lets out some expletives but then those are the only

213

words spoken between us. I bandage both his hands and before I can stop myself, I give in to the urge and gently kiss over the taped knuckles.

"Tessie," Cole groans, his hand cupping my cheek.

"I'm so sorry, Cole." I choke out the tears coming full force now.

"Hey, hey, Tessie, look at me. Shh, baby, it's okay. I'm okay, please look at me."

I'm overreacting, I know I am. It was just a brawl but I can't stop crying, knowing I've somehow caused this. He's hurt because of me, he's fighting with his brother because of me and all I can do about it is cry.

"C'mere." He pulls me into his arms, tucking my head under his chin. I allow myself to cry some more and get rid of all the anxiety and tension that's been building up inside of me after the confrontation with Nicole. Once there are no more tears left, I let myself drown in Cole's scent. Breathing him in, I let timid, shy Tessa fly right out the window and press my lips to his neck. I smile against his skin when I feel his breath hitch and his heart pound.

Cole pulls back slightly and stares into my eyes as if seeking permission. I all but throw myself at him by linking my arms around his neck. Moving closer, I allow myself to be bold for once.

"Tessie?" His voice is so low and gruff that I almost don't hear him speak.

"Yes."

"You've never been kissed before, have you?"

Shame and humiliation washes through me. Of course he knows this; my inexperience is as obvious as the Scarlet Letter. Here I am, desperately trying to get closer to this guy, but how could I have forgotten the fact that I don't know the first thing about making someone want me. If anything, I must be putting him off with all my clinginess.

"I . . . I . . . no, I haven't." My words are laced with shame, which he picks up immediately.

"It's a good thing, in fact it's the best news I've had all day. You're mine, Tessie, and if another guy had touched those lips of yours I would lose it right now."

My heart soars at his words. Time and time again, he proves that he's too good for me. He epitomizes perfection and I'm the one who gets to be with him.

He inches his face nearer, one hand lifting from my face to cup my cheek and the other going to the back of my neck and angling my face closer to his.

I concentrate on his smoldering eyes. I never want to forget this moment and if I get amnesia and the only memory I can retain is this one,

I'll die a happy woman.

"God, I've been dying to do this," he breathes and then in a split-second, he closes the space between us and presses his lips against mine.

CHAPTER TWENTY-ONE
Girl Hospitalized for Checking out Cole Stone's Chest

You know what's funny? We spend our entire lives waiting for that perfect moment, for that perfect boy and that perfect kiss. All you can think about as soon as you start considering boys as more than disease-carrying rodents is what would happen when you fall head over heels for one. Then most likely all of high school is spent in the hopes of catching the eye of that cute boy in your algebra class and when he does notice you, all you can think about is what his lips would feel like against yours.

You read the novels, watch the movies, and dream about the endless possibilities, but let me tell you one thing. Nothing and I mean absolutely nothing can come close to the feelings that course through you when it actually happens. The Harlequin novels on your bedside table? Yeah, they don't cover half of what it's actually like. Ryan Gosling in all his knee-wobbling glory cannot possibly compare to the all-encompassing emotion you feel for the boy who gives you your first kiss.

Every thought, every carefully planned move flies right out the window as soon as Cole's lips touch mine. They are everything I could've imagined but even more. Soft, yet just chapped enough to cause a delicious friction between our movements. My eyes flutter shut as like the ghost of a touch he brushes them against mine, once, twice, and then a couple of times more until I'm almost ready to beg for more. His hands still gently cradle my head and I'm too afraid to move, like if I even shifted slightly I'd ruin this amazing, magical, mind-blowing moment.

Then it happens. His lips touch mine with an increased pressure and I respond almost immediately. I don't know what I'm doing but I've seen enough movies to have a general idea. Our lips begin to move in sync and fireworks burst behind my eyelids. Oh God, this feels so good. Why haven't we done this before? He's been in town for months and we could have been doing this for ages. All the time I've wasted being a deluded moron and I could've been kissed by the most awesome kisser in the history of kissers.

I gain encouragement from how he's not pulling away. It means I'm not that bad, right? My hands travel up his chest and one comes to rest just above his heart. It's hammering away and the thirteen-year-old inside me is squealing with joy because I know I affect him like this. He moans into my mouth and it's the best sound I've ever heard. Thrilled by his response I curl my arms around his neck and press myself closer to him. The need to get rid of the space between us is as foreign as it is urgent but he seems to be on the same page. We kiss slowly and languidly as he pulls me into his lips. My skin sears where it touches him and jolts of electricity shoot through me. It's the most wondrous feeling on earth.

Being out of breath is what causes us to pull apart. Stupid human weakness for air, I want to pout because I never ever wanted to stop. But I guess since we're both breathing heavily, we needed to stop.

"Whoa," Cole rasps and rests his forehead against mine and I can't help the grin that spreads across my face. Cole, the guy who has probably been with more girls than I'd like to figure out, liked kissing me.

"I know." I breathe out, trying to hear myself above the relentless pounding in my chest.

"That was . . ." I begin.

"Amazing, awesome, the single most spectacular moment of my life?" He grins and I mirror his expression.

"Probably even more."

If we smile any wider, our cheeks might not be able to handle it. I touch my still-tingling lips and stare at Cole, completely awestruck. The way I'm feeling can't be described. It's a mixture between the high that you get when you come off a really fast roller coaster ride and the rush that accompanies eating an entire tub of strawberry ice cream.

Cole cups my face and his gaze zeroes in on my thumb, which is still tracing my bottom lip. I see his eyes darken and he leans in again. My insides melt away in a flurry as I prepare myself for round two, this time feeling more prepared.

A knock on the door has us flying apart. Cole curses under his breath as he jumps off my bed and settles into one of the chairs. I busy myself in putting all the things back in the first aid box as Cole grabs a random magazine from the pile I keep in my room. Mom pops her heads inside the door and smiles at the two of us. I can see her red-rimmed eyes so it's obvious that her fight with Dad didn't end so well. Usually she tries her best to not be affected by him but sometimes things tend to get a little out of control and tonight would be one of those times.

"Hey, kids. Honey, can I talk to you alone for a second?" She looks at us apologetically.

"Oh-kay," I mutter, knowing this isn't going to end well. Cole squeezes my hand as I pass by him and the small gesture warms my heart.

Walking outside to the hallway I wrap my arms around myself due to a sudden chill in the air. Call it premonition or whatever else you want but I can sense that something's about to go horribly wrong. My parents usually avoid Travis and me after one of their fights.

"What's going on?" I ask her as she paces in front of me.

Her meticulously prepped outfit has seen better days. Her shirt is wrinkled, the slacks have multiple creases in them, and her cuffs have been rolled up haphazardly. This is not the woman my mother has grown to be. Her broken expression and appearance remind me of the woman who'd once been lost at the prospect of a ruined marriage. The feeling of loss turned into indifference and then she became numb. The numb version of my mom is what I've lived with for the past four years so I can't be blamed for not knowing what to do right now.

"Your father and I . . ." She stops pacing to look at me, as if trying to find the correct words to tell me something I already know. I want to tell her that it's okay, that I understand. I know my parents hate each other, I know that my dad may or may not be having an affair with someone, and I know that my mother's more or less addicted to prescription drugs. What more could she possibly have to say?

"We've been having more problems than usual and both of us have decided that we need a break."

Right, a break. Of course they're too stubborn to realize how toxic they are for each other, how they'd be better off if they just decided to go their separate ways but that can't happen. Dad needs Mom's money and Mom needs the security blanket of a marriage. Nothing would estrange her from the women in the country club more than a divorce.

"So you're leaving?" I ask, wrapping my arms around myself. This is happening; it's finally happening.

"Yes, I'm leaving for your grandparents' in the morning. I need to talk to my dad, figure some things out. It's better this way, honey, trust me. I need to do this."

Being abandoned by my own mother should be a little more devastating than how I'm currently feeling but I blame my parents for this. They changed; they left me, so if now I can't really feel anything for them then I'm not to blame, right?

"Okay," is what I say after a while and she seems surprised. I'm not sure what it was that she'd been expecting. Am I supposed to yell at her, cry, or something akin to that?

"Your dad will be here, Travis too. If you need someone to talk to . .
."

"It's fine Mom," I offer her a small smile, "I'll be okay. I've managed it so far, right? You should get some sleep, you look tired."

She opens her mouth as if to say something but like always she holds back. Like always she's numb and can't even feel her own emotions, let alone relay them to me. Nodding her head in acknowledgement she turns her back on me and heads downstairs for her room. I stare at her retreating back wondering if she'll ever come back.

Cole understands that I don't want to talk about whatever it is that happened with Mom. In fact I don't want that memory to taint that of our first kiss. He holds me as I lie on the bed, my back pressed into his chest and I relax into him, loving that he's here. I love how he always knows what to do and I'm also scared to think about what's going to happen when he isn't with me anymore.

"Cole?" I say into the darkness.

"Hmm?" he whispers against my neck and the movement of his lips against my skin causes butterflies to erupt in my stomach.

"You won't leave me, will you?"

He's quiet for a while and I'm afraid that I've asked the wrong question. It's too soon for me to ask something like this from him. I don't know what possessed me to just do that. Okay, so maybe the fact that my mom's running out on me has me a bit unnerved, but why the heck did I just do that? I might as well do a Taylor Swift and start working on our breakup album right now.

To his credit, Cole doesn't pull away. His arms tighten around my waist and he nuzzles his face into my neck. I can almost see what's going on in his head. He must be thinking that I'm one of those girls who reads too much into a kiss and begins forming a ten-year plan. I prepare myself for the blow, for him to tell me that he isn't sure about me anymore, that maybe we, just like my parents, need a break.

"It's not a choice for me, shortcake. I couldn't leave you if I wanted to, tried it once before, didn't work out so well. You're stuck with me now." He seals his promise with a kiss to the spot beneath my ear which instantly has me breathing faster.

Does he have a book, like a version of *Being the Perfect Guy for Dummies* somewhere? How is it that every time I expect the possible worst, he says something and everything becomes okay?

My heart's basically doing the tango against my rib cage. I savor the moment and let the protective feel of his words wrap itself all around me. I want to say something, anything to tell him what he means to me. But, I am as usual tongue-tied when it comes to really expressing myself. I can insult him on demand and all through the night but ask me to tell him how I really feel then all I can afford is . . . nothing. So I do the only thing that comes to mind; grabbing my phone I choose a song that'll tell him what he is for me.

Taking a deep breath I play a song that instantly reminds me of Cole, "Just a Kiss" by Lady Antebellum. I feel him smile against my skin and I know he understands what I'm trying to say to him. That's what the best part is about us.

***

Eventually Cole has to go home. His phone won't stop buzzing and I think his parents are trying to get ahold of him. We'd almost forgotten about the Jay incident since we were so wrapped up in each other but now that he's leaving, I'm starting to worry. I don't want him to get in trouble because whatever happened is my fault. He'd only been trying to protect me and Jay is partly to blame, but I guess when they see the damage done to him, Cole would undoubtedly bear the brunt. I can only hope that Alex has worked a miracle and Jay doesn't look half as bad as he did when we last saw him.

He kisses me again, a good-bye kiss at the door as I'm walking him out. It's short and sweet but the emotion it contains is more than any open-mouthed kiss. I'm half tempted to pull him by the jacket, drag him inside my room again and never let him leave. But the guy's got to go home, right? "Meet me tomorrow?" he asks as he's about to leave and I nod. I need him; always, but tomorrow I think he's going to need me. Whatever problems he has with Jay are coming to the forefront so I'll try to support him as much as I can.

Nodding, I watch him walk away and my heart squeezes in despair as soon as he's out of view. I miss him already; it's terrifying. I've gotten so attached to him that I can't help but be afraid. All the people I've let myself get close to in the past have in some way or the other left me. My parents, my best friend, Jay, and even my brother, but I'm lucky that I have him back. I don't think, however, I'll be able to survive if it's Cole that walks away.

Before going to bed, I text Megan and tell her we got home okay and that Cole's simmered down. She replies immediately telling me that they didn't have to take Jay to a doctor after all. Apparently Alex is an expert in dealing with broken noses and was able to help Jay out with some painkillers and a frozen bag of peas. Alex took him home and told Sheriff Stone that it had just been a minor scuffle at the party and that he should see what the other guy looks like. I shake my head at this one, as if Sheriff Stone would encourage violence. The guy only had to see Cole's bandaged knuckles to make the connection. I'm afraid for when he does that.

Sleep doesn't come easily to me tonight. It's been a big day, or night seems more appropriate. I witnessed two guys fighting over me, I had my first kiss, my mom tells me she's leaving me. You couldn't make up such situations even if you wanted to.

After tossing and turning all night, I fall asleep only to wake up to the sound of a car engine revving and tires screeching against the road. Rushing to the window, I see my mom's car speeding down the road and just like that she's gone. She didn't even bother to say good-bye.

I get a head start on the day even though it's a Saturday, which by rule should dictate a day in but when even I can't sleep till the afternoon, you know something's wrong. Feeling a sense of determination, I decide to do something today that I've been putting off for a while. If I want to make sure that Cole and I don't have any more problems like the one we had last night then it's time.

Getting dressed, I grab my cell phone and bag. No one's up yet, so easily grabbing a granola bar, I'm out of the door. I take a detour on my way to the Stone residence and grab a pie from Rusty's; it's a blueberry one and it's his favorite. Bringing a peace offering might surely help me escape the conversation unscathed. Physically, I know he won't hurt me again; emotionally I might be scarred for life.

Cassandra opens the door for me when I ring the bell. She smiles at me but it's not her usual infectious one. There's a solemn look on her face and I can probably guess why it's there. Guilt starts spreading through me again as I imagine being in her position. She loves Cole like her own son and having to choose between him and Jay must be difficult for her. She loves them both equally and I basically parted the two in the middle like the sea.

"I thought I'd be seeing you here soon." Her greeting is warm as she lets me in.

"I wanted to see if everything was okay after last night. Jay, he didn't look so good, so I thought I'd bring him his favorite pie." I hold up the box in my hand, like it's proof of the fact that I come with good intentions.

"Well, yesterday wasn't either of my sons' best moments. I guess I can be happy about the fact that they didn't lie to us. I'm sorry, Tessa; I apologize for my son's behavior."

"You don't have to . . ." I protest but she places her palm out to stop me.

"Like I said before, I know Jason's made mistakes. The way he behaved toward you isn't the son I raised. But I'm proud that Cole's made you happy. I'm glad you chose the right guy. Jason has a lot of growing up to do before he's in a relationship with a good girl."

She shakes her head, as if to emphasize her disappointment. A knot forms in my throat; there's nothing I can say to her. This seems like a family affair but then I also need to defend Jay.

"He's a nice guy. I know the way he's been acting lately isn't the best proof of that but he's been my friend for so long. He protected me in his own way and I guess I don't like him that way anymore but he's an amazing guy, Cassandra. I know that and that's why I . . . I liked him like that. That guy's still in there somewhere and I want to help bring him back."

My throat constricts at the end of my speech. Cassandra places her hand over mine and squeezes it. Wanting to take her sadness away, I'm more determined than ever to get my message through to Jay. His mom deserves better and I'll be damned if I let some stupid high school drama hurt this amazing person, the closest thing I have to a mom.

After the talk with Cassandra, I quietly make my way up to Jay's room. Cassandra told me that Cole won't be up for another hour or so, so I'm a little relieved. Not that I like going behind his back but he's not going to be happy about this and I really need to have this conversation. I knock on his door, the dull sound of music coming from the room alerting me that Jay's awake. He opens it for me and his eyes widen in surprise, hands freeze on the doorknob. He backs away just a little and his mouth gapes open. The aftershocks of last night are still visible, the bruises looking more prominent after the shower it looks like he's just taken. I suck in a breath as I notice the purple skin above his right eye, the crusted blood on his upper lip and his slightly swollen nose.

"Hey." I offer him a small smile as he stands there, gaping at me. Feeling a little self-conscious, I push the box with the pie in it in his direction. His gaze is locked onto me so he doesn't even notice the gesture until I speak.

"I brought you this; it's your favorite, right?"

"Huh?"

Okay, this isn't going anywhere fast. I repress the urge to look over my shoulder and glance at Cole's door. I know I shouldn't be this worried about his reaction, after all this is just a harmless meeting, but somehow its feels like I'm being disloyal to Cole.

"The pie, Jay, I thought you'd like it."

He shakes his head, as if comprehending my words for the first

222

time, and takes the box from my hands. He mutters thank you and opens his door all the way to let me in. His room is the exact opposite of Cole's. It's neat and tidy, off-white walls with blue accents. A made-up bed with a basic blue bedspread, a study desk piled high with books. Baseball uniforms through the years framed and hung on the walls. A small television mounted on the wall opposite his bed, above the only similarity his room has with his stepbrother's, the biggest collection of DVDs you'll find this side of the Atlantic.

"I'm sorry, Tessa, I'm so sorry," he says in an agonized voice as I take in his room. The moment is surreal; I've always wanted to be alone with him here but now that I'm actually standing in the place, I can't wait to rush to the room opposite this one.

His eyes are glassy as I turn to face him. He's sitting at the edge of his bed, holding his hands between his knees. Taking a deep breath, I sit beside him and nudge my shoulder with his.

"I'm not mad at you. I understand why you acted like that and I want you to know that I'm not mad at you."

His shoulders tremble as a frustrated groan escapes him. "I can't believe I hurt you! All I ever want is for you to be happy and look at what I do? I fucking hit you."

He looks at me then and the pain in his eyes cuts me deep.

"I am happy, Jay. I'm happy with Cole and I need you to know that."

Shaking his head, he gives me a bitter smile. "That's what I deserve, right? I let you slip right through my fingers and out of all the people you could end up with, it's Cole. He can't do anything wrong, can he?"

There it is, the bitterness toward his brother. That's what I need to take away but it's not going to be easy.

"Cole didn't ask for anyone to pick him over you. I get why you feel this way but he's never intended to hurt you. You're the closest thing he has to a brother; he would never do that to you. As for me, I think it's always been Cole. Even when he was bullying me, making my life miserable, he made me feel special. I felt like there was someone who cared, someone who was a daily fixture in my life. I could count on him like no one else, even if he was pushing me into mud puddles. I guess my crush on you was misplaced."

He winces at my choice of words and I rush to correct myself. "I liked you, Jay, I really did, but with Cole the lines were always blurred. Somewhere down the line though I realized that no matter how he acts around me, Cole's the one I trust. I trust him to never let go of me."

"That's what I did wrong, didn't I? You can't trust me because of how I treated you after Nicole and I started going out."

223

I wave my hand dismissively. "I'm over that. Yes it hurt at the time and I wanted to know why you'd do that but I realize something now. You were the popular jock and she was the prettiest girl in school. It made sense for the two of you to be together. Being with me would've been a lot of trouble and I get why you weren't willing to go through all that at the time."

He's quiet. That's what tells me that I've nailed the explanation. It makes me feel better somehow, knowing that I'd been rejected for the sake of reputation and not just because I was me.

He takes a deep breath before responding to my conclusion.

"I thought I could like her. I mean she was your best friend, right? I thought she'd be just like you and that that way I'd be around you all the time. When she cut you out of her life like that, I was angry at her and even angrier at myself. I was weak, I cared about my reputation so much that ending the relationship never came to mind. For the first time ever, I was the one who had everything, not Cole. I knew she bullied you but I . . ."

"It's okay, I'm over it, Jay," I try to assure him but he shrugs it off.

"You should hate me. I have no right to be jealous of Cole after how I've treated you but damn it I am! It's not even about him, it's me and how big of an asshole I am. You deserve better but I can't seem to let you go. I want you to look at me like you used to, Tessa. Please just give me a shot."

I'm stunned into silence. Did he just say that to me? I came here to mend fences between Cole and him, not to hear a love declaration. This can only get worse.

"I . . . I can't. I'm sorry," I say, feeling dazed.

"Will you just think about it? We can finally happen, Tessie, we'll be amazing together, I know it."

"It's Tessa."

"What?"

"Call me Tessa. Only Cole gets to call me Tessie."

There's an uncomfortable silence between us again. It gives me time to regroup and collect myself. Getting up, I turn to him. "Cole and I are together and if we're ever not together then it'll be because he's the one who leaves me. I'm never going to let go of him, Jay. I hope you understand that and respect my decision."

There's a grim expression on his face but he nods his head. I don't know what I've accomplished here but I've said what I came here to say and there's nothing more I can do. If even after all this, he's going to keep acting like an a-hole then I'll leave him in Cole's capable hands.

I rush out of his room; the space had started suffocating me. Downstairs I come to a standstill. Cole's in the kitchen, shirtless, only in his boxers and drinking OJ straight out of the box.

He's smiling at me as I gawk at him and I swear he must have planned this. Slowly he gulps down the juice so that I'm mesmerized by his throat muscles, and don't even get me started on the chest.

"Girl Hospitalized for Checking out Cole Stone's Chest." That would make one good headline.

"How's my Doctor Phil doing today?" he asks once he's done torturing me. We stand on opposite sides of the kitchen island and I cannot get my brain to function. I'm in a lust-infused fog and I'm totally about to give Cole enough ammunition to tease me till I'm eighty.

"Not balding and overweight?" I offer and he laughs, eyes crinkling, dimples coming out in full show.

"So I guess your heart-to-heart with Jay went well?" He screws the cap on the juice and places it back in the fridge without marking the container. If it were anyone but him I'd be disgusted but I'm too focused, burning a hole into his back. Those muscles ripple!

"Not exactly, but we've reached a peaceful agreement."

"I guess that's good. If I hit him again, my dad's going to have me spend a night in prison with the local motorcycle gang." He shudders at the thought and I laugh. Just like that we fall back into our easygoing banter.

"So you're not mad?" I ask him hesitantly. He doesn't look angry but then again even if he was, he'd never take it out on me.

"I could never be mad at you, Tessie. I know why you wanted to talk to him, I know you want to fix my relationship with him but that's my problem, okay? I appreciate what you're trying to do but don't worry about it, okay?"

I nod. He grabs my hand and interlinks our fingers. We stare at each other, smiling like idiots for a while until I become more and more aware of his half nakedness. I flush immediately and he notices. Chuckling, he rounds the island and pulls me closer. He leans in and whispers in my ear, "Spend the day with me?" I nod in response.

"Great, let me put on some clothes and we'll go out."

I pout and he laughs at my disappointed expression over the thought of him covering up. Placing a deep, hard kiss on my mouth that renders me speechless, he walks away, but not before adding, "Soon baby, soon."

Suffice it to say I'm redder than Rudolph's nose.

CHAPTER TWENTY-TWO
I Asked You to Make Soup Not Babies

I should have done this sooner. Really, I should have because now that I've started it I just can't stop. Call me a floozy if you will but if you're going out with someone as hot as Cole Stone you wouldn't be able to keep your hands to yourself either.

"We have to go to class soon," I say breathlessly, trying to put some distance between us.

"Don't worry, we won't be late." Cole's lips continue their merciless assault on my neck and I arch my back wanting nothing more than to meld my body to his. What on earth have I been doing with my life before? I've had him so close to me for months and I could've been riding this high forever but my thick-headedness made me blind to the obvious mind-numbing attraction there is between us. Oh well, better late than never.

It's not the ideal situation, to have barricaded the supply closet, but we didn't have another option. The last time we kissed was when Cole picked me up for school and since then we haven't had a moment alone. All day long he's been teasing me, giving me looks that made me want to maul him with my lips. At lunch, he kept a hand on my thigh the entire time and I hadn't been able to swallow a single bite. That's when we'd both made a lame excuse of having to borrow some books from the library and had made a mad dash to find some solitude.

No one bought the excuse, obviously. Alex had even oh so charmingly added his words of wisdom, "Don't forget to wrap it up, Stone!" That's what he had yelled for everyone to hear but by that time Cole had almost been deaf to the outside world. Typical boy, only had one thing on his mind.

"Cole . . ." I whine but it comes out as an embarrassing moan. His eyes light up like a Christmas tree as he takes in the obvious effect he has on me. He kisses me again, deep and long, until we hear the first bell ring. I untwine my arms from around his neck but he doesn't let go of me. We just stare at each other goofily before another shrill ringing sound destroys the moment.

Cole groans and tugs me by the hand. "Come on, Tessie, after school I'm finding a better spot to make out."

I giggle at his obvious frustration but it's thrilling that he's as obsessed with the idea of kissing and, well, touching in general as I am. The last thing I want is to become some clingy girlfriend who wants to spend all her time holed up in the bedroom. As appealing as that sounds, I think Cole would get cabin fever after a while.

The rest of the day passes similarly. We give each other secret smiles, well I smile at Cole but he winks at me, insinuating something and as usual I blush. I get it now, the hype about being in a relationship. According to Megan, who is now our resident relationship expert, I'm in the honeymoon phase and it's going to last a while so that's awesome. The only damper on the day was seeing Jay and Nicole. Funny how I'd always thought that I'd be so happy when they weren't together anymore. I guess I was suffering for all my ill wishes. Yes, when they'd been a couple I was miserable but now I just wanted to disappear. The looks they'd shoot me, the guilt they wanted me to feel, proved that the two really did belong together. But I'm not letting them get to me, not much, that is. I have Cole; I have my friends, so it's not particularly bad. Though the thing is, I get why Nicole hates me. Unintentional as it was, my burst of honesty has left her on the outside looking in. She doesn't have any friends, even her minions have abandoned her in search of a new Queen Bee. Nicole's still on the dance team but from what I've heard, they've basically made her a pariah. I guess you really can't afford to be dumped by Jay Stone. Jay is just a puzzle and I have no idea how to get all the pieces to fit together. Yes I snubbed his advances, but was he really expecting me to come running to him? Give me some credit here. He's being an utter tool with how he's acting toward Cole and me. If I were him, I wouldn't be testing my stepbrother's patience—a little caution would be preferable since he still has the bruises to show for his last confrontation.

***

On Saturday, I put aside the ever-present drama in my life and trade it for nerve-wracking, butterfly-inducing excitement. Cole is picking me up in an hour and we're going on a date! It's the first time we're going out since our relationship's become more serious. He'd been grounded for a couple of weeks following the incident with Jay and for sneaking out with me the next morning. Sheriff Stone was all for sending him back to military school but Cassandra calmed down. Of course it was after everything went down that Jay fessed up that he'd started the whole thing. In hindsight, I'm trying to remember why I liked him so much in the first place.

I wear a purple wrap dress made from jersey material and pair the outfit with my high-heel ankle boots, which I know for a fact that Cole loves since he doesn't even try to take his eyes away from my legs when I'm in them. I like how honest he is about his gawking; it's endearing, really. I'm working on my makeup when the doorbell rings. Since the mascara wand is still in my hand and I don't want to blind myself, I take some time to finish with my lashes. Rushing downstairs, cautiously enough so that I don't fall to my death, I halt when I see that it's Travis who has met Cole at the door. I gulp, watching the two have a stare-down. Their relationship is still a mystery to me. I understand that my big brother is a bit wary of Cole because of his past but I wish Travis could see how different things are now. If that happened things wouldn't be so strained right now.

"Hey guys," I break the building tension in the room and get their attention. The change in expression is almost comical. The hardness in Travis's eyes melts away and is replaced by concern and the defensiveness and hardened look on Cole's face disappears almost as quickly. His eyes light up and a smile tugs at the corner of his mouth. My heart skips a beat, knowing that somehow I'm responsible for making him look like that.

"You were going somewhere, Tess?" Travis has upped the level of protectiveness since our mom left. He'd always taken care of me but now he's taking it to an entirely new level.

I make my way to Cole and he's brave enough to take my hand and whisper, "You look beautiful, shortcake," in my ear. Travis's eyes zero in on our entwined hands and he frowns.

"Yes, we're going out for a couple of hours. I'll be back in time for my curfew."

"But you can't go," Travis says smoothly, not missing a beat.

Before I can process his words or begin to formulate a reply, I feel Cole's fingers tighten around mine to the point of being painful. He responds before I ever get a chance to.

"Why not?" he bites out, jaw flexing, and all Travis does is smirk at him. He is so not helping the situation, knowing Cole's history, the last thing my brother needs to do is instigate him.

"Because I'm sick and I need her to take care of me."

Narrowing my eyes at him, I study him closely. "You look fine to me, Trav."

"Aah-choo." He gives the fakest sneeze in the history of fake sneezes and checks his forehead. At this point I'm seething. I know he isn't going to let me go if he's this desperate; what I want to know is why he's doing this in the first place.

"You expect her to buy that shit?" Cole growls and I feel the need to step in between the two men. I position myself in front of a very amused-looking Travis and cock an eyebrow at him while placing a hand on my hip.

"You're not sick so why are you doing this?"

"I am sick, you just can't see it. Don't tell me you're going to abandon me in my time of need, little sis." He pouts, giving me the face that no one has ever managed to say no to. This is how he gets girls to fall all over themselves for him. Granted, I'm his sister and I know all the tricks of his trade but I can't help myself either.

I sigh heavily, pinching my forehead. "And what is it that you need me to do? You seem fine. How am I going to take care of you when I don't know what's wrong with you?"

This brightens him up immediately and I hear Cole mutter something under his breath. I bet the other girls he's dated don't have families half as dysfunctional as mine. I bet they don't fall for their brother's blatant lies and don't have moms who'd rather sunbathe in Miami than actually fix their marriage.

"You can start by making me some soup. I'm famished, couldn't keep anything down yesterday."

I look between the hopeful expression on his face and the disgruntled one on Cole's face. It's like asking me to pick between a KitKat and strawberry ice cream—impossible. How do I handle this? If I stand Cole up, the chances of him dumping me are sky-high. If I leave Travis, when he obviously doesn't want me to, then I'll feel guilty all day.

"Okay. Okay, I'll stay and I'll make the dang soup but I have one condition."

Travis grins his infamous grin and crushes me in a bear hug, choking me to death. When he pulls away I can see he's smug about his victory, but his plans are going down the drain.

"Whatever you want."

See? Big mistake right there.

"Well I guess that means I'll see you later," Cole grumbles behind me and I whirl around grabbing his hand. Without looking at Travis I say something that's not going to make him very happy.

"Cole gets to stay here and you're going to be nice to him. You leave us alone and do the online coursework that I know you have. If you try to get into a fight with him then I'm leaving and you can kiss your soup good-bye."

My words manage to hit the Cole Stone smile jackpot. He doesn't give me his usual half grin but the full-fledged version of what you would call a panty-melting smile. I repress the urge to fan myself because I really don't want my brother to know that I'm feeling incredibly turned on right now.

There's silence but after a while Travis gives a noncommittal response which sounds a lot like a "whatever" and leaves us alone, stomping up the stairs.

"So I guess we've got some soup to make." I look at him apologetically, feeling horrible for ruining his expectations of our "date." Whatever he'd wanted, it must not have included playing house with me. Why he still insists on being with me, I have no idea.

"Tessie . . ." he starts but I can't stop myself from talking.

"You don't have to stay if you don't want to. I didn't mean it like that; you shouldn't have to suffer through this. I don't know what I was thinking when I told Travis that. Go out, do something fun, whatever it is you guys do. Why don't you try to catch an NFL game and maybe Alex . . ."

I never get to finish my sentence since Cole places his hands at the nape of my neck, brings me forward, and kisses me before I have time to react. My eyes widen in surprise at first but then as I feel the pressure of his soft lips on mine, I give in to the basic instinct and kiss him back. I don't care if Travis is upstairs or that my dad might come home from work anytime. All I can focus on is Cole and how wonderful his kisses feel. Wrapping my arms around his neck, I crush myself against his hard chest. He growls, his hand traveling downward to my butt.

We break away when I begin to feel a little dizzy and a lot breathless. Cole chuckles as he tucks a strand of hair behind my ear and kisses my cheek. It's a chaste gesture compared to what we were just doing but it's just as knee-melting.

"I think that answers any doubts you had about me staying."

Since there are still fireworks going off in my head it takes a little while for the words to make sense to me. I nod like an idiot, every inch of my skin still tingling from his touch. Does this happen to everyone? I need to send out a survey just to reassure myself that I'm not some nymphomaniac.

"Yeah . . ."

He chuckles again and drags me by the arm to the kitchen, depositing me at the kitchen counter since I still haven't fully recovered the use of my legs. I watch in a kind of daze as Cole rummages through the fridge and takes out whatever he needs to make the chicken noodle soup. It's when he steps in the space between my legs that I focus on something besides the wonderful feelings coursing through me.

"You do know that I'd mop the floors if that's what it took to spend time with you, right?"

I love him.

It's not just what he's just said to me but it's just a culmination of every moment I've spent with him that leads me to this conclusion. Before he walked back into my life, I felt like I wasn't good enough. That's what my poisonous obsession with Jay and his even more toxic relationship with Nicole had led me to believe. I thought there must have been something wrong with me that everyone would pick someone else over me. My parents picked their personal problems, my brother picked Jack Daniel's, my best friend picked popularity, and the supposed love of my life picked reputation. So you can understand why I didn't have the highest self-esteem. I let Nicole walk all over me because I thought that was what I deserved but I know better now. People will treat me better if I learn to treat myself better and that's what Cole has taught me. He's the person who's made me feel better about myself and made me accept myself for who I am. He's shown me how to give people second chances and to believe that they can change for the better and not just for the worst.

Hence I love him and am most probably in love with him. It hits me like the combination of a lightning bolt and a freight train. Were I not sitting, I'd definitely collapse from the force of it. The look on his face, that light shining in his eyes, tells me that he might feel the same way but I'm still not brave enough to tell him. It's too soon and I'm scared. I don't want to chase him away, especially not now.

"Well, luckily you won't have to do that but I believe you."

His hands rest on my hips, his thumbs rubbing themselves in circular motions. He does things like this a lot now and I don't shy away from him. It's like we've crossed an invisible bridge and are much more comfortable now, free to grab untaken liberties.

He leans forward and pecks my lips. "Good," he whispers against my lips and pulls back. He starts to cook and I watch him, completely mesmerized. Homemade soup will probably warm Travis toward Cole more than my attempt to heat something out of a can so I let him do the work. He moves so incredibly well in the kitchen, it's like an art, and the way he carries himself so assuredly is sexy beyond belief. Plus the man cooks like a god, so you know you can't help but love him.

"Where did you learn to cook like that?" I muse as he chops vegetables like the knife is an extension of his arm.

He doesn't look up from the board when he answers me. "I needed a job back in military school. Dad wasn't being very generous with my

231

allowance. The cook, Mrs. Montgomery, liked me and I asked her if I could get a job in the kitchens after school. She taught me everything I know," he reminisces.

I realize then that we don't really talk about his time at military school so much. Whenever I bring up the topic he changes the subject smoothly enough that I don't even notice. Lately however, I've begun to pick it up more and more. I wonder if he's ready now.

"How was it there, military school, I mean? Is it as bad as the movies?"

He shrugs, his knife not halting, but I notice his shoulders stiffening. "It's just like any other boarding school but stricter. It's a lot more, disciplined, I guess. You'd think they'd have a lot of people with juvie records but mostly it's just rich kids whose parents couldn't be damned to spend time fixing their problems."

It's the most emotion I've gotten out of him regarding this topic ever. I can see the anger rolling off of him. I have to keep going; he needs to talk about this stuff and get it all out. All this time he's been helping me fight my own personal demons but now I need to do the same for him.

"Cole, surely you don't think your dad . . ."

He gathers the vegetables and throws them into the pot with the butter. As he sautés them, he shrugs once more. I think it's part of his defensive mechanism, pretending that something doesn't affect him when it obviously does.

"I went because I wanted to. Dad suggested it when I started acting out more but he didn't force me to go."

This is news to me. I'd always thought that Cole never had a choice but to go. He didn't seem like the kind to volunteer himself for a punishment like that. Why would he do that? I ask him just that.

He concentrates awfully hard on stirring the pot in front of him. "I was a coward, Tessie. I took the easy way out."

He looks at me and must have seen the confusion on my face, which makes him explain himself.

"I told you once before that I thought I had to get away from you to get over you. It was driving me insane; I don't do well with jealousy. You were so convinced you were in love with Jay that it was like you never saw me. I had to do some pretty bad things just to make you notice me. You hated me, sure, but at least you knew I existed."

I try to speak past the golf-ball-size ball in my throat. "I always knew you existed, Cole. I was always aware of you."

"You were terrified of me," he scoffs and I can see the self-loathing in his eyes. "I left because I didn't want the situation to get worse. I thought that in time you'd just remember me as the kid who annoyed you in grade school and I would be happy with that."

"But . . ." I prompt.

"I couldn't stay away. Trust me, I tried. There were plenty of distractions and I acted like a complete asshole but I guess I was always looking for you."

I know I should be touched by his confession but I can't help but wince when he says he had plenty of distractions. Of course he had. Girls must have fallen all over themselves for him. Immediately I hate all of them, anyone who'd meant something to him. But then again those girls didn't force him into skipping town and going to military school because of their obliviousness.

"Why did it take you so long to come back? You were gone almost four years, you didn't come back once, not even during the holidays. What made you decide that you wanted to return?"

I try keeping the hurt and accusation out of my voice but I guess I don't do a good enough job. Cole looks shamefaced as he runs a frustrated hand through his hair. Avoiding any eye contact, he moves closer.

"I did come back."

"What?"

"I came back this summer, just for a day. Cassandra called me, she was really upset. She blamed herself for me wanting not to come back. I don't know why, I guess she thought I had never learned to love her like I loved my own mom. I had to come back to make her feel better."

Cole's mom had died of a heart attack when he was four. As a kid, I didn't get around to knowing her well but my mom always told me that she was a wonderful woman and that Cole looked just like her. I know he's telling the truth, I believe his sincerity.

"So why didn't you come see me?"

"I tried. I came by the house. I didn't know about Travis or his drinking problems but when he saw me he lost it. I tried to tell him that I just wanted to apologize, to say sorry for everything I'd done to you but he wouldn't have it. I guess I pissed him off a lot since he practically broke my nose."

"What?" I shriek, jumping off the counter in one go. I place my hands on Cole's shoulders and force him to look at me.

"Please tell me that's not true," I beg.

"I don't blame him for hitting me. I'm the prick who terrorized his sister, I deserved it."

"No, you don't understand. Travis always knew you liked me. He wouldn't do that; it must have been the alcohol. He's not that person anymore."

"I know, Tessie, I do. You don't have to defend him. It's just that I know he never told you about seeing me, did he? Not when I was leaving and then again when I came back."

I shake my head, feeling angry and sad at the same time. He should have told me; Travis had no right to keep a secret that wasn't his to keep. But then I remember what he'd been until very recently. His days and nights consisted of alcohol and nothing more. He hadn't been in his right mind, how could I expect him to hold a civil conversation, let alone remember one?

"But I saw you, you know? When I was leaving, I saw you from my car and that's why I came back in the fall."

Even more confused, I study his face for a clue and try to understand what made him come back.

"You were sitting on the sidewalk. Even though you had your head down on your knees I could still tell it was you. That hoodie of yours, the Batman one you wore every day to school for a week was pretty much all I had to see to know it was you. Your shoulders were shaking but I couldn't tell if you were crying or laughing."

I remember the day he's talking about and the memory turns my face crimson. If he saw what had happened next, I would feel even more pathetic about how much of a pushover I'd been. The events play in my mind as I recall the particularly nasty confrontation with Nicole and her silicon soldiers. I'd gone to the café near my dad's office after an extremely grueling college discussion session with him. He'd been stressing on Dartmouth when all I'd ever wanted was to go to Brown. Then that floozy secretary of his had basically fallen into his lap in front of me and the two had flirted like there was no tomorrow. I had stormed out, craving one of my only two weaknesses post Fatty Tessie—ice cream. I'd ordered a double scoop topped with rainbow sprinkles and that's when I'd been busted.

Nicole's bully radar had pointed her straight to me and to the gigantic cone in my hand. She gathered half of the dance team and stalked toward me. I'd already started feeling embarrassed having been caught pigging out. I still didn't feel comfortable with my body even after having lost all that weight and Nicole was surely going to pick me apart.

Which she did—brutally, I might add. By the time she was finished with me, I wanted to crawl into a hole and die. I dropped the ice cream right there and ran out. Running as fast as I could, I ended up near the outskirts of town, collapsing on the ground and then sobbing my eyes out.

Then I did something which I hadn't forgiven myself for forever. I hadn't done it ever again but the urge was strong and in a moment of complete hopelessness, I made myself throw up. Right there on the street that I thought had been deserted. Guess I was wrong. "You didn't . . ."

"I did. I'm sorry baby; I know you never wanted me to see it but I . . ."

"You came back because you felt sorry for me?" My voice is too high-pitched and screechy like it always gets when I'm mad but it's worse— I feel completely naked and vulnerable.

"No!" He grabs my arm forcefully, stopping me from running. "I came back because I knew I couldn't stay away from you. I had to be near you, I had to make sure you were okay. When I saw you crying, it felt like someone had ripped my heart right out of my chest, damn it! Then when you . . . did that it just broke me. I wanted to kill the person who made you feel like you had to do that to yourself. Don't you see? It wasn't pity; it was how I felt about you! How I've always felt about you."

Tears sting my eyes as I stare in wonder at him. Should I believe him? Does he really not feel sorry for me? I'm baffled; I don't know what to think. I want to believe him but it seems too good to be true.

"Tessie, please believe me. I'd never lie to you, you know that, right?"

"I . . . I believe you."

His entire body slackens after my words. The kind of love I feel for him surges through me and I all but attack him, jumping into his arms. I bury my face in his chest and take in the smell of him as he wraps his arms around me, lifting me off the ground.

"Thank you, thank you, thank you." I kiss a trail up his chest, feeling the pounding of his heart against my skin.

His voice is husky and throaty as he asks, "For what, baby?" before kissing the top of my head.

I pull back and kiss him gently on the mouth before cupping his face. "For saving me."

His eyes glisten before he crashes his lips to mine, growling low in his throat as he does so. He urges me to wrap my legs around him and I do so. My hands fist themselves in his hair and his roam underneath my shirt. His tongue sneaks out and darts against my lips. The feeling is so exquisite that I'm instantly greedy for more. Hesitantly, I open my mouth allowing our tongues to touch for the first time and it is sheer bliss. I moan as I'm filled with the taste of him, pressed up to every inch of him. He backs me into the counter so that the edge of the granite top presses into my spine but I'm too busy floating in the clouds to care. He kisses me fiercely like his life depends on it and I try to keep up with him.

"Hey guys, I asked you to make soup, not babies."

There are some things you wish your brother would never come across. This includes any underwear, sanitary products, and texts from your boyfriend. Having him watch you getting hot and heavy in the kitchen with a guy he supposedly hates would top that list.

But then again, this is me we're talking about and things like this just have to happen.

CHAPTER TWENTY THREE
It's Like the Freaking *Jungle Book* in My Stomach

I've had a bad week. Scratch that, I've hit the mother lode of bad weeks and even though it's Friday and school will be over in an hour or two, I feel like I've been enduring this agony for eons. See, I'd been living the dream recently, what with Cole in my life and all. He's the most attentive and loving boyfriend you could ask for. The fact that even he failed to cheer me up just makes the situation all the worse.

My mom texted my dad, I repeat, she texted him and declared that she wouldn't be coming back anytime soon, spouting nonsense about discovering herself. It's a little early for her to have a midlife crisis if you ask me but that's the point here, no one asks me. My father couldn't care less; he hasn't cared about her in years past my grandfather's funding. He's just moved on with his life—and his secretary, who I'm pretty sure gave him a hickey the other day.

Mom will come back; that's not the problem. She's all about saving face and a long-term absence will raise questions. This would explain why she's asked us to tell the country club wives that she's in some remote village in Africa, helping improve maternal health. I worry for my mother's soul, I do. She might not be a great parent but it's not like I want her to burn in hell for the rest of eternity. The real problem is that she seems to think she's not just leaving her husband but her kids as well. Neither Travis or I have heard a word from her and it's making me mad.

All this coincided with "that week," you know, the one where you want to chop off everyone's head with a blunt ax? I have major abandonment issues and my mother's blatant dropping out of my life has just fueled those insecurities to a point that I think I've become psychotic. I've taken a leave from a job I only have to go to twice a week. I haven't been paying attention in class and ditched a girls' night with Megan and Beth. No one's pushing me though; they all know what's wrong with me. I'm glad that they are so understanding, especially Cole. He understands what I'm like during what he refers to as my "lady time" and gives me the space I so desperately need but I'm indefinitely worse this time. Thanks a lot, Mom.

What I have a problem with is how easy it was for her to just uproot her entire life and move on. When the going got tough, she hitchhiked the first ride she could get ahold of and is now all set to reinvent herself. How could she just up and leave without even putting into consideration the amount of damage she'd leave behind? Fine, she wasn't much of a parent in any case but at least she was there. Now I hear stories about her and cabana boys and it is sickening. What my parents have is a disgustingly open marriage, an embarrassment for the institution. Why can't they just get divorced and give us all some peace of mind? At least then I'll know it's over but no, they like toying with my feelings.

With that thought, I slam my locker shut and basically stomp my way to the last class of the day. It's the one I share with the Brothers Grimm and Nikki the ho bag. If she so much as looks at me in the wrong way today, I'll poke her eye out with a blunt number two pencil. My hormones and I have had too much of her brooding and glaring, it's time to move on, sister.

"Hey," Cole says tentatively as if he's testing the waters. I'm not a shark, I want to scream. It bothers me that I'm so completely crabby right now but then I can't even attempt to act differently.
I give him a small smile that takes every ounce of willpower in my body and begin digging out my economics book. We still sit at the very back but Cole helps me with my notes now. We're a good team and ever since we've started studying together, my grades have skyrocketed. I should be grateful for that but right now I'm just mad that I can't see the whiteboard and that my teacher is too lazy to speak just a little louder. Then I see Nicole right up in the front and I want to strangle her—
with a barbed wire. I really could use some KitKats right now, these violent thoughts can't be normal.

The class goes by in a hurry and my notebook remains empty. I doodle a little in the corners, watch the clock some more and ignore the fact that Cole's staring at my profile. All I want is to go home and hole up for the weekend. When the bell rings, I'm the first person out of the seat.

"Tessa, wait," Cole calls from behind me, quickly shoving his own books into his backpack, which he slings onto one shoulder. My God, he looks so good doing that. I'm blindsided by lust, let's just blame the crazy hormones. People say you get butterflies when you look at someone you have feelings for but then there's me. One look at him and it's like the freaking *Jungle Book* in my stomach. He sweeps a hand through his hair, messing it up, and catches up with me looking adorably concerned.

He takes my hand and pulls me away from where the miserable two, Jay and Nicole, are watching. Sadly for them, they're partnered for the rest of the year. I guess I should feel sorry for the awkwardness of the entire situation but I can't muster up an atom of sympathy for them.

"I'm still giving you a ride home today, right?"

I nod, feeling a bit guilty. This morning I'd opted to ride with Megan instead of him just because I felt particularly catty. Megan knows how I get since she's somewhat like the Hulk on steroids during her own "week." We have a silent understanding over how terrible our mood swings are so it makes sense that we try to spend as much time together as possible, just to spare others the horror. Beth avoids us like the plague during those days and rightly so. For all her intimidating boots and dark eyeshadow, she's as mellow as a hippy all year round.

But I can't push Cole away anymore since he looks sort of hurt. I haven't been myself the last few days and have been taking out all my anger on him. If there's one thing I should be able to do, it's to act like a human being for the sake of the guy I'm in love with.

"Yeah, if you don't mind."

He looks at me like I've lost my mind and then nudges my shoulder with his as we walk hand in hand down the halls. "I won't mind, that's the farthest thing from how I'd feel, Tessie."

Leaning my head on his shoulder, we walk to his car and I strap myself in. So far so good, no more Hulk moments. I can do this, yes, hormones, you are going down. Watch me take you down like a bitch. I am the master of my own fate, the captain of my soul. We've been studying some hardcore Henley in class; it's bound to mess with my head.

"What are you doing this weekend?" he asks as he places his free hand on my jean-clad thigh. He's always doing this; I want to superglue his hand at that very spot and never let him move. He's a salve to all my anxiousness and nerve-wracking mood swings but then my emotions are the most heightened when I'm around him. That's why I've been trying to avoid him so much this week. Yes, he gives me the highest highs but one wrong word from him and I end up crying my eyes out in the girls' bathroom.

"I'm not sure, staying in, I guess."

Actually I have it all mapped out in my head. As soon as Cole drops me home, I'll gather the necessary supplies such as ice cream, KitKats and plenty of string cheese. Then I'll take out the most comfortable blanket I have and snuggle up into my oldest onesie. After that I'll spend my weekend with McDreamy. Megan gave me a boxed set of *Grey's Anatomy* for my birthday; she understands the therapeutic powers of Dr. Shepherd.

"And you're sure you don't want me to come check up on you?"

"I'll just bring you down as well. It's okay, Cole, I'll survive. You should have some guy time."

We've been spending a lot of time together and it makes me wonder if he's getting sick of me. But there's another part that knows we're good. After last week, knowing what he saw and why he returned, my faith in him has just grown beyond the acceptable point. I believe him, blindly. So maybe I should just stop questioning every little thing.

"I was going to talk to you about that. Some of my friends from military school are in town for a couple of days. I told them I'd come see them so I'll be leaving today and coming back on Sunday."

He's watching me, waiting for a reaction. I don't know how to feel. I want to be left alone and for him especially to stay away until I stop biting his head off. This is exactly what we need but then why do I feel like he just struck me right in the jugular?

"Tessie?"

I'm aware that we're parked outside my house now. But I just sit there, lip quivering and eyes watering. I've become unhinged and it's officially time to call the nut house. The urge to get mad and throw a tantrum is strong. Out-of-whack hormones coupled with my mom's abandonment are all of a sudden too much for me to take. He's leaving too, probably to have a wild old time with his delinquent friends. There will be girls too, hot, tattooed, edgy biker chicks that have piercings in places I shudder to think about. Before I know it, he'll be hooking up with someone called Yolanda and telling me to take a hike because I'm not badass enough for him.

"Fine, go, have a great time." The sarcasm pouring out of my mouth stings even my own ears but I can't stop. Grabbing my backpack, I scramble out of my seat and slam his car door shut. He's getting out too, from what I can hear and every noise he makes is grating at my nerves.

"Hey, hold up. Did I do something wrong?"

I clench my teeth. Why are boys so clueless? Doesn't he know that it's a terrible idea to even look at me right now? I'm ready to explode, desperately in need of chocolate and all but want to crawl into a hole in the ground.

"Please just go away. I don't want to talk about it."

"No, I'm not going to go away. I get it, Tessie; it's been a tough week because of your mom and other stuff." His faces flushes as he mentions the latter and I want to die. I cannot believe I'm discussing my period with Cole.

He continues, not really aware of my discomfort. "But you can't just shut me out. I'm not letting our first fight be about something as stupid as this."

"Stupid? You think my mother leaving me is stupid? Well I'm sorry to have taken up so much of your time by talking about my stupid issues!"

He groans. "That isn't what I meant. I meant my leaving for a few days. If you don't want me to go just say so. "

"By all means, don't let me and my stupidity stop you from having fun, Cole. Go, do whatever you want, just leave me alone." He grips my arm when I try to leave and I'm just about to unleash some major fury when Travis walks onto the porch. I assume he heard us fighting, or rather me being a complete nightmare.

"You should just leave, man. It's best to listen to her when she's like this."

He looks apologetic and that's when I realize how neurotic I'm acting. If Travis is forced to apologize to Cole on my behalf then it's got to be really bad.

"I'm so sorry!" I cover my mouth with my hand and push past them both, stomping up the stairs and into my room. Falling face-first into my bed, I try holding in all the pent-up emotion but I'm not quick enough. A frustrated scream leaves my mouth as I punch my pillow repeatedly. I will not cry, I will not cry, chanting the mantra like it would actually help. It doesn't help and I cry, bucketsful.

I don't even know why I'm crying. Maybe it's because of Mom, maybe it's because of Dad but mostly I think it's because I might have just ruined the one good thing in my life. I want to run to Cole to beg him for forgiveness and to tell him that I didn't mean to fight with him but he must be long gone by now. It's been hours since I locked myself up. My rumbling stomach tells me that it could be late evening, entirely too late to kiss and make up.

Changing into a pair of ratty old pajamas, I wobble like a duck into the kitchen. My head feels like it weighs a ton and my eyes sting. Couple that with the monthly curse and I am the picture of misery. I feel slightly better when I smell a delicious aroma coming from the kitchen. It's Travis, he's bent over a pot and stirring it constantly. It looks like he's making his world-famous and my favorite chili; instantly I start to salivate.

"Hey," I mumble feebly as I take a seat on the counter.

He gives me a sympathetic smile and puts the lid on the pot, lowering the heat. He comes and sits by me, slinging an arm around my shoulder and I place my head on his. It's comforting and I close my eyes, letting myself unwind for the first time in days.

"How're you feeling?"

"Like I was run over by a bus, twice."

He chuckles, mussing my hair. "You sounded like you were crying for a while up there."

We're silent for a while before I finally answer. "I hate what Mom did. I hate how selfish she is and how Dad doesn't care. I hate that they don't just split up and stop pretending."

"Tess, we know our parents are screwups. We've grown up knowing that their reputation is everything for them. I wish they were different too but they're not and it's hard to accept that but you have to. You can't let them do this to you, trust me, they aren't worth the tears."

I snuggle further into his shoulder. "But they weren't always like this. I remember them being good, being happy. We were a normal family once, Trav. What happened?"

He sighs wistfully. "I don't know. Maybe they were always unhappy in their marriage and we never picked it up. It got worse after Dad became the mayor and after that it was just like watching a train wreck. I'm sorry I couldn't be there for you during that time, Tess, I swear I'd do anything to go back and fix it."

I snort, "Don't apologize. You were more of a parent to me than they ever were."

He hugs me closer. "Thanks, baby sis. Maybe we'll make it out of here alive after all. Just no more crying over those two ever again."

I nod. "Okay."

"Oh and Tess?"

"Yeah?"

"Call Stone, will you? He's been bugging me all day."

***

At 10 p.m. I find myself in front of the Stones' door. I have no idea what I'm going to do but what I do know is that I have to be near Cole right now. He didn't leave to see his friends, Travis told me so. He's been checking up on me all day and I feel so bad for treating him the way I did. Even worse than the guilt is how much I crave his presence. It's insane, like someone ripped me into two and took the other half away. He needs to know that I'm an idiot, a stupid girl who is in way over her head with him and sometimes doesn't know what to do with her over-the-top emotions.

Due to never-ending misfortune, it is Jay who lets me in. He looks startled to see me, or maybe he's just put off by my appearance. I didn't really try too hard, simply changing into jeans and a simple white V-necked sweater. My hair's a little ratty but I managed to run a comb through it despite my hurry and there's just a hint of lip gloss on my lips.

242

"Hi." He sounds a little breathless and I don't like it. He needs to stop acting like I affect him so much. If Cole ever sees the kind of looks Jay sends me when he thinks no one's looking, I'm pretty sure we'd have a brawl on our hands.

"Who is it?" Cassandra's voice comes from the living room and I immediately begin fretting. What's she going to think of me, showing up to see her son at this hour when he's probably spent the day upset.

"It's Tessa," Jay says without taking his eyes off me. I'm starting to get weirded out right now; he has got to stop checking me out before I punch him into tomorrow.

"Hey, Mrs. Stone." I offer Cassandra a meek smile as she comes my way.

"Hi honey, I didn't know we were expecting you."

I look down apologetically. "You weren't. I just needed to speak to Cole about something."

She analyzes me and a smile tugs at the corners of her mouth. "Does this something have to do with why he's been locked up in his room all day?"

My cheeks turn red. She must hate me; Cole deserves to be treated so much better than this and here I am callously playing games with his heart.

"We . . . no, I . . . I made a mistake and I need to tell him I'm sorry."

"You guys had a fight?" I resist the urge to throw Jay a glare. He looks triumphant and I want to take that smug look off his face with the help of a butcher knife. The words *mind your own dang business* are at the tip of my tongue but I can hardly say them with his mother in the room. The same mother who must probably hate my guts right now.

"Please go to your room, Jason. That wasn't a question you could ask so freely." As she chastises him I fall in love with this woman even more.

"But Mom . . ."

"Your room, Jason."

"Fine." He sounds sullen but leaves us.

Cassandra places her hand on my arm and gives it a gentle, motherly squeeze. Her eyes are full of understanding and warmth as she nods in the direction Jay just went. "You should go see Cole. I'm sure you two will work out whatever there is to work out."

"Thank you." I'm sure my eyes are watery by this point but I don't care. I rush to get to Cole's room and when I open the door, glad that it's unlocked, I freeze.

243

He's shirtless and only in pajama bottoms, sitting on the edge of his bed. His cell phone is clutched in both hands and his eyes are pressed up against both fists. His shoulders are heaving, the muscles of his abdomen rippling as he breathes heavily.

"Cole." My voice comes out a little hoarse but he hears it all the same and it's like he immediately knows it's me.

"Tessie." He stands up as his cell phone falls noisily to the ground. We stare at each other in silence from across the room. The quietness is suffocating and it's so not us. We have such an easy aura around us now that this tense moment feels all wrong. I have to fix this since it's entirely my fault.

"I'm an idiot," I stutter.

"Tessie . . ."

"A moron, a jerk, a bonehead, imbecile, nincompoop, ninny . . ."

He takes two large strides and is in front of me, cupping my face.

"Did you just say nincompoop and ninny?" He's squishing my cheeks so I have fish lips now.

"Yesh."

He plants a quick but intoxicating kiss on my lips and then starts to laugh, like really laugh.

"Say it again."

"Nincompoop, I am a total and utter nincompoop, emphasis on the *poop* part."

He laughs even harder. "The other one too!"

"Ninny, Cole. I. Am. A. Ninny." I start laughing too and soon we both fall into bed, laughing like crazy hyenas.

As is his habit, he interlinks our fingers. "Do you have any more of those?"

"Shut up," I mumble into his skin, burying my face in the crook of his neck. I'm perfectly aware of his lack of clothing and yes I prefer him like this.

"No, seriously, that was priceless. I want more!"

"Too bad, you're not getting any."

"Ain't that the truth."

I smack his shoulder playfully. "That's not funny."

"Kidding, I'm kidding, sorry!"

He wraps an arm around me and pulls me tightly toward his side. We lay in silence, just enjoying each other. The day has been tough on both of us and I guess we just want to make sure that the other's still there. The thought of losing him is terrifying and I can only hope I never pull another stunt like the one I did today.

244

"I'm sorry, Cole."

"You don't have to apologize, shortcake."

"I have to. I shouldn't have yelled at you like that. It's just . . . everything with my family is messed up."

He hugs me tighter to him, kissing the top of my head. "I know, sweetheart. You don't owe me an explanation."

"But you had the chance to go see your friends today and you didn't go. You stayed because of me. I can't believe I guilt-tripped you into ruining your weekend," I mumble.

He clicks his tongue. "As long as I'm with you, I'm good. Besides, they're there till Sunday so I can make the trip tomorrow."

Oh. Okay, so I admit I really wanted to spend tomorrow with him. The hormones are becoming controllable and I've missed being with him. But he has a life of his own and I can't keep gate-crashing into it.

"There's just one thing, though . . ." he continues, unaware of my pity party.

"What's that?"

"I told them that I'd be bringing my girl with me."

My heart leaps and it soars. I'm floating, light as cotton candy, the pink kind, of course. I hide the huge grin that swallows me whole and kiss his neck; on the exact spot he always kisses me.

"You want me to come with you?"

"If you want to? I don't think I'll make it past city limits if you aren't next to me."

The L-word is on the tip of my tongue. I want to shout it from the rooftops and have it tattooed across my forehead. I want to tell him, and then kiss the life out of him but now isn't the time. We're both a little scared, both a little vulnerable. He wouldn't take me seriously even if I tried.

"I'd love to meet your friends."

I feel his smile against my skin and it makes me giddy to know I could affect his moods so drastically. Meeting Yolanda will be a small price to pay for this guy's happiness. I'd do practically anything for him.

"Great, I'll pick you up at seven in the morning."

Note how I said practically anything; some things are strictly out of bounds.

"You're joking, right?"

CHAPTER TWENTY-FOUR
You're a Tweedlewart

The fact that I can sense another person's presence in my room would be considered useful. It would mean that even when I'm asleep, my super ninja powers will protect me. However, on a Saturday and at the unholy hour of seven a.m. it's more like a curse. Sleeping Beauty, consider yourself lucky. Imagine all that uninterrupted sleep and you don't even age! How is that even a curse?

As I start to become aware of someone creeping toward me, I'm reminded of a tacky horror film. If I weren't so lazy, I'd just get up and scream "NOOOO." There's an inner battle going on within me. Half, well more like about ninety-nine percent is content to keep sleeping while the other measly one percent reminds me that Cole is probably here and might possibly witness me drooling on my pillow. Drooling in my SpongeBob pajamas no less.

Guess who won that showdown?

"Tessie."

I pull the covers tightly around myself so that my body is cocooned by them. My head's buried in the pillow and I try to block out his voice. I love the guy, of course I do and his voice is just divine but nothing and absolutely nothing sounds appealing to me at this hour.

"Come on, shortcake. Don't make me bust out the big guns," he says in a singsong voice and I feel him plop down on the bed beside me. At this point, I more or less resemble a mummy, what with being wrapped up in the sheets and all.

"Mmph." This is the only sound of protest I can stand to make. Too tired and too lazy to do more, coupled with what remains of my PMS, has me struggling to gain coherency.

"I don't understand sleep-obsessed Tessie, can I order the regular version please?"

246

"It's too early for me to make a wisecrack," I mumble, or at least that's what I hope I mumbled. From what my ears manage to pick up I sound like someone stuffed a boxing glove in my mouth. Coherence obviously isn't at its peak at the moment.

"Tessie, come on. I'll buy you donuts and even let you get the one with the disgusting frosting."

He's bribing me with donuts. That much I can process and so lured in by sugar-coated goodness, I pop one eye open and then the other. Suddenly the world has clarity and I have a purpose to actually make it out of this bed.

Donuts, yummy Nutella-filled donuts with an extra large coffee.

Once he's convinced that his method of bribery has worked, he leaves me alone after a kiss to the top of my head but not before I have the last word.

"Tweedlewart."

"What?"

"You're a tweedlewart."

"Is that supposed to be insulting, Tessie?"

"It sounded a little bit more intimidating in my head."

***

It definitely is the perfect start to my day. To say that I'm not nervous would be the kind of lie that would set an infinite amount of pants on fire. Cole's friends are ex-felons, well, most of them anyway. Not that I'm judging them, it's me that I'm more concerned with. I'm a dorky blonde and the closest I've come to getting a tattoo is Photoshopping one onto my arm when I got bored in computer class. What if I make it all one big awkward disaster? Cole hasn't seen them in a while and I would hate to be the reason that he doesn't get the opportunity for the kind of quality time that he requires with them.

Before I can psyche myself into not going, I rush to the shower. Once standing between the steady streams of hot water, it's easier to think of Cole's friends as human and not Russian mobsters. Cole went to military school too and he's perfectly normal, right? Well, *normal* isn't a word likely to be associated with him; he's extraordinary.

My point is that it is wrong to be presumptuous. I don't know what they'll be like so there's no need to be terrified. Then again if they don't like me then that'll definitely not bode well for what Cole and I have finally managed to establish—a healthy, drama-free relationship. If Beth and Megan hadn't approved of him, I'd be having second thoughts about Cole too.

I dress simply but assertively, jeans and a graphic T-shirt with an old pair of brown suede studded boots. It took me a couple of times to nail the look but I'm satisfied now.

Downstairs I find an odd picture in my kitchen. My father, from what it looks like, is trying to maintain a conversation with my brother and Cole. He and Travis try to make sure their timings never match, which is why it's exceptionally weird seeing the three of them have breakfast like they were in Little League together.

"Well I'll be damned. Who knew my daughter would actually be able to get up before noon?" My father chuckles and I make a face at him. Traitor! We're all big on sleep in this family, so what if I happen to love it more than the rest of my bloodline?

"Told you I could do it, now pay up." Cole grins at my brother, who grudgingly gets out a wad of bills from his wallet and hands them to my soon-to-be-dead boyfriend.

"You guys were betting on whether or not I'd get out of bed?" I narrow my eyes at the three of them sitting behind the kitchen island. It takes all of my cranky morning will to not dump my freshly brewed nectar of the gods onto their heads.

"Honey, you don't exactly have the best track record. Trying to wake you up early on a weekend is like poking a bear in hibernation. Remember the time your mother tried to get you up for the visit to your grandparents."

A booming laugh escapes Travis and despite the teasing, I feel warmth spread through me. Not only is this the first time Dad has remembered Mom fondly since she left, it's also the first time Travis and Dad are actually acting normal around each other. If embarrassing me with sordid details of my sleep-obsessed nature is the key to get them to get along then hey, come at me.

"You mean when she 'accidentally' set off the fire alarm in her room and you guys had to spend the rest of the day figuring out what was causing the beeping?" I bite my lip in humor at the memory. Those scented candles are more useful than most people assume. Just hide them in some discreet corner and you can get a peaceful amount of sleep while everyone else figures out the cause of something that might potentially burn your entire house down. All while having a room that smells like peaches. You tend to pick up some things when spending considerable time with Cole.

I see him looking at me with a mixture of amusement and adoration in his eyes and it makes gargantuan butterflies burst in my stomach. Now that I'm looking at him, really looking at him, my mouth waters slightly. In my sleep-induced hatred for all human beings, I somehow managed to overlook the fact that there's something different about him. Of course he always looks mind-numbingly hot but today there's a kind of rugged, dangerous, bad-boy edge to him that wasn't there before. Whether it's the threadbare concert shirt, the dark-washed jeans, or the leather cuff on his wrist, Cole is emanating his dark and dangerous appeal today. Usually, he's rather subtle about the bad boy that he truly is, especially since coming back. With me he's been the perfect gentleman but I've caught glimpses of the pre-military school Cole, especially when Jay's around. Today is the day his appearance stresses who he really is and it is swoon worthy.

He waits until we're all eating breakfast to point out the fact that he noticed my blatant ogling. "I like it when you stare at me openly; you should do it more often, shortcake."

Blushing is second nature to me, it truly is. Out of the corner of my eye, I watch my dad reading his morning paper and Travis going through his phone while shoveling spoonfuls of cereal into his mouth. They're both distracted enough so I let my gaze drop to Cole's lips.

"I like the view."

His eyes darken in a way that makes me wish we were alone. I've become quite adept at flirting if I do say so myself. He's an excellent teacher and now I don't feel like a moron when expressing how I feel. Confidence is key and he's the one who taught me that.

He places his hand on my knee beneath the island and my heart skips a beat. My skin feels like it's on fire and I wonder if I'll ever get used to this heady feeling I get when I'm around him.

We share a moment when our gazes lock and I see a strong emotion flit across his eyes that terrifies me. It's like he's trying to convey something important with just that one piercing look and it has me all kinds of frightened. Some people may say that it's not too soon for us to be feeling this way, that what we feel is too strong to wait for what's considered the right time. But I can't do it.

Of course I'm in love with him. What sane or even slightly unhinged girl wouldn't be, but I can't chase him away. Loving people and I don't exactly have the best history. Whether it's my parents or my brother, even Nicole—I've just been let down so many times that even with someone like Cole it is a bit daunting to have that kind of expectation, especially with the L-word.

***

We leave shortly after breakfast, tons of coffee and promised donuts later

I'm fully functional and my nerves return. My eyes keep going to that cuff on his wrist because it's so foreign to the everyday image I have of him.

"What's going on in that overcomplicating but adorable head of yours?" Cole asks, driving with one hand on the steering wheel and the other on my knee.

"Can I ask you something?"

His brows wrinkle and he looks at me like he's trying to read my mind but still nods.

"What were you like in military school? We never talk about it or not much and I want to know that Cole, just to get an idea of what I'm going into."

He stares right ahead for a while, concentrating on the windshield, but then he squeezes my knee and leans over to kiss the top of my head. He exhales heavily before starting something which I guess means a lot to him.

"At first I was mess, a smart-ass who mouthed off a lot."

"So a lot like your usual sunny self." I chuckle and am punished with a poke in the ribs.

"Yeah, I was a lot like I was back here. But then I learned the hard way that it's not a great idea to be a hothead in a place chock full of them."

Ah, a legion of Coles. That must have gone well. I let him continue, truly interested in his story. He knows how I spent the last three miserable years of my life so it's only fair that I know about him too. Growing up with him meant that I'd always had him in my life. He's well acquainted with every aspect of it and I've got so much to learn about his.

"The teachers were tough, and the first year I just kicked myself for landing in the hellhole but then I met some guys whom I could actually relate to, you know?"

I nod, understand dawning. For being as close as they used to be, Jay and Cole have always been polar opposites. Like my brother, Jay fit the image of golden boy to a tee. Cole's always been a little controversial, a little louder, and a whole lot of trouble.

"There's Landon, but don't call him that, ever." He gives me a mock-stern look as a smile twitches at the corner of his lips. "Lan's a lot like me and we discovered that after nearly beating the shit out of each other the first day we were made roommates sophomore year." He must have seen my shocked expression since he chooses to elaborate.

"Let's just say we weren't big on sharing space with egos bigger than the size of our room. Things got better after that. Lan introduced me to a couple of really cool guys, all of whom you'll be meeting today. They're great, shortcake, I wouldn't take you to see them if they weren't." Then almost shyly, with a light flush coloring his cheeks, he adds, "It means a lot to me that you're coming with me, you know. Feels nice to show my girl off."

I beam at him, filled with warmth. God, I love this boy.

***

An hour goes by quickly. Sometimes we talk each other's ear off and sometimes there's companionable silence. The drama of yesterday is forgotten and I feel a lot like myself given that my "girl time" is nearly over. As Cole talks about his friends, I begin to relax. They sound like really nice, normal people, which makes it all the more important that they like me.

I think of that as I run my fingers over the cuff on his wrist absentmindedly.

"You've been paying this thing a lot of attention. Do you like it?"

Yes! It's completely hot and so very bad-boy but I can't tell him that, now can I?

"I've never seen you wear it before. It's . . . interesting."

"Interesting good or interesting 'it makes you look like a girl and I hate it'?"

I laugh at his exaggerated question and slip a finger beneath the band and trace his wrist. It's one of his moves and it always turns me into jelly. So when his breathing hitches, I discover it affects him somewhat in the same manner.

"Definitely interesting good." I grin at him and he gulps audibly. I lean back in my seat. Tessa: 1, Cole: 100 gazillion. Ah, how beautiful are small victories.

As we enter the city limits, my nerves start acting up again but it's better than before. Hearing all the hilarious stories Cole's just told me about them makes them more real and less intimidating. It still doesn't do much to help me deal with my meeting-new-people anxiety.

"Hey, look at me."

Cole parks in the parking lot of what looks like a five-star apartment complex.

"Don't be nervous, everyone's looking forward to meeting you. I've talked about you so damn much that they already know you and I bet are just as crazy about you as I am."

I gulp and break into a sweat. This is me at my worst; the lack of confidence, the crushing shyness and awkwardness is why I keep to myself.

"I . . . umm, I can't . . ."

"Deep breaths, Tessie, deep breaths."

His hand rubs up and down my back and he says soothing words to help calm me down. I'm seconds away from a Hannah Montana song when he leans in and kisses me. Just like that, all my worries disappear. I forget why I'm so stressed out, why I'm acting so neurotic, and why I'd rather launch myself in front of a tractor.

He kisses me slowly, languidly, like he has all the time in the world. As always, my eyes shut on their own accord and my hands tease the hair at the nape of his neck. We kiss and kiss until I lose all sense of time and place and then when it's getting difficult to breathe, he pulls away and rests his forehead against mine. We're both panting slightly and my lips are tingling, swollen from his ministrations.

"We good?"

I grin at him, suddenly filled with euphoria. "We're great."

"Lan's dad owns the apartment but he's always on business trips so this is more like Lan's bachelor pad," he says as we walk down the polished floors of the lobby, the door of which was opened by a very prim and proper doorman. I'm familiar with posh places because of my parents and grandparents but still not very comfortable. Growing up around money meant constantly being judged for it, so you tend to disassociate yourself from those titles and authority.

"This is nice," I say as we take the elevator to the fifteenth floor. Consciously, I study my image in the mirror and Cole wraps his arms around me, pulling me into his chest.

"Beautiful" he says, kissing my cheek and I snuggle into him.

With a ding the elevator approaches our destination and hand in hand, we walk out. He knocks on a door just on the left of the carpeted floor and gives me a reassuring smile, squeezing my hand. I've got to do this for him. He's changed my entire world so the least I can do is get along with the people who obviously mean a lot to him. Nothing bad could possibly come out of this.

Except for the nearly naked platinum blonde who swings the door open with a shit-eating grin on her face and launches herself onto my boyfriend, attacking his lips with hers.

I spoke too soon, now let me at her.

CHAPTER TWENTY-FIVE
The Lecherous Ho Has a Point

For a few minutes, my mind is simply processing why a leech is sucking the life out of my boyfriend. It's like staring at a piece of abstract art and trying to figure out what the artist was trying to portray. Everything's a blur of shapes and colors and you're just standing there trying to console yourself that you're not an idiot and it's the artist that lacks talent.

There is a girl, a girl wearing next to nothing and she's wrapped herself like a spider monkey to Cole. I think I'm going to be sick. I might be making really painful sputtering sounds but I don't really care. What matters is that there is another girl with her hands all over MY guy.

"What the fuck, Kimmy!" I hear growling. Someone is growling and the leech is pushed away. She makes a sound of protest and is ready for another attack but someone grabs her arms and pulls her in before she does some more soul-sucking.

"But *Coleee,* I missed you." Okay, so the leech speaks.

"That's enough, Kimmy. Don't make me bring out the tranquillizers." A heavy male voice tries to control the leech, who is struggling in his grasp. What is wrong with her? Is she epileptic, is she having a seizure?

"Goddammit Lan, you said she wasn't going to be here."

My head whips around and then I realize it's Cole who is growling and rubbing his lips very, very vigorously. Well, too late for that, buddy. You have her saliva and germs all over you now. I shudder, pitying the poor guy, but that's when I take in the crestfallen look on the leech's face and suddenly it all makes sense. She's pouting but looking at Cole like he's her entire world. I recognize that look; I wear it more than often myself.

"Yolanda," I gasp and all three people turn to look at me with various expressions on their faces. Cole looks apologetic and panicked, like he's waiting for me to storm out of the place. I can't exactly do that even if I want to since he's my ride. I then face Yolanda, the leech, and she's glaring at me with a kind of viciousness only rivaled by that of Nicole's, and then there's Lan.

Lan is as tall as Cole and has a similar build. Tall and lean with arms that aren't overly muscular, a T-shirt stretching over his biceps, emphasizing them, and his toned chest. He has a head full of thick, dark hair and when my eyes finally land on his face I realize he has really stark green eyes, which are watching me with wariness and something akin to shame.

"Who the hell is *she?*" I have come to the realization that Yolanda the leech emphasizes a word in every sentence she says and it is kind of funny. But it's hard to find the humor in the situation when all I want is to take a chainsaw to her neck.

I feel a hesitant hand placed on the small of my back and feel the warmth of Cole's body next to mine.

"This is my girlfriend, Tessa, and you better damn respect that, Kimmy." His voice is hard enough to cut steel and I'd pity the person being on the receiving end of it if it were anyone else but her.

She gives me the basic bitch once-over. I've faced it quite a lot so it doesn't make me as insecure as it used to. She scrutinizes every inch of my body, her lips tilted up into a vicious snarl.

"*That's* who you're dating?" Her face scrunches up in disgust and I feel Cole's body tense even more, if that's possible. To save the poor thing from becoming a pummeled mess, I speak up.

"I'm afraid so, but at least you should be glad that he's upped his standards since you."

"Meoww."

I assume that's Lan but I'm too busy having a stare-down with Yolanda, who looks like she wants to deck me. Cole chuckles next to me and pulls me closer, exhaling in relief. Ha, he thinks he's off the hook but I am so not done with him. This must be one of his "distractions" from military school and I don't know what that says about him. It hurts more than I expected and we'll need to talk about it, but after I put the leech in her place.

"How *dare* you!" She stomps her foot, actually stomps it and I stifle a laugh. She is such a walking cliché it's not even funny. "You have no *idea* what the two of us shared. He's just using you as a rebound until we get back together," she hisses and I snort. If I didn't trust Cole the way I do, I would have believed her but there's too much history for me to doubt. The girl is clearly delusional and obsessed with Cole in a way that's nowhere near being something akin to love. She's a brat who hates the fact that she can't have what she wants. I'm well acquainted with the type; I was best friends with her for a long time.

"I'm sorry but from where I'm standing, it doesn't look like he's in too much pain being away from you. If anything you might have just traumatized him trying to suck his lips off. Does that particular technique work for you?" I ask with a straight face but Lan ruins the effect when he bursts out laughing. Yolanda shoots him a poisonous glare and then closes in on me.

"Back off, Kimmy. You don't want to do this." Cole steps in front of me with warning ringing clearly in his voice.

Ah, my Yolanda is actually a Kimmy.

She looks back and forth between me and Cole, as if gauging how much more she needs to work on destroying what we have. I thought people like her only existed in the trashiest of romance novels. The unrelenting, psychotic ex who goes to great pains to come between the hero and the heroine. She's even doing the crazy eye twitching, which always creeps me out. What the heck did Cole see in her?

Or maybe it wasn't her sunny personality that attracted him. The thought makes me sick to my stomach. "Come on, Kimmy, don't make a bigger fool of yourself than you already have. Just go to your room and we'll forget this ever happened."

Lan is once again playing mediator and manages to get through to her. With one last withering stare, she huffs and turns around, her circle skirt flashing all of us as she does so. Huh, she wears thongs, why am I not surprised?

Standing in the hallway we hear a door slam and there's a general sigh of relief. Cole and Lan are having a silent conversation and it's almost comical how I can almost guess what's going on. I decide to break the straining silence and do the polite thing, which is to introduce myself to Lan.

I extend my hand to the towering guy. "Hi, I'm Tessa. You must be Landon; Cole has told me so much about you." I purposely use his full name just to tease him a little and get back at him for introducing Kimmy the leech into my life. He winces but takes my hand nonetheless, surprising me by kissing it instead of shaking. My cheeks heat as Cole's fingers dig into my spine.

"Lan, please call me Lan. It's a pleasure to finally meet you, Tessa. The guy's talked my ear off about you." He grins charmingly and I find myself smiling back.

"Nice to meet you too, even though you have questionable taste in houseguests."

I'm rewarded with an embarrassed laugh from Lan, and Cole

tucking me closer. "I'm so sorry about that, Tessie. My soon-to-be-dead friend here told me she wouldn't be here." He glares at Lan, who holds up his hands in defense.

"That chick is crazy. I accidentally let it slip that you and the guys were coming up and she managed to talk her mom into letting her out of the nut house."

To me he explains, "She's my stepsister. Though I'd rather chew my arm off than be related to her."

By this point we've walked into the huge apartment, obviously decorated by a professional, and take a seat on the massive leather sectional. I turn toward a brooding Cole. "And how do you know her?"

He scratches the back of his neck. It's his tell and I'm pretty sure I'm not going to like what comes out of his mouth next. Preparing myself for the worst, I hold my breath.

"We . . . uh we . . . she went to military school with me. Her dad, he's a teacher there and we . . . God." He runs his hand through his hair and tilts his head back, squeezing his eyes shut.

"Remember how I told you I was sort of messed up during the time I spent there? Well she's a part of that mess."

"So you two . . ." The insinuation hangs heavy in the air.

He's made it quite obvious what kind of relationship he shared with "Kimmy" and it's painful enough without him putting it into words. In spite of myself, my mind conjures up images of him through the years with many other faceless girls. Ouch, that just hurts.

"Yeah, we did."

I swallow heavily and try my best not to act like a manic, jealous girlfriend. It's all in the past, well a past where he was supposedly pining away for me, but still. Something inside my chest hurts and I feel lightheaded. He slept with that . . . thing out of all the possible girls he could've hooked up with?

Lan twists knife in deeper. "If it's any consolation, Kimmy has slept her way through the entire school. When you're with her, you know exactly what you're getting into. A meaningless, hard and fast f—"

"Dude, shut up! Don't you think you've done enough already?"

Lan looks sheepish but his face softens once he obviously takes in the state I'm in. "Listen, I'm sorry, Tessa. She just showed up out of the blue and I couldn't kick her out. If it's any consolation, she's a lot better than Erica."

Now who the hell is Erica? My face scrunches up in confusion and Lan bites his tongue like he's said something he wasn't supposed to. Cole groans beside me as I turn to him.

"Erica?"

"She's a family friend." He stresses the last word. "We stay with her family at their beach house during the summer and Lan hates her because she turned him down." He scowls at his friend and that's the end of it.

I nod and try to smile but I'm pretty sure it comes across as a grimace. I'm as comfortable in this situation as someone having a root canal and bikini wax at the same time.

"Right, that's why I hate her. But Tessa, seriously, if I had any idea Kimmy would do this I'd have kicked her out no questions asked."

"It's okay. I understand. I know all about having a dysfunctional family," I tell him with all honesty.

To Cole I say, "Why her of all people? Is that your type?" I scrunch my nose and he laughs, understanding that I'm letting it go for the time being.

He leans in and kisses the top of my head. "I learned the hard way that she was entirely the wrong shade of blond for me."

***

We spend some time waiting for two of Cole's other friends to arrive. Lan is an amazing host, warm, funny, and charming. I'm horrified at myself for being so judgmental of him before even meeting him. He is nothing like I imagined him to be and if he stopped dropping hints about this Erica, he'd be perfect. I'll have to get Cole alone to tell me more about the girl.

Kimmy stays in her own room though I do hear the whiniest pop songs blasting through the door so I'm guessing she's in a mood. Cole's still pretty embarrassed and he's showing that by being extra attentive toward me. Yes, imagine how wonderful he usually is and multiply that by like a hundred. I almost get the urge to put the guy out of his misery but then a more vindictive part of me is enjoying this very much. Currently he's in the kitchen since he's the resident cook of the group. When the rest of his friends arrive, they've planned to just relax at the apartment first and then there's some college party.

Yes, I'm also perfectly well aware of my history with parties. But then Cole's asked me about a hundred and one times if I'm "okay" with the plans. It might be his guilt talking but still it's awfully sweet of him to be so considerate, and the last thing I want is to ruin his plans so I say yes. There's no Nicole here and things might actually go okay.

"I really am sorry, you know. Kimmy's always been a pain in the ass but lately it's like she's channeling the love child of Britney Spears and

Miley Cyrus."

Lan sits down next to me and I have to laugh at that comparison; it's so apt and I'm not even the one coming up with it.

"Did he, umm, did Cole date girls like her a lot?"

I use the word *date* since saying what he actually did with them would be utterly embarrassing.

He understands what I'm trying to say and hesitates a little. "I'm not sure I'm supposed to answer that question."

"Bro code?"

"Definitely."

"And Erica? Should I be worried?"

He sighs but tells me anyway, "He'd chop off his right arm before hurting you, I know that for sure. But that girl is something else. Just promise me if you ever come across her, don't let her play her mind games with you."

"I don't understand, I've never even heard about her before."

"Her family and Cole's are pretty close. I've spent summer breaks with him and Erica's always around. She's obsessed with Cole, Kimmy times ten, and he doesn't even see it. I won't bring her up unnecessarily but she's been asking about him a lot lately. I keep tabs on her just in case she gets wind of your relationship and decides to act up. I don't want you to be blindsided by her if you ever meet her."

***

Lan's words about the mysterious Erica and Kimmy declaring nuclear war on Cole's mouth are constantly swarming my head. I shrug and smile it off when Cole asks but in my mind I think that it's even worse than I imagined. He's been with so many girls that even his best friend refuses to tell me the extent of his philandering ways. This is one of the classic moments where the girl asks the guy for a list of every woman he's been with. I can't do that with Cole.

There's not enough paper in the universe, apparently.

***

"If you don't take your hand off my girl, McGinty, I might have to rip it off."

I'm trying not to laugh at the raging jealousy on Cole's face but it's too hard. His friends Seth and Jameson arrived about an hour ago and ever since then Seth's been making an active effort to get killed. The guy is as smooth as butter and he's decided to put the moves on me today. If it's not the hug he engulfed me in the moment he entered then it's the almost-snuggling on the couch. Cole's hands have been fisted for a really long time and I think it's about time we stop torturing him.

"Relax, Stone. I'm just getting to know her after all the time you've spent drooling over her. She's even more beautiful than you described."

I don't know if he's only teasing Cole but that just makes me blush and Cole growls as Jameson and Lan snicker. The boys are playing video games; well, two of them are playing video games while the other two are engaged in some juvenile caveman role play. Seth places an arm around my shoulder, which immediately has me tensing.

"So Tessa, do you have a sister?"

"No, she doesn't, and your brother is about to become an only child if you don't stop touching her."

"Calm your tits, man. You're so whipped, but I'd be too if she were mine." He winks at me and while another girl would've swooned, I can only laugh since this guy is helping me take sweet, sweet revenge from Casanova over there. I feel so empowered, it's not even funny.

"Don't encourage him." Cole glowers at Seth and almost drags me to his side of the couch.

"He's just being friendly Cole, relax."

I'm given the stink eye and he pouts like a petulant child, muttering, "A little too friendly" under his breath.

Seth is more muscular than Cole and Lan, because he's on the wrestling team. He's got light blond hair which is cropped close to his head and has the lightest blue eyes I've ever seen. He's a total flirt and the womanizer of the group, it seems. But I like him since he does everything in good humor. If anything, he seems a lot like pre-meltdown Travis. Jameson is a bit like me, in the way that he's quiet and seems a little shy almost. It doesn't seem like he talks much even on a regular basis but he seems to fit the group perfectly. His looks complement his slightly brooding personality. Tall and lean with messy dark brown hair, gray eyes, and a nose that looks like it's been broken at some point. I also catch my first glimpse of a tattoo as it peeks out from under the sleeve of his shirt. It's a foreign script, but I couldn't gawk at it as much as I would have liked to without appearing like a freak.

"We're still going to that frat party, right?" Lan asks, switching off the game. There's a unanimous grunting of yeahs and I sigh inwardly. I've read a lot about frat parties and most of them end with someone falling asleep naked in the bathtub. I hope to God it's not me.

"Sweet, I'll let my cousin know."

"I'm not exactly dressed for a party," I mutter once the rest of the boys are distracted and Cole turns to me.

"You look great. What's wrong with what you're already wearing?" He frowns. Ah, sweet, adorable, naïve boy.

"It's your job to tell me I look good but honey, I need something better than this to wear if we're going to that party."

He's still frowning. "You always look amazing but if you want to we could go shopping."

My heart melts at his sincere suggestion. He would really ditch his friends to take me shopping and that breaks through all the doubts I've been having throughout the day regarding his past. It may or may not be guilt but I shouldn't be questioning the integrity of his feelings for me, not when he's shown me so many times.

"We're going to the mall?" The two of us whip our heads around to where Seth is standing, stuffing his face with a BLT. I grin at how excited he sounds and how Cole immediately gives his caveman grunt.

"The mall? Cool, I hear the arcade got a couple of awesome new games. Hey, Jameson, we're going to the mall!" Lan calls out to him as he too emerges from the kitchen. Suddenly everyone's buzzing and making plans. I giggle at the absurdity of it all and laugh even harder at the look on Cole's face. He's so not happy about this.

But then suddenly everyone's up and getting ready to go out. We're waiting for Seth to finish taking a call when Kimmy crawls out of her lair and walks over to the door, twisting the doorknob and then shooting us all an impatient look.

"What? I thought we were going to the mall, hurry up."

***

Shopping is fun generally but shopping with four boys is downright hilarious. When I told them that I needed an outfit for the night, being the gentlemen that they were, all of them agreed to accompany me. Hard as I stressed, they wouldn't go and do their own thing. I realized shortly that they were trying to stop Kimmy from ambushing me.

"That's really pretty."

"You look great."

"Damn, girl, you look hot."

The last one is Seth, obviously. Cole just grunts.

I'm standing outside the dressing room wearing a pair of black skinny jeans and a basic red boat-neck top that's really flattering. I don't know whether I'm supposed to trust their judgment since they've said the same thing about the last three outfits I tried on. Cole's not being much help with his moody possessiveness. Seriously, how is he even upset when I have slutty Barbie probably plotting a painful death for me?

"Cole?"

He's still acting like a four-year-old throwing a temper tantrum so I get an idea. He needs to assert his "ownership" and while that is not the healthiest thing in a relationship, I can't let his immaturity ruin this day.

"Could you come here for a second?" His face softens as he sees the discomfort on my face and together we enter the dressing room. It's sectioned into two areas, a curtain separating the actual changing room and a sitting area.

He's staring at his shoes, avoiding eye contact. "I can't find something good to wear. Would you mind picking something for me?"

If he recognizes what I'm doing he doesn't show it. Instead he looks pleased. "Yeah, of course." Bending down to kiss my forehead he leaves the changing room in a much better mood.

***

Once accompanied by shopping bags containing the outfits Cole got me and insisted he pay for, we roam the rest of the mall. The boys go the arcade while I get myself some coffee. Wandering alone without the guys flanking me turns out to be a bad idea. Just as I take a seat at the café, with my drink and blueberry muffin, I'm ambushed almost instantly by Kimmy.

"So you're *still* around." She smirks at me and pulls out the chair opposite to mine.

"And you obviously still have issues understanding the concept of personal space."

It takes her about a minute to process what I just said and when it finally hits home she glowers at me.

"He may think he wants you, a little Goody Two-shoes, but *trust* me I know what he really wants. He likes them bad and wild and honey, you're *never* going to be that."

Well then, the lecherous ho seems to have a point. It's not like I have something substantial to deny that with. Cole's past sure as heck favors her but then there's everything he's told me and how I can't convince myself that he's lying.

"Do you know his middle name?"

"Huh?" She looks like we just launched into a discussion about astrophysics.

"Do you know what his favorite food is?"

"What does that . . . ?"

"Do you know the exact shade of blue that his eyes are?"

By this point she's stopped trying to make sense of what I'm trying to do and just watches me, cautiously, like I've lost my mind.

"My point, Kimmy, is that whatever you two 'share' can't be that great seeing as how you don't even know the first thing about him."

She opens her mouth, closes it and repeats. It's quite entertaining to watch. I've never been one to deliver the verbal bitch slap but today I seem to be on a roll. I have to give credit where it's due though, this girl is such an easy target.

"Whatever!" she huffs, getting up, "I don't need to hear this." Then in her signature style, she stomps away.

***

"Sorry I acted like a jealous ape."

I'm in one of the guest rooms, finishing getting dressed, when Cole walks up behind me and wraps his arms around me. He nuzzles his face into my neck causing my eyes to shut on their own and that's all it takes for my body to go haywire.

Somehow I find my voice. "You bought me shoes. In girl world, that makes everything okay," I joke and feel his laugh reverberate through his chest.

"And God, the whole Kimmy disaster. I'm so sorry about that, shortcake."

I shrug the best I can when he's holding me like this. "I'm not too worried about her. That girl's got more bleach in her head than brain cells."

"You never have to worry about her, ever. She's a mistake, but you, Tessie? You're it for me."

And despite the day we've had, despite what I've learned about him today, I believe him. Maybe a while ago I'd have brushed aside his statement, laughed it off and made a joke about it but not anymore. It's a matter of having faith, finally realizing that not everyone you care about will eventually leave you and when that's firmly ingrained in your mind, you stop being afraid and just accept.

"You're it for me too," I tell him and then we kiss.

CHAPTER TWENTY-SIX
Cole Is Stone Cold Sober. Get It? Stone Cold?

"Where's the Justin Bieber song?"

I squint at Cole through the dim lighting, trying to figure out his angle. I mean come on, he's a guy. No guy would voluntarily bring up Justin Bieber unless there was a really cruel joke somewhere in the middle of it all.

"What?"

He slings his arm across my shoulder and pulls me to him, saving me from being shoved into by yet another drunken college student.

"We're at a party and you look comfortable. I'm waiting for you to burst into a song that'll make my ears bleed any moment now."

I scoff and push away from him, nudging him with my elbow. "I'm sorry; I didn't know my singing made you so miserable. Or is it just my voice in general? Maybe I should just stop talking to you. Maybe I should just go and find Seth."

He narrows his eyes at me and then at the red Solo cup hanging loosely in my hand. He grabs it before I can stop him and throws it in the trash. I might possibly have been drinking a bit more than usual but it's just to calm my nerves, honestly.

"I'm cutting you off, Tessie, no more beer."

I cross my arms defiantly over my chest and lift my chin. "We're at a party, Cole, and we're supposed to be drinking cheap, disgusting, warm beer and having the time of our lives. Why do you want to ruin the mood?"

His eyebrows shoot up and he sighs before pinching the bridge of his nose. He exhales heavily before hooking an arm through my elbow and dragging me behind him.

"I forgot you're a mean drunk."

I pout and drag my feet on the hardwood floor, just to be annoying but he doesn't give. Instead he leads us through the throngs of dancing bodies, up the stairs. The guy Brandon hosting the party is a friend of Cole and the guys and was a couple of years ahead of them. From what little time

I'd had to get to know him, he seemed . . . nice. Okay, so he was completely stoned and asked me if I knew his great-grandma Myrtle.

"And you're a sourpuss."

He chuckles, pulling me along, down a corridor, before coming to rest in front of the last door. He digs out a key from his back pocket and unlocks the door, ushering us in. Then he locks the door again and pockets the key. Whereas I'm a little tipsy, Cole is stone-cold sober. Get it? Stone cold? You know because his last name . . . forget it.

I'm in a typical college boy bedroom. Messy with clothes strewn all over the floor and an unkempt queen-size bed. There's a study desk shoved in a corner, piled high with books and a laptop. Soft music plays from the iPod dock and the open window lets in a chilly early spring breeze.

We're shrouded in darkness until Cole switches on the light. He leans against the door and watches me as I take in my surroundings. Admittedly I'm only partially interested in that particular task. It's just something I'm doing to ignore the crazy flips my stomach's doing. I'm alone, in a locked room with my boyfriend. There's no parental supervision, no nosy brother and no restriction whatsoever.

"Sit," he says simply and I obey, taking a seat at the very edge of the bed.

He walks over to the minifridge and grabs a sealed water bottle and rummages around for food. This must be Brandon's room if he's so casually going through his stuff. He grabs an unopened bag of chips and tosses it to me.

"Drink." He hands over the water bottle and it's not until I've unscrewed the cap and am gulping down large amounts of water that I realize that I'm parched.

"Now eat."

And as I begin to munch on the salty, greasy goodness I feel the headiness go away. Immediately I feel more like myself. Of course that's never a good thing. My nerves are shot. I'm at a party, alone in a locked room with Cole. Haven't I seen this movie enough times? But then the funny thing is I'm not panicking because I don't want something to happen. I'm panicking because I know I might suck at anything second base and beyond. Maybe I suck at first base too, who knows. Well Cole knows but it's not like he's going to tell me.

"Would you relax? You look like you're ready to run the minute I let you." He crouches down on the floor in front of me and takes my chin in his hand and rubs my cheek with his calloused thumb. I wonder if he can tell that I just want to grab him by the neck and mash our mouths together, for eternity. I wonder when he'll realize that I'm not brave enough, confident enough to actually do what I want to, especially with him.

"I only brought you up here because I don't want you drinking more than you already have. The people here . . . it's just not a good idea. I don't know if I'll be able to take good care of you."

"I trust you," I whisper.

"So you weren't thinking that I locked you into this room to take advantage of you?" He gives me an amused grin but I can see that my answer matters. It's the seriousness in his eyes that he can't pretend to hide.

"You can't take advantage of the willing, Cole."

My eyes concentrate on my shoes. I cannot believe I just said that. Place me in a ring with that Kimmy and I'll take her down but put me in confined spaces with my boyfriend and I'm a mess. Does he think I'm like all those girls downstairs who have literally been throwing themselves at him since the moment he walked through the doors?

Cole notices the second my cheeks turn pink and cups my face between his palms. I'm forced to look him in the eye and what I see puts me at ease. He looks . . . he looks at me like I'm the most important thing in his world, and the look is staggering.

"Hey, don't ever be embarrassed to say what you want to me. I like it when you're honest, in fact I love it. It makes me feel like I'm the one person you trust the most."

"You are," I say hoarsely and his eyes fill with so much happiness that my heart squeezes with joy.

"I am?"

I nod, smiling at his disbelief. Time and time again, he does things or says things that show me that he cares about me. I don't put myself out there nearly as much and maybe it's because of my shyness or maybe it's because I'm always waiting for the other shoe to drop. But then again, how much more does he need to do to make me believe that he's not going to leave or break my heart?

"Hey, Cole?"

"Yeah?"

"Please kiss me."

He doesn't have to be asked twice. Staying in the same crouching position, he leans in and presses his lips to mine. It's a gentle caress at first, our lips hardly brushing against each other's. I make a noise of impatience at the back of my throat, causing him to smile against my cheek. That's when things really start moving along. He gets up, moving me right along with him until I'm on my back on the bed. Slowly he moves over me, his body hovering over mine. The proximity causes me to lose my breath. I stare at his enigmatic blue-green eyes and he looks at me with such adoration and tenderness that I almost lose my mind.

He cups the back of my neck, bringing me closer to him and kisses me again, harder this time. My arms wrap themselves around his neck as I try to push myself closer and try to erase the distance. I gasp when his tongue darts out to lick the seam of my lips and then we're a blur of tangled limbs and heated kisses. His tongue enters my mouth and I meet each thrust of his tongue with one of my own. The taste of him overwhelms me. He hasn't been drinking tonight and whereas I might taste of cheap beer, he is something else. A mixture of spearmint, and something else that's purely Cole. It's intoxicating and I'm so very drunk on it.

My hands move on their own accord, traveling down his back and then under his shirt. His muscles tense where I press my fingers against the bare skin and he growls into my mouth. His kisses turn frantic as I trace the hard ridges of his spine. He moves his lips to my jaw, peppering it with kisses until he moves on to my neck and I arch into him, greedy for more.

This feels incredible! Why don't we do this all the freaking time? Now I know why Megan and Alex have stopped hanging out with us as much as they used too. They must be busy locked up in their rooms doing this! I don't hold a grudge, seriously.

My heartbeat turns frantic when Cole slips his hand under my top. This is new, yeah this is definitely new and I love it. It's then that it dawns on me that I'm wearing an extremely easy access skirt, definitely convenient. But then all thought flies right out the window as his hand edges up my torso. Momentarily I forget how to breathe. He pauses, only to look at me, asking if it was okay and I let him know that it was even better than okay. I wanted his touch so fiercely that it scares me. I could feel every part of me coming to attention, every sensation seems to be heightened, and every touch seems to cause an array of emotions. I'm on fire and it's the most wonderful feeling ever.

I want more, more of this skin-searing touch. I tug at the hem of his shirt and he rises, sitting on his knees and reaching over his shoulder. He pulls the shirt over his head in one smooth go and throws it on the floor. I take in his naked chest, all those defined muscles, the abs . . . Oh dear God the abs.

"I forgot you had an eight-pack." I gulp, not being able to take my eyes off them.

He chuckles, nipping at my lips as he once again covers my body with his.

"They're all yours." As if knowing what I'm dying to do, he takes my hand and places it on those lickable abs. I touch them in absolute wonder as Cole sucks in a breath. My fingers move over the muscles which contract beneath my touch. His skin is smooth but taut, rippling muscles and hard edges.

I take my time exploring him as he kisses my cheeks, my forehead, my eyelids, my nose, and eventually my lips. His heated kisses travel down my neck and I can feel my eyes roll back into their sockets as he approaches my chest. He hesitates before trailing his tongue over the swells of my breasts. I gasp as he pushes my shirt down, just a bit and not all the way. He then follows the trails of his tongue, with his lips. I'm a quivering mess of emotions and feelings.

Cole buries his head in my neck and nuzzles his face into it. His breathing is as erratic as mine and I realize that my hands are still roaming over his body. I grip his shoulders, trying to catch a breath but it's a bit difficult with his warm breath fanning my face. My nerves are in hyperdrive.

"That was even better than anything I'd ever imagined."

"You . . . you thought about me?" I stutter.

When someone who looks like he does, tells you that they fantasized about you it's kind of hard to believe. He raises his face and props himself onto his elbow. Looking right at me, he gives me another knee-knocking kiss, the end of which has me in danger of cardiac arrest.

"All the damn time."

***

After a little, okay, a lot more hands-on making out we straighten our clothes and prepare to head back downstairs. The plan is to crash at Lan's for the night and then head back tomorrow evening. I check my phone just in case Travis is being his usual paranoid self and am shocked to find dozens of missed calls from Megan. There are a bunch of voicemails from numbers I don't recognize and some texts, again from Megan asking me to call her ASAP.

"Hey did you—"

My fingers are already dialing Megan's number as Cole comes to stand in front of me. From the looks of it his phone's been pretty busy too. We exchange worried looks and I assume he calls Alex. My heart's racing once again but this time for a completely different reason.

Maybe Megan's just being Megan. I don't have to automatically assume the worst. Everything's going to be okay. She's a drama queen, I know how she is. Her mom must have discovered her and Alex in a compromising position or worse, come across her Judy Blume collection. But the longer she takes to answer, the more my heart sinks. I'm going to be sick. Pick up the damn phone!

"Tessa, thank God!" My friend sounds breathless, her voice shaky. It sounds like she's been crying.

I immediately assume the worst and pray that the images flashing through my mind are nothing of consequence.

"W-what's going on?" My knees feel weak and I have to sit down on the bed before they give way. I'm struggling to breathe at this point. And then I see Cole come into view. His face is somber, serious like something's really wrong.

"It's Beth," she cries and I grip the sheets tightly, swallowing hard.

"What happened? Tell me!"

"Her mom, Tessa, her mom's dying. There was an accident." Megan begins to sniff and I realize that I'll lose her in a few seconds. She struggles to catch her breath before continuing.

My chest feels heavy; it's like someone reached inside it and is squeezing my heart. "She was driving drunk and . . . and she hit another car. They're okay . . ." She hiccups, on the verge of tears. "But Marie lost a lot of blood and . . . Oh God, please come back, Tessa."

That's when the call ends and the phone drops from my hands. Darkness blurs my vision; I see spots and my arms begin feeling numb. Blood is rushing to my head as I try to understand what I've just been told. Beth's mom is dying, Marie is dying. No matter what their relationship is like Beth loves her for who she is. My best friend is about to lose the only family she has left.

"Come on, Tessie; let's get you out of here."

I let Cole gather me in his arms and steer me downstairs, not aware of him telling his friends we're leaving. It's all a blur and then we're in the car. All I can think about is Beth; she doesn't need this. Her life's been difficult enough. She's never known her dad and now she's going to lose Marie too.

"It's going to be okay." Cole grabs my hand with his free one and squeezes it. It's meant to be a reassuring squeeze but all I can think is how I don't even feel the pressure. That's the funny thing about tragedy, right? You never expect it to hit you so when it does, you just can't process it. The longer you take to process it, the more you prolong the inevitable pain. Wouldn't it be easier to just deal with the pain and get over it? Why push it away? Why make it worse?

"She doesn't have anyone else," I say, my voice sounding strange to my own ears.

Cole glances at me from the corner of his eyes. It's a busy road, he shouldn't be distracted. I should keep quiet.

"We don't know what's happening, Tessa. Her mom might make it."

"Did Alex say that?"

He looks away and I know that he knows how bad the situation is. Knowing him, he's probably already talked to Cassandra. She must know the truth. She must've told him how bad things are.

"You have to be strong for her, Tessie, please. We have to be there for her. Stay with me baby, just stay."

I press my head into the back of the seat and squeeze my eyes shut. I'm reminded of the day I first saw Beth. She'd been the new kid, the freak no one wanted to associate themselves with. But the truth was, everyone wanted to get to know her. The girls felt insecure because she was so beautiful, without even trying, and the boys felt intimidated by her strength, despite being attracted to her. She wore her leather pants, her biker boots, and her Beatles shirt, walls up and impenetrable.

Then Megan had offered her a place to sit during lunch and I'd seen it. The vulnerability, the fear of rejection and the relief at acceptance. Of course she'd concealed the reaction immediately but I'd seen it and I knew that she was someone real. Nicole's rejection had scarred me and I had trust issues a mile long. Megan had slowly broken down my walls, not all of them but enough to make her own place. But then Beth had arrived. She saw through my bullshit and forced me to speak up. I became my old self, especially around them, and that's when I realized how important this complicated, strong girl was to me.

And now she could possibly lose her mother. I had to be strong for her. Cole's right, I couldn't lose it when she needs me the most.

"Thank you, I needed to hear that," I tell him and he gives me a small smile, reaching for my hand again.

"We're going to get through this. Together, Tessie, I'll be right with you."

And somehow that made all the difference in the world.

***

The strong smell of antiseptic hits us as we walk down the familiar hallways of Farrow Hills Hospital. With Cole's hand in mine, I square my shoulders and head toward the ICU. The drive was excruciating. We'd been in constant contact with Megan and Alex and so far things were going from bad to worse. Marie had sustained critical internal injuries, significant brain damage, and heavy blood loss. She'd slipped into a coma two hours ago and the doctors didn't know how much longer her body would be able to fight.

A small crowd has gathered around the white doors leading to the ICU and I see the familiar red hair immediately. Alex is holding Megan, who's watching the doors intently. My gaze wanders to some of Marie's friends that I've seen occasionally at Beth's house. They seem different . . . sober.

Then I see her, curled into a ball in a corner, with her knees pulled up to her chest and her arms wrapped around them. Her alabaster skin is bordering on dangerously translucent and her eyes are bloodshot. Her entire frame is shaking but not with tears. She looks paralyzed by shock.

Her head is resting on a man's chest. I wonder how I missed that. Now that I concentrate, she's curled into him like he could be the one to save her. The man lifts his cheek from on top of her hair and shock runs through me when I see a face I know as well as my own.

Travis.

His arms are wrapped protectively around her and he keeps kissing her forehead. Momentarily I'm stunned, the image of the two of them together not seeming to piece itself together.

Cole's standing stock-still next to me but I can feel his eyes watching me, awaiting my reaction. Honestly, right now I couldn't be happier for them. It sinks in now, all of a sudden, that she's the girl who made my brother work to win her heart. As horrible a time as this is, at least something good's come out from it. Travis and Beth are perfect for each other.

I wipe a tear and give Cole a reassuring smile; he exhales. I walk the short distance between my brother and my best friend and sit down next to her. Travis's eyes widen when he sees me but I give him a watery smile and mouth, "It's okay." His pale face gains some color and he gives me a small smile of his own. He mouths, "Love you" to me.

I take ahold of one of Beth's hands. Like I knew, she's bloodied her palms by digging her fingernails into them. She lifts her head slightly to see who's there and when she sees me, she breaks down all over again. I hug her close as sobs wrack her body and cry with her until she has no tears left. Megan joins us as all of us sit and wait.

CHAPTER TWENTY-SEVEN
Not All Boys Are Giant Douche-cicles

"Hey."

I look up from my phone to find a familiar head of blond hair heading in my direction. Quickly chasing away the nervousness that always now seems to surround me whenever I see him, I put a small smile on my face. He's my boyfriend's stepbrother, if nothing else.

"Hi Jay, what are you still doing here?"

He takes a seat next to me on the school steps. I'm waiting for Cole to come out since his class is taking a test. I'm a bit wary about where this could go. Whenever I try to have a conversation with Jay, things just tend to get a little dramatic. It's been a while though since anything's happened and he's kept his distance. I just hope he understands the kind of situation I'm in these days and respects that.

"Practice ran late. I saw Cole's car and thought you guys would be around too."

"Yeah, Mr. Vaughn just gave them the two-hour test." I shudder, thinking of the algebraic torture device I'd taken in my junior year. My poor Cole will need a whole lot of R & R to recuperate from the trauma he's going through right now.

"Ah, the algebra one, right? God, I can still remember how I felt after that, like my brain just got hot-wired."

I laugh, remembering that we'd taken the class together. It's nice to have a civil conversation with him, one which doesn't end in a fight.

"So how's Beth? I-I came to the funeral to pay my respects but she didn't seem like . . ."

I gulp and concentrate on the screen of my phone, twiddling my thumbs unnecessarily. It's still too soon to talk about it, too painful. Marie's been gone for just two weeks and in that period I've seen Beth break down a million times. It's heartbreaking to see my strong, determined best friend

271

crumble like this. She's not just grieving; she's also blaming herself for her mom's death. All she does is think about the what-ifs. What if she'd been home? What if she'd gotten Marie the help she needed? What if she'd hidden the booze in a better place? There's no consoling her. No amount of time spent making her understand is able to pull her from the dark place she's in. I've never felt quite so helpless in my life.

"She's . . . she's going to be fine. She will be, I mean with time."

He nods in understanding. Beth lost a parent, the only parent she had. You can't possibly guess what amount of time will make the pain go away.

"Well, I'm sure she will be. She's got you and you're the best kind of friend there is. I was an idiot but I'm sure people are smarter."

There it is, that poorly timed sentence that makes everything awkward. Why does he do this? Just when I think that I've put the Jay history exactly where it belongs—in the past—he pops up again like a jack-in-the-box. We've been doing so well lately, ignoring each other, and that's been perfect for me, and here he goes rocking my perfectly balanced boat.

"Jay . . ."

"No, hear me out, Tessa. I'm so sorry, about everything." He looks up at me with those blue eyes that do nothing for me, they're entirely the wrong color, the wrong blue.

Speaking of blue eyes, brother, if Jay doesn't put more of a space between us and doesn't stop leaning toward me like he is, we could have a problem on our hands. I scoot away but he just closes the distance again and continues talking.

"I ruined everything and it can't be fixed, I get that. We can't happen right now and I accept that but can we be friends? Like we used to? I'd really like your friendship back, Tessa."

"Look, I—"

"I know Cole's not going to be happy with this but you don't have to listen to everything he says. We can go back to being what we were before he got back."

That's it, my bullshit tolerance meter has reached its limit for today. He's about to get an earful and only because he asked for it.

"We weren't friends, Jay, not the right way, at least. You knew how I felt about you, and you still dated Nicole. If you cared about me in any way you wouldn't have done something as low as that. You stood by and watched her bully me day in and day out. But I was that stupid, huh? I always made excuses for you, always thought that you didn't know what your girlfriend was up to, but not even you could be that blind. Fact is you were too embarrassed to be seen with me when I was fat and unpopular, so why should I let you do that now? You haven't given me a single reason to trust you."

It feels good to get all of it out and I hope I've gotten the point across. The nerve of him to come up to me and imply that Cole somehow controls me was the straw that broke the camel's back. I could easily have ignored the rest of his pathetic tirade but he does not get to give his opinion about my relationship.

"And as for Cole, he and I are none of your business. I'd appreciate it if you would keep your deluded opinions to yourself."

I stand up with a huff, yanking my backpack from the ground in an attempt to run away from him but he's got ahold of my wrist faster than you could possibly imagine. He looks remorseful and apologetic.

"That came out all wrong, I'm sorry. I keep making a mess of this." He exhales and inches closer to me.

"I just . . . I wish things were different. I wish I hadn't pushed you away and that we could have our shot but I now see that it's not going to happen. It makes me so mad that I threw away what we could've had for someone like Nicole. Please just give me some time? I could be your friend, Tessa, and I swear I'll do a better job this time."

I just stare at him at a total loss for words. I never thought I'd see the day Jay Stone begged me for friendship and declared his feelings all in one go. Of course I dreamt of it, like that naïve weakling I was, but that's all in the past. Now I harbor no such wishes or dreams. It's kind of ironic.

"I'm . . . I can't think about this now. There's too much going on and right now I just need to be there for Beth. I can't do this, not right now. I'm sorry."

He lets go of my hand and steps back, shoving both his hands into his pockets.

"I understand, I'll wait. It's what I deserve, right?"

"You don't have to—"

"But I will." He gives me a small smile and walks away. I slump down to the ground feeling a bit dizzy. That interaction was definitely not what I'd anticipated for my day when I got up in the morning. It's a bittersweet moment; I'm happy that I'm strong enough to stand up for myself but it also seems like the end of an era. The melancholy doesn't last for long since as soon as Jay gets out of sight I'm surrounded by a smell that's so mouthwateringly delicious that it can only belong to one person.

"I think we have something to talk about." I squeeze my eyes shut at the sound of his voice, confirming what I already know. He must have seen and heard at least some part of my conversation with Jay. I'm being silly by

273

fearing his reaction. It's not like I nose-dived into Jay's waiting arms and then mauled him with my mouth. We had a purely platonic mature conversation that ended in a way I least expected.

"Open your eyes, Tessa."

Tessa? Uh-oh, the dreaded full name. Curse you to the depths of burning hell, Jason Stone!

"I can't." My voice is squeaky; I'm in complete panic mode right now.

"I'm not going to ask you again, open your eyes."

I shake my head. I'll do anything at all to avoid this conversation. If it means never seeing anything again then that's all right.

"Fine; you asked for it."

In a heartbeat I'm upright and in the next I'm flung over his shoulder and my world turns topsy-turvy. What makes it worse is that my eyes are still sealed shut and the dizziness plus the sensation of blood rushing to my head becomes stronger. If I don't open them now I'll puke all over Cole and give him enough ammunition to torment me till I'm old and gray.

"Fine! They're open, my eyes are open. Put me down." I half scream, half beg, and he purposely skips down the steps so that the movement jostles me even more. I can feel my lunch making a reappearance and all I can think about is how I'll never be able to eat a tuna sandwich ever again.

"Nope, I asked nicely and you didn't listen so now we're going to do this."

He hops off one step and then the other and again on the next one. My head's spinning. I'm not one for motion sickness but this is just horrible. I know he's annoyed about the whole Jay situation, he's made it pretty obvious in the past that he doesn't like it when Jay's around me but he has to know that I was practically ambushed today.

"If you don't put me down right now I'll puke all over your backside!" It's not a threat really; it's kind of a prediction which has a great chance of becoming true. If he values his designer-jean-clad derriere then he'll put me down.

"Fine," he grumbles as I'm put down on the beloved ground and it takes a while for my head to stop spinning. Once I'm sure I'm not going to face-plant into the ground I punch Cole in the stomach.

"That was mean." I glare at him and he rolls his eyes.

"You try walking in and seeing your girlfriend and brother all over each other. I'm going easy on you, woman."

"What!?" I shriek and punch him again. "All over each other? Are you out of your mind? We were not all over each other."

"I saw what I saw. I thought I told you to stay away from him." He's flailing his arms about, his face reddens and his hair's becoming more and more disheveled by the second. I don't know whether to slap him or kiss the life out of him. Then Jay's words come back to my mind and creep over every crevice like a poisonous vine. He assumed that Cole controls me, my actions, and my thoughts. While it may not be true, I do tend to mostly do what he says because he's right—almost always. But that doesn't mean he gets to dictate who I do or do not talk to. Granted, every conversation with Jay turns out to be a complete disaster, but this is unacceptable.

"Oh you told me? You told me? I'm sorry I disobeyed you, master. How ever will I earn your forgiveness?"

My emotions are all over the place so I don't try to rein in the smart-ass comments; if he wants to pick a fight for no good reason then he shouldn't expect me to be the rational one.

"Okay now you're just being difficult. Damn it." He kicks a rock, which goes flying away with so much force that I'm just now able to gauge that Cole's mad. He's hurt and he's angry. But I didn't do anything wrong and don't deserve to be treated like this. After all he's the one who's taught me that others will only respect me if I respect myself.

"I'm tired and you need to cool down. Just take me home."

He thinks about my request for a while before nodding and walking off toward his car, leaving me to follow behind in silence. He still opens the door for me and waits till I've secured my seatbelt but that's that. The rest of the car ride is filled with a tension that we've hardly encountered during the length of our relationship. It's strained and full of barely repressed fury. I'm so mad at him. How could he assume that I'd even think about Jay like that? It's like he's slapping my old self back into my face, reminding me of how pathetic I used to be.

When he stops outside my house, I grab my stuff and get the heck out. Slamming the door behind me I run to the house, resisting the natural urge to look over my shoulder. He doesn't give me the opportunity though, peeling away before I'm in the door.

The door slamming continues and like a little child having a tantrum, I throw my backpack on the floor and kick our futon several times. Curses leave my mouth as I continue to fume and it's only when I've expelled some of my anger that I notice the fact that I've got an audience.

"You done?" Travis asks through a mouthful of Lucky Charms. I scrunch my nose in disgust at my brother, who's simply smirking at me. He's just had a full-on view of my freak-out, which means he'll be asking questions. Brilliant, on top of everything now I'm going to have to stop my brother from killing my boyfriend.

"Not quite." I kick the futon one more time before collapsing down on it.

"Relationship troubles?"

I wave it off. I'm back at my house, which means all my attention is now on one thing alone and that's Beth.

"How is she?"

Travis finishes off his snack and after rinsing the bowl places it in the dishwasher. He then comes over to me and sits down next to me. Sighing, his places his arms on his knees and holds his head between his hands.

"The same. I got her to eat a bit but that's it. She hasn't really eaten in days and she's starting to lose a lot of weight. Nothing I say seems to get through to her."

"What do we do? She can't go on like this. You know her doctor recommended therapy but she refuses to go. I'm just . . . I don't know how to help her."

We sit in silence, both pondering how best to help the person we both care about. Beth's been staying with us ever since she came home from the hospital ten days ago. When we got the news from the doctor that Marie's body had given up and saw how a big part Beth just . . . died along with her mom we knew we couldn't let her go back to her house. Surprisingly, my dad stepped in and actually acted like a responsible adult for once. He sympathized with Beth and ordered us to bring her home. I know that even now he's been devoting a lot of his time getting in touch with Marie's lawyers and figuring out how to take care of all the legal issues following her death. He planned the funeral so that Beth had a minimal role in all of it—which she preferred. He left for some business only yesterday, after making sure we were all in a good place.

I'm still having a hard time understanding what Travis and Beth's relationship is. I haven't pressed for details, given the situation, but my curiosity is getting the better of me. They knew each other before, that much is obvious, but I wasn't the one who introduced them. When Beth and I became friends, Travis was in a bad place and when he got better, Beth rarely had time to come over and hang out. Of course she'd seen my brother in photos around the house but they were from the time we were kids and Travis looks a lot different now.

But when I see them together, it's obvious that there's a connection there. Sometimes it looks like he's the only person holding her together and I've never seen Beth like that around a boy. She doesn't date much, always claiming that she's so busy being a mother to her own mom that adding a boy to the mix doesn't make sense.

But I know from experience that my brother's different. He's a nurturer, he likes taking care of the people he loves. Yes he's been through a rough patch in his life but that doesn't mean that he's always been like that. When he's sober, Travis is one of the most caring and loving people out there.

"Do you want me to push the therapy thing? I could try," he asks but I shake my head. She needs some time, it's too soon and that's why she's not ready. Yeah she should probably get some professional help but not until she's ready to ask for it.

"I'll go and check up on her. Get some sleep, Trav, you look really tired."

He does. There's two-day-old stubble on his face and there are hollows between his eyes. He's two seconds away from dropping dead and I feel guilty. Between school, homework, and Cole I've been leaving him with Beth for way too long. I try telling him that I can watch over Beth for some time so that I can let him get some sleep but I doubt he'll go to bed voluntarily. "I'm fine," he says, but even as he says that a yawn escapes him.

I push at his shoulder. "Go to bed. I'll take good care of her, I promise."

He winces. "I know you will, Tess. She's your best friend first and my . . . whatever she is later. You can't be comfortable with this situation, can you?"

I shrug and pretend to think about my answer for a while, just to mess with him. He's watching me attentively, like my answer has a kind of life-or-death importance. It's sweet that he cares so much. Not all boys are giant douche-cicles.

Then I nudge him with my elbow and grin at him; he sags on the back of the futon in relief. "I'm really glad she has you. Whatever kind of relationship you guys have, I'm happy that you're in each other's lives. You'll be good for her and when she's back to who she is she'll be really good for you. Now go sleep before I have to sedate you."

Smiling, he gets up. Leaning over me he ruffles my hair and kisses the top of my head. Walking backward toward the stairs he says, "I'm here for you too, you know, so if you want to talk about whatever Stone's done to get you all riled up my door's always open."

"Yes, Yoda brother, I will seek you out when I need to."

"You think Yoda stops teaching just because his student does not want to hear?" my goofball brother says in his infamous *Star Wars* imitation. I chuck a cushion at him and he ducks, chuckling all the way to his room.

Then I go up to check up on Beth, who's staying in the guest bedroom. All her stuff is still in boxes and Megan and I have only unpacked the essentials. She doesn't move from her position on the bed except to use the bathroom or to eat the little she does. She's lying like she always does, on her side facing the window and staring out into the distance, her face expressionless. Her body's curled with her legs tucked in toward her chin and her head's resting on her folded hands. She looks like a fragile, lost child and it breaks me.

"Hey," I say softly and she acknowledges my presence with a glance in my direction and then goes back to staring out the window.

She doesn't talk much or at all. All we can do is tiptoe around her, waiting for the moment when she's ready to deal with what happened. Right now she's coping by shutting everything and everyone out. It's how she's protecting herself but damn it, it hurts to see her like this.

I lean against the door and rack my mind for something trivial to talk about. I should tell her what an asshat my boyfriend is but I don't think she'd appreciate my whining right now.

"Mr. Vaughn brought that horrible algebra test back, you know the one we took last year? Do you remember how bad it was and how we wanted to stuff Megan in the trunk of her car because she couldn't stop crying over how she got one question wrong?"

No response, nothing.

"And the cafeteria lady's been trying to sell us that casserole again, the one in which someone found a fake tooth? I've never been more grateful for vending machines in my life." I persevere, not letting her silence get to me.

"Oh and I almost forgot, Megan spilled OJ all over one of Nicole's ex-minions. It was hilarious, the girl was all over Alex and Megan got all up in her face and dumped the entire cup over her head."

When I'm met with more silence, I give up since it hurts too much to stand here knowing I can't do anything to lessen her pain. She's always been there for me, always been so strong and it's shameful that I can't be there for her when she needs me the most. I place the plate of food in my hand on the nightstand, hoping she'll nibble on something and then leave, closing the door quietly behind me.

***

After ending a call with Megan and telling her all about the progress with Beth for the day, I pick up my Kindle and hope that a good book will give me some peace. Cole hasn't called or texted me, nor have I reached out to him. He's the one who should be apologizing, not me. His verbal attack was completely uncalled for and there's no way I'm breaking down and calling him until he says he's sorry and that he was wrong. But God, I miss him. I miss hearing his voice right before I go to bed. I miss the stupid things he says to make me laugh. I miss talking to him about Beth and hearing him tell me that everything's going to be okay. Then just as I am a second away from grabbing my phone and calling him, it buzzes, letting me know that I have a text. I reach for it, my heart thudding violently, but then the disappointment is just as crushing. It's completely the wrong person that's texting me. I don't want him to text me!

Jay: Cole's in a mood. You guys have a fight?

Yes, you ignorant idiot, we had a fight. It was about you, now go hide before I stab you where it'll really hurt. I toss my phone aside, not bothering with a reply.

Trying to lose myself in a cheery, lighthearted romance is difficult given my current situation so I switch over to a sci-fi where everyone dies. Yup, that's much better. Doom, death, and despair is much more my cup of tea at the moment. My eyes are drooping and the Kindle begins slipping from my hands when there's a knock on my door. My first thought is Beth and that she better be okay. Praying silently, I rush to the door throwing it open but it's not Beth.

"What are you doing here?"

He looks bewildered for a moment or two before his eyes dart toward my braless chest clad in—ironically enough—one of his T-shirts. Of course he'd come when I was in my pajamas and completely vulnerable to his gaze. I cross my arms in front of my chest and wish my short shorts would automatically elongate themselves.

"I want my shirt back," he says defiantly but then I notice how he's swaying on his feet. I step closer and the stench of alcohol becomes stronger. Fantastic.

"You're drunk," I state and he does a comical mixture of both nodding and shaking his head.
"Shirt," he says again. The swaying becomes worse and I realize that I need him to lie down before he injures himself.

"I'm not taking my shirt off, Cole, now come in."

I support his huge body the best I can into my room and toward my bed. He's mumbling incoherently under his breath all the while but doesn't struggle against my hold. Finally, after the kind of workout that should make up for a month at the gym, I push him so that he plops down on my bed.

Placing my hands on my waist, I give him my most disapproving look. It's hard though, especially when he's looking this vulnerable and lost.

"How much did you drink?"

He squeezes his thumb and index finger together leaving about an inch of space between them but then reconsiders his answer. He spreads his arms apart, looking pretty pleased with himself. "This much."

Holy Batman. Did he just raid Charlie Sheen's liquor cabinet?

I begin pulling off his shoes and pull the covers over him. There's no way he's going home tonight.

"Why?" I ask as he begins humming the national anthem.

"Because you like him better. You'll always like him better," he states like it's the most obvious thing, halting my movements.

My heart breaks on the spot. Is he still worried that I could have a thing for Jay? I think about all the time we've spent together and wonder if I've not shown him enough what I feel for him. The feelings I have for him trample all over the ones I have for Jay. They're nothing alike in any way whatsoever. But he's still conscious of it and that makes me feel inexcusably guilty. This boy has changed my life and I'm too much of a coward to tell him that I love him. That I'm in love with him.

"You're wrong," I whisper softly but he's already passed out by this point.

I sigh and crawl into bed next to him, draping myself all over his chest and swinging my legs over both of his. My arms go around him, holding him closer, and I breathe the scent of his shirt. It's only slightly marred by vodka but it's still him.

Tomorrow, I clear all his misconceptions.

CHAPTER TWENTY-EIGHT
You're as Lickable as Your Ice Cream Namesake

He's gone.

I know this even before I open my eyes and face what has suddenly become a horrible day. We all have the basic senses, right? Sight, smell, taste, touch, and hearing. While these five things continue to fail me on a daily basis, I've developed a new sense that has yet to disappoint. It's the Cole sensor.

When he's nearby there's a hum of electricity in the air. My nerves are on high alert and whether or not I choose to acknowledge it, a part of me knows that he's there. Every single bit that I consist of is attuned to his presence. The Cole sensor is as freaky as it is a godsend. It gives you the kind of thrill you get when the roller coaster suddenly dips, the feeling that can only truly be matched by free fall. And right now, I'm horribly attached to solid ground.

I pat the space next to me, refusing to acknowledge something I already know. He left. He came brokenhearted and trashed out of his mind yesterday and slept with me in his arms and now he's gone. I roll over onto my back and stare at the ceiling, blinking back tears. It's not hard to convince myself that I'm just being melodramatic. It's not like we had this major relationship-breaking argument, it was just a minor misunderstanding which needs to be cleared immediately.

The thought forces me out of bed, thus preventing me from moping around all day, eating my weight in ice cream. Old Tessa would have no problem doing that since it was the norm for her. But I'm so sick of being the helpless little girl who always needs to be rescued. How many times has Cole put himself out there for me? How many times has he braved his fears and been honest? So yes, it's the least I could do for him.

A sort of determination leads me through the process of getting ready. I blaze through getting ready, hoping that my eyes aren't still red rimmed. Before leaving, I check on Beth. She's asleep but what's surprising is the fact that Travis is in the bed with her. He's been sleeping in his own room because Beth wouldn't let any one of us stay with her but that seems to have changed now. I smile as I watch them. Both are on their sides, facing each other. Their hands are joined, between their two bodies, and it's like they fell asleep just talking and holding hands. I suddenly miss Cole so much that it's staggering.

Not even bothering with breakfast, I fly down the stairs and rush outside my house. The five-minute walk seems like eternity but I finally make it. Huffing and completely out of breath since I ran all the while, I ring the doorbell. I have just enough time to stop looking like a panting dog before the door opens. I try to hide the disappointment when I see Cassandra. It's okay, I tell myself. Cole must be asleep or trying to get rid of the hangover from hell right now. He won't be waiting for me, dying to open the door when I show up.

"Hey, honey. Come on in." Cassandra smiles at me kindly and lets me in. Taking me by surprise, she engulfs me in a warm hug and I hug her back. She's been such a rock for me lately. Not just me, in fact. She's helped Beth in whatever way she could. The hospital is such a blur to all of us but I remember her taking care of Beth and allowing her to deal with her grief while understanding that she couldn't have done anything to help Marie.

So it's good to be here with her, letting her comfort me. I think about my own mom, who's reportedly shacking up with a guy Travis's age. It hurts, of course it does. I've seen her gradually become someone I could never respect. She went from being a great mom to a good, partially there listener to a stranger. I have Travis now, family-wise that's all I could ask for. Dad's changing or trying to change. He's been more attentive, more caring, but that still can't make up for the years of neglect or how his job destroyed our family.

We sit down on the living room couch and my eyes wander around the room of their own accord. The Cole sensor isn't blaring out and I know even before she tells me that he's not around. My heart sinks, stomach turns, eyes water.

"I take it you two had a fight?"

She clasps my hands in hers but I can't meet her gaze. I feel gutted, like things are spiraling out of control and I don't have a way to stop them from doing so.

"Not a fight . . . he just misunderstood something that happened and he didn't give me a chance to explain."

She sighs. "I would have stopped him if I knew he was running away from his problems again. I'm sorry, Tessa, but he left an hour ago with an overnight bag. All I got was a note on the fridge. If it makes you feel better he said he would be back tomorrow."

No, it doesn't make me feel better. Cole has a full twenty-four hours for him to convince himself that I'm in love with Jason—the source of all my problems—Stone. If it weren't for the love and respect I have for the woman sitting next to me I'd take a cleaver to her son's head.

In a sort of a daze I walk out of the Stones' house, all my earlier determination having dissipated. The world around us has always caused problems but Cole and I have always been okay with each other. That's what makes being with him so perfect. He's always there for me, always. To know that he's hurt because of me and that he's mad at me crushes me in the worst kind of way. A guy like him comes only once in a lifetime, I know that. I've seen more than my share of dysfunctional relationships. I've seen men cheat, get drunk, and even abuse their partners. High school kind of makes you immune to the idea of love and commitment, but Cole changed that.

And now he's gone.

I pick up my phone and despite the small voice inside my head asking me to give him some space, I text Cole. I text him the one phrase that I know will get his attention. We have it for emergencies and this qualifies as an emergency. I'm losing my mind here. For all I know he could've run into the waiting arms of Kimmy or Nicole or the other multitude of women just dying to sink their claws into him.

I need you.

I press Send without a second thought. The phone weighs a ton in my hands as I stare at the stupidly unchanging screen. He might not even have his phone on him. The battery could be dead, he could have dropped it, or there might be no reception in Kimmy's evil lair. And then the most wonderful feeling in the world, my phone buzzes! I can hardly control the relief that courses through me. I can see the words, I don't care if there are only three of them but they make my heart soar. It may be slightly pathetic of me but at least he cares.

Are you okay?

No.

What's wrong?

Before I can formulate a reply, one which states that he's breaking my heart in a less self-pitiful way, my phone starts ringing. The ringtone I've recently set for Cole, 'The Only Exception" by Paramore, blares out as my shaking finger slides over the screen so that I can answer. We both speak at the same time.

"What's going on?"

"Where are you?"

I repeat my question, "Where are you?"

"Tessie, just tell me, please. Are you okay? Are you hurt?"

"Yes and yes to the last question," I mumble and I hear him draw a heavy breath on the other side. I could just imagine him running his hands through his hair, tugging at it painfully.

"Don't do this to me. What do you mean yes? Please tell me what's going on," he begs and for a second I feel cruel. He left me. He just up and left after last night, making me go through hell. I want to make him feel the worst. I want him to suffer but then again I'm so in love with him that the idea of hurting him is preposterous.

"You left. You didn't even talk to me or let me explain. You just left." I emphasize the last three words and hope he gets the importance of them. He knows I still struggle with my abandonment issues. If he still just up and left despite knowing that about me then he should feel guilty. I can't possibly handle another person in my life deserting me because I wasn't enough.

"Please, shortcake, don't be angry . . . I just needed some space."

"Space?" I nearly screech and it sounds hideous even to my own ears but now I'm just angry. The concept of "space" has been invented to get men to leave their relationships and do as they please. It's just as bad as wanting a "break." You're basically in the same confused state, not knowing whether you are or are not in a relationship. The women sit at home by the phone, weeping and eating copious amounts of chocolate while the men sow their wild oats; they show these things on TV all the time.

"You needed space so you run? Did you not for a second think how much that would hurt me? I've been going out of my mind here. If you wanted to leave me you could've just said so."

My breathing's hard and I'm fighting back sobs. I hate him, I love him but I hate him so much right now.

"I'm sorry, I'm so sorry. I didn't realize what I'd done until I was too far away. I'm a dickhead, baby, but I'd never leave you."

"Guess what? You already did. You couldn't trust me enough to stay. You never gave me an opportunity to explain and that's unfair, Cole."

I hear the sound of traffic in the background so he must be talking while driving. It's dangerous, especially for someone who's hungover. We can't have this conversation over the phone and I don't want him to get hurt.

"I was wrong; I shouldn't have left like that. Just listen to me, Tessie, I . . ."

"You should focus on the road. We'll talk later."

"No, you're not hanging up on me. We have to talk about this. I'm sorry, okay, I'm so damn sorry."

"Bye Cole, drive safe."

I end the call and toss the phone aside. It rings and rings again but I let it go to voice mail. So the driving thing is partly why I don't want to talk to him. What he said about space hit a nerve. I'd been told that before. When my best friend decided I wasn't good enough to hang out with anymore, she told me she needed space and look how well that turned out.

Pushing back thoughts of doom and despair, I busy myself with schoolwork. Before I know it I've finished three days' worth of homework. It's surprising how much you can get done when you have so much on your mind that you can't bear to lose focus on something mundane. It's no surprise that by the time Travis knocks on my door to let me know about dinner I've basically completed all the college applications I'd pushed to the side.

College, yet another problem.

***

"How is she?" I ask my brother as we eat Chinese takeout.

"The same except she said she wanted to go back to work again."

There's silence and I know neither of us is happy about that prospect. She's not ready to go to the five odd jobs she's always got lined up. Cassandra insists that Beth try therapy and that only then will she be able to move forward. I agree; she carries too much guilt to function properly. I know her and when things get too much she'll self-destruct. She'll shut us all out and recede into the dark crevices of her own mind.

"How do we get her to go to therapy then? She needs to talk about . . . everything to someone who knows the right thing to say."

Dropping his elbows on the table, Travis hangs his head low between his hands. I know he's worried just like I am and that it's killing him to not be able to do something to help her. He's a problem-solver and it's in his nature to be protective and a constant source of comfort.

"I had an idea but I don't know if she's gonna go for it. I thought about seeing someone about the drinking, you know . . . how sometimes I still get the urge. Maybe if I go or suggest group therapy or something she'll agree."

"I didn't know that you were . . ."

"It's not serious, I promise, baby girl. But sometimes things get too much, you know? I'll never do that to you again, I swear."

I beam at him but on the inside there's a clawing at my chest. He still feels the compulsion to relapse? How have I been so blind that I couldn't see him struggling? I feel like the worst sister on the planet. My selfishness lately has been insurmountable; all I think about is me or Cole or both of us.

"Well I think it's a brilliant idea. If you're there with her, she'll definitely think about going. Talk to her, she needs to do this."

He nods his head and when he asks me about Cole, I tell him we're okay.

***

"Hey."

It's him. The Cole sensor is going haywire and so is my heart. I stand by my bedroom window, turning my back to him. He sounds breathless, like he ran all the way here. That somehow lifts my spirits a little.

"Tessie, talk to me, please."

I hear his footsteps closing in on me. Before I know it he's wrapped both arms around my waist and pulled me to his chest. His head's buried in the crook of my neck. A shudder passes through my body as I feel him kissing the spot above my collarbone. God, he makes me so weak.

"You left." My voice trembles.

"I'm sorry," comes his muffled voice.

"Stop saying that. Stop apologizing and tell me the real reason why you couldn't stand being with me."

His arms become ironclad restraints. I don't struggle because it's not like I ever want to move. I just want him to explain what I'm trying so hard to understand.

"I was drunk last night. Seeing you with Jay messed with my head. It made me feel like that stupid kid again, the one you never looked at with anything but hate. Every bad memory I'd repressed came back. I thought I'd lose you again. I was scared, baby. I thought when you woke up you'd tell me you didn't want me anymore."

His entire body is shaking and so is mine. The emotions are too overwhelming and all-consuming. He's never been this vulnerable before. I'm so used to him taking away my insecurities that I've never thought about his. Seeing him like this, hearing these words come from him rips me into two. He's with me so selflessly and wholeheartedly that I feel shameful about being afraid of my feelings for him.

I take a deep breath; I have to do this now. Fears be damned.

Turning around in his arms, I take in his haunted face, his messed-up hair, and eyes that seem more glossy than usual. Every pore of me aches for him. How have I not yelled this from the rooftops before when it's so damn obvious?

I lean forward and press my lips to his, putting all my feelings into the kiss. I kiss him slowly, savoring the feel of his lips against mine. He immediately responds, his arms tightening and pressing me further into him, thus eliminating every inch of space. I feel him smile against my lips. Well, buddy, the smile's about to get a whole lot bigger.

I pull away and push up on my tiptoes, cupping his face between my hands. He stares at me and the look in his eyes is so tender that it takes every ounce of willpower for me to not kiss him again. Here goes nothing.

"I love you."

Silence, that's what follows. If you try hard enough, you could even hear how furiously our hearts are beating right now. Mine threatens to crash right out and land between our feet in a bloody mess.

Suddenly I'm mortified, what if I've made it totally awkward? What if he doesn't reciprocate my feelings or maybe just isn't ready for a confession like this? I've ruined everything. I can't cry, I won't cry, at least not now.

But then the most glorious thing in the world happens and I feel my tattered heart start to piece itself together.

Cole smiles! Well, *smile* would be putting it mildly. His lips stretch into a grin so wide that I'm actually scared for his poor face. His eyes gleam, his face regains color and then at last he mashes his lips against mine. I feel the grin throughout the kiss. The kiss itself? Well, it's damn near maddening. His tongue seeks entrance and I allow him more than willingly. We're greedy for each other, hands running all over each other's bodies. Tongues are tangled, lips nip and bite and taste. It's a whole new feeling, a new thrill now that I've said what's always been missing.

When we finally pull away to catch our breaths, Cole rests his forehead against mine and gives me a soft kiss.

"I love you, so much, Tessie. God, you have no idea how much I love you."

My breath hitches and tears sting my eyes. It is the absolute worst time to cry but I can't help it. He'd shown me through the kiss that he felt the same but the words mean oh so much. I'd always dreamt of a love like this but never thought I'd actually find someone like him.

I launch myself at him, jumping up and wrapping my legs around him. I hug him to me tightly, my head resting against his neck and drinking him in. He holds me up firmly and repeatedly kisses the side of my head.

"Say it again," I breathe.

"I love you and I always have, Tessie. The second I saw that little girl with her green eyes and pigtails, I knew I'd never be the same."

I sniffle and he pulls me to him tighter. My arms are around his neck, my face still hidden and I'd like to keep it that way. It's embarrassing that I'm crying but how could you not? How can you hold in all that emotion when you have a guy like Cole baring his soul to you?

"God, you're perfect. Are you sure you're real?" I joke, half laughing, half crying.

He nips lightly at my neck with his teeth and I jolt while he chuckles. "Real enough for you?"

I smack his back but then sigh, leaning into him again. "Where did you go?"

He walks backward until he sits at the edge of my bed and swings me sideways so that I'm draped all over his lap, my head on his chest. I free my hands and trace patterns over his shirt. He shudders visibly under my touch and I feel a sense of satisfaction. He loves me!

"I went to see someone who'd knock some sense into my head."

He kisses the top of my head again.

"Who?"

"Nana Stone."

I laugh as I think of all the scenarios I'd pictured and how I tortured myself the entire day. But hey, on the flip side, I can probably scratch my plans for a double homicide now.

"What did she say to you?"

"She said some things I'd already figured out by the time I got there. Mostly about how I was a bumbling idiot who was letting the best thing that had ever happened to him slip out of his hands. Though it was much more effective when she said it."

"I bet it was."

"Hey, Cole?"

"Yeah?"

I look up at him and just like him, I can't stop kissing him. I lean in for a deep kiss and when we break for air I tell him again. "I love you."

"I love you too," he says with a wide grin and shining eyes. It's the happiest I've ever seen him and it makes me giddy to know that I'm responsible for it.

***

"Hey, did someone ever tell you, you sound like an ice cream?"

"What?" His chest vibrates beneath me as he laughs but I look at him seriously.

"That's a huge reason why I'm with you, Stone, don't laugh."

He pretends to be serious for a while before bursting out laughing. "How do you even come up with this stuff?"

"But it's true. I'm telling you that's what brings in all your fangirls."

"Fangirls, huh? You sure they're not there because of my amazing looks and irresistible charm?"

"Nope, it's definitely because of the ice cream factor."

"Now I just feel objectified." He pouts and I kiss it away.

"Don't worry, though. You're as lickable as your ice cream namesake."

It's close to midnight and we're lying in my bed. Well, Cole's lying on my bed, I'm lying on top of him, draped over his body. We've been like this for the last two hours or so, occasionally getting up for rigorous rounds of kissing. Now that we've exchanged the L-word it's even more difficult to keep our hands off each other. The feeling of being in love is exquisite. The high you get is just . . . beyond the power of words. To know that there's someone out there who loves you so unconditionally and irrevocably makes everything feel . . . perfect.

"About what happened yesterday," he starts before swallowing heavily. I wait for him to finish because I know it's important to him.

"I don't know why I did what I did or said what I said. Seeing you two together, I just couldn't handle it. I know it's stupid of me to expect that you'll never see or talk to Jay again but I guess I wasn't prepared. You said to stop apologizing but I have to. Showing up at your house, drunk like that . . . I could've hurt you. I'll never forgive myself for that."

When he's done, I hold him closer and take his hand in both of mine.

"I understand. I get the insecurity because I spent the entire day planning different ways to kill the girl you were with." He laughs at this point and I continue, "But you have to talk to me when you feel this way. You have to let me tell you that Jay means nothing to me, not anymore. If it makes you feel better, I also actually felt the urge to behead him today."

The laugh this time is loud and booming, reverberating around my room. It's the best sound ever.

"Wow, you were feeling really sadistic today, weren't you?"

"It's all your fault. I keep hanging out with you and I'll end up turning into the town serial killer."

"But you still love me," he says sounding reassured and confident.

I sigh dramatically. "Sadly, yes. The heart wants what the heart wants."

"And you want me?" There's a hint of nervousness in his voice that the teasing tone can't hide.

"Always."

"That's my girl."

CHAPTER TWENTY-NINE
I'm Thinking about Jumping Your Bones

It's definitely unsettling how your entire life can change when you least expect it. I started out my senior year praying for some reprieve from the continuous cycle of torment and hurt. I'd hoped that I would go unnoticed, hidden until I could get the freedom I so badly craved. I'd come to accept that the only guy whom I could ever love would never love me back. There was also the fact that my best friend had turned into a person I could never be able to connect with again. My family was a mess; my brother had lost his way; hence the year would in no better words—Suck.

Funny how things change, right?

I walk languidly down the hallways of my high school, trying to push back the nostalgia that creeps through me. Let's face it; this place hasn't exactly been a haven of joy and happiness for me. In fact the years I've spent here have been downright the worst in my life. My freshman, sophomore, and junior years were as painful as pulling off a fingernail. With the exception of meeting my best friends, those years had sucked me into a vortex of what I considered inescapable gloom.

But then everything changed. A smile creeps up on me as the corner of my mouth lifts up as a surge reminiscent of happiness courses through me. In the last few months, in these very halls my life changed forever. I found someone who made me love myself, who made me realize that I could choose happiness and who finally broke through the vortex. My superhero.

These are the thoughts I mentally play in my head as I walk toward a very familiar sight. Nicole is leaning against her locker, tapping her high-heel-clad foot restlessly on the ground. She glances at her watch and then looks around. When her gaze lands on me she straightens up and gives me a nod of acknowledgement before starting to walk.

I tug the strap of my backpack higher up my shoulder and hug my notebook to my chest. Following her out to the football field, I try not to bring my personal issues with Nicole to this interview. When I volunteered to be on the yearbook committee, I knew that at some point I'd have a run-in with her. Of course I hoped it would never happen but it's me and despite my personal lucky charm called Cole, things like this do tend to happen. I'm supposed to be interviewing all the captains and co-captains of the various clubs and sports teams the school has. So far it's been good, except for the highly awkward ten-minute disaster that happened with Jay. The man has grabby hands, let me tell you.

Nicole takes a seat high up on the bleachers and I follow. We're both wrapped up in layers upon layers of clothing and although her choice of venue is problematic, I guess that she needs to find a place that she's comfortable while answering my questions. I've prepared a list of questions and hopefully this won't take long. Each person barely gets half a page so it's not like I'm writing an exposé on the seedy underbelly of science clubs in high schools.

She sits down and brushes off imaginary lint from her coat. In recent years, Nicole has become very "refined." She's always impeccably dressed, never a hair out of place even during dance rehearsals. The woman it seems is incapable of sweating or looking ugly, for that matter. She's even got a tanned glow to her face in the middle of winter and her dark hair is generously streaked with gold toward the ends. The well-fitted cream sweater she's wearing sets off her complexion magnificently. I might hate her but the fact is that she's stunning. So far neither of us have brought up our obviously strained relationship. This is extremely awkward but for the sake of journalism I'll simply have to persevere.

"Okay, so this won't take a lot of time." I get out the recorder and my notepad that has my questions and where I can scribble additional notes.

Nicole stares blankly into the distance as I ask the questions. She appears to be completely disinterested, narrating rote answers and inspecting her fingernails as she does so. My blood begins to boil and I have to remind myself to keep a lid on it. I can't toss her down the bleachers; the dance team would not appreciate that. Maybe if I stare viciously at her profile some more, she'll evaporate into thin air.

For the most part Nicole's left me alone. After her huge social downfall and break up with Jay, she's been off the radar. Her minions have scattered, only a few daring to be around the new outcast. I should feel sorry for her, having been in the same place as her, but when she acts like this it's hard to empathize. Even now, she's so . . . ice cold, unreachable, and locked up in her own mind. If I could be bothered with it, I would ask her what the hell happened to turn her into this person. But through the years I've realized that no length of an olive branch would be able to repair what we've lost.

Once I've gathered enough material to please the editor, I start packing my things. Nicole doesn't even blink in my direction and I'm more than happy to get away from her. Cole is waiting for me in the parking lot and the sooner I get to him, the better. If it's one thing that I've learned this year it is to recognize and treasure the people who love you for who you are. Changing yourself to fit into someone else's life is never a good idea. People should love you for who you are, not who they want you to be.

I'm finished packing up and about to leave when she addresses me. I stop midstep and wait for her to continue.

"Look," she exhales heavily and begins examining her fingernails, "We're all graduating this year and I'm getting out of this hick town as fast as I can."

Understandable. Nicole's always been fascinated with New York City. That combined with an early acceptance to NYU means there's nothing really stopping her from like she says "getting out of this hick town as fast as she can."

"Okay." I study her face, trying to find more clues as to what she really wants to say to me. My gut tells me it'll be something along the lines of the closure I've subconsciously always sought. You don't just stop being friends with a person you've known for almost all of your life and not need closure. So I might not want it but maybe I need it.

"Before I go, there's some stuff I need to do, clear all the misunderstanding, you know? I heard karma's a bitch so this is my attempt to put all the bad stuff behind me."

I'd hate to tell her that maybe it's too late for repentance. The things she's done over the past few years, or well ever since we hit puberty aren't really going to be washed away so easily. I've seen her do a lot of ugly things, most of them to me. Even if we forget about what she's done to me, there's still a list as long as the Burj Khalifa, the world's tallest building, of all the destruction she's caused. Karma might not be the nicest person to her.

"Is this you apologizing?" I cut to the chase. It's kind of bittersweet, I want to be here but not be here at the same time. There's this sense of finality in the air, like all the four years behind us are leading up to this moment. I've never been good with endings. I read the last Harry Potter book a page a day just to extend the time I had left with the characters. So yes, it took me a while to get through it but I relished every second. I'm tempted to run away right now.

"Kind of." She begins tapping her foot restlessly against the ground; her icy demeanor is starting to thaw. I can practically feel the anxiety rolling off her. Whatever she's got to say is going to be really tough to hear as well.

"I want to confess, Tessa, not apologize. Yeah okay maybe I owe you an apology too, maybe a shitload of them, but telling you the truth is more important."

My brows furrow; clearly I have no idea what's to come.

She takes a deep breath. "I like Cole. I really, really like him. Maybe you've always known that but you don't know that I'm in love with him too. When I was nine, my dad beat the crap out of me and I was hiding in the boys' bathroom at school the next day crying my eyes out. I didn't want you to see me like that. You always had the perfect family and I began to hate you for that. Cole found me that day and he . . . he was so nice to me. He took care of me, told me his dad was a cop and he'd make the bad people go away. Of course I didn't tell him about my dad but it was enough, to feel safe. To know that this beautiful, kind boy would always take good care of me."

I suck in a breath and my jaw drops. In no possible way had I expected that; you could've told me that my parents adopted me from a remote village in Zimbabwe and I would have believed you but this . . . Oh God. I always knew she liked him but always based it on Cole's bad-boy charm or just plain physical attraction. I knew she'd tried to get with Cole in the past and he'd refused but I didn't know how deep her crush went. And the thing about her dad hurting her . . . how come I knew nothing about that? How come I didn't know that she hated me for a family that's currently in shambles?

She must sense my shock but apparently she isn't going to attempt to lessen the blow. "I think that was the point when I started hating you. Before, yeah I was jealous of you but then I saw how Cole would always be around you. How he'd always find a way to talk to you, to tease you and how he'd pay so much attention to you that he never even looked at me. I just . . . I couldn't. But even nine-year-old me knew that I had to stick with you if I wanted something with him."

Words fail me, ironic considering I am here on a journalism assignment. In my mind, the reason Nicole stopped being friends with me was because I wasn't good enough for her. I'd been overweight, awkward, and generally unpopular. It'd made sense that she wouldn't want to be my friend. But the fact that she's never truly been the best friend I always thought her to be stings big-time.

"I could say I'm sorry but it wouldn't be enough, would it? I should've told you the truth, shouldn't have faked a friendship for that long but I was selfish. I wanted Cole and when I couldn't have him . . ."

"You took Jay. You didn't even like him, did you? You just took him because you knew that would hurt me," I say more to myself than to her.

Even though my feelings for Jay have been more or less vaporized I can still remember the hurt I felt then. When I thought I'd been in love with him, my heart had literally been ripped to pieces to see him with Nicole. Nicole, my best friend, had taken the guy I was in love with. Yup, that had been enough to make me sob for weeks. And she'd done it just to spite me.

"He was the only way I could make you feel how I did. Maybe I crossed a line. Later, I realized that you never did anything intentionally, that you didn't ask for Cole to love you the way he did."

I open my mouth to argue but she stops me. "Please don't. I think you were the only person who didn't realize that the boy was madly in love with you. Everyone saw it but you were too busy obsessing over Jay to notice it. That made me angrier, how oblivious you could be."

"Why? Why are you telling me all this now? What do you expect me to do?"

"Nothing. After everything I've done I expect nothing from you, not even forgiveness. The things I've done the last few years don't really deserve that. But I want you to know that I admit I was wrong. I'm glad you have the kind of friends now that you deserve and . . . I'm glad you have someone like Cole. He loves you and now you love him too. Just hold on to him, okay?"

Words jumble up inside my head when I try to string together a sentence. It's like there's this whirlpool forming around me brain, leaving me incapable of thinking. Yes, what she's just told me definitely erases the confusion I've felt for a long time, but this is worse. Nicole was never my friend, she hated me when I thought of her as the best friend I'd ever had. She'd been the person I considered my support system, and all the while she was possibly sticking pins into voodoo dolls of me.

"I feel like I should say something," I choke out, "It's probably a good idea if I get it all out today. I feel sorry for you, Nicole, that you fell for someone who doesn't love you back. Trust me I know how that feels. I'm sorry that you thought you had to go through such lengths to get him to love you. If there's one thing I've learned this year it's that if you're meant to be with someone, it will happen. You can't force love. So even if it means that your first love becomes unrequited, then you should move on because maybe there's someone better for you."

I can see her eyes getting watery; it's the most emotion I've seen from her in years. "I'd also like to thank you. Maybe if you hadn't cut me out of your life and gotten rid of that fake friendship, then I never would've met Megan and Beth. I haven't really let myself admit it but being friends with them definitely felt different than being friends with you. What I have with them is what real friendship is supposed to be like. And we're all moving on with our lives; I don't want to carry this kind of baggage with me when I leave, so you know what? Even though I should probably hate you for what you've put me through I'll just say that I hope you have a better life from now on. Find a guy who loves you for who you are and friends you genuinely like. Speaking from personal experience, those things kind of change your life."

Leaving her still sitting on the bleachers, I rush to where I know Cole's car is. When he sees me running toward him he gets out of the Volvo and begins walking toward me, concern etched onto his handsome face. I all but throw myself into his arms, wrapping my arms around his neck and burying my face into his chest. His scent immediately calms me down. Warm, familiar, safe, and enthralling all at the same time. It's easier to understand now why someone would fall in love with him at the drop of a hat.

Maybe my mom dropped me on my head a lot when I was a baby. That would totally explain why I didn't see how he felt all that time ago.

"You okay?" His arms tighten around me and I nod into his chest. I just need him to hold me. I need to know that he's still with me and that I'm the lucky girl he's chosen to fall in love with. Knowing that girls that look like Nicole would do anything to be in my place has just made me all the more aware of the fact that he is a one-in-a-million kind of guy.

He's my guy.

"Are you sure?"

Reluctantly after some neck sniffing, I pull away and grin at him. "I'm wonderful. So what's this surprise you keep telling me about?"

He looks puzzled for a second, trying to figure the situation out but then his face breaks into a breathtaking smile.

"Get in the car." He nods his head toward it and I eye it skeptically. He's being really mysterious but I like it. Today is a good day for the unknown because obviously nothing is how it seems, as exhibited by my conversation with Nicole. I'll talk to Cole about it soon, but not now. Now I just want to be with him.

"Oh-kay. Are we going my house first? Because I need to check up on . . ."

"Beth is with Travis and he's going to take good care of her. I just got off the phone with him and he told me that she's ready to talk to a therapist."

"What?" I gasp, feeling thrilled. "How did that happen?"

"Well, he told her that he'd go if she did and . . ."

"She's doing this for him. She's going to therapy because of Travis,"

I say in awe, feeling a surge of happiness. The fact that she's put aside her fear of talking to someone about her relationship with her mother for Travis, makes me realize that she loves him.

"Then are we going to your house? Because Cassandra asked me the other day to—"

He stops me again. "Just get in the car, Tessie. I'll explain the rest."

He opens my door for me and as I'm putting on my seatbelt I notice the bags in the backseat. My carry-on bag is immediately recognizable and I become even more intrigued. I see one of Cole's bags as well and the excitement builds.

He sees I've figured something out when he gets in.

"We're going somewhere?" I ask in excitement and he chuckles, but there's a light in his eyes that I know is only there when he's really, really happy.

For a second he looks nervous, possibly uncomfortable when he scratches the back of his neck. "I thought maybe we could go out alone for the weekend. I asked your dad and everything, I talked to Travis too . . . but maybe I should've asked you first, right? If you don't want to, I get it but I just . . . I wanted to spend some time alone with you and . . . shit, I should've thought this through."

Since he looks so darn adorable when he's rambling I let him go on for a while. I know I need to put him out of his misery but this is so much fun. Most of the time in our relationship, I'm the one who's blushing and just being an overall awkward moron so this is fun for me.

"Cole, stop!" He looks at me, his face still tinged with a bit of red and eyes looking a little panicked. I shift in my seat until I'm facing him and lean over to kiss him softly. He closes his eyes and groans as his hand immediately goes to the back of my neck to hold me in place. We kiss slowly and deeply until I feel all the tension leave his body.

When we break apart, he grins goofily at me. "You should shut me up like that more often."

"I thought you were going to have a panic attack and I'd have to administer CPR."

"Well I wouldn't have been opposed to that. I love a girl who's hands-on," he says cheekily and I smack his shoulder.

"Get your mind out of the gutter and tell me where we're going. And yes I want to go, I'd love to go, and you are an idiot for ever thinking that I wouldn't want to."

That earns me another searing hot kiss that has my toes curling.

"Okay then, if that's the case then sit back and relax. It's a bit of a drive."

"You're not telling me where we're going?" I pout, crossing my arms over my chest which just makes his grin wider.

"God, I love you."

That melts my insides and even when I'm pretending to be annoyed at him I can't help but say, "I love you too."

***

From what I can tell we've been driving for a while. It's given me enough time to start hyperventilating. We've been traveling in comfortable silence exchanging kisses here and there but then the silence just gave my darn overactive mind something to freak out over.

I'm going to be alone. Alone with Cole. For two whole days. No adult supervision, not even Travis.

The kind of images that spring to mind would make a nun pass out.

Yes, I've slept in the same bed with him a couple of times but that's always been with the knowledge that any family member of mine could walk in on us at any given second. This feels different and I know it's because of how highly charged the emotions between us are now. Exchanging the L-word changes everything. We've gotten more possessive, more into touching each other and just overall craving each other's company more. Sometime we get a little too carried away and have to stop.

My heart starts beating faster; my face begins to burn as images of being intimate like "that" cross my mind. Is it getting hot in here or what?

"What are you thinking about, Tessie?"

I don't want to answer that question. If I did it would be something like, "I'm thinking about jumping your bones."

"Nothing," my voice comes out impossibly squeaky and I feel like slapping myself across the face multiple times.

"This is the second time today you've tried to lie to me, you know. Whatever you're thinking about it's clearly embarrassing you. Look at how red you are."

"Well, you do call me 'shortcake' for a reason. And yes I hope it's not because you're saying I'm short. That would suck."

He chuckles, a hearty sound that's doing NOTHING to stop those darned thoughts from invading my mind.

"I call you 'shortcake' because that's all you ate through second grade. I'd see you with your Little Mermaid lunchbox and you wouldn't touch the sandwich. I think you gave it to that scrawny kid who barely ate and then you'd just sit there nibbling on the strawberry shortcake."

298

Huh. It's a day for revelations.

"How come I never noticed that you paid so much attention to me?"

A sad look crosses his face and once again I feel like doing myself physical harm for hurting him. Whatever he's thinking about right now must not be pleasant.

"Wait, don't answer that. That was just . . . stupid. I'm an idiot and I shouldn't have been that oblivious."

"No, Tessie, don't put yourself down," he scolds. "I had the worst way possible to show you that I liked you. Let's just forget about all that crap for now. I want to spend time with you, alone, and just think about all the good stuff. Let's do that—deal?"

"Deal."

We're near the ocean, I can tell from the smell and it feels divine. I realize that it's somewhere near the place where we came to see Nana Stone, the day everything changed. Rolling down the window, I breathe in the fresh saltwater smell and inhale deeply. Despite the obvious chill in the weather and it not being peak season anymore, there's something about being near the water that puts you in a summer state of mind. As if realizing my happiness, Cole places his hand on my knee and squeezes gently.

"This is perfect," I tell him as he slows down toward a bend in the road. The Volvo turns into an open driveway which leads to an opulent two-story glass beach house which sits on a large expanse of sand. I'm in a trance, looking at the breathtaking structure. It's gorgeous! You can see inside the glass and see the entire spacious interior. The house itself is a mixture of both modern and traditional architecture with its driftwood flooring. I gasp as we near it since I see the clear blue water behind it. Private beach!

"Oh My God."

"Do you like it?"

"It . . . it's gorgeous! Whose house is this?" I turn toward him, nearly jumping in my seat as I take in all the beauty around me.

"My parents bought this a couple of months ago from their college friends. I . . . I've wanted to bring you here for a while but I guess the timing was never right."

"Wow, Cole. This is really amazing, I can't believe your parents own this place!"

He shrugs casually. "I've been here a lot in my childhood. My parent's friends . . . they're moving outside the US and they wanted to sell this place. Cassandra thought we had too many memories attached to the house to just let it go so they bought it."

299

"I can definitely see why she wouldn't want some stranger to own it. It's so . . . wow."

"So would you like a tour, Ms. O'Connell?" he asks gesturing toward the house and I all but rip my seatbelt off and sink my feet into the sand. I'm quick to take off my boots and socks since the cool sand feels wonderful on my feet, despite the colder temperatures.

"Definitely."

***

As expected the house is as beautiful on the inside as it is on the outside. I'm in the bathroom of the master bedroom, which is one of the six bedrooms in the house—yes, six. Cole's put our bags in the same room and he's in the kitchen making us dinner. My heart is doing its usual gymnastics routine whenever it comes to Cole. Splashing some cold water onto my face, I try to get my hormones under control.

If I keep thinking about "it" for the rest of the weekend, everything's going to be a mess. I'll never be able to act normal around Cole at this rate. He has given no indication of the fact that he wants something to happen so why am I psyching myself out?

"You can do this," I tell my image in the mirror and maybe I'll fool myself into believing that.

I take a cold shower since I hear that's what you're supposed to do but really, it didn't do much to my racing heart or out-of-control thoughts. Standing in the bedroom in just my towel, I realize that Cole's right across the hall from me and I'm nearly stark naked right now.

Shaking my head, I rummage through the bag Cole brought for me until I freeze when my hand lands on a certain lacy garment.

Oh No.

With trembling hands I pull out the pair of black lacy panties Beth gave me as a gag gift after declaring that I'd be a virgin for life. I haven't touched them since my birthday last year. They've been stuffed in some dark, untouched crevice of my underwear drawer.

Which only means one thing . . .

As quickly as I can, I get dressed. Scrunching the panties in my hand, I rush toward Cole, feeling infuriated and embarrassed beyond words. Unluckily for him he's standing next to a frying pan full of hot sizzling oil.

"Hey, I thought I'd make . . ."

He stops when he catches the expression on my face.

He holds up his hands defensively. "Whatever it is that you think I did, I probably did it and I'm sorry."

I grit my teeth. "You did not go through my underwear drawer, did you?"

He bites and tugs on his lips and I swear I can see him hiding a smile, that smug bastard!

"Well . . . someone had to pack the necessities."

"Oh My God! I can't believe this." I cover my face with both my hands, feeling absolutely mortified.

"Tessie, come on, it's not that big of a deal. Please don't be embarrassed. It's just me. I'm sorry, I should've asked your permission but I wanted to surprise you and I wasn't thinking. Don't be mad, sweetheart, I mean it's not like I'm never going to see you—"

He stops himself just at the same moment my head whips up to hear him finish the sentence.
Holy shit.

"Holy shit," he breathes, repeating my thoughts.

"Uh, forget I said that. I'm . . . I'm going to go finish dinner." He looks a bit dazed as he jerks his thumb toward the kitchen area, staring intently at the ground.

"Yeah . . . yeah that's good. Do that. I'll . . . I'll go call my dad and tell him we got here okay."

"Okay, good."

"Yeah."

"Right."

"Well I'll go now, see you umm, see you in a bit."

I hurry back to the bedroom and fall face-first on the mattress. So . . . . I'm not the only one feeling the tension then, huh? I gulp. This could be quite the weekend.

CHAPTER THIRTY
I'm More Clueless than a Kardashian Without a Camera Crew

Breathless and shaking all over I turn around so that I'm on my back. My trembling hands reach for the phone as I do what I've done in, well, not similar situations but close enough. In five seconds flat I'm in a conference call with Beth and Megan.

"Will you guys first please tell me whether my brother or my boyfriend's best friend are within hearing distance?"

"No." They answer simultaneously and I sigh in relief, my head making a thudding sound as it comes into contact with the pillow and I breathe through my nose.

"So we have a code red situation," I tell them and am immediately bombarded with questions from both of them.

"But you're with Cole, right? He was going to surprise you and he told us . . . are you okay?"

"Do you want me to bring out my steel-toed boots and kick him? But I should warn you, then you won't get to have those genetic-lottery-winning blond-haired, green-eyed babies Megan's been fantasizing about."

"What?" I half shriek and Megan groans on the other end.

"I just said that if Cole and you ever had kids they'd be the cutest things ever! And I get dibs on being the godmother because Beth's going to be their aunt anyway."

"Hey!" Beth shouts in protest and I can almost see her pale skin becoming tinged with a deep shade of red. If I weren't seconds away from a certified panic attack I'd find this conversation very confusing.

"Guys, would you listen to me! Did you forget what I just said about code red?"

"Right, so what's going on? Did you and Mr. Godsend have a lover's spat?" Beth asks wryly.

"No . . . uh." How the heck did I even consider doing it when I can't even talk about the subject with my best friends? This is how pathetic I am and Cole expects me to . . . I'm going to die. I know it, I'll die right here in this very bedroom and I'm about to tell two people the most embarrassing cause of death that's ever been recorded.

"Tessa, what's going on? You're scaring us." Megan's voice is soothing and calming, like she's dealing with a frightened little child, a child I'm clearly acting like. I'm sure the mature thing to do would have been to sit down with Cole and discuss my feelings and then plan a route of action—or no action—but look at me. I'm hiding, cowering beneath the comforter and running to my pseudo-mommies.

"I think I want to take the next step with Cole." My voice is barely above a whisper. My face is flaming red and I've basically buried my head between my knees as if expecting a physical blow in response to my words. There's complete silence on both lines. You can almost hear the imaginary crickets chirping.

It's Beth who cuts the very palpable tension surrounding us and when she speaks, it's the last thing I could have ever expected.

"What the hell? You two haven't slept together yet?"

A scandalized gasp leaves my mouth the same minute Megan starts shrieking at Beth for being too crude and insensitive. I can't breathe; I just can't. My lungs struggle to function, as hysterical laughter bursts from within me. Now I can't stop laughing. I laugh until tears start pouring out of my eyes as my best friends continue fighting on the other end.

"I can't believe that's what you guys thought!" I say once I manage to calm down and catch my breath. If Cole's heard anything alarming then he doesn't make it known. But then I think the day has reached its saturation point of embarrassing moments. It can only get better, right? Of course, Tessa, of course it will. Believe that.

"Well what were we supposed to think? You guys are always glued to each other's side. You're alone all the time doing God knows what if you weren't even hooking up."

"Beth shut up, just please shut up." Megan groans and tries to make sure I don't have another panic attack.

"What she's trying to say is that you two just always seem so in love. We thought that it was only natural that . . ."

"That what? We were . . . we were sleeping together? I can't believe you guys just assumed that!"

"What's so wrong about that, Tessa? Come on, it's no big deal. You're eighteen and still hanging on to your virginity despite having the perfect boyfriend who's crazy in love with you. That's just . . . wrong." Beth snorts and I use a pillow to muffle my cries of frustration.

These two were supposed to be helping me. Telling me what to do, whether it's too soon and if I should wait some more. But this is going all wrong.

"It's okay if she wants to wait, Beth. I personally think she should only do it if and when she's ready."

"But how will I know when I'm ready?" I half whisper, the words barely making any sound.

"You just will. Everything will feel right. I mean you'll still feel scared to death but in your heart you'll know that you can trust the person you're with to not hurt you. And you'll be in love with the person, obviously," Megan tells me with such certainty in her voice that I begin to breathe easier.

Until.

"Wait a second, does that mean you and Alex . . ." I leave the question incomplete, unable to wrap my mind around the idea that my sweet, naïve, and slightly neurotic friend might have actually done the deed before me. Plus her parents are practically prison wardens. There's no way . . .

"Yeah right, have you met her parents? She couldn't have escaped their hold long enough even for a quickie in the backseat."

"Megan?"

"I'm right, aren't I, Megs?" Beth asks and I know we're both holding our breaths. She's quiet, way too quiet.

"Well," she stretches the word and I gasp, the same instant Beth exclaims her choice swear word of the month.

"WHAT!"

"Come on, guys." She whines sounding terribly embarrassed, "I knew you'd react like this!"

"But you . . . how, when? I can't believe you didn't tell us!" My voice is coming out squeaky, like I've inhaled helium and the urge to crawl under the covers and never come out is stronger than ever. Nothing is what it seems. Ex-best friends have tragic, haunting pasts, boyfriends think about you naked, and current best friends lose their virginities without letting you know about it.

"I still can't believe you and Alex did it before Colessa."

"What? Colessa? Did you just couple name us, Beth?"

"Sure, everyone does it. You two are so sickeningly perfect together, it totally warrants a couple name. Personally I like Colessa but there's a variety out there for you to choose from."

"Okay then, that's just creepy. And off topic. Megan! When did this happen? And . . . how was it?"

She contemplates her answer for a while, my heart racing like crazy as I wait for her to make up her mind. Beth has already told us about her less-than-great experience. She was sixteen and had just been about to move to our town. Her then-boyfriend, a rock star wannabe with a beat-up old truck, had told her he loved her and coerced her into sleeping with him. She said she did it out of curiosity and that it had been pretty lackluster. So it's quite obvious that Megan's answer matters hugely.

"Well, it was a little awkward and a little painful but that part's totally biological and had to happen, right? Alex was really sweet and he took great care of me. In the end, I did feel great and more, well, more in love with him if that makes sense? I think it brought us even closer and we connected on a whole new level."

"That's what she said."

"Beth!" We both exclaim at the same time before all three of us burst out laughing.

"I swear I didn't mean for it to come out like that." Megan is laughing her crazy hyena laugh where she occasionally snorts. I join in feeling a lot lighter and relieved. So it's awkward for everyone, right? Good, that's good. It's a relief, but does that mean that I'm going to go ahead with it?

"But Tessa, listen, you'll know if you're not ready. I mean if you're still thinking about it as much as you are then maybe you and Cole should talk about it. It sounds horribly awkward but in the end it's better to just be clear about these things. You don't want to give the other person the wrong impression or hurt their feelings."

"When did you become such an expert on sex?" Beth sounds slightly dazed and I feel the same way too. This is Megan. The nerd, the one with dictator-like parents who probably expect her to become a nun. It's weird, hilarious but weird. But I'm happy for her, glad that she has someone like Alex. Knowing from Nicole and Beth that some guys take a girl's virginity for granted it's good to know that guys like Alex still exist.

"Who's a sex expert?"

The blood drains from my face.

"Is that my brother?" I ask in a barely there voice.

"Wait, is that my sister? Are you talking to my sister about sex?" Travis shrieks.

"I gotta go, guys. Bye, love you, and if one of you wants to kill me then just donate my music to a worthy cause."

Beth hangs up.

"Tessa?"

"Did that just happen, Megan? Did that really just happen?"

"I'm afraid so."

"Oh God."

"I know."

"I think I'm going to go throw myself in the ocean now. Bye Megs, talk to you later."

"But Tessa, no, wait . . ."

I end the call and decide that once I go back I will do a research project on how it is possible even if not statistically proven to die of utter humiliation.

***

When I finally decide to come out of my room, I've simmered down a bit. Of course I turned my phone off, expecting Travis to start bombarding me with calls and text messages which threaten Cole bodily harm. The fates hate me today, which is why it is possible that Travis may have contacted Cole. If he has then Cole doesn't show it. I find him in the living room, watching a movie on the huge flat screen. Well, I'd use the term *watching* loosely. He's mostly just staring at the wall in front of him while Reese Witherspoon continues being *Legally Blonde*. Cole would never watch *Legally Blonde*, ever. This is definitely a state of emergency.

I take a seat next to him tentatively and you can feel the tension rolling off of both of us. I'm as aware of his every move, every blink and facial expression as he is of mine. We're weird like that, so attuned to each other that I could tell you his exact movements blindfolded.

"Hey," I whisper softly, placing my hand between the both of us.

It's a peace offering, a way to break this awful tension.

"Hey." His voice is throaty, his eyes downcast but his hand still meets mine in the middle as he interlinks our fingers.

"Did you talk to your dad?"

What? Why would I . . . Oh, right. I told him I was going to go talk to my dad.

"Yeah I did."

"Good."

Not this again! It's time to take this into my own hands then.

"Cole, listen, about what happened earlier . . . " I take a deep, calming breath which really doesn't serve its purpose but oh well.

"I think we should talk about it, right? That's what people who are in relationships do, they talk about things. We should talk too. What happened before . . . let's not allow it to make things awkward between us. I'm not mad at you for what you said, I get it." Before saying the last part, I squeeze my eyes shut and tighten my grip on Cole's hand. "In fact I've been thinking about it too."

I hear his quick inhale of breath. His fingers hold mine in a death grip and I felt a shudder pass through his body. But then maybe it's my own shivering that I'm passing off as his. But then I can't regret being honest with him. He needs to know that he's not the only one having these urges. That I'm on the same page as him but he also needs to know that I want to wait.

"But I don't think I'm ready, not yet. It's me and all the messed-up things in my life. I need some time to clear it all up. I just . . . now's not a good time. I'm sorry if you expected . . ."

"Tessie," Cole groans and places his hand behind my neck pulling me to him. He begins kissing me furiously. So furiously and passionately that I forget everything I'd been rambling about. But that's all he does, he kisses me. Our hands are folded between us and it's like he's telling me he loves me for the first time all over again, this time with his lips.

I moan against his mouth and feel him smile. My hands itch to run through his hair but he's restricting them. Finally when we pull apart, panting for breath, he places one last kiss on my forehead and my heart turns into a bloody, gooey mess.

"I love you," he breathes, pulling me close to his chest. "And I'm a lucky bastard that you love me back even when I monumentally fuck up."

I'm a bit sensitive to his second-last choice of word right now, but oh well who's asking?

"You didn't. I told you I understand; it's okay," I mutter into his chest.

"Yeah right. I made you feel like you had to . . . Christ, I keep finding new ways to mess things up with you. At this rate we might not even make it till prom." He groans and I laugh.

"Don't knock yourself down too much. I'm sure we'll manage."

He snorts. "Don't sound too confident."

I lie content in his arms, just inhaling his scent and enjoying the quiet. This is good, this is perfect.

"Hey, Tessie?"

"Yeah?"

"You know I can wait as long as you want, right? In fact if you want to live a life of celibacy I'd totally be . . ."

"Ugh! Would you shut up, please?" I whine, ducking my face into his neck. There's a flush creeping up my neck and I can feel Cole's body reverberating with laughter. Now the jerk-wad is just enjoying himself.

"I'm just giving you your options, that's all."

"How about you just forget I ever said something, okay?"

"But then I wouldn't be me and you wouldn't be you. Does that make sense?"

"Strangely so," I muse. "And Cole? If you ever go through my underwear drawer again, I'm going to be listening to nineties boy bands. A lot. So much so that you'll find yourself becoming a Nick Carter fanboy. Just saying."

He shudders. "Touché."

***

By the next hour we settle into a comfortable rhythm, all awkwardness forgotten. We eat the reheated dinner and watch some television. It's the perfect night for cozying up in front of a fireplace but before that we attempt to brave walking on that beach, beneath layers of warm clothes. We stroll close to the shoreline, hand in hand and there's something so sublime about the solitude. I know, I know it's so cliché but the immensity of the moment cannot be ignored.

"Nicole and I had a talk today." He's surprised. I don't look at him but I can feel the stiffness of his body and how he suddenly comes to a standstill. He's checking for battle scars, eyes washing over me from head to toe. I let him have his scrutiny since he's only doing it because he loves me.

"It's not what you think. We didn't have a WWE smackdown, we just talked. A lot. Well she talked and I listened."

We slowly make our way back to the house and settle in front of the fireplace. We take off our warm coats and wrap ourselves in blankets instead. I curl into Cole's side and tell him all about it. When it comes to the part where I tell him that Nicole's in love with him, he seems genuinely shocked.

"Look, I thought that she always hit on me because it was some messed-up way of showing you up. She got Jay and she rubbed it in your face. When we got closer, I thought she wanted to try the same thing."

He rubs his palm over a slightly scruffy jaw. It's a different look for him since he's always clean-shaven but I find it quite appealing. It just adds to the list of things I love about him. The list is never ending though, so I could be borderline obsessed.

"Do you remember the incident? The one where you found her in the boys' bathroom?"

He sighs and nods hesitantly. "I wanted to tell you, I did. But . . ."

308

"It wasn't any of my business. Cole. I didn't have any right to know. It was Nicole's secret to share, not yours. I understand."

"I just helped her out a bit and looked out for her a while. It was pretty easy since she was always around you. But then she seemed fine and there weren't any obvious bruises so I . . . ." He chokes before getting the last words out, "I forgot."

"You feel guilty." It's not really a question. This is Cole we're talking about. If anyone knows how he likes to be the rescuer then it's me. He rescued me but that doesn't mean I'm the only one. Does that make me jealous, yeah sure, but everyone needs someone like him at some point in their lives. And if it's the actual thing then what more could you possibly want?

"That might explain why I tolerated some of the crap she did. It was obvious to everyone but you that she didn't treat you like you should treat a best friend. She was . . . she was all darkness, Tessie, and you were always light. But I thought that you knew her secrets and that's why you stayed. But when I left and things got bad, the guilt stopped being so important once I came back."

We're both quiet for a while. I let his words sink in. Nothing is what is seems to be; there's a history and a story behind everything. The fact that I've never managed to realize this is rather astounding. Have I always been this clueless?

Taking a look at the boy sitting next to me, who tells me he's been in love with me since the day we first met, answers the question. I'm more clueless than a Kardashian without a camera crew.
"So are we done with the heavy talking for the night?" Cole jokes and I lean further into him.

"Only if you tell me you have what I want for dessert. If you don't, then we have a problem."

"Why, Tessie, are you trying to take advantage of me? I have the right to say no if I'm not in the mood." He finishes with a flourish and I slap my hand over his mouth, my face burning.

"What is wrong with you? Is your brain like wired to turn everything I say into something that sounds completely wrong and . . ."

"Sexual?" His voice is muffled beneath my fingers but I can feel his lips curling up into an arrogant smirk.

"You're evil." I glower, narrowing my eyes at him and pulling away with a huff. Crossing my arms over my chest, I twist my body away from him and stare right ahead.

Childish, yes, but the man is totally enjoying my embarrassment right now! Let's make fun of the blond virgin. I'm sure one of those is as

309

rare as a Komodo dragon with a unicorn's body.

"I think you meant sexy," he coos in my ear, successfully trapping me in his arms so that his chest presses against my back.

"Unlike your other legions of fangirls I do not spend my days thinking about how hot you are, Stone," I huff. It's a lie. It is such a lie but maybe since he can't see my face he can't tell.

He twirls a strand of my hair between his fingers and a shiver passes through my body at the lack of space between us. His breath fans my ears. "That's too bad because I do. I think about you a lot. I miss you when you're not with me. I want to hear your voice first thing in the morning and the last thing before I go to sleep. I want to be where you are, Tessie, always."

I sigh involuntarily, my body relaxing into his. My defenses disappear when he starts talking like this. Every pretense that I carry, acting like he doesn't matter as much as he actually does to me just . . . the act vanishes. And then I'm just a girl who's hopelessly in love with her boyfriend.

"Wow."

He chuckles as he kisses my cheek. "I'm so glad you're here with me now. This is as great as life gets."

"Mmm-hmm." My eyes shut as sleep pulls me in. It's been a long day and exhaustion is setting in, especially when I'm so comfortable in Cole's arms.

"Before I take you to bed," he says in a gravelly voice that has me jolting out of slumber and twisting my body toward him with wide, wide eyes. "Literally speaking, babe. I'll just carry you to bed, that's it." He stifles a laugh as I elbow him. "Tell me, why is Travis blowing my phone up?" I bite my lip. Uh-oh. He might possibly break up with me after this.

"About that . . ." I let my hair fall across my face so that he can't see me. "You might want to consider hiring a bodyguard. It's nothing serious," I add quickly, "But there might have been a little accident while you were cooking."

"Tessie . . ." he says slowly, sweeping the hair away and turning me fully to face him, "What's going on?"

So I tell him. Well obviously I omit the more embarrassing parts of the conversation I had with my best friends and tell him the crux of the matter. However I spin it, it sounds bad. He looks rather pale by the end of my spiel.

"Huh."

"Listen, I know it sounds bad but trust me, I'll talk to Travis. He'll understand that nothing happened and . . ."

"He's going to castrate me. Or he'll try at least. I could probably put up a fight. Things would get ugly. Oh man, my dad's going to kick my ass. I can't go to jail again or be responsible for someone else ending up in jail at least for the next six months. I can't end up in the emergency room either. Cassandra said if I come in after a brawl she'll tell the authorities I'm some deranged kid with mommy issues from Wyoming."

I can't help it. I laugh hysterically until tears start pouring from my eyes. Clutching my stomach I fall backward onto the couch and attempt to catch my breath. My sides ache from exertion but for the love of me I cannot stop laughing.

"Go ahead, laugh. You're not the one taking possibly what could be my last breaths."

I snort, "Don't you think you're being a little dramatic?"

"The guy thinks I took his little sister's virginity AFTER I promised him I would keep my hands to myself and you'll return exactly the same as you left."

My mouth hangs open as I gawk at him. "When the heck were you two discussing my . . . when did you talk about this?" I nearly shriek.

"Can we forget about that and focus on the bigger picture, Tessie? I mean I might possibly be six feet under soon, do you really want to be mad at me?"

"I don't believe you. Oh God. I'm going to kill you both, that's it. Problem solved. I'll kill you both with my bare hands."

"Damn, you O'Connells really need some anger management classes. How about I give you a card to my shrink?"

With that I lunge at him. And no, not even remotely in a sexual manner.

CHAPTER THIRTY-ONE
What It Feels Like to Get Your Heart Broken

I flex my fingers around the handle of the spatula and gingerly open one squeezed-shut eye. The thing that's on the pan is not an egg, nor does it remotely resemble one. If an egg could be passed through hell and then back, it wouldn't look as burnt as it does now. The thing is scorched beyond belief and the sight of it makes my stomach heave.

There are footsteps leading into the kitchen so I know he's there, obviously. My Cole senses are tingling and his freshly showered scent hits me like a truckload of bricks. But I must resist and not fall for his boyishly charming ways. Squaring my shoulders, I put up a defensive front and pluck the frying pan from the stovetop, dumping its contents into the trash can.

Something cooked is out of the question now so fruit bowl it shall be. Or I could forget about fitting into my prom dress and slather my favorite chocolate spread onto a butter croissant. Now that I think about it that would be a great idea since my date to prom will probably be dead before the day arrives. And my brother will be in jail. Reacquainting me with Fatty Tessie doesn't seem that big of a problem. Heart attack and clogged arteries on a plate it is.

"I can cook something for you if you want me to."

"No thanks," I mutter and shove past him to go to the fridge.

Even though his voice sends all kinds of tingles through my body, I'm still mad at him. Honestly, I feel humiliated beyond belief that he and my brother would discuss my personal life without actually including me in it. Having spent a long time cast in Nicole's shadow and not really having much control over my actions has made me a little paranoid about things like that. My life is supposed to be mine and it's not an open forum for discussion.

Say I actually wanted to sleep with him, then what? Would he have said no because he'd made a deal with my brother? My brother who is in a relationship with my best friend, a relationship I've never questioned or stood against. I give them their space, don't interfere, and generally stay out of their way. Could I not expect the same? Yeah, sure Cole's being a gentleman and Travis is being a protective older brother, but you have to draw the line somewhere, right?

"Tessie, come on, I said I'm sorry. I shouldn't have discussed our relationship with Travis, especially not that part of it, but I really wanted you to come here. He wouldn't have been cool with it otherwise."

I grab the jar of chocolaty goodness and nearly slam it onto the kitchen island.

"I'm eighteen years old, for Christ's sake! He's my brother, not my keeper, Cole. Why was it so important for you to make sure he's 'cool' with it?" I ask, starting to feel angry.

"Because," he sighs, "because he's not my biggest fan and he's your brother. I know how much you love him and how important he is to you. I just, I need him to trust me with you."

"I don't get it. He's always pushed me toward you. Yeah, he was a bit skeptical at first but he's never outright told me to not be with you. But there's something there, something between the two of you that you haven't told me. It's why you feel the need to be accountable to him, isn't it?"

His eyes widen, like he wasn't expecting me to make the connection and I know I've hit the nail right on its head. This runs deeper, I know it does.

He doesn't speak so I continue, "You told me you came to see me before you left for military school, right? That you were going to apologize, tell me everything. Travis never told me about that, why is that? He said he always knew that you had feelings for me, then why would he do that?"

He roughly shoves a hand through his hair as his jaw tenses and the vein in his neck pulses. His eyes stay trained on the floor and he curses under his breath. My voice is softer now, even though I'm scared to death of what could possibly come next. A lot of worst-case scenarios flash through my head and I struggle to keep it together. He needs to be handled carefully, I can't be too harsh or demanding but at the same time, I just need to finally know.

"Can we not do this now? Can we pretend that the last part of yesterday and this right now, it didn't happen? I want to spend this time with you not thinking about our problems. When we go home, I'll tell you. Please just trust me, whatever it was, it's in the past and it doesn't matter. But right now can we just be us again?"

It's the pleading, puppy-dog look that does me in. I'd been prepared to stand my ground and demand answers but when he's looking at me like that and being so vulnerable, my heart can't stand to say no. And I'll probably pay for being so accepting of his temporary need for denial but he's right. We're in this beautiful, heaven-like place with a just over a day and a half for some alone time and I want to spend it being, like he just said—us.

"Okay," I breathe and his face lights up, "But only if you tell me everything as soon as we get home."

He grins and hugs me close to his chest, kissing the top of my head. "Promise."

***

Around midmorning, Cole leaves to get some groceries and I lounge around the house in the coziest pair of pajamas that I own. I'm just about to really get into the *O.C.* rerun when the doorbell rings. Hmm, that's weird. We have a visitor? Straightening up, I walk lightly to the door, glancing through the peephole. There's a girl out there that I can't see clearly but she doesn't look like an ax murderer.

And Ted Bundy didn't really look like a serial killer, now did he? Talking myself out of all my slightly neurotic thoughts I open the door to someone who appears to be a goddess of a girl.
I should've really put on some lip gloss or mascara or brushed my hair or well, worn something less homeless-person-like because this girl is seriously gorgeous.

In complete awe, I watch her smile at me as she moves in to hug me. "You must be Tessa! Wow, it's really good to finally meet you."

My first thought is that she looks a lot like Megan. She's pretty and not tacky, cake-face-Kimmy pretty. She has thick, long, vibrant red hair and the greenest eyes I've ever seen. I have green eyes, so I know what I'm talking about. Mine do not . . . sparkle like that. She's pale with alabaster skin but only in a way that redheads can carry off. She's a bit taller than I am and dressed so, so much better. Her body is the real killer though. She's tall and willowy, those devastatingly haunting figures that rule the runway but she's not stick-thin. Her body's toned and there are slight hints of curves which are emphasized by her emerald hued sweater and tight fitted jeans. There's a coat draped over her arms. Her long, lean legs appear even longer in her thigh high boots.

Who is this girl and why is she looking at me like I'm the sister she's never had?

I pat her back awkwardly, clearing my throat as she pushes back to beam at me.

"I'm sorry, I don't know who—"

"Erica? Is that you?"

314

Wait, this is Erica? The creepy stalker Lan warned me about? With everything that's happened I'd all but forgotten about her. Now, when she's right in front of me I can't help but shrink back, feeling intimidated.

Cole comes into sight, walking toward us carrying the grocery bags. He puts them on the ground as soon as he sees Erica and she rushes toward him, jumping into his arms. I watch, completely stunned as he returns her hug and then kisses her on the cheek as he lets go of her. Grabbing her hand he walks her toward me, where I'm still standing utterly paralyzed on the doorstep.

"Tessie, this is Erica. I've known her—"

"Practically your whole life, right?" She grins and looks stunning while doing it.

I want to pull a Joker and put that smile permanently on her face, with a knife.

"I . . . I'm sorry; I didn't know. I've heard about you of course but didn't expect to meet you," I say stupidly, looking at the two of them absolutely stunned.

"That's Cole all right. I mean you guys have been dating for several months and he doesn't introduce you to one of his oldest friends. I should be offended but I'm used to it." She shrugs casually before elbowing Cole in the side.

We're still standing at the door and it seems stupid. So I invite her in but it's not like she needs an invitation and I figure out the cause soon. As Erica and Cole catch up, I make quite a few discoveries that Lan missed out on. The weirdest thing is watching Cole and Erica together, they look stunning, like Hollywood stunning. I'm on the armchair as she and Cole sit on the love seat and I observe her edging closer and closer to him as she talks animatedly. So far she hasn't given out any psychotic vibes but hey, it's still pretty early so putting my guards up doesn't hurt.

"But I thought you wouldn't be here for another two days." Cole looks happy and not uncomfortable like he is around most girls who have a thing for him.

Does he know that she has a thing for him? Because it's glaringly obvious to me right now.

"I got an earlier flight and this one didn't have as many stopovers as the other one. Then I spent a couple of days with Mamaw and Granddaddy at the farm before coming here. It's just a short visit though, I have to get back to school for the next semester soon."

There are so many things that beg to be questioned about her answer. She seems mysterious, and interesting. Everything that I'm well, not . . . so I start with something that won't make me sound as horribly curious

315

as I am.

"You're in college?"

She looks at me like she'd forgotten that I was even in the same room. I understand though, Cole has that effect on people. Especially people who might be obsessed with him.

Still, Erica doesn't miss a beat and rattles off what sounds like a much-practiced answer. "Yeah, I'm a year ahead of you guys because my parents homeschooled me until my freshman year of high school. They're anthropology professors, archeology to be specific. So I've basically spent a lot of time around dead people." She shrugs. "They're on a sabbatical as we speak. I took a semester off to stay with them, well actually I really wanted to go to Italy." Grinning, she focuses her attention back to Cole.

"You won't believe how beautiful Pompeii is, Cole! I wish you and the rest of the family could have visited us when I was there. It'd be just like old times."

"Erica's parents and mine are friends. Actually they're the friends who sold this house so technically until a couple of weeks ago this was her house."

Now I'll feel totally uncomfortable staying here.

"Yeah, and they've traded this place for a farm! Can you believe that? My grandparents are going crazy with excitement since they're caretakers but I'd rather be at the beach."

"Wait, where are you staying? I don't see any bags and I told you, you could stay here as long as you want to."

My eyebrows go up but I quickly straighten my expression. I'm hurt but it won't be the best idea to show it and be crowned the heartless bitch while Ariel over there becomes the victim. Obviously I'm thinking about what Cole said to me earlier, about wanting to be alone with me and forgetting about everything else. Having a houseguest who has feelings for him kind of goes against that, doesn't it? How can he not notice the hero worship that's in her eyes as she talks to him? Doesn't he see how she eliminates any space between them whenever he tries to create it and that she's always finding little ways to touch him? I know the signs of an unrequited crush when I see one.

Lan was right. Erica's crazy about Cole and he refuses to acknowledge it.

"No, no, don't be stupid, Cole. I don't want to interrupt your time with Tessa. I'll just be in the way. There's a bed-and-breakfast not that far away from here and I've already checked in. I'm not staying here," she protests but it's half-hearted; she wants to be here.

"Tessie doesn't mind, she's not like that. I'm right, aren't I?" He

316

turns to me and all I can do is nod.

"Of course, please, stay here. You've got more of a right to be here than me at least."

Cole looks at me weirdly when I say this but Erica quickly grabs his attention with some anecdote about her farm life and I take the opportunity to get away. It's suffocating to see them. A girl who I'm convinced now is in love with my boyfriend and said boyfriend who has no idea, it seems.

It's too much like the Jay situation and that would make me Nicole. Dang it, I don't want to be Nicole. But now that I'm in her shoes, I can see why she was so mean to me. I'd done all but drool over her boyfriend and Jay had always been really friendly. Fat or not, that must have bothered her and made her bring out the claws.

Entering the bedroom, I collapse on the bed and wonder where the day's headed. This isn't what I pictured our weekend to be like. Not the thing about Travis and certainly not Erica. Everything's going downhill and there's this feeling in my gut that tells me that it's not going to get better anytime soon.

***

A couple hours later, I'm roused from a nap when my phone starts to ring from its position on the dresser. Erica and Cole spent the afternoon catching up and I escaped quietly, claiming a headache. If I didn't already have one, I'd get it from seeing them interact. She's vicious and knows what she wants. Cole's in denial and seemed pretty confused when I left. Well I'm confused too. I've never seen Cole so . . . clueless and have no idea how to approach the situation.

It seems like the universe is trying to send me a big fat sign because when I finally pick up my phone, the caller's Jay. My hands tremble as I answer, sitting down on the very edge of the bed. Chewing the inside of my cheek, I mutter an incoherent hello.

"Tessa? Are you there?"

"Yes," I take a deep breath, "I'm here. What's up?"

"I was just worried . . . I know you're with Cole at the beach house but there's something, or well someone you should know about."

"Let me guess, her name's Erica and she's more beautiful than any woman on the face of the planet?" I say dryly, feeling my heart sink. If Jay's calling me only to mention Erica then there really is something going on.

"Shit. You've met her already, haven't you?"

"Yup."

"She's still as lovesick as ever then?"

317

"Yup."

"And Cole's still clueless?"

"Well he is your brother."

"Ouch. Right, I deserved that but I just wanted to make sure you're okay. Erica can be a little . . . well a little like a lovestruck puppy on crack when she's with Cole. She called the house to make sure he's still at the beach house. I knew that you were there so . . ."

"You thought you'd warn me. Thanks, but I've already witnessed it firsthand. But how can Cole not see that she's crazy about him? Christ, I could tell the minute she laid eyes on him."

"Well, like you said we're brothers and guys in general tend to be . . ."

"Morons? Blissfully ignorant, in denial? Pick one, Jason."

He chuckles nervously. "They haven't seen each other for a while. Maybe it's not as bad as it used to be."

"Oh it's bad all right, it's really bad. It's so bad that I want to catch the first bus and get as far away from them as possible."

"I can come get you if you want?"

"Do you have a death wish, Jay? Cole would go ballistic." I sigh, knowing that I'm stuck here. I hear my door opening and I know it's him. "Listen, I'll talk to you later but thank you, you know, for calling."

"Anytime, Tess. Take care and remember Cole doesn't feel that way about her."

Cole staring at me with a small frown on his face. "Yeah, I get it. Bye, Jay."

Cole's jaw ticks as I end the call and put the phone back on the dresser. He closes the door behind him and leans against it, somewhat casually. But his body's gone all still and he looks slightly pissed off.

"What did he want?"

"He just wanted to tell me that we might have a guest soon so that I don't get caught by surprise."

His tone makes me angry so I snap at him. I don't want to fight again but he has no right to be angry with me for just talking to Jay. He's the one with a girl who's madly in love with him, hanging out downstairs.

His brows crinkle in confusion. "Erica? Is this about her? Are you mad that I didn't tell you about her visit? I didn't think it was a big deal, Tessie."

"Not a big deal? Are you blind? Can't you see she's in love with you?" I nearly shriek but then remember that Erica's probably downstairs.

"Come on," he groans, "You don't actually believe the bullshit Lan fed you about her, do you? Or did Jay say that to you? I'm going to fucking kill him. You know he's just trying to mess with us. There's nothing between Erica and me. We're friends, we've been friends for a long time and that's all we'll ever be."

"For God's sake, Cole, Jay isn't brainwashing me. I can tell just by looking at her that she likes you, that she really, really likes you. How can you not know that?"

"I've known her my whole life," he says incredulously. "She's like a sister to me. It's not like that between us."

I take a moment to calm down so that I don't bash his head into something. But if there's one thing I know it's that I'm not going to become Nicole. I'm not going to flaunt my relationship around a girl who couldn't help who she fell for. Erica doesn't threaten me, much. I know for a fact that Cole's telling the truth when he says that she's like a sister to him but she doesn't know that. She'd be devastated if she did.

"You might not like her that way but she does, Cole. She loves you and I can't be here, hurting her feelings."

"Damn it, Tessa! I'm not Jay and she isn't you! This isn't your pathetic little love triangle. Not every friendship is as twisted and screwed up as that! Grow up, for fuck's sake."

I stop breathing, I can't breathe.

Tears sting my eyes and my hand immediately comes to my mouth to contain the sobs. Cole's eyes go wide once he realizes what he's said. He opens his mouth to apologize but he won't mean it. Right now he'll do anything just so that I forgive him. We'll sweep it under the rug, just like we've done it with everything else.

"Leave."

"Tessie . . ."

"Please just leave. I don't want to fight anymore. Give me some space."

He tries to say something but I turn away from him and lock myself in the bathroom. The slam of a door tells me that he's gone and only then do I come out. That's how the day passes and then the night. Given how eerily quiet the house remains for that period, I can tell that I'm the only person here. I stay in the room and do not hear from Cole all day. But late at night, I hear footsteps coming up the stairs and a hesitant knock but when I don't answer, Cole doesn't try again. That night I sleep with the door locked, crying into my pillow. His words hurt me more than anything else. The next morning, I make a decision. Gathering all my things, most of which are still in the carry-on, I make the call which might well further doom our relationship.

***

When I come downstairs, there's no one there. It's early dawn and a nagging feeling inside me wonders where Cole could be, if not camped outside my door. I wonder what Erica thinks about me. She must think I'm a complete psychopathic girlfriend who isn't good enough for Cole. She may be right but today I won't feel guilty. He crossed a line and he needs to know that I'm not going to accept that kind of behavior, not anymore.

I let myself out unnoticed and walk back the way we came. Remembering the diner I saw on the way here, I follow the same path until I can see the red neon sigh. I text my ride to meet me there, and I'm told that they'll be there in half an hour. It's been a few hours since the fight. After I refused to open the door to let him in last night, Cole hasn't tried to contact me and I'm not sure what I would do even if he did try. Still, there's a voice inside my head that's questioning why is it that Cole hasn't tried harder. It's okay, I tell myself. I asked him to give me space and I couldn't probably be around him either. Still I can't help but feel disappointed.

I sit inside the pleasant and neatly kept space with friendly looking waitresses and order myself a cup of coffee. What's going to happen once I get home isn't really clear to me. What I do know is that the beach house is cursed. There is no way I'm going back to that place. Cole and I were good before we got there. And now we're totally messed up.

I'm nursing the last bit of coffee in the mug when the door opens and Travis walks in. He sees my tear-streaked face almost immediately in the mostly empty diner and I rush to him. Forgetting my annoyance with him, I hug my brother closely and he runs his hand over my hair, calming me.

"I've got you Tess," he coos. "It's going to be okay."

"Thank you for coming to get me." I hiccup into his chest and he hugs me closer.

"I'm always going to be there for you, little sis, no matter what. Come on, let's get you home."

Travis hastily pays for the coffee and tips the waitress before leaving. We sit in his car and he turns the radio on to my favorite station. They're playing The Civil Wars right now and it's just what I need. Closing my eyes I lean against the window and fall asleep.

***

"She's with me . . . No, I'm taking her home. She's upset, asshole; I'm not bringing her back. Yeah whatever. I'll tell her when she gets up but only if she's feeling better. Just back off for a while, okay? Yeah, I'll tell her. I'm driving man, I'll text you later."

Bits and pieces of conversation filter through my ears as I struggle to open my eyes. My head feels heavy and there's an ache starting to set in. It takes a bit for me to get my bearings straight but then I remember everything. The fight, leaving, and then Travis coming to pick me up. I feel like vomiting. How did everything get so bad?

"Hey, you up?"

It's midday outside the car window, so we must have been driving for a long time. The two-and-a-half-hour journey looks like it'll soon come to an end.

"Hey," my voice is husky from sleep and from the lack of use. I rub my eyes and straighten up, avoiding looking at the questions in my brother's eyes.

"So we'll be home in about twenty minutes. Beth's making your favorite pasta for dinner."

I groan, hitting my head repeatedly against the seat. "You guys were supposed to have fun this weekend! I can't believe I screwed it up. Great, perfect. My own disaster of a relationship wasn't enough, I had to go butt into yours as well. I'm on a roll, aren't I?"

He chuckles. "You're being a little dramatic. Beth and I weren't going to do something crazy while you were gone. Movie night and Chinese takeout was the only plan we had so you're more than welcome to join in."

"Gee thanks," I say dryly and then remember the reason I woke up.

Jolting up in my seat, I look at my brother suspiciously. "Was that Cole you were talking to?"

"Yes. He wouldn't stop calling you. I guess you didn't tell him you were leaving. The guy was worried out of his mind. I told him you were with me."

"Oh."

I feel kind of bad now. Terrible, actually, but I can't deny that I wanted to torture him a little by leaving unannounced. Now that my objective has been achieved, I just feel guilty.

"Did he . . . did he tell you what happened?"

"No, but he wants you to call him. Whenever you're ready, Tess, there's no hurry."

I might just need the time.

***

Beth takes one look at me and knows that I'm not in the mood to talk. But she looks better, for the first time in weeks her face has some color to it and she's enjoying herself as she cooks. A day of therapy and it already seems to be helping her; I'm beyond happy for my friend. She deserves to be able to live her life without the guilt of her mother's death plaguing her every single second. She hugs me tightly and tells me that Cole and I will figure it out, because we're meant to be together.

Hanging out with my brother has made her quite the romantic. I on the other hand am one step closer to turning into a crazy cat lady. An extremely obese crazy cat lady, I correct myself later as I'm shoving spoonfuls of strawberry ice cream in my mouth.

My phone rings and only one person could be calling me at two a.m. As my heart races wildly, my fingers tap uncertainly over the phone. Cole's breathtakingly beautiful face weakens my resolves as it flashes on the screen. I nearly answer but then remember how he shouted at me and the words he said. I end the call and then turn off the phone.

As expected I don't get any sleep and I twist and turn until it's dawn and then watch as the sun rises high into the sky from my window. Today, I'm throwing myself a pity party, which means that I'm in my pajamas and don't plan on leaving my bed. They're showing John Hughes movies all day today so entertainment is taken care of. Travis knocks, Beth knocks, but I only come out for food.

Then there's a different knock. A softer one, a much more hesitant one.

I start shaking and scoot further into my cocoon of blankets.

The door isn't locked. If he really wants to come in, he will. I glance at the clock on my wall and it tells me that it's just after noon. When did he leave last night? Where was he after he left me? I haven't switched my phone on so I don't know if he's tried texting or calling again. I'm being a coward; it's not exactly news but I'm more afraid now.

"Tessa, can I come in?"

My heart breaks when he calls me Tessa. It literally shatters but I still don't say a word.

"Please. I just need to say a few things to you and then I'll leave. Please just talk to me."

No! Why is he talking about leaving? Why isn't he being his usual stubborn self? The Cole I know would have barged right in and made me talk to him, whether I like it or not. That's what I expected of him, that he would magically fix everything like he always does. But he sounds so different now, defeated and scared. My heart falls into the pit of my stomach.

"Okay," I say loudly enough so that he hears me but not so loud that he hears the trembling of my words.

The door opens quietly, not making a single noise, and then Cole comes in, just as noiselessly. He's still wearing the clothes from the day before yesterday and he hasn't shaved. His eyes are bloodshot and his shoulders slouched in defeat. Something's very wrong.

"You were right. I'm an asshole and you were right," he says almost immediately as he stands a couple of feet away from me, very near to the door. He looks like he's ready to bolt any second and he's yet to look at me.

"Cole . . . I . . . overreacted. Maybe I shouldn't have left like that . . . I . . ."

"She likes me. Erica, she says she's in love with me."

My vision blurs with tears and my heart very nearly stops. The way he says these words tells me something much worse is going to follow.

"I was upset with you and about what happened with us. We were talking and drinking a little. She started crying. She told me she's always loved me and then . . ."

"Then what, Cole? THEN WHAT?" I shout hysterically, my entire body shaking violently.

"We kissed. She kissed me and I . . . fuck!" He curses loudly and kicks my door, "I kissed her back. I was hurting, Tessie. I was so mad at you, at Jay, and at myself. I felt guilty for hurting both you and Erica and when she kissed me I thought that I could at least do one thing right. That was bloody stupid of me, wasn't it?"

I'm pretty sure I'm going to puke. Bile rises at the back of my throat but I force myself to stay put. My mind is racing, my heart's breaking, and I can't stop shaking. It's cold, it's so damn cold in here.

"Did you . . . did you do more than kiss?"

I don't know how I got that out but I need to know.

Cole looks like he's going to cry. "No . . . No, I didn't have sex with her but I'm not going to lie to you, not now. It got close before I had the sense to stop."

That does it, I rush to the bathroom and everything I've eaten in the past twenty-four hours comes right back out. I throw up for what seems like forever and when I'm done, I realize that Cole's sweeping my hair away from my face and stroking my back.

I shove away from him and collapse on the tiled floor. "Go away. Get the hell away from me." I'm shouting. I yell so loudly that Travis comes rushing in and once he sees the state I'm in he forces Cole to leave.

"I'm sorry. I love you, I love you so much, Tessie. I didn't mean to hurt you."

But I can't process a word he's saying because I feel so dead on the inside.

This is what it feels like to get your heart broken and smashed, right? If it is, then why do people even bother falling in love? And the thing is, the harder you fall the more painful it is when you finally hit the ground.

I fell hard, I fell with my body and soul, with everything I was made of. So when the free fall ends, I'm pretty sure there's not a part of me that's left intact.

CHAPTER FOUR
Cole's POV

Here's the thing and I'll be honest about it, in life there's very little that fazes me. By the age of eighteen I've done more crazy, outrageous, adventurous things than people dream of. Therapists that my father liked to stick on me said that I had turned out the way I did because I experienced loss at a very early age. Apparently, losing your mom to an aneurysm and developing the habit of challenging authority figures go hand in hand. I'm not sure how it works but if that man with the degree on his wall says so, then it must be true.

Back to the topic at hand, out of all the crazy things I've done in life and rest assured they were crazy or I wouldn't have ended up in military school, there's nothing quite comparable to women. I'll be the first to admit that before, relationships used to scare the crap out of me. I would honestly break out into a sweat at the thought of having a girlfriend. Which was why at military school, I kept my hookups brief and simple. Neither party was looking for a serious relationship, we'd clear that up in the beginning to avoid unnecessary drama when things ended. Every girl knew the deal and few complained.

I stuck to the rules of my game.

But guess what? When it comes to the one girl I actually want? I don't even know how to make the first play.

Ever since I've gotten back, I've been trying to do my best to gently ease myself into Tessa's life. Before I left, I'd been nothing but a constant thorn in her side, annoying her just as a desperate means to get some attention. My pranks, all the teasing, all the wars we constantly fought were just a stupid way to get her to notice me and make her forget the still-nonsensical crush she had on my stepbrother, Jason. But things didn't really work out the way I wanted them to and I guess I really shouldn't blame her for not seeing through all the hell I unleashed on her. That's too much pressure to put on a girl, especially one that's in love with someone else. But now that I'm back, after nearly four years with the intention of trying to win her back, trying to make her smile a little more, trying to make her life a little happier, I've been trying to do the opposite of what I'd done before. I'm not using the game per se to win her over because every coherent strategy and plan that I try to use flies out the window where Tessie's concerned.

I sound a little lovesick and a little foolish. Childhood love is unrealistic, that's what I get told from the few people who know how I feel but it is what it is. I'd taken one look at the little girl in the playground and had found some sort of a comfort in her beautiful green eyes. I don't know what it takes to make a kid that young fall in love but I did and maybe for the wrong reasons. She'd been friendly, she'd had hair like sunshine, a smile that'd light you up from the inside out and she radiated happiness. Even as a child, I lacked that natural exuberance and lightness that came with being a kid and not having any problems. Losing my mom as young as I did, having a father who worked most nights and being left on my own till my grandparents could look after me would do that to a person.

Tessie made me think I could be as happy as other kids my age and I realize now that I shouldn't have made her responsible for my happiness or the baggage that came with suddenly losing your mother. Nobody could make me feel something that I didn't want to, not even the little girl who became the closest thing I had to solace. But pushing her in a ditch the first time I saw her wasn't probably the best way to get her to be my friend. Because that's all I wanted in the beginning, for her to like me, to be her friend, to be the person she smiled at and shared her KitKats with but from the very first day, she was drawn toward Jay and I was drawn toward her. That's just how things were.

But he's always been blind toward her feelings and to make it all that much shittier, he's dating her ex-best friend. I'm not sure how long I'll be able to watch him hurt Tessie like that.

But if I want her to let me in enough to help her then I need her to understand that things are different now. But my attempts at starting any kind of a relationship with her have been huge disasters so now you understand why I'd rather jump off a plane without a parachute than try to figure out women.

***

We're currently sitting at a table in the cafeteria, a table that's not near the trashcans for once. It makes my blood boil to realize just how badly Tessie and her friends are treated at the school, and all the cruelty's the

326

result of someone that Tessa considered a best friend. I won't get into my own sordid history with Nicole Bishop but knowing what I do about her, I'm not surprised that she turned on someone who trusted her.

Though since joining the high school, I've made a considerable effort to put an end to their mistreatment. I do realize that it comes with a price and that the girl I'm trying to woo would rather have the ground swallow her whole than live with the kind of attention we're getting right now. She hates the fact that people are staring, at her, at me, at *us,* and I feel the guilt picking at me. I don't want to make her uncomfortable or make high school more of a hellhole for her than it already is but in order to get people to treat her the right way, I have to push her out of her comfort zone, just a little.

So at lunch, I do a little more of the pushing Tessie out of her comfort zone thing and ask her and her two friends about their plans for the weekend. I'm not surprised when Tessa tells me that their wild, wild weekend involves mostly a trip to the mall. I'm not blind, I see the way people look at the three of them, the way Nicole controls how they're treated. I'd use my fists and roar in anger if I could because the last person who deserves this kind of a treatment is Tessie. But that's not how you approach someone like Nicole because I'm dealing with years' worth of damage and people treating these girls like pariahs.

One step at a time it is then.

I call out to Jared, one of the jocks who's been after me all week to let him throw a party since I'm back now but I wasn't interested, at least until now.

"Hey, man you still up for the party on Saturday?"

He's sitting at the same table as Nicole and Jay and by the looks on the couple from hell's faces I can tell they're not happy that I'm disrupting their little table hierarchy. But the buzz has already started as people prepare themselves for what's already looking like the party of the year.

I turn to Tessa and the girls. "That guy's been after me all week to throw a welcome home party. I didn't want one since you know he's a tool but you're welcome."

I look at the three of them, expect a stronger reaction than the silence I'm greeted by, especially from Tessie. You would expect her to be thrilled or honestly, ready to chop my head off slowly and painfully with a butter knife but she sits there like nothing's the matter. But she finally begins to catch on when her friend Megan shows the kind of enthusiasm you'd expect from a six-year-old who gets a pony for their birthday. She makes a high-pitched noise and claps her hands, forcing Tessa to finally ask, "What?" with an adorably confused look on her face.

"We now have plans for the weekend," I explain and she glares at me; yeah, I'm doing a great job of wooing her. Her face contorts into the least-threatening scowl I've seen in my life.

"Who says I'll go?"

"It would be the polite thing to do, besides it'll be fun." I shrug.

It probably won't be anything spectacular than cheap alcohol and pizza but it'll be a chance for people to see that she's no longer willing to be a doormat.

"No, no and no! I will not, I cannot, and frankly I should not for the sake of my own well-being go to this party."

"What's with her?" I turn to Megan but that doesn't turn out any better because the redhead seems to be at a loss for words whenever I directly address her.

"I-She . . . her . . . I mean that . . ."

But Beth, ballbuster that she is, finally pieces it all together for me as she takes out her earphones. "What she's trying to so eloquently say is that we've been banned from parties. If Nicole sees us at one we're done for and while I don't give a damn about her, these two are too scared to actually face her."

My first reaction is that I'm happy Tessa's got someone like Beth by her side; she's tough and the little time I've spent around her tells me that she won't take shit from anyone and she's protective of her friends. I've got to give her props but even as the thought crosses my mind, I feel anger coursing through me, the kind of anger and fury that sent me to military school in the first place.

"How long has she been doing this?" I know the answer but I would still like to know just how much damage I've got to undo and just how long my brother's been sitting there silently while his girlfriend bullies the person who thinks the world of him.

"It doesn't matter," she tells me and even as I pin her down with my eyes, she squirms in her seat as though she'd be more than willing to up and leave if she could. I know we've got eyes on us, people aren't even pretending to not watch and it's the attention that Tessa hates but I need answers and I need them now. I do, at the same time, understand why I'd be the last person she'd share memories of her tormentor with because, rewind three years and I was the tormentor. Maybe I didn't take things as far as Nicole but maybe to Tessa, she and I are the same thing. If I wasn't dying of guilt and remorse before, I am now.

"How long?" I ask again and she slumps in her seat, her shoulders sagging in defeat. It seems as though a thousand different thoughts run through her mind and it breaks my heart to see the pain that's etched across her face.

"Like I said it doesn't matter, I'm handling it."

"Oh you are? Because from what I've been seeing for a whole week your idea of handling is letting her stomp all over you with her giant-ass feet."

Finally, finally she laughs and I feel like patting myself on the back.

"She does have huge feet, doesn't she?"

Her attempt at avoiding the subject is so weak that I can't help but groan and laugh at the same time.

"I saw her toes once up close and they're so freakishly long," Megan chimes in and I'm as surprised as she is by her ability to articulate a fully formed sentence.

Turning to Tessa, I remind her, "This doesn't mean that I've forgotten what this conversation is about." But something about the look on Tessa's face stops me from further questioning her on the subject, maybe it's enough for today which is why instead of digging deeper, I smile and tell the three girls, "I'm taking you three to that party and I'm going to teach you to have fun."

***

The thing with reinventing yourself in someone else's life is that you've got to take the initiative. If I'd sat and waited for Tessa to accept the new and improved Cole and let me into her life, we'd both be waiting until we were about sixty. So desperate measures are definitely in order. I've been driving her home for a week and every day I feel like, grudgingly as it might be, she gives in a little.

While Tessa does seem wary and it looks like she expects me to pull one stunt or the other at any given moment, that's expected because of my reputation. I'm trying my best to get her to trust me though and if that means imposing myself in her everyday life to a point that's kind of ridiculous then I'm more than okay with it.

Today as I drop her off, I don't just make the short drive back to my house and instead bite the bullet.

"So I was thinking, since we're spending all this time together . . ."

"Involuntarily."

"Right." So far so good Stone, she still hates your guts.

"I know I'm still not your favorite person and odds are that I never will be but what about a peace offering? How about I make you lunch and we talk?"

I'm making this up as I go along but food is always a good way to go right? And it turns out that I do something right because she says it's okay for me to come in and she follows me inside her house. I think I scared her with the word 'talk' because I can almost feel the nerves radiating off of her. "So what is it that you want to talk about?"

I smile to myself but it's devoid of all humor. She can only see the back of my head so she can't tell just how much I'm beating myself up right now. This is all my doing, this girl for whom I have every possible complicated feeling in the world is always on her guard around me.

"Relax shortcake. I'm not suddenly going to declare my undying love and devotion toward you. If we're going to be friends, I thought it'd be nice if we spent a little more time together, actually talking and not arguing."

"I didn't think you were capable of that kind of emotional maturity."

"Usually I'm not but hey, I'm willing to give it a good old college try if you are."

"And why would I want to do that? Try with you I mean."

"When life gives you lemons and all that jazz, shortcake. The thing is, you're stuck here with me for at least a year. You could either choose to ignore me or we could try and build something great. I vote for the latter."

And on that note, I use the spare house key her parents gave me and unlock the door. And the move has the kind of reaction I'd expected.

"Why do you have a key?" She squeaks and I can practically see our ship sink. She hates the idea, it's probably not going to lead to love from here on out.

"Your mom gave me one the other day. She told me to make myself feel right at home."

"Excuse me?" Her voice remains shrill.

"Well she said you have a tendency to forget your keys and since both your dad and her might not be home to let you in, I was entrusted with the responsibility. I take it you're not so happy about that?"

And with that, I let the two of us in.

***

So one of the things I'd wanted to achieve with this homecoming was to make sure Tessa's life was a lot happier than what it used to be. I'm not sure if her falling for me would ever be a reality but something I do want to do for sure is to slowly start distancing Tessa from anything that'll give her a reason to be unhappy.

"Hey, Tessie?"

I ask her this as I'm sprawled across her bed, my large frame overtaking the entire thing. Remember how I spoke about imposing myself onto her, well there's no such thing as doing too much of it because the more I seem to push her, the more she seems to give in.

She's huddled in a corner of her room, sulking as she pretends to do her homework but I'm well aware of her watching me so I flex my muscles just for fun.

"Yes?" She answers as though she can't stand me.

"Would you mind if I asked you something?"

Even as the words leave my mouth, in my head a montage of a car collision plays out. I'd been meaning to ask her a question for so long and maybe I should've waited for the right moment but the more time I spend with her and the more I notice it, the more my worry grows.

"You've never really cared about what I thought before. Why are you asking now?"

I still think about it, whether I really want to do this. I'm not following a script and I don't know what to say but I've opened this can of worms and now I need to go through with it.

"Look, this might totally not be my place. Actually, I'm pretty sure I'm way out of line asking you this but . . . is there a reason why you barely touch your meals?"

She becomes absolutely still and I kick myself mentally, over and over again. I shouldn't have approached the subject like this. Maybe I should have waited for a better time, when she accepted me. I don't mean a thing to her now and she doesn't owe me any explanations. I almost want to take it back but it's too late.

Her response is to throw a badly aimed cushion at me, which I catch easily.

"W-what do you mean?"

I hate the tremor in her voice, like she's afraid of her secret being exposed. But I want her to know that if she's in pain, if she's hurting then it's okay for her to share that with the people who're supposed to love her.

"Look, just tell me if I'm imagining things." My own voice catches but I continue.

"But, even at school you pick at your food. Whenever I eat with your family, you take a bite or two and then leave thinking that your parents don't notice. We've been back from school for two hours and you didn't even eat half of what I made. Please tell me that I'm wrong, that I'm seeing something that's not there. I . . . I know it's not my place to bring this up but Tessa, I'm just worried."

"Maybe it's because you repulse me and I can't stomach food when you're around."

I don't think she realizes that the only thing that could hurt me is if I was never part of her life at all. As long as I'm here and as long as she'll let me, I'll do what I can to be there for her.

"I'm not joking, Tessa. If there really is a problem then I want you to be able to talk about it, to someone you trust if not me. I don't know what to do here, maybe I'm just making a huge idiot of myself but I want you know that I care and that if you ever need someone to talk to . . ."

She takes some time to formulate her reply and I can't help but smile at the childish, "Mind your own business."

"You are my business, Tessie."

If I look at it from her perspective, I know it looks completely insane that someone who'd been so committed to pulling pranks on her all through our early years would do a complete three-sixty and try and be a better person. If I were more patient, I would give her time to adjust to the idea but I've been preparing for this for the past three years. I've already wasted so much time, I don't think I have more to waste. So I'm pleasantly surprised, well more like shocked to hear what she says next.

"How about we come to a mutual agreement to talk about this on a day when I'm ready and you've literally not come at me with it out of nowhere?"

"Oh, okay. Will you be willing to do that then? Talk?"

"I might as well since you've somehow made it you job to worm yourself into every possible area of my life."

She couples this with a grunt and I take that as an opportunity to lighten up the moment.

"You might want to tone down the grunts, Venus, or your brother might think we're playing the kinky kind of tennis."

I'm happy to play the part of the pervert if it keeps her from freaking out.

***

Here's the thing about Jay, everyone looks at him and thinks he's such a great guy. God knows I've been compared to him enough times to know that I'm the black sheep of the family, and if he could, my father would definitely trade me in for another one of him. However, I like to think that people will soon see him for what he is, weak and manipulative.

Those are pretty harsh words to describe someone you're related to by marriage, someone you'd once considered a best friend but truth be told, after the way he's treated Tessa and how he's allowed Nicole to treat Tessa, I'm done with this guy. He's a user, someone who's more than okay with stringing a girl along as long as it boosts his ego. The more I think about how he's mistreated Tessa and taken advantage of her feelings toward him, the more capable I am of manslaughter.

Which is why when I see him talking to her in the hallway at school, I have to resist the urge to pummel him into the ground. Instead I walk casually toward them, and in a not-so-subtle manner warn him to back off. I sling my arm across Tessa's shoulders and pull her into my chest.

"There you are, Tessie, I've been looking for you everywhere," I say as I ruffle her hair.

She immediately resists, little fighter that she is, and elbows me before making an attempt to fix her hair. I can't help but laugh at the difference between how she acts in front of Jay, all solemn and heartbroken, and the spitfire she becomes in front of me.

"Ah shortcake, always so affectionate."

I return my arm to around her shoulder as she attempts to attack me by stomping on my foot.

"Let go of me, you oaf! In the name of your pea-sized balls I say unhand me!"

The downright insulting and completely untrue statement is followed by a painful stomp on my foot that has much more power to it, enough to make me wince and give Tessa the opportunity to slip away.

"My balls are not pea-sized!" I protest.

"Whatever makes you sleep at night." She glares at me and backs away a little as if expecting me to jump her; the corner of my mouth twitches at how hilarious she is. But the moment is ruined by Jay; of course it is.

He clears his throat and I'm surprised by just how angry he looks as his eyes look from Tessa to me. I'm not surprised by the reaction, he's always been a jealous prick but I'm angry because the asshole has no reason to react the way that he is. He shouldn't get to think he has any kind of ownership over Tessa and she shouldn't be worried about what he thinks or feels.

But I know that she is and it kills me.

"Don't you have a class, brother?" The sooner he leaves, the faster I can work on making sure Tessa forgets that he even exists and that's a little difficult to do if he's constantly sniffing around her like a lovesick puppy.

"I do, actually Tessa and I have the same one so I was hoping we could walk together."

Yeah, not in your wild, wild, dreams, jackass.

"No can do, she's coming with me."

"I am?"

"She is?"

You're damn right she is. I don't trust him around her now, not when I know he's useless when it comes to protecting her from whatever hell Nicole plans on unleashing on her.

"I know you didn't get to do your homework last night because of me so I got us out of class by offering to do some stupid volunteer work in the AV room."

"You two were together last night?" He has the nerve to sound wounded, but it's a ploy of his. He wants Tessa to feel sorry for him, for her to pick him over me and validate his belief that he's still got her wrapped around his finger but things need to change, starting now.

"We were and now we really need to go." I don't give Tessa a chance to respond, I simply steer her toward the AV room and try to ignore the jealousy when she still turns and takes one last lingering look toward Jay. I can't stop myself from telling her, "He's not worth it." She's quiet and pensive, as if still reeling from the hurt of seeing Jay. I want to tell her that Jay isn't worth an ounce of her feelings and maybe, just maybe if she let go of her childhood crush, she'd see him for what he really is. But that'd be too much for now. I can't be too honest, too vulnerable because it'd be easy for her to reject me. So I go with my signature immaturity that she's so found of.

"Trust you to fall for the uglier brother. I can bet he has a smaller pe—"

On cue, I have feisty Tessie back and she slaps a hand over my mouth.

"Stop talking or I will throw up on those three-hundred-dollar high-tops of yours."

Yeah, this girl knows me so well.

CHAPTER ELEVEN
Cole's POV

I think I've made some headway into making Tessa look at me like I'm a person and not a recurring nightmare. In the month or so that I've been here, I've done my fair share of stupid things, things that were intended to do good but that just went horribly wrong. All of it was done to win Tessa over in some way, to make her see me, for her to realize that the feelings I have for her are not the kind she thinks. But in doing so and in trying to shake her life up a little, I've also brought her the kind of pain that she'd been protecting herself from. Thinking about taking her to that party and it all going wrong in the worst possible way still keeps me up at night. I took out a lot of my anger on Hank, I don't think the man will be capable of a fully functioning body for the rest of his adult life but there's nothing that can get rid of the guilt, no matter what Tessa says. I shouldn't have forced her to go to a party she never wanted to go to in the first place. The more I interfere in her life, the more I end up ruining it all for her. But something makes me try harder every time not to screw up. I want to be there for her whenever she needs me and I may mess things up on the way but I want to be someone she can lean on.

I've tried telling her that she can't let Nicole get away with what she's done to her but I'm aware that Tessa's a little wary of my plans and I don't blame her, especially not after everything that's happened. But I can't help but insert myself in her life any way that I can, given that she's been trying so hard to keep her distance. Case in point, the tutoring thing.

I don't need to be tutored, not really. School has always been easy for me and I don't take that for granted because if I had had bad grades with the kind of shit I've pulled in the past, military school wouldn't even have been an option, I'm sure my dad would've killed me first.

But he doesn't need to know about the little tests I'm failing here and there, just to make sure the administration thinks I need a tutor. I'll bounce back and make up for the bad grades but getting that extra time with Tessa is necessary. Though I'm not sure how I'll manage to do that when I'm six feet under the ground after she's successfully managed to kill me.

I'm watching her argue with our calculus teacher, Mr. Goodwin, trying to talk her way out of tutoring me and I stifle a laugh because the man's holding his ground. Between him and the principal, they really want me to do well and I'm sure I won't even need to intervene to get Tessa on our side.

"Megan is so much smarter than I am, sir, I'm sure she'll be able to do a better job."

She sounds pretty desperate and I almost feel bad for pushing this on her but then I remember just how vicious Nicole and her cronies can get and for some inexplicable reason, I know that right now it's my responsibility to protect Tessa from them. I'll wait until she's ready to stand up for herself but until then I'm more than okay with being a thorn in her side.

"You know you guys should stop talking about me like I'm not here," I remind her, not because I think that'll make her spare my feelings but because the sooner we cement this agreement, the less the chances are of Tessa sweet-talking the man into letting her off the hook. God knows she can make me do just about anything if she asks nicely.

"Ah, Mr. Stone, just the man I was looking for. As you've heard, Ms. O'Connell will now be tutoring you in most of your subjects and I'm sure together you two will manage to make the situation much better."

Oh yes we will. Then again, if the murderous look Tessa throws my way is any indication of how well we'll work together, it's a good thing I don't actually need her help with my grades. Were it up to her, I know my GPA would drop faster than your dignity when you accidentally get sucked into binge-watching *The Real Housewives of New Jersey*. Oh believe me, it happens.

"Oh and Ms. O'Connell, if Cole here gets passing grades on his midterm report card, I'll write that recommendation that you've been asking me for."

I did not ask him to say that, genius as it is; I don't like that he's literally manipulating Tessa into helping me. He's overpowering her, putting her in a position that makes her weak and I'm not into that. Maybe Goodwin and I need to have some words. I get out of my seat and walk to the door, leaning against the doorframe to watch Tessa seal the deal.

"Okay, fine. I'll do it, I'll tutor him."

Mental fist bump even though she's still staring daggers at me.

"Then we have a deal, you have until the end of the semester to make sure that he's improved and that his grades are consistent."

She tries to smile at him, but it comes out as a barely concealed teeth-baring snarl, "Don't worry, Mr. Goodwin, I've got this."

Heaven help us both.

***

There's something to be said for playground tactics when it comes to impressing girls. Sometimes they work, mostly they don't. You can't pull their hair and treat them like crap and not expect them to run to the good guy, you know the one who plays baseball and gives you flowers. Not the dumb football jock who accidentally lands you in the emergency room one time too many.

But some playground tactics do have merit.

So I continue poking Tessa in the shoulder and she continues ignoring it. It's like we're right back to kindergarten.

"Hey, shortcake." In the cafeteria, she concentrates on her food in an attempt to forget the fact that I exist. Well at least she's eating and now that that's out in the open between us, I'm happy to see that she's eating a lot more. The silent treatment continues for the length of our lunch period and I'm only amused by it. I can't help it, she's cute when she's angry.

"Shortcake, come on, why are you mad?" I shouldn't be goading her, I really shouldn't be; it's what makes us, us.

She continues to ignore me, focusing on every other person sitting at our table. She'll come around soon, I think.

I hope.

But as I let her continue her attempt at matchmaking Megan and Alex, I also think about how to make up for this. I know that I sprang the tutoring thing on her and that maybe it's not quite something she has time for, or frankly is interested in. Mr. Goodwin took it a little too far when he tried bribing her with the recommendation letter for Brown but even as the thought crosses my mind, I know that I'm going to have to push, to bend the rules a little and cross a few lines to get her to open up to me.

I'm finally able to get her alone as the bell rings and everyone gets up to leave for class. Since the group at her table knows that I'd like to talk to Tessa with some privacy they are quick to leave and she stares after them like a deer caught in the headlights. I can almost see the pulse thrumming in the base of her neck. Is she nervous to be around me? The kind of emotions I want her to feel toward me are the furthest thing you can think from fear or hatred. And I think, it's time to remind her of that.

"So you're not going to talk to me?" I face her. Around us, even as people leave for class, their eyes are on us and I couldn't care less. She tries to walk past me but I won't let her go this easily. She started the whole silent treatment thing and it's time to have a little fun with it.

I place a finger under her chin, forcing her to look right into my eyes. I know it does something to her, I feel the tremble of her skin and it thrills me to know that I have that effect on her. Bastard that I am, I decide to take advantage of her temporary state of dazed and confused.

"You're going to just stand there and let me do this?"

My own heart pounding viciously, I try to hide just how much my hand is shaking as I reach out and place it at her waist. She doesn't make a sound as my thumb glides over the silky soft skin of her stomach. The hitch of her breath makes the entire world disappear and for the life of me I can't figure out how we ended up here, with me touching her and her not shoving me away.

I wait for her to stop me as I caress her skin but even as she starts to tremble in my arms, her mouth remains sealed shut and I dare to push it even further. I know desire when I see it in her eyes because if I even for a second felt her be afraid or disgusted with my touch, I'd never go near her.

Not until she asked me to.

"If I do will you tell me to stop?" I lean in closer and my breath fans her ear. And right there, in the emptying cafeteria, with people still lingering to watch us, I feel as though I lay my claim on her a little. Taking her earlobe between my teeth, I bite it gently and she gasps, which does all kinds of wonderful things to my body. Continuing to caress the skin of her waist, with my lips dangerously close to hers, I make sure to never break eye contact.

"Speak up, Tessie, tell me what you want."

She doesn't say a word but her body language speaks volumes.

"You should really ask me to end this."

But I hope and pray to every single God out there that she doesn't.

I'm not sure if this is how I want our first kiss to be, with Tessa barely uttering a word and with an audience that does not seem intent on leaving. But I can't help myself and as I close in, my lips hovering over hers, so temptingly close to kissing her for the very first time I realize that I don't have much self-control left. My hands creep up her top, something that just illustrates that I've lost my mind because I'm feeling her up in the middle of the day, at school.

She needs to be the one who stops this.

But she doesn't and I'm almost certain that this will be it, the moment that changes everything.

"Cole!"

I don't back off immediately because I know that's not Tessa's voice but whoever it is, the moment's interrupted and it's like having a bucket of ice-cold water thrown over me. What the hell am I doing? I thought the plan was to take things slowly and ease Tessa into knowing my feelings for her. If I'd kissed her right now, chances are that she'd freak out and we'd be over before we even started.

So as I turn to face the person who might've just saved me from making a colossal mistake, I find it kind of ironic when it's actually Nicole Bishop, standing there looking so hurt and wounded, as though I'd kicked her puppy and then some. My first instinct is to make sure she doesn't even get to look at Tessa, memories of what she's done to her are too fresh and I don't even want Nicole breathing the same air as Shortcake. Just the way she's looking toward us, the hatred in her eyes tells me she's capable of far worse than what she's already done.

"Nicole?"

"W-what are you two doing here?"

Her attempt at being nice to me only makes me want to throw up. I don't want any attention from this girl. She's a whole lot of nasty and only someone like Jason would be totally oblivious to that.

"I don't see how that's any of your business."

She stalls, her attempts at trying to get my attention getting more and more desperate by the second until the sickly sweet scent of her perfume threatens to choke me.

"The principal just called for a special assembly for us seniors and since I'm class president I'm supposed to get everyone together."

"Thanks for the concern, we'll be right there."

And maybe it's the tone, the fact that I'm not prepared to take any more of her bullshit or let her pollute the air with more of her vileness that finally gives her a clue. With one last glare at Tessa, she leaves and I can finally breathe again.

"That was awesome!" The smile on her face, how happy she looks right now? Well, I'd take a million showdowns with Nicole if I could get her to beam like that at me.

"Talking, are you? You weren't looking so keen a while back."

She blushes profusely, looking so adorable that all I want to do is kiss her. But I know better now. Patience, Stone, you've just got to be a little more patient. You don't rush girls like Tessa, especially not if you're going to be their first kiss.

Which you bet your ass I will be.

339

***

Our first "tutoring" session is right after school as we've got both the principal and Mr. Goodwin on our case and we've got to give them regular updates. But Tessa and I both know, I don't really need help with studying, so it pleases me that she's still going with the little charade. The events of the cafeteria are still fresh and maybe it's just me, but I feel like we've finally broken down a barrier between the two of us, something's shifted and changed and I like the direction we're heading toward.

We're in my room, eating lunch and trying to study but all I can do is take in the fact that she's in my bedroom and my messed-up brain links that up with how close I actually was to her in the cafeteria and I want to do more of that; I can't help but wish.

Shit, what a time to be turned on.

But I obviously can't act on it since Tessa's been distracted and lost in her own thoughts since we got here. She hasn't said a word to me but she's thinking so much, I can practically hear her brain processing everything that's happened.

"Why are you so quiet?"

The fact that she doesn't answer me and just gets lost in her own head tells me that I might need to back off a little and give her the space that she deserves. I don't have the right to just walk in and pretend to fit right into the life that she has now. We're both different people than who we were three years ago and maybe it's just damn confusing for her to come to terms with who I've become while I've been away.

So I try to go back to someone familiar.

"Tessie?" I try to get her attention again, genuinely worried about just how hard she's had to think about me, about us. Do I really stand a chance here?

"What?"

"Are you okay?"

"Why wouldn't I be?"

"Well, you look a little dazed. That must have been some daydream."

"Trust me when I say you didn't star in it."

And she's back, I mentally applaud myself. So that's how you get her to not have a panic attack, keep things light and no matter what you do, don't talk about feelings, at least not just yet.

Got it, I'll need to put on the kid gloves. I decide to change the topic so that neither of us is thinking about what we almost did, or just how amazing it could've been.

340

"So now that you're done daydreaming about me, have you thought more about what you want to do to Nicole?"

"I wasn't daydreaming!"

"You were looking at me with hearts in your eyes; I'd say you came pretty close to it."

I'm right and she knows it but who would Shortcake be if not a little firecracker.

"Please, like I'd ever be interested in you."

Oh we're going to have so much fun with that.

I move in closer from where we're both sitting cross-legged on the ground. And I know I just said that I want to take things slow, but there's nothing wrong with a little harmless fun, right?

I push out of our way the books that no one's studying from and the dishes, because my lady does get impressed by my cooking skills, and invade her space for the second time today.

"You want to try saying that again?"

And there it is again, the look in her eyes that tells me that my nearness does something to her, and if it's anything close to what I feel then my job just got a whole lot easier.

"I . . . I—I . . ."

"Think Cole is a sex god."

I move away just to give her enough space to breathe but not to be totally coherent.

"You don't need to say something for me to hear it, Tessie, I know you, and I know that's what you wanted to say to me."

And guess what? She nods.

Score!

The moment she realizes what she's said, her fiery temper makes a comeback and she lunges for me. I sprawl on the floor laughing my ass off as she tries but in vain to hit me. I don't help my case by not being able to stop laughing and she gets up, making sure to quickly collect her stuff and heads right for the door.

"Come on, shortcake; don't get mad, I was kidding." And that would sound a whole lot more believable if I could manage to keep a straight face on for more than five seconds. She's getting increasingly embarrassed if the color of her cheeks is anything to go by and when she leaves, I'm on my feet, ready to chase her and apologize.

But she stops at the top of the stairs, causing me to run into her. I'm about to ask her if she's changed her mind when I realize what it is that's caused her to come to a halt. Jay's on the phone with someone standing at the entryway to our house, at the bottom of the stairs. He doesn't hear us approach and I feel Tessa backing into me, like she doesn't want him to notice her. I'm immediately on guard because I know the kind of dynamic the two of them have is also changing, especially after the incident with Hank.

I'm prepared to let Tessa hide in my bedroom until he leaves but before I can do that, the idiot literally destroys any chance of me actually considering him a decent human being.

"Yeah man, I'm really going to have to work to get that scholarship. The last thing I need is to end up a loser like Travis O'Connell."

Tessa stiffens, her entire body locks up and the hurt is so very evident on her face. She's protective of her brother, to the extent that she'd go head-to-head with anyone who dared insult him. He's her weak spot and I'm guessing Jay just majorly screwed up.

"Tessie."

I don't want her to hear any more of this because I know what's about to come is uglier. Jay doesn't really let his true colors show when he's around people, but when he gets the opportunity? He's an absolute asshole and even though it would help my case, for Tessa to see him for who he is, I don't want her getting hurt.

But she refuses to move, daring me to even try to take her away. So we stand there together and listen to the train wreck of a conversation.

"That guy's a total screwup, even Coach says so. He had everything and he lost it because he was too stupid to write a paper."

He pauses and then spits out the most disgusting thing I've heard from him for a while now.

"I wonder if Jenny's still single. She's just a couple of years older and she used to be so hot."

The fact that he's brought up Travis's old girlfriend and is talking about her the way he is, the girl who ditched him when he was at his lowest and very publicly broke his heart, makes me sick to my stomach and I can only imagine how Tessa's feeling. I don't think she should be hearing any more of this so I try again.

"Tessie, come on; let's get you out of here."

And she lets me because she's hurt. She's hurt because she's starting to realize that the idea of the person she'd built in her head for so long, who she truly thought Jay was, has drastically changed and I know it can be a lot to take in. She's clung to him for so long, for the feelings she developed for him when things were completely different that I know it'll be painful for her to let go. But I'll be there for her every step of the way.

**

342

In the security of my bedroom, I kneel before Tessa, who's sitting on my bed, her face ashen. I take her hands in mine; my only priority is to make her feel better and not gloat. Because I'm not getting a kick out of how she's stumbled upon Jay's true nature or just realized the fact that he isn't Mr. Perfect.

"He crossed a line; he shouldn't have said all that. I'm sorry, shortcake."

It seems as though it takes her a while to process it but she surprises me by agreeing.

"I know a lot of people think that Travis is a loser but I never thought Jay would be one of them."

She's upset and has every right to be but I'm relieved that she's realized this. Jay's toxic for her; the minute she lets go of him, she'll realize just how much better off she is without being hung up over him.

"You think you know him but he's not Mr. Perfect, Tessie, he's a good guy but he's got flaws too, flaws you don't want to see."

She doesn't disagree.

"Come, I'll take you home." I give her a small smile, one she returns that makes my heart do a weird somersault kinda thing inside my chest. And as we leave my room, I feel as though, just like the incident at the cafeteria, something massive has shifted between us.

And I can't wait for how things unfold for us now.

ABOUT THE AUTHOR

BLAIR HOLDEN (@jessgirl93 on Wattpad) is a twenty-three-year-old college student by day and Wattpad author by night. Her hobbies include and are limited to obsessively scouring Goodreads and reading romance novels, with a preference for all things new adult. Her own work usually contains lots of romance, humor, angst, and brooding bad-boy heroes. Caffeine and late-night Gilmore Girls marathons help her find a balance between completing her degree and writing. She writes for herself and also to make readers swoon, laugh, and occasionally cry. Her book, *The Bad Boy's Girl*, has amassed nearly 170 million reads, which absolutely baffles her. Her dream is to see her readers holding a published copy of her books and remembering how far they've come together! Find her on Twitter as @blairholdenx and on Facebook and Instagram as @jessgirl93

Made in the USA
Monee, IL
18 March 2020